"What possible motive did you think I had?"

Cade's darkly challenging stare made the fine hairs at the nape of Emma's neck rise. "Let's see…" His gaze performed a leisurely inspection of her bedraggled person. "Well, there's always the possibility you might want to trade the use of your delectable body for a new wardrobe, some hard cash and plush living conditions."

Emma's corset seemed to have instantly shrunk. She couldn't get a decent gulp of air. And, from the heat flaming across her cheeks, she knew her face must be scarlet.

"It's not very flattering that the thought never entered your mind." He sounded disgruntled.

"But why should I have thought that you'd…?" She swallowed. Her mind was suddenly filled with images of what he'd been thinking she was capable of doing. Kissing him. Letting him kiss her. And surely much more, though she wasn't precisely sure what the "much more" entailed. She had some strong suspicions disrobing would be involved….

Dear Reader,

When a homeless schoolteacher is taken in by the wealthy uncle of one of her students, falling in love is the last thing on their minds, in Pat Tracy's terrific new Western, *Cade's Justice*. Don't miss this first book in her series set in Denver, Colorado, called THE GUARDSMEN, from an author who always delivers a fast-paced and sexy story.

His Secret Duchess is a heart-wrenching new Regency romance from Gayle Wilson, a RITA Award finalist who is also making a name for herself with her spine-tingling mysteries for Harlequin's Intrigue line. In this month's title, a nobleman presumed dead returns home after seven years of war to discover his "secret wife" on trial for murder. And in Linda Castle's new book, *Temple's Prize*, rival scientists fight their mutual attraction when they discover that they are both after the same prize.

And popular author Suzanne Barclay returns to her bestselling series, THE SOMMERVILLE BROTHERS, with her newest medieval book, *Knight's Rebellion*, the stirring tale of the leader of a band of outlaws who finds himself unable to resist the mysterious woman whom he has rescued.

Whatever your tastes in reading, we hope you enjoy all four books, available wherever Harlequin Historicals are sold.

Sincerely,

Tracy Farrell
Senior Editor

Please address questions and book requests to:
Harlequin Reader Service
U.S.: 3010 Walden Ave., P.O. Box 1325, Buffalo, NY 14269
Canadian: P.O. Box 609, Fort Erie, Ont. L2A 5X3

PAT TRACY

CADE'S JUSTICE

Harlequin Books

TORONTO • NEW YORK • LONDON
AMSTERDAM • PARIS • SYDNEY • HAMBURG
STOCKHOLM • ATHENS • TOKYO • MILAN
MADRID • WARSAW • BUDAPEST • AUCKLAND

ISBN 0-373-28992-8

CADE'S JUSTICE

Copyright © 1997 by Pat Tracy

Printed in U.S.A.

Books by Pat Tracy

Harlequin Historicals

The Flaming #121
Winter Fire #188
Saddle the Wind #273
Beloved Outcast #333
Cade's Justice #392

PAT TRACY

lives in rugged Idaho. No longer a country mouse, Pat recently moved to the city of Idaho Falls, population 49,000, where she writes, practices karate and dreams of times when rough-and-tumble heroes had their hands full dealing with independent, lofty-minded heroines.

Pat loves to hear from her readers c/o P.O. Box 17, Ucon, Idaho 83454

Dedication:

In honor of my heroine, Emma January Step, a tutor of refined young women, I would like to dedicate this book to Carolyn Horowitz, who taught English and literature at La Puente High School. This wonderfully insightful teacher encouraged me to write and rewarded my efforts with lots of lovely A's. I don't know where you are, "Mrs. Horowitz," but I want to thank you for loving English (you did, didn't you?) and teaching your students to think for themselves.

If any of my readers happen to know a Carolyn Horowitz who taught at La Puente High School, California, 1963-1964, please write to me at P.O. Box 17, Ucon, Idaho 83454. I would love to send her an autographed copy of this book.

****

SPECIAL ACKNOWLEDGMENTS

Maxine Metcalf, friend for life. Thank you for your generous proofreading services. You saved my skin. Again.

Flora Jorgensen, Debbie Ricks, Sherry Roseberry, Martha Tew and Vonda Wilson. You're the critique group from heaven. Thank you. Thank you. Thank you.

Chapter One

The wrought-iron gate leading to Gideon Cade's brick mansion stood ajar. In Emma January Step's present mood, it wouldn't have mattered if the gate was padlocked. She would have found a way through it.

She proceeded up the rain-slickened flagstone path. During the two-hour walk from the academy, the strips of newspaper she'd tucked inside her worn shoes had dissolved into squishy clumps. The numbing chill that seeped through to her feet added to her discomfort.

Emma sensed more than saw the dark blur that streaked past her. Before her startled eyes, a shadow materialized from the damp mist shrouding the front porch of the three-story residence.

She pressed a palm to her racing heart. "Good grief, what are you doing here?" The less-than-cordial question was directed at the huge, hairy hound now blocking the doorway.

"You followed me, didn't you?" she demanded of the drenched creature. Without a flicker of apology, the dog's steady gaze met hers. "And you raced ahead at the last moment to beat me here. I should have known it was a mistake to feed you."

Emma continued up the stone path. Shrewd intelligence gleamed back at her from the disreputable mutt's black eyes. Clearly, it *had* been a mistake to smuggle him table scraps from the academy's kitchen. Obviously, the motley beast had decided he could count upon her as a source of food.

"You've followed me in vain," she informed him in no uncertain terms, gingerly maneuvering herself around him on the porch. "I haven't a morsel of food on me."

She drew her damp cloak more closely about her and steeled herself against the reproach she detected in his unwavering canine regard. After all, one could hardly be expected to remember such minor details as feeding a stray animal when one's world came crashing about one's shoulders. From the dog's point of view, though, she supposed being fed was a matter of vast importance.

"I'm sorry." She sighed, unable to endure this added burden of guilt. "I should have thought to bring you something to eat. Just go away for now, and let me conduct my business without interruption."

Guilt weighed more heavily upon her. "I promise to bring you a giant soup bone when we return home."

Emma bit her lip. The academy where she taught was neither her nor the dog's home. She couldn't speak for the beast, of course, but, as for herself, she hadn't known a place that could be so termed since she was three years old. Because she couldn't remember anything of her early years, that meant that to all intents and purposes she'd never experienced living in a real home.

"Shoo," she said forcefully, determined to accomplish her mission.

The animal's lower jaw went slack. Looking for all the world like a fallen banner, his pink tongue drooped from the side of his mouth. Even though he cocked his head in an attitude of submission, the dog stayed put.

"Suit yourself, but I'm warning you. If you expect any more food from me, you better be on your best behavior." Resigned to the dog's presence, she reached for the oversize brass knocker that decorated the tall, ornately carved ebony door.

Emma engaged the knocker. A series of reverberating clangs broke the early-morning stillness. As she waited for someone to answer, she wiped the soles of her muddy shoes on the front mat. The potent stench of wet dog fur reached her. She could only hope that whoever opened the door wouldn't think it was she who reeked of rainwater mixed with what was surely years of collected dirt and fleas.

Trying to dismiss the thought, she focused upon the fortunate coincidence of Gideon Cade's residence having been pointed out to her the day before. She and several of her students had been returning to the academy after occupying a pleasant afternoon contemplating the beautifully rendered paintings and statues displayed in Mr. Burke Youngblood's nearby private art gallery. As their rented conveyance passed through the affluent Denver neighborhood, Mr. Cade's niece, Courtney, had proudly gestured to the brick mansion and identified it as her uncle's home.

Emma was about to re-employ the knocker when the door suddenly swung open.

The best means of compensating for both her humble origins and a distressing lack of height, Emma had learned, was to get immediately to the point. "I must see Mr. Cade at once."

The large, disheveled man glaring down at her said nothing, nor did his unfriendly expression alter.

From the frayed condition of his drab blue robe, she deduced that he was a servant and not the notorious Gideon Cade of whom she'd been reading in the daily newspapers. According to vitriolic editorials, the ruthless and incredibly rich freighting tycoon was hardly likely to be traipsing about his mansion in such shoddy garb. From the scores of unflattering stories being circulated about him, he would far more likely have been found strolling about with a crown upon his head and wielding a smoking pistol for his scepter. A recent article had portrayed Courtney's uncle as a cross between a vicious vigilante renegade and an arrogant foreign potentate.

Emma returned the servant's belligerent stare. "I trust I do not need to repeat myself, sir."

The yellowish splash of light provided by the lamp on a table behind him made the shocks of white hair sticking up from his scalp look like oily shafts of lightning. Despite his giant frame, the man glaring down at her resembled an irate troll guarding the castle gate against any who had the temerity to trespass upon his master's domain.

"Have you any idea of the hour?" the scowling troll demanded, his bushy eyebrows converging over his remarkably huge and pitted nose.

"Certainly." Emma pushed back the cloak she'd worn to blunt the night chill and consulted the timepiece pinned to her gray bodice. Unfortunately, the light was so poor she couldn't make out the position of the hands upon the inexpensive watch. "My best estimate is that it's half past one. Now, please be so good as to fetch Mr. Cade."

"In the morning," the troll intoned balefully.

"That's right." She refastened her cloak. She'd checked on Courtney at 11 p.m., expecting to see her settled in bed. The subsequent seven-mile walk here had consumed a lot of time. "Now that we've established the hour, you may summon Mr. Cade. I'm here on a matter of grave urgency."

The servant chuckled gruffly. "If I disturb him again tonight, it will be grave, all right. Yours and mine."

"Now see here—"

"Miss," he said, interrupting her, his droopy eyes and tone unexpectedly conciliatory, "you best come back at a decent hour."

Emma had no intention of leaving without telling Mr. Cade his niece had disappeared. She inched closer to the doorway. If she had to, she would push her way past him. Returning her gaze to the dishearteningly massive figure of the overzealous gatekeeper, she realized she would hardly emerge victorious in a show of brute force.

Perhaps, if she pretended to swoon, he might catch her and carry her across the threshold he presently blocked. It was more likely, however, that he would leave her lying on the step until dawn.

Thoughts of Courtney wandering Denver's often rowdy night streets sent a tremor of increased distress through Emma. "Sir, you don't understand. I'm an instructor at Loutitia Hempshire's Academy for Young Ladies. I have terrible news and fear the worst.''

Astonishingly, the troll seemed to take her announcement in stride. He didn't so much as raise one caterpillar-size eyebrow. Emma wondered if perhaps butlers and stray dogs shared a distant but common ancestry. What would it take to startle the morosely self-contained man? She doubted a cattle stampede of longhorn steers rampaging down Larimer Street would shake his unflappable reserve.

He rubbed his jaw. She didn't know if he was debating the truthfulness of her claim or the relevance of the news to his employer. When his cannon-size nostrils began to twitch, she realized he must have picked up the mongrel's foul odor. Fearing he was about to slam the door in her face, Emma decided bold action was required. She would awaken Mr. Cade herself.

With little forethought, she launched herself through the puny space left between the uncooperative servant and the doorframe. That she wasn't big meant she could move quickly.

''Hey, now!'' the troll yelled, making a lunge for her.

His beefy paws closed around her cloak, dragging her to a skidding halt. A second later, the sound of ripping fabric heralded a burst of freedom. She sprinted past him into the entry hall.

Though Emma scarcely had time to catalog her elegant surroundings, an impression of quiet opulence struck her. With subtle impact, she perceived immense chandeliers, gilt mirrors, velvet draperies and mahogany furnishings. The scents of freshly cut flowers, leather and linseed oil reached her. The thought flashed through her mind that the combination of tasteful fragrances was probably how a vault full of money smelled.

Once inside, Emma wasn't sure what to do next, but she had only seconds to make up her mind before the troll caught up with her.

She noticed a curving staircase. Surely at the top of those stairs she would discover Gideon Cade, nestled snugly in his bed. She vowed to check every bedchamber until she found him.

"Not so fast." The servant's fingers closed around her arm.

Emma turned to explain why it was imperative that she speak with his employer. Before she could speak, a feral growl froze the blood in her veins. Her gaze swung to the open doorway where the stray dog had staked its territory.

"Oh dear."

"A bit of an understatement, I'd say."

Emma glanced at the man who held her. His florid face had paled to the color of parchment. "Uh, I think you ought to let me go…before he attacks."

"You'd best heed the lady's advice, Broadbent."

At the sound of the unfamiliar voice, Emma looked toward the staircase where a tall man now stood. His dark green dressing gown appeared to be made of silk. The garment probably had cost more than she earned in a year. Obviously, she was making the acquaintance of Gideon Cade. In the privacy of his own home, he'd evidently forgone wearing a crown. Nor did he carry a scepter.

Even though the horrible events that had transpired thus far tonight were not directly his fault, she felt a wave of resentment. In a fiercely uncertain world, it was obvious at a single glance that Gideon Cade was the kind of man who knew exactly where he fit in the greater scheme of things. She was certain he considered his place to be at the top, not only in business, but in other venues, as well. When he spoke, he expected to be obeyed. Without delay *or* debate.

"Broadbent, you'd best release the fair damsel you've captured."

The snideness of the man's observation was not lost upon Emma. She knew she was neither fair nor in that category of select females who might be called "damsels."

"Your only alternative appears to be having your throat ripped apart," he pointed out mildly. Carrying a lamp, he descended the final stair.

Over six feet tall, with wide shoulders that clearly didn't need a tailor's skill at padding to achieve their daunting proportions, he projected the aura of a commanding general being called upon to chastise a troop of inept soldiers. Even his thick pelt of mussed black hair added to the forbidding image.

"I'm inclined to agree with your assessment, Mr. Cade," the servant acknowledged, responding with his own brand of ironic dignity.

Emma hid a smile. From the troll's less-than-subservient demeanor, it was obvious he didn't hold his employer in complete awe.

She felt the constraining grip loosen, then disappear. Returning her gaze to the doorway, she slowly lowered her arm. The beast ceased growling, yet remained at rigid attention. As if charged with pulsating energy, his dirty coat of black fur still bristled outward.

"Call off your animal."

The velvet-voiced order came from behind her. Not wanting to make any sudden moves, she kept her focus upon the stray dog.

"He's not mine," she felt obliged to explain.

"From his protective stance, he views your relationship differently."

The soft but steely voice was closer. It took all Emma's control not to turn her head to keep track of the man. Having him at her back aroused her survival instincts to full alert. Still, she didn't feel it prudent to take her gaze from the ill-tempered beast who had invaded Mr. Cade's entry.

"It's true," she protested. "He's not mine. I don't even know if he has a name. Our only connection is the dinner scraps I've fed him."

"With a stray animal, that's enough to forge a bond for life."

The gritty observation sounded as if it had been spoken directly into her ear. Realizing that unless the hound relaxed his attack stance there would be no reduction in the escalating tension between herself, the dog and the men, Emma forced a smile to her stiff lips.

"Uh, nice doggy… Everything's all right now. The mean

man let go of my arm.'' She added the last remark for the
troll's benefit, lest he think she'd forgotten his rude treatment.

Almost imperceptibly, she saw the dog's hostile bearing
eased. He cocked his head, as he'd done on the front porch.
She moved forward. "You're just unhappy because you're
hungry, isn't that so?''

The animal whined softly, then moved toward her. His toe-
nails clicked against the hardwood floor until the sound was
cushioned by the oriental rug. The revolting smell of wet dog
hair soon filled the entry. She didn't consider herself a particularly demonstrative person, and yet, despite the beast's
rank odor, she felt he deserved a pat on his head for coming
to her defense. In her entire life, no human had performed
such a selfless act on her behalf.

She lightly brushed her fingertips through his black fur.
"That's a nice doggy.''

Her consoling gesture elicited another heartfelt whine and
the startling assault of the animal's wet, scratchy tongue upon
the back of her hand. She flinched but didn't pull away from
the contact.

"It appears, Broadbent, that 'Beauty' has tamed the
'Beast.''"

"Aye, so it does, sir.''

At the wholly facetious compliment, Emma's cheeks grew
warm.

"While he's evidencing such tender devotion, I suggest
you escort him to the kitchen and provide him with something
to eat, Broadbent.''

Following his master's edict, the servant approached the
hound and held out his hand. He let the dog sniff it. Soon
Broadbent's thick fingers were being energetically licked.
Telling herself it was foolish to feel betrayed by the animal's
fickle affection, Emma's arm fell to her side.

"Come along…'' The servant paused and affixed Emma
with a disapproving glance. "He really does deserve a
name.''

"You name him.''

"Very well.'' The man pondered for a moment, deepening

the lined indentations upon his ruddy brow. Then his reflective expression cleared. "I'll call him Duncan."

The name, coming as it did from nowhere, meant nothing to Emma, yet she saw Mr. Cade stiffen.

"Is that acceptable, sir?"

Her gaze flicked between the waiting servant and his frowning employer. For reasons unknown to her, the name Broadbent had selected must hold special meaning for both men.

"I couldn't care less what you call the mongrel."

At the indifferent response, a look of sorrow seemed to touch the troll's eyes. "Aye, sir. Come along, Duncan. I'd say you've waited long enough for your supper."

After flashing a reproachful glance at her, Broadbent sank his fingers into the fur at the back of the dog's neck. The animal allowed itself to be led a couple of steps before stopping. Having only a vague idea as to its basic disposition, Emma tensed again.

The servant wisely removed his hand from the animal. Whimpering softly, it trotted toward her.

"Go along with Mr. Broadbent," she urged, feeling awkward at having others overhear her stilted admonition to the uncooperative canine. "He's going to feed you. There now, be a good doggy. Uh…Duncan, I'll be perfectly all right on my own."

He held her stare, as if by looking into her eyes he could somehow fathom what was expected of him. She smiled reassuringly, aware from the corner of her eye that Mr. Cade was studying her.

Without any warning, the hound planted its paws on the rug and shook his hairy body free of the excess moisture he'd been obliged to carry. A misting spray of rainwater, mingling with disgusting, foul-smelling dog residue, enveloped both her and Mr. Cade.

Emma jumped back. "Oh! Stop, you naughty dog!"

Mr. Cade stepped aside to avoid the full brunt of his dirty baptism. Mortified by the animal's rudeness, she closed her eyes.

"He really isn't my dog," she said, again compelled to disavow any connection to the unruly stray following Broadbent from the room.

"So you've said, Miss—" Mr. Cade broke off, his lethal gaze fairly boring into her. "I assume, whereas yonder hellhound has no name, you, on the other hand, come with both a first and a last one."

The man's sarcasm was a chore to overlook. Nevertheless, considering that desperate circumstances had brought her to his home in the wee hours of the morning, she strove to contain her growing dislike toward Courtney's uncle.

"Of course I do."

"And that would be..." he prompted mockingly.

His insulting tone made her feel like a common beetle who had strayed beyond its prescribed territory and was in imminent danger of being squashed beneath Mr. Cade's finely stitched leather slipper.

"Emma January Step," she pronounced through clinched teeth, intimidated against her will by the man's arrogance.

He raised a black eyebrow. "And what is it you want, Miss Step, other than to invade my home and terrorize those in my employ?"

A hot blush singed her cheeks. "I apologize for the dog. I had no idea he would follow me." She pushed at the strands of hair that had fallen into her eyes. "You see, I have a matter of the utmost urgency to discuss, and your servant wouldn't summon you so I could explain what's happened."

"I must remember to give him a raise."

"A *raise?*" she repeated, infuriated by the man's puffed-up attitude.

He nodded. "I value any employee safeguarding my privacy." His lips curved mockingly. "Especially after I've retired for the night."

Emma rolled her eyes. It was a bit much to hear the conceited man pronounce such high-handed drivel. Even without a crown, he was more overbearing than any far-eastern potentate she'd read about. Had Broadbent been present, she wouldn't have been surprised to see Mr. Cade pitch *him* a bone, or perhaps pat the servant on his head. Goodness, it required little imagination to picture Broadbent licking his master's hand in the same devoted manner as the dog.

"How much?" Emma inquired briskly.

"I beg your pardon?" Mr. Cade drawled softly, still viewing her with all the warmth he would have bestowed upon that upstart beetle.

"How much of a raise will you give Mr. Broadbent?"

Growing up as an orphan, Emma had learned one lesson above all others. People might occasionally make generous offers, but it was rare indeed for any of those teary-voiced promises to be fulfilled. It probably didn't reflect to her credit, but she had a passionate aversion to hollow pledges and the people who issued them.

"Are you thinking of an additional dollar a week?" she continued, undaunted by Mr. Cade's now glowering countenance. "Or did you have something more substantial in mind?"

"Miss Step, am I to believe you and your hairy mongrel invaded my home in order to negotiate an increase of salary for Broadbent?"

Recalling abruptly the urgent business that had sent her flying out the academy's door in the wee hours of the morning, Emma winced. "No, sir, of course not. I'm afraid I have very distressing news."

"And that would be…"

"It's Courtney." Emma closed the small distance that separated her from the girl's uncle. "I regret to inform you, she's run away."

Chapter Two

Emma waited for an outburst of alarm from Mr. Cade. He stunned her by remaining unruffled.

"I see."

Frustrated by his lack of emotion, Emma's hands clenched. "As I told your servant, I'm a teacher at the Hempshire Academy, and your niece is one of my students. I spoke earlier in the evening with Courtney and shared some disquieting news regarding the school's future. I decided to look in on her before going to bed. That's when I discovered she was gone."

"I see."

If he pronounced that inane, wholly useless phrase again, she would slap his insolent face.

When that ferocious thought imprinted itself upon Emma's mind, she flinched. Good grief, she was not the kind of woman to entertain visions of violence. She was a tutor of refined young women.

"I realize how upset you must be," she said, deciding to credit the man's lack of emotion to acute distress. "I imagine you are somewhat in a state of shock."

"Am I?"

Emma nodded. "Perhaps a glass of…sherry would calm you."

He tilted his head. "Do I appear to be *uncalm*, Miss Step?"

Actually, he looked irritatingly unaffected, but she could

think of no other explanation for his lack of concern. It was inconceivable that she faced a monster incapable of caring about his own niece's welfare.

Instinctively she reached out and touched his silk sleeve. "I collect that being awakened from a sound sleep and discovering a hostile dog holding one's servant at bay would discomfit anyone. To be informed of Courtney's disappearance on the heels of such a misadventure is bound to have discombobulated you, sir."

"I wasn't exactly in deep slumber."

"No?"

He shook his head. "I was already on my way downstairs, to get some work done in my study." His speculative gaze lowered to where her fingertips rested upon his sleeve. "Do you still think I require a glass of sherry to...*fortify* me?"

Self-consciously Emma removed her hand. "I have it upon good authority that spirits may be used for such medicinal purposes."

He inspected her features with a dispassionate intensity that scraped her composure. "Then I leave myself in your capable hands, Miss Step. If you believe I require a drink to deal with this situation, by all means let us adjourn to the library where we may indulge ourselves."

Emma experienced a surge of relief. Perhaps Mr. Cade wasn't as unfeeling as she'd supposed. "Lead the way, sir. Time is of the essence."

He did not precede her, however. Rather, his fingers closed around her upper arm. Startled by the unexpected contact, Emma's gaze flew up. His harshly sculpted features were blandly inexpressive.

The golden lamplight pooling about them in the vestibule accented the harsh lines of his formidable countenance. Her stomach curled. Uncomfortably aware of being alone with him in the silent house, Emma licked her suddenly dry lips. She realized her heart was beating as rapidly as if she'd just sprinted up three flights of stairs.

His hold tightened. "Come along, Miss Step."

There was a silkiness to his tone that raised the fine hairs

at the nape of her neck. Surely it was only her imagination
that made his touch and suggestion seem faintly improper.

She was the one who'd thrust herself into the alien situation
of being alone with a man in the wee hours of the morning.
She could hardly demand that he dash upstairs and put on a
shirt, trousers and topcoat. It was entirely reasonable that he
wore a dressing gown. She slid him a sideways glance. Still,
she was certain the trousers would have made her less aware
of the large male body at her side.

Making no comment, she allowed herself to be guided by
his forceful grip down the hallway and through the first open
threshold they passed. A small cocoon of light accompanied
their passage, increasing the sense of intimacy tugging at
Emma. The indisputable strength of the fingers wrapped
around her arm made her feel as if the man were doing something more significant than leading her into a darkened chamber.

She shivered and told herself the dual shocks of the Hempshire Academy closing and Courtney running away were af-
fecting her nerves.

Mr. Cade released her. She tried to rub away the tingling
sensation in her arm. His shuttered gaze tracked the instinctive gesture, and she stopped. Turning from his disturbing
scrutiny, she absorbed her surroundings.

Again she was struck by an impression of understated opulence. The shifting shadows cast by Mr. Cade's lamp lapped
at towering bookcases filled with leather volumes. There was
the resonant clicking of an ivory-and-gold clock on the mar-
ble mantel above a cold, dark hearth. A lacquered Chinese
box, a gold candlestick and a cut-crystal bowl graced a
leaf-carved mahogany lowboy.

It was obvious that Gideon Cade had created an eastern
oasis for himself in the West. From the corner of her eye, she
was aware that he was lighting several more lamps. The subtle, strangely sensual sound of his silk robe rustling against
his hard frame accompanied his actions.

He gestured toward one of the two padded high-backed
chairs grouped before the desk. Vivid green-and-gold striped

material covered padded armrests and seats. "Sit down, Miss Step."

Emma complied. She wanted this discussion over with as quickly as possible. They needed to be searching for Courtney.

Instead of taking the chair behind his desk, Mr. Cade went to a cherrywood cabinet and opened its carved doors. There was the faint clink of shifting crystal. She saw the play of powerful muscles along his upper back beneath the robe.

When he turned, he held two glasses. One was a squat tumbler filled with a rich amber-colored liquid; the other was a fragile-stemmed vessel containing a thimble-size swallow of a dark reddish fluid. The startling contrast between the glasses made her keenly conscious of the contrast between herself and Mr. Cade.

His impressive stature and the energy radiating from his somber eyes dominated the chamber. The shadows might have retreated to the room's farthest corners, but the tight line compressing his mouth made her think there were shadows to this man that would never be banished. His brooding, assessing eyes added to the effect of "secrets kept."

He extended the dainty glass. "Here."

For one contrary moment, Emma wanted to reach for the tumbler instead. The urge to ruffle Gideon Cade's complacency caught her by surprise. Usually she made it a point to get along with everyone.

She hesitated only a moment before accepting the more delicate of the two vessels. No matter how tempted she might be, it wouldn't be prudent to antagonize this man.

Her fingers curved around the glass. "Thank you."

For a fraction of a second, she wasn't sure he intended to surrender the drink. Perplexed, she looked beyond his strong, leanly sculpted hand and encountered his hard stare.

Again she had the feeling that he was inspecting her as if she were an insect who'd blundered into his exalted domain. She didn't think she'd ever been studied with such penetrating awareness. She couldn't imagine what caused those ruthlessly intelligent eyes to gleam with interest. There was nothing noteworthy about her.

She tugged lightly at the glass. Her fingers grazed his. The subtle friction did something unexplainable to her stomach. For a frozen moment, Emma's surroundings faded to insignificance. It seemed as if she and the man towering above her were the only two beings left in the entire world. She had the feeling that the heart beating within his wide chest shared the same rapid rhythm as her own racing heart.

The pressure of his grip eased. She took the glass into her trembling hands and raised it to her lips. That her own nerves needed steadying was an abhorrent admission. For as far back as she could remember, her only true sense of security had come from the inner knowledge that she could keep her head when everyone else was in danger of losing theirs.

As she drained the drink, she decided it was Cade's aggressive stare causing her uncustomary bout of self-consciousness. She added rudeness to his growing list of faults.

He circled his desk and seated himself behind it. "Why the scowl, Miss Step? Surely the sherry isn't that bad."

The hint of humor tingeing his harshly defined features surprised her. She sensed Mr. Cade wasn't given to casual smiling. The sweet aftertaste of sherry that lingered in her throat wasn't unpleasant. "The drink is fine."

"I'm relieved to know my liquor supply meets your standards." He sipped slowly before setting aside his tumbler. "Now that we've both had the opportunity to calm ourselves, why don't you tell me what the *hell* is going on?"

The mildness of his tone momentarily distracted her from the profanity. When it did register, her fingers tightened around the empty glass. Gone was the earlier amusement that had briefly tempered his arrogant expression. She restrained herself from chiding him about his foul language. To do so would be too much like challenging a wild panther with whom she'd inadvertently become locked in the same cage.

Best to placate the creature, she reflected, since she knew the news she carried would darken his already beastly mood.

"As I explained in your foyer, Courtney has disappeared."

"Surely not into thin air."

The sardonic quip dug deeply into Emma's remaining reserve of patience. "Of course not. I told you, she's run away."

"How can I be sure you haven't misplaced her?"

"But that's preposterous," Emma sputtered, deeply affronted.

"On the contrary, any institution run in such a slipshod fashion as the Hempshire Academy could easily misplace a student or two."

"We haven't *lost* her—she's run away! And for your information, the Hempshire Academy is a wonderful school."

"I have difficulty believing a 'wonderful' school would maintain such poor control over its students that it's possible for a young lady to slip out in the middle of the night to roam the streets."

A red haze lowered over Emma's eyes. She shot to her feet, exerting every bit of willpower she possessed *not* to hurl her glass at Mr. Cade's arrogant, thick head. "We can affix the blame later. For now, our attention must be directed at finding Courtney."

"Sit down, Miss Step."

His order, spoken with whiplike command had her knees buckling in compliance. Her mind kicked in, however, before her bottom connected with the chair.

"You should know that, unlike Broadbent, I won't obey high-handed commands."

"And you should know that *I* do not run into the night half-cocked. Experience has taught me it's better to have a complete grasp of the facts before taking action."

She was tempted to circle the desk, grab the perfectly pressed lapels of his dressing gown and shake him into mobility. The thought brought with it a sudden awareness of the white linen nightshirt beneath the green robe. The black chest hairs curling above the border of tiny pink rosebuds created a ludicrous contrast of masculinity verses femininity.

No article of clothing in her possession was half so elegant.

That such a potent specimen of masculinity as Gideon Cade enjoyed parading about in such feminine clothing was difficult to accept.

Emma sank back into her chair. "What precisely is it you wish to know before we organize a search?"

"What makes you so certain she's run away, what was the news about the academy's future you imparted to her, and what made you come here tonight?"

Emma reached into her pocket, grateful that she hadn't forgotten Courtney's note. "This was all the explanation she left."

She extended the folded paper. Reluctant to risk another disturbing encounter with his fingers, she considered flinging the note across the desk. He was already leaning forward, however, and she was coerced into allowing him to retrieve the paper in a more civilized manner.

She braced herself for the contact. His thumb and forefinger gripped the corner. Before she could let go, something compelled her to look up. His enigmatic gaze was locked squarely upon her. She wasn't sure she remembered how to breathe. She loosened her hold. The paper slid from her grasp. There was no physical contact. Still, her stomach took a peculiar dip.

She forced herself to glance away from him and take a deep breath. When she looked up, he was smoothing the note's creases. As he began to read the hastily scribbled message, his dark eyebrows drew together.

He looked up, catching her stare. "Well, one thing is clear."

"What's that?"

"Whoever teaches penmanship at your institution has failed miserably on Courtney's behalf."

"Is that all you can say?" Emma couldn't believe the man could be so insensitive about the note's contents. She'd committed the message to memory.

My dearest Miss Step,
Don't be alarmed. I've gone to seek help for the acad-

emy's desperate situation. I hope to return with good news. Fortunately, there's someone I can turn to for assistance.

> Your most devoted and loyal student,
> Courtney Gertrude Cade

Emma touched a trembling hand to her hair. The rigid rein she'd exerted on her roiling emotions was slipping. "I thought if I came to you, you would want to find her."

"Is that why the school's headmistress sent you?"

"I—I saw no need to awaken Miss Loutitia." The thought of informing Miss Hempshire of Courtney's disappearance during this traumatic period of the older woman's life made Emma shudder. Loutitia Hempshire was the kind of person who, even in the best of times, wasn't able to keep her high-strung sensibilities under control.

"If she can't keep track of her students, she deserves to have her sleep interrupted," Mr. Cade stated dispassionately.

To Emma's horror, warm tears blurred her vision. Not trusting her voice, she refrained from pointing out that having a hysterical school matron on her hands was hardly conducive to finding Courtney.

"Well, have you nothing to say?," he inquired chidingly. "Don't tell me you've run out of words? I wouldn't have though you so weak-spirited."

At the barely veiled insult, Emma tensed. Now she knew why people took such delight in deposing tyrants by bloody methods. She could imagine the satisfaction of wielding a sword against a bound and gagged Gideon Cade.

"While we're debating the matter in the comfort of your library, Courtney is alone and unprotected." Emma's voice caught. "We have to find her. She's young and innocent and totally at the mercy of any dishonorable man who might want to take advantage of her."

"You don't believe this exhibition of headstrong rebellion warrants whatever disaster befalls her?"

Emma recoiled at the heartless question. "No!"

"But what about the danger she's placed you in?"

"Me?" she asked in confusion.

"By running away, Courtney caused you to leave the security of the academy and race recklessly into the night. Surely the terrors facing an innocent young girl would also endanger you, Miss Step."

"Courtney's welfare takes priority over my own."

"Does it?" he asked softly.

She shifted uncomfortably. "I...I shouldn't have left her alone after confiding the problems the academy was facing."

Emma's words dwindled to silence. Guilt grew within her at the knowledge that her own concerns had blinded her to how upset Courtney must have been. With the Denver institution closing, the girl would surely be sent to an eastern finishing school. It was a mystery to Emma, but evidently Courtney wished to remain in close proximity to her coldhearted uncle.

"My niece is old enough to be held accountable for her own actions."

Emma refused to suffer the man's insensitivity another moment. "Courtney is a bright and brave young woman who deserves our best efforts to find her."

"She's also willful," he interjected quietly. "Come now, there's no need for tears or self-recriminations, Miss Step. You've already expended your best efforts."

Emma's control finally snapped. "If you weren't an unfeeling monster incapable of basic human sentiment, you would be looking for her right now!"

His dark eyes turned frigid. "Is that how you view me?"

"It's how the whole world views you!" she shouted back. "*Everything* the newspapers say about you is true!"

It was the foulest insult she could think to hurl.

He shrugged. "I find what's printed in newspapers generally isn't worth the time it takes to read them. And as for my niece..."

He had Emma's full attention now. "Yes?"

Drawing out the moment, he leaned back in his chair and steepled his fingertips. "Since she's fast asleep upstairs in her bedchamber, there's little point in searching for her, is there?"

Chapter Three

Gideon watched Miss Step's eyes darken to a deep shade of smoky slate.

"What did you say?"

Her question trembled with barely contained outrage. An ordinary man would have been cowed by the fury shimmering in her wrathful gaze. Gideon felt an inner quickening. He didn't consider himself ordinary, and the woman sitting across his desk, looking as if she would like to supply the rope at a lynching held in his honor, didn't intimidate him. She provoked a different response—one that challenged him on a profoundly elemental level.

"You heard me. Courtney is upstairs asleep."

Miss Step rose slowly. Her eyes continued to reproach him. Gideon was startled by the twinge of guilt that pricked him. He reminded himself he'd had good reason for not revealing the girl was safe. He'd wanted to teach the woman whom Courtney repeatedly described as a "paragon of magnificence" that, when one was in charge of a minor, one damned well ought to keep track of her!

"You...you..."

Gideon had the feeling the redoubtable Miss Step was rarely at a loss for words. He inclined his head. "Yes?"

"You are a fiend."

He swallowed a laugh. If that was the worst she could come

up with, she'd led a sheltered life. "I was merely teaching you a lesson."

"You were playing a game of cat and mouse!"

The accusation carried a measure of truth. He didn't mind a game of cat and mouse—provided, of course, that he played the role of cat.

"When one misplaces a young woman, one needs to suffer. That way, the episode will not be repeated."

Her hands clenched.

He wasn't given to fanciful observations, but in that moment he would have sworn twin lightning bolts flashed in her eyes, transforming the turbulent gray to shimmering quicksilver.

"When one is consumed with worry about the future, one can't be expected to know in advance what a sixteen-year-old girl will do!"

"Come now, surely a woman of your age and experience must realize young ladies are generally an unpredictable lot."

Miss Step's creamy complexion became a shade of pink that was in stark dissimilarity to the streak of grime smudging her delicate jaw. She'd probably picked up the smear when she petted the flea-bitten mongrel who'd followed her to his house. It surprised him that he found her disheveled state appealing. No doubt his interest was held by the contrast of the pristine princess and the woebegone commoner sharing the same lithe body.

Gideon noticed other details about the furious woman. She was compact in stature and dressed in a drab gray gown that covered everything except her face and hands. Spatters of mud clung to the hem. The dress's cut and material were clearly second-rate, though he had to admit there was nothing second-rate about how the still-damp garment outlined her feminine curves.

"I was worried about her! That's why I went to her room to check on her."

Gideon mentally counted the tiny fastenings running up the gown's conservative bodice and sleeves. His gaze narrowed. There had to be forty black buttons holding her dress together.

"But when you found out she was missing, you didn't alert the headmistress." He gestured toward her. "If you were so concerned about Courtney's welfare, why did you choose such a difficult gown to get into? It must have taken you an hour to secure those buttons."

New color climbed her cheeks. His comment about the time it took to get into her gown had probably offended her. Should he make an observation as to how long it would take to get *out* of the garment, she would most likely swoon.

"I was already dressed when I checked on her."

Gideon's interest sharpened. Was it customary for the schoolmistress to keep such late hours? It wasn't any of his business, of course. The only point of relevance between them was that the woman and the institution for which she worked had failed in their responsibility to safeguard his niece.

And yet Gideon wondered how Miss Step occupied herself at night. He often stayed up late, pursuing the amusements available to a man of his age, temperament and social position. There were fine cheroots to be smoked, vintage wines to be savored, games of cards to be played, and worldly women with whom to satisfy his more basic needs.

How did Miss Step pass the time between midnight and dawn?

"You keep late hours," he confined himself to remarking. "Satisfy my curiosity and explain why you didn't wake the headmistress?"

Miss Step pushed back the tendrils of light brown hair that had sprung from the coil fastened at the nape of her neck. In the process, she managed to spread the dirty smear from her jaw to her cheek. It was ridiculous to find her unraveling condition intriguing. Yet damned if there wasn't something charming about the fastidious woman's progressively unkept appearance. She reminded him of a delicately wrapped package being opened by invisible hands. Her wrappings might not be fancy, but beneath the frippery, Gideon suspected, the gift would be unexpectedly lovely.

"To understand that, you would have to know the

woman." Courtney's teacher looked away. "Miss Loutitia is prone to…"

"To what?" Gideon asked impatiently, missing the touch of Miss Step's gaze upon him. He liked the way her wide gray eyes exposed her changing feelings. The sense of sincerity she radiated spawned a powerful reaction within him, making him feel as if she were standing utterly naked in his library. The blood in his veins heated. As much as his mental picture shot shafts of fire though him, he found the prospect of peering into her unguarded soul even more exciting.

She looked up. "I'm afraid Miss Loutitia has a somewhat overemotional temperament. When things go the least bit wrong, she becomes hysterical."

Gideon hadn't met the man yet who wouldn't rather face gunfire than an overwrought female.

"I can see why you'd want to avoid such a scene. Tell me, Miss Step, are *you* prone to overemotional outbursts?"

She shook her head. "Of course not. What is, simply is. I've learned not to rail at fate. Doing so accomplishes nothing."

Another silken strand of hair settled softly along the side of her face. A curious tightness gripped Gideon's chest.

"I've made the same discovery."

She moved toward the door. "Now that I know Courtney is safe, I'll be on my way."

"Not so fast."

His words were harsher than he intended. Her back stiffened, straight and unyielding as an iron post set in rock-hard mortar.

"Since our business is completed, there's no point in my remaining."

You could always join me upstairs in my bedchamber. We could while away the next few hours between my sheets….

When that rogue thought materialized in his brain, Gideon's skin grew hot. The militant Miss Step was the last female on this good earth about whom he should harbor lascivious feelings.

He pushed back his chair and stood. It had been an act of

calculated rudeness to remain seated after she rose to her feet. He'd wanted to see if she had the fortitude to chastise him for his churlish behavior. He imagined restraining herself had been taxing.

"I'm sure you understand why I can't let you leave, Miss Step."

She whirled around. "What do you mean?"

It probably wasn't a good sign that her widened eyes and the slight waver in her voice fueled his growing interest.

"Good manners won't permit me to let you go dashing into the night unescorted."

She stared at him as if he'd just recited the preamble to the Constitution, or something else equally irrelevant.

"*Good manners?*" she repeated, clearly stunned.

He nodded.

"But you haven't displayed a single bit of mannerly behavior!"

"Of course I have. You just weren't paying attention."

She drew herself up to her full height, such as it was. "Not more than three minutes ago, you remained seated after I had stood. Practically the first lesson a boy learns is to rise when a lady stands."

Gideon was sure she felt better for getting the reprimand out. "A small oversight when compared to abandoning you to the likelihood of being murdered on Denver's wild streets, wouldn't you agree?"

"I'm perfectly capable of returning to the academy without getting myself killed," she responded with cold disdain.

"Perhaps you are, but I've no intention of putting the matter to the test."

"It's not your choice!"

Damn, she was stubborn. What she didn't realize was that after committing himself to a course of action, he never backed down. "This streak of childish rebellion is wearing my patience."

"Then I'd best leave."

The woman actually had the misplaced gall to try walking

past him. Gideon's hand shot out and closed around her arm. A look of indignant astonishment swept her features.

"My way," he said softly. "We'll do things my way."

"Why, you conceited, overbearing tyrant."

"And here I thought you were having trouble understanding me."

He didn't know why he was taunting her. But he did know he wasn't going to yield to the powerful temptation of turning himself inside out to please her.

"You can't make me believe this rusty bit of chivalry with which you insist on bullying me is anything more than an example of your perverse nature." She tugged her arm. "Now let me go."

Strange how her absolute lack of coquettishness made him incredibly aware of her femininity. Standing this close to her, with her upturned face just inches from his, he was bombarded by her subtle beauty. Her skin was flushed with color. Her soft, parted lips trembled. Her eyes, sheltered beneath thick, dark lashes, beckoned him to pull her more tightly to him.

"My 'perverse nature' likes to make sure I get a sound night's sleep. I won't be able to do that if I'm kept awake by visions of you running for your life from some drifter who never got that first lesson on manners. Nor do I like the thought of you getting caught in another rainstorm. Unless you like my hand on you and want to prolong this useless argument, I suggest you accept my offer of a carriage ride." He couldn't resist adding, "With an appreciative smile."

Her eyes spat fire. Her feminine ferocity was oddly invigorating. For too many years, cynicism and bitterness had formed the bedrock of his character. This woman straining futilely against his hold glowed with enough earnest outrage to thaw the most frigid soul. Her obvious devotion to duty and her spirited nature lured him closer.

She struggled briefly before giving in to the inevitable. Her breathing was fast and shallow. The stench of dog had dissipated. For the first time, her female scent teased his nostrils. His body hardened.

"All right. I'll accept your offer."

Her brittle capitulation seemed a major victory. "Where's the smile?"

She bared her teeth with surprising indelicacy. If she was tamed to his handling, it would be a pleasure to feel the tips of those teeth lightly scraping various parts of his anatomy. In her present state, though, he doubted his hide would escape serious damage.

"Now, that wasn't so hard, was it?"

Her eyes silently burned him at the stake. He watched her take a deep breath. He'd lost count of how many times during their encounter she'd done so. He would have liked to watch her chest inflate, but he couldn't tear his gaze from her face.

"Are you going to release me?"

"Of course." He did so reluctantly.

"I'll wait here while you change," she said coolly.

"Change?" They would be here until the next century if she expected him to change his basic nature.

"You'll catch a chill if you go outside dressed as you are."

For the first time since coming downstairs, Gideon became conscious of his attire. He felt Miss Step's gaze drift to the ridiculous nightshirt he'd been compelled to put on in order to greet his overemotional niece.

He couldn't recall the last time he'd experienced the heat of embarrassment crawling up his neck. Having Miss Step see him in the frilled, embroidered nightshirt he'd received several Christmases ago from a former lover with peculiar taste in men's clothing would be enough to make any man squirm.

The alternative would have been to come downstairs with nothing beneath the robe, which, of course, he couldn't do with Courtney in the house. He usually slept naked and hadn't even known he owned a nightshirt until he'd rummaged through his dresser. A cruel and malicious fate had decreed this nauseating beribboned garment to be the only thing with which he could quickly cover himself.

Gideon shoved his fingers through his hair in disgust. It was amazing that Miss Step hadn't broken into gales of laughter at the sight of him in rosebuds and pink ribbons. It annoyed the hell out of him that she probably assumed it was his habit to wear such feminine-looking apparel.

He cleared his throat. "It won't take me long to dress."

"If you would just be reasonable about letting me—"

"We settled that argument. I won. You lost. Remember?"

He knew he sounded like the very tyrant she'd called him, but he refused to continue standing there dressed as he was. When this confrontation ended, he intended to have his pants on.

"I have an excellent memory," she said with surprising calm.

Had she finally learned which of them was in charge?

"Wait here," he instructed briskly.

She opened her mouth.

He raised an eyebrow, daring her to balk at his command. A half second passed. Obviously, she was weighing the ramifications of further rebellion.

"All right."

It was nice to know that the universe had returned to its proper course, a course where Courtney *and* her intrepid schoolmistress yielded to his authority. "Help yourself to another glass of sherry. I won't be long."

Emma watched Courtney's uncle stride from the room. She had no intention of having more sherry, *or* of cooling her heels while he went upstairs to dress. It was time the insufferable toad learned he could not bend everyone to his will. A flash of satisfaction swept through her as she thanked the Creator for the honor of being allowed to prick the overinflated bubble of Gideon Cade's pride.

She wasted no time in vacating the library, moving quickly through the hall. It occurred to her that, if Miss Hempshire closed the academy as immediately as she'd announced she would, Courtney might not return to school. Emma experienced a pang of sadness that she wouldn't have the opportunity to say goodbye.

When she stepped into the entry, the sight of her torn and muddy cloak hanging from the coatrack next to the front door stopped her. It seemed as if a dozen years had passed since she first entered Mr. Cade's residence. As she spread the time-worn garment over her shoulders, she remembered the dog.

Drat, she had no desire to burden poor Duncan with the likes of Courtney's coldhearted uncle or his bizarre butler. Even though she hadn't the means to support even herself for long in Denver, she impetuously decided to take the hound with her.

Emma altered her path and followed the direction Broadbent had taken when he led the dog away. She walked through a faintly lit hallway, past a spacious dining chamber and down a short flight of stairs. Another turn brought her into a large, well-scrubbed kitchen.

The dim light leaking from a trimmed lamp revealed large copper kettles hanging above an immense brick fireplace. There was also a substantial cookstove. On one of the wide counters sat a blue ceramic bowl over which a white cloth had been spread. A small bulge pushed upward at the draped cloth, indicating that bread dough was rising beneath it. Two apple pies cooled beside a deep steel sink. A large smoked ham lay next to the short-handled pump. Various tall cabinets and a sturdy wood table surrounded by half a dozen chairs added to the room's aura of secure abundance.

At the rich aroma wafting from the apple pies, smoked ham and expanding bread dough, Emma's steps faltered. She'd been so upset by Miss Loutitia's news about the academy closing that she'd paced her bedchamber instead of going downstairs for supper. Emma's stomach growled in recognition of how long it had been since she ate. She sympathized more keenly with Duncan for having to depend upon the kindness of strangers to supply him with food.

Forcing herself to ignore the thickly crusted apple pies' siren call, she looked around the meagerly lit room in hopes of finding the stray hound.

"Duncan, where are you?"

Only her own rapid breathing disturbed the chamber's silence. She saw the vague outline of a door through the shadowy darkness and walked toward it. She'd almost reached it when her right foot slammed into a chair leg. Pain shot from her toes through her entire body.

"Ow! Ooh, oh, that hurts!" She didn't know which was louder, her cries or the raw scrape of the chair against the wood-planked floor.

Standing on one foot, she leaned forward and massaged her throbbing toes. It was difficult to see past the tears that had sprung to her eyes, but she forced herself to limp the rest of the way to the door. It opened to the outside. She was dismayed to discover a thick fog had drifted into town.

"Duncan," she called again. Then she realized the fickle mutt probably didn't comprehend that he'd been newly christened. "Here, doggy, it's time to leave."

Nothing disturbed the dank grayness that enveloped her. "I'm going now. I'll be at the academy." She was wasting her breath. Even if the dog was hiding nearby, he couldn't possibly understand her.

She waited a moment longer, listening for a canine whine or whimper. Hearing nothing, she shifted her attention to the misty, otherworldly landscape that surrounded her. In even the best of circumstances, finding her bearings was challenging. In this macabre situation, she felt utterly disoriented.

She tried to visualize the position of the side doorway she'd stepped through in relation to the mansion's exterior as it faced the street. It seemed that, if she walked straight ahead for a couple of yards and then turned right—no left—she would be heading toward the flagstone path she'd used to reach the front porch. When she found that path, she would go in the opposite direction and turn left...or was it right? No, a left turn would point her in the direction of the academy. Well, she hoped so, anyway.

Emma drew her thin cloak about her and tried to remember why she'd been so opposed to having Courtney's uncle give her a ride in his carriage.

Oh, yes, he was an arrogant cur who terrorized others so that he could have his way. Also, there was a predatory look in his brooding eyes that made her skin tingle and her heart pound. She didn't like how she felt when he was breathing down her neck, as if she were melting from the inside out and not in control of her mind and body.

Hoping for a stroke of good fortune, she surged forward into the fog. A fresh bolt of pain radiated from her right foot. It did little for her tranquillity to realize she would be limping all the way back to the academy. She tried to dispel the feeling that she was an injured warrior surrendering the battlefield to a superior foe. Besides, if she had been vanquished, it was only because he'd employed unfair tactics.

She took only a few steps before she smacked into what must have been a brick wall. Her injured foot registered its anguished protest. Emma braced one hand against the wall and reached down to comfort her battered toes.

The wall shifted unexpectedly, and she lost her balance. "Oh!"

Amazingly, the wall reached out to steady her.

"Well, Miss Step, now that we've established your word is worthless, shall we be on our way?"

As he'd certainly intended, the insulting question stung her pride.

She refused to feel one iota of guilt for trying to escape his odious company. "I was under no obligation to stay."

"Only the obligation of having agreed to do so."

"You...you bullied me into agreeing to wait."

The powerful fingers gripping her arms tightened. She didn't delude herself that she possessed the strength to pull free. He wasn't hurting her. He was effectively demonstrating that his strength was superior to hers.

"I don't resort to bullying to achieve my goals. I simply insist that those who deal with me abide by the laws of logic."

Had her foot not been in such agony, she would have kicked the smug man soundly. And the blow would have landed where Johnny McGuire had taught her all men were vulnerable. While he was doubled over in pain, she would have sprinted away.

"Would you do me a favor?" she asked with as much calm as she could muster.

"What is it?" Definite suspicion laced the query.

"Put your lips together and keep them that way until we bid each other farewell." That event could not come soon enough for her.

"Considering your age, don't you think it's time you stopped lapsing into such childish baiting?"

Emma choked down a hiss. Why did he insist on harping about her age? Just how old did he think she was? "Not that it's any of your business, but I'm twenty-four."

"Really? I'd thought perhaps you were thirty."

"Let me go."

"Now I've upset you."

Upset her? She was miles beyond upset. How dare he make such a cruel and thoughtless remark! He might have just as easily said she looked like a shriveled old maid with a hump on her back and had the word *spinster* branded on her forehead. Oh, she knew thirty wasn't such an advanced age, but when a woman was single, she tended to be sensitive about such observations.

"Take me to your carriage."

"I've noticed that even when you're being reasonable, Miss Step, there's a definite edge to your voice."

He released his hold. Before she could celebrate the victory, he moved beside her and cupped her elbow in a guiding gesture. She gritted her teeth and began walking. Blasted, aggravating—

"Why are you limping?"

"Because one of your kitchen chairs attacked me before I could gain my freedom from this monstrous edifice you call a house."

He stopped and knelt down. "What were you doing in the kitchen?"

"I was looking for that stupid dog, of course."

He began to fiddle with the hem of her skirts. "You planned on taking him with you?"

"I considered it my duty to liberate him from—" She broke off and tried to back away. When had he suddenly become fascinated with her petticoats? "What do you think you're doing? Stop that!"

She batted ineffectually at his roving hands. Instead of answering, he pulled her unceremoniously to the ground. She landed in a sitting position.

"I said to stop—"

"Hold still."

"I will not! Get your hands off my limbs."

"Relax, I'm just raising your skirts."

"If you think I'm going to let you molest me in your yard, you've lost what little sense you have."

He looked up. Because his face was so near, she had little difficulty making out his rugged features. "Miss Step, I have no doubt you are right. I do seem to have lost my senses where you're concerned, however, I can assure you that I would never molest you in my yard. Believe me, there are more comfortable places to become acquainted with what's beneath your skirts."

"You blackguard! No matter how *nefarious* your behavior, all you dwell upon is your own comfort."

"On the contrary, it would be your comfort I'd be considering. Now behave yourself. I want to judge how badly you damaged yourself while in my 'monstrous' house."

"It's too dark to see anything."

"Damn, you're right." He pulled her skirt down.

She was in the middle of a sigh of relief when he stood and swept her into his arms. The world tilted alarmingly. "Put me down!"

"Miss Step, has anyone ever pointed out that you are an extremely bossy woman? In the short time we've known each other, you've barked out more orders than Sherman probably issued on his march to the sea."

She was bossy? Clearly, the man suffered from delusions. She refused to say anything else until... She envisioned no circumstance wherein she would exchange further conversation with him.

"Would it kill you to cooperate?" His tone was at once aggravated and strained.

"If I'm too heavy, you'd best set me down."

"It's my intent to carry you inside," he growled softly.

The low, hostile sound put her in mind of Duncan. "Then do so."

"I will—as soon as you let go of the hairs on my chest."

Emma's face went hot. Immediately her fingers relaxed their death grip on his shirt. "Uh, I'm sorry."

"Apology accepted," came the gruff response.

He proceeded toward the house. Even her guilty embarrassment couldn't compel her to twine her arms around his neck. With her hands folded in front of her, she suspected she was an awkward bundle to manage, but that was his problem. She'd been willing, after all, to limp along beside him.

She was relieved when they reached the slightly raised step at the side of the house. Being transported by Courtney's uncle through vaporous, otherworldly mists was surely the stuff of nightmares.

While shifting her weight to one arm, he reached forward to unlatch the door. Even though she knew she wasn't heavy, she was still impressed by his strength and admitted he was a splendidly formed man. Too bad his character didn't measure up to the rest of him.

"If you'd put your arms around my neck, this would be easier."

"Stop playing Sir Walter Raleigh, and you'll have both hands free."

"I bet you've lost count of the times you've been called overbearing." He leaned to the side, managing to get the door open. "They must call you General Step at the Academy."

He carried her through the side door into the kitchen. She tried to ignore the leashed male strength at his disposal. He sat her on the kitchen table and turned the nearby lamp to increased brightness.

She assured herself it wasn't concern that tightened his expression. He raised her skirts again. She said nothing, even though her stockings and lace-bordered pantalets were exposed to his view. Instead, she crossed her arms and imagined she was tucked safely in her own bed.

"Which foot is it?"

He didn't look up as he asked the question, and she continued to have an unrestrained view of his thick pelt of black hair.

His head jerked up. She was pinned by a pair of relentless dark eyes. Swallowing, she decided she would limit herself to strictly necessary speech.

"The right one."

He looked down again. She felt him gingerly remove her shoe. Despite his obvious care, a flash of pain spiraled through her. She flinched and sucked in her breath.

"Sorry," he muttered, his head blocking her view of the proceedings.

His warm fingers strayed upward, above her knee, where the garter beneath her pantalets held her gray stocking in place. There was no point in ordering him to cease his outrageous liberties. Other than crowning him on the head with the smoked ham by the sink, she'd learned, there was no way he could be stopped.

The throbbing in her toes lessened as her awareness became centered on the strangely hypnotic feel of his gentle touch. She closed her eyes. The stocking came down slowly. The caress of air stirred against her bare foot. She raised her eyelids. The scandalous sight of her limp gray stocking dangling over one of Mr. Cade's broad shoulders greeted her. Against the flimsy garment, the black suit jacket he wore looked as rigid as armor.

"Damn, you really hurt yourself."

For no reason at all, tears came to her eyes. She did feel hurt, perhaps even battered. The fact kept intruding into her thoughts that in less than two weeks all she would have between her and starvation was the meager funds she'd secreted beneath her mattress.

He cradled her heel in one wide palm while pulling a chair forward. Never taking his focus from her foot, he sat down. "I don't think you broke any toes, but they're swollen and turning purple."

With him sitting, she could see the results of the chair's

assault. At a time when she needed to search for employment, she was going to be reduced to hobbling from place to place.

"One thing's certain, you won't be running any footraces soon." His tone was unexpectedly sympathetic.

The warm pressure of moisture built behind her eyes. What a wretched time for him to start acting kindly. It was easier to deal with Mr. Cade when he was at his nastiest. How dare he unsettle the last of her composure by sneakily changing tactics.

At that moment, she would have given her soul for a clean white hankie. Instead, she was reduced to wiping her nose with the edge of her cloak. Seeing her worn, muddied shoe tossed heedlessly a few inches from the heel of his brilliantly polished boot made her feel even lower than the beetle she'd fancied herself earlier. Bits of matted newspaper littered the floor. Sitting on the table with her bare leg exposed to her knee—which was where he'd shoved the hem of her pantalets—her dress flecked with mud and her toes turning purple, she felt downright pitiful. Courtney's uncle would probably have rather had a sack of soiled laundry on his table than her own sorry self.

She sniffed.

He raised his head. The dark eyes lancing into her didn't hold a trace of pity. No, it was something else, something elemental and...shockingly intense. Her stomach turned over. It abruptly occurred to her how improper it was for her exposed limb to be thrust forward for his examination. While her thoughts were diverted by her threatened circumstances, he'd removed his grip from her heel. It rested with bold familiarity upon her inner thigh. She forgot anything so mundane as throbbing toes.

He must have read something of her panic, because his fingers curved around her ankle before she could pull her foot from its inappropriate perching place. His thumb idly rubbed the sensitive skin along the inside of her heel.

"The best thing you can do tonight is stay off your feet," he said in a reasonable manner that was at odds with the growing heat in his unwavering gaze. "Allow me to extend an invitation to stay here."

Emma's breath caught. Surely it was her own fevered imagination and woeful ignorance about men that was turning this bizarre incident into something more than Mr. Cade performing an act of simple Christian charity. He was merely playing the role of Good Samaritan. There was no reason to imbue his offer with impropriety. No gentleman would invite a woman who was a total stranger to conduct herself...improperly. Of course, she'd already concluded that his actions were significantly less than sterling.

"That's a generous invitation, but I really must be on my way."

Somehow his gaze became even more intense. "Why?"

Why? Well, because... For no reason at all, she trembled. "You know as well as I do that it's impossible for me to remain."

"On the contrary, it's both highly possible and eminently sensible," he countered. "Naturally, you would occupy the guest room next to Courtney."

Emma knew she was flushing again. "I assumed as much."

A strong sense of self-preservation, however, reminded her that there was no way a single female could share lodgings with a man who wasn't her father or brother or husband. Considering her limited resources, an unblemished reputation literally meant the difference between life or death. If she was foolish enough to deviate from the straight and narrow path of circumspect behavior, all future doors of employment would be slammed in her face.

Despite Gideon Cade's occasional lapses in gentlemanly conduct, he must know the strict rules governing the social etiquette between men and women. Either his thoughts were more chaste than hers, or he found her so unappealing that it would never occur to him that anyone could misinterpret his motives in having her stay. Emma found both possibilities deeply demoralizing.

She could not, however, ignore the fact that rich, devilishly handsome men didn't entertain lascivious thoughts about plain, impoverished schoolteachers. And she knew for a certainty that she _was_ plain. For as far back as she could remember, her adult caretakers had repeatedly said her appearance was sadly lacking.

"I take it you're not enthusiastic about my suggestion."

Mr. Cade's thumb continued its subtly rhythmic stroking.

"I want to go home," she said quietly.

Neither smile nor frown altered the straight line of his mouth.

"All right."

"Thank you." She glanced at her abandoned shoe. She hated him seeing the newspaper she'd used to compensate for the almost worn through soles. Having him know the extent of her poverty grated sharply on her pride. The idea that he might be silently laughing at her cut to the quick. Making no comment, he reached for the soggy piece of footwear. Had there ever been a night in her life when she felt more beleaguered? Seemingly lost in reflection, he sat the shoe on the table next to her.

While he looked for all the world like a cynical, jaded version of Prince Charming, she boasted no princesslike attributes. Loutitia Hempshire was no fairy godmother. Her waterlogged shoe in no way resembled a glass slipper. And the wayward mongrel who'd complicated tonight's events was in no danger of being transformed into a magnificent stallion fit to pull a golden coach. On the bright side, though, there wasn't an evil stepmother or sister in sight.

"Take heart, Miss Step. In less than an hour, you'll be tucked safely in your own bed. By noon tomorrow, tonight's disagreeable chain of events will be only a faint memory."

Chapter Four

Emma sat beside Gideon Cade in his covered coach as it navigated Denver's predawn mist. She cast a sideways glance at Courtney's uncle. His profile didn't reveal his thoughts. It was hard to believe this stranger had carried her in his arms, run his fingers over her bare foot and looked at her naked leg. It staggered her that, in the space of a few hours, she'd experienced so many intimacies at his hand. They'd exchanged the most barbed of insults.

Incredible… She was a woman who'd grown accustomed to being isolated. Yet a single encounter with the brash Mr. Cade had cracked the social barriers she'd erected to survive in a world that accepted her only on *its* terms. From a very young age, she'd taken those terms to heart. *Be competent, be silent unless spoken to, and hold all personal emotions deeply within yourself.*

One of Gideon Cade's remarks returned—that the evening's events would be quickly forgotten. *Not by her.* A lifetime wouldn't be long enough to erase this strange interlude with a man who'd managed to shatter the reserve that had become the bedrock of her character.

The carriage proceeded at a snail's crawl toward the academy. Emma decided her companion was too big to share such cramped quarters with another person. His broad shoulders took up entirely too much room. There was no getting used to his thigh rubbing intimately against the side of her leg.

Nor could she relax with his arm draped across the back of their seat. His jacket's sleeve brushed her hair. The subtle friction was enough to keep her off balance. In her present mood, she deemed his booted feet overly large and encroaching. He was probably taking up more than his fair portion of air, too. Though she had to admit that the faint whiff of hair tonic emanating from him was preferable to the smell of wet dog.

She hazarded a quick glance around him. He had plenty of room on his other side. Instead of scrunching her between himself and the carriage's inner wall, he could have easily slid half a foot to his right. Contrary man.

"What can you tell me about the financial trouble facing the academy?"

The unexpected question made Emma start. She should have known he wouldn't allow their ride to pass in silence.

"Only what Miss Loutitia confided to me."

"Out with it, Miss Step. Don't keep me in suspense."

Emma resented the hint of boredom that laced his inquiry. A matter of grave consequence to her was only mildly noteworthy to him. She wondered how he would like it if his world were suddenly turned upside down. Realistically, however, it was impossible to imagine anything of sufficient magnitude to threaten a man of Gideon Cade's abundant resources.

"She told me there isn't enough capital to keep the school operating for more than another ten days."

"She must be an extremely negligent businesswoman."

"How can you say that? You've never met her."

"When you consider the girls attending her school belong to some of the wealthiest families in the West, it stands to reason only an incompetent could run the business into bankruptcy."

"I won't sit here and listen to you insult Loutitia."

"Even as short as you are, Miss Step, I think you would have trouble standing in my carriage."

"I'm not short!"

"You're not?" he drawled with maddening humor.

He was staring at her with those damnably assessing eyes of his. She stared right back at him. It was best that they got this business about her height cleared up.

"I am merely less tall than some."

"Less tall?"

If he wasn't careful, he might actually smile. While the thought of the implacable Mr. Cade actually doing something as human as smiling wasn't totally disagreeable, she didn't want the smile to come at her expense.

"You'll probably think it a matter of semantics, but I happen to detest the word *short*. Nor is it accurate in my case."

"It isn't?"

"Certainly not. Tempers grow short, young men's pants are short, and so are fall days."

"I stand corrected," he said softly.

Unprepared for his surrender, Emma blinked. The lamp that hung in the carriage was turned to sufficient brightness for her to notice the subtle easing of the harsh lines marking his face. The shadow of an evening beard darkened his jaw.

"I have an entire list of things that are short," she ventured, in case he wasn't convinced.

"It won't be necessary to go through it. Why are you so protective toward Miss Loutitia?"

"Her offer of employment gave me the opportunity to begin a new life in the West." At the reminder that she was about to become unemployed, fear squeezed Emma's stomach.

"How did that come about?"

The man was full of questions. Answering them lessened the silent tension. "There was an advertisement in the *Philadelphia Sentinel* announcing teaching positions west of the Missouri."

"What were you doing before you responded to the advertisement?"

"Teaching." She saw no need to elaborate. The school where she'd previously taught was run by a small religious sect. Everyone had been kind, but she wasn't of their faith and had felt an outsider.

"So you came to Denver to begin a new life?"

"Yes."

"No doubt you were looking for excitement and adventure."

If tonight was any indication, she'd certainly found it. "Everything I'd read about Denver suggested there would be more excitement here than in Philadelphia."

"The thought of cattle rustlers, claim jumpers and train robbers didn't alarm you?"

"Denver has its own band of protectors looking out for its citizenry." One of the lures that made the western town so fascinating had been the legendary group of men who'd banded together to combat the area's lawless element. The eastern newspapers had made much of their noble exploits.

He regarded her in open amusement. "You're referring to the 'Guardsmen,' I assume."

She bristled at his disparaging tone. "I am."

"I'm surprised you put so much stock in what newspapers print. There's no proof the Guardsmen actually exist."

"Of course there is. Almost every time someone tries to rob a stagecoach, they're caught and turned over to the authorities."

"That's not proof there's an underground group of vigilantes at work."

At his mention of the word *vigilante*, Emma realized they had strayed to a dangerous subject. She abhorred vigilante justice. No man or group of men had the right to take the law into their own hands and administer their justice, especially at the end of a rope. Rumors were rife that Gideon Cade was such a man, that he ran his freighting empire with an iron fist and anyone who challenged him wound up dead.

During their extraordinary encounter, she'd forgotten with whom she was dealing. Emma shivered. "The Guardsmen are different."

"Not that I'm admitting the group exists, but why?"

"Because, they don't perform their own...er...executions."

Uttering the last word was a bit like reminding the devil of his agenda for wreaking havoc.

"And, of course, that's what the newspapers imply I'm guilty of."

She hadn't expected him to openly refer to the charges that had been made against him.

"Getting back to the Guardsmen," she said, wanting to avoid an argument that was bound to put them on opposing sides. "You have to admit their methods are ingenious."

"Some might say farcical."

"They would be wrong," Emma replied, warming to her defense of the anonymous group. "Remember last week, when they left those trussed-up cattle rustlers at the church in the middle of the night?"

"Who can forget?"

She didn't appreciate his levity. "Along with a list of their misdeeds, the names of two wranglers who'd witnessed the crime were provided. Had the Guardsmen not appeared on the scene to save those witnesses, they would have been killed. Now they can testify."

"And that wouldn't have happened without your masked band of do-gooders?"

"Of course not." Really, the man could be quite dense. "Even if the wranglers hadn't been killed, they would have been too intimidated to testify in court. Part of the Guardsmen's success is based on the protection they offer people. I'm sure Sheriff Beckman and his deputies are extremely grateful for the extra help they've been receiving."

"You think so?"

She nodded. "Of course. After all, it must be extremely disheartening for an officer of the law to have so much crime going on under his nose. I imagine he wishes he knew their identities so he could thank them personally."

"Interesting idea."

"Well, there's one thing for certain."

"What's that?"

"Whomever they are, I'll wager they're some of the bravest and most intelligent men our country boasts. They deserve to be recognized for their courage and selfless devotion.''

Instead of commenting, Mr. Cade stretched. Somehow, in the process, his arm lowered, and the back of her head became cradled against him. She was about to extricate herself when he spoke again.

''I suppose you agree with the editorials that condemn me for operating a toll road to the mines.''

''Now that you mention it, it does seem a tad...er...excessive to charge men to travel to and from their own gold claims.''

Even though it was her custom to employ tact when dealing with others, Emma resented being wishy-washy with this man.

''Are you aware there wasn't a passable road until I had one surveyed, dynamited and laid through the mountains?''

''Well, no, but—''

''And that I happen to own the land through which the road passes?''

''No, but—''

''And prior to my freighting teams, complete with drivers and men riding shotgun, miners were unable to get their gold to Denver?''

''But—''

''And without the rail spurs that took two years to build, it would take more than a century to transport the ore from the mountains?''

''Still—''

''Unlike your Miss Loutitia, I know how to run a business.''

His rigid tone discouraged rebuttal.

''She isn't *my* Loutitia,'' Emma pointed out. ''But she's successfully run the school for the past few years, and has a reputation for kindness.''

''Being known for one's kindness hardly qualifies someone to run a business,'' came his scoffing rejoinder.

''That's just what one would expect from a coldhearted businessman.''

The words slipped out despite Emma's best intentions to avoid a quarrel. The disagreeably arrogant man had a knack for provoking her. If there had been a way to call back the barb, she would have done it.

"I assure you my heart is no colder than any other part of me."

What exactly did that mean?

"I spoke out of turn." She was amazed she didn't choke on the apology. "I merely meant that as a…businessman, you're inclined to look at the facts as they're written on sheets of paper. The rest of the world tends to look at things differently."

"As you've separated me from the rest of the human race, explain how so-called *normal* people will view Loutitia Hempshire's business failure."

The command was brusquely issued. Had her observation wounded him? Immediately she chastised herself for being so foolish as to think she could hurt Gideon Cade's feelings.

"Instead of condemning her, most people will sympathize."

"An utterly pointless exercise."

The man specialized in cold pronouncements.

"What do you plan on doing when the academy closes, Miss Step?"

The last thing she wanted to discuss was her uncertain future.

"I'm looking into several possibilities," she said vaguely.

If only the academy could have kept its doors open for another year. By then, she would have saved enough money to invest in the new institution Jayne Stoneworthy was beginning. Both Jayne and she had been recruited by Miss Loutitia to come to Denver. Jayne, however, had decided she had enough funds to establish the fledgling school.

"That's what people say when they don't know what they're doing."

She shivered at the accuracy of his observation, aware suddenly of her clammy clothes, the chill in the air and her throbbing toes.

"You're cold."

"I'm f-fine."

It was ridiculous. She wasn't any colder than she'd been a moment before. There was no reason for her teeth to start chattering.

"Sure you are."

Before she knew what he intended, he had vanquished the infinitesimal distance between them and was drawing her into his embrace. Stunned by his sudden boldness, she let precious seconds flit by without protesting. The now familiar sensation of powerful arms closing around her rocked her equilibrium. When the dust settled, she was seated upon his lap.

"You should have worn a heavier cloak."

"If I had one, I would have," she snapped, for once not trying to conceal her impoverished state. Futilely she attempted to dislodge herself from on top of him.

"Settle down, I'm just warming you up."

She continued to try to wrestle free. "Ha! You can't fool me."

"I can't?"

His voice was a husky murmur that flowed directly into her ear and seemed in danger of thundering out of her palpitating heart.

"You're the kind of libertine who takes every opportunity to get his hands upon a woman." Every squirming movement seemed to deliver her more tightly into his embrace.

"You have to admit, you've given me plenty of opportunities."

The carriage took an unexpected turn. Had he not held her so firmly, she would have been tossed to the floor.

"I haven't given you anything!" She looked up at him in frustration. "You're just acting true to form."

He pressed a wide palm to her back. "What form is that?"

Because of the close way he held her, she was forced to notice his warmth. She refused to enjoy it. "That of a robber baron, of course."

"Of course," he conceded lightly, sliding a hand around her waist and securing her sideways on his lap.

She was effectively captured, her resistance limited to the hand she'd wedged between their snugly pressed chests.

"Stop shivering as if you were a kitten left on the step in January."

His words were more accurate than he knew.

"I'll stop shivering when you release me!" That didn't sound right.

He rubbed his hands over her back and arms. "Hush now. There's nothing wrong with sharing our warmth."

His deep voice washed over her in heavy, shattering waves. Gideon Cade surrounded her. His thighs cradled her. His musky scent, at once alien and strangely enticing, teased her senses. Freeing herself from his bold trespass became of paramount importance.

She tried wiggling.

"Miss Step... Oh, hell, I refuse to say, 'Miss Step' one more time. Your first name is Emma, right?"

"Yes," she answered absently. She was beginning to feel light-headed from her exertions. Nor was her corset helping matters. "But I haven't given you leave to address me by my first name."

"You're a thorny little thing, aren't you?"

Her thoughts turned to the practical logistics of gaining her freedom. There was no help for it. She was going to have to push against his chest. Before this contest was over, she intended to demonstrate he couldn't put his hands on her every time he felt like it.

"You do realize there's no point in trying to break free, don't you?"

She detested his almost whimsical tone. "I realize you are indeed the bully I called you earlier."

Her efforts to push free accomplished nothing. Desperation joined her growing sense of frustration. Being caught in his embrace against her will was too much a model of her life's present disarray. Getting free represented gaining control over that which overwhelmed her.

"If you don't release me this instant, I shall blacken your eye."

His husky chuckle tickled her ear. "Better men than you have tried and failed to do so."

She doubled up her fist.

"I'm giving you fair warning—"

The carriage stopped abruptly.

"Oof!" The involuntarily sound accompanied the air whooshing from her lungs. He took the opportunity to squeeze her more intimately against his unyielding chest.

"You all right, honey?"

His ill-mannered familiarity and his hands brushing fleetingly across her writhing person sparked a strange response from Emma. Unfortunately for her peace of mind, it wasn't one of loathing. No, a series of alarmingly thrilling tingles now competed for her attention.

Both furious and frightened by the powerful tremors skating through her, she felt the last layer of her control disintegrate.

Without any warning—either to herself or to the thug holding her against her will—her clenched fist smacked him in the jaw. One second she was his prisoner, and the next she was... Well, she was still his prisoner, but now he held her with one arm wrapped around her, instead of two. Her fist throbbed as painfully as her toes. Good grief, by the time full daylight struck, she was going to be confined to a bed.

"I'll give you that blow, Emma."

Slowly he allowed her to slide from his lap and reclaim her space on the seat next to him. *He* might concede that she'd had every right to hit him, but Emma was horrified by her unrestrained behavior. She rubbed her aching fingers and wondered if she had been around Miss Loutitia too long and was in danger of becoming one of those females prone to hysteria.

Her only question was how this vigilante robber baron would choose to retaliate. After all, it was rumored he hunted down those who crossed him. She swallowed. From the way her fingers stung, she'd clearly struck him a vicious blow. No doubt his head was still ringing from the pain, and that was why he was staring at her as if she were a new species of mammal.

A mysterious source of light permeated the carriage's interior. Mr. Cade's features were cast in a reddish glow that created the sinister illusion that she was gazing into Lucifer's harsh features, lit by the fires of never-ending perdition.

A fierce pounding assaulted the coach's door. "The school is on fire!"

The driver's announcement brought with it the blistering sensation of heat. The horses whinnied their distress, and the vehicle lurched forward.

"See to the team, Hennesy," came Mr. Cade's curt command. "Wait here, Emma, while I find out what's going on."

He stepped from the carriage, closing the door behind him. Sound exploded around her. A coarse litany of shouts shredded the cocoon of silence that had engulfed her and Courtney's uncle. She looked through a small window. Clusters of men lined up in bucket brigades.

Dismissing Mr. Cade's order that she remain inside the coach, Emma swung open the door and jumped from the carriage. The flash of pain in her foot barely registered.

Towering columns of flames held her rapt attention.

Had it not been for the recent rain, she suspected, the entire block would have been lost. She jerked herself free from the conflagration's hypnotic spell. The sudden need to make sure everyone had escaped safely swept through her.

"Emma! Emma!"

The sound of her name being frantically screamed above the blaze's crackling roar had her looking in all directions. Through the wild din of confusion, Jayne Stoneworthy rushed toward her.

"Thank God, you're alive!" Jayne cried when she reached her. The fellow instructor's smoke-blackened robe was torn. Tears and a layer of soot streaked her face. "We thought we had lost you...."

Emma accepted her friend's tearful embrace. "I'm fine."

Jayne straightened and rubbed her red-rimmed eyes. "We haven't been able to find Courtney."

At her fellow teacher's stricken features, Emma's heart twisted. "Courtney's safe, too."

"I don't understand. Where were you, and where's—"

"Miss Step!"

Loutitia Hempshire's shrill shout cut Jayne off. Emma had no difficulty making out the headmistress's plump form as she waddled purposefully toward her through the melee of men, wagons and bystanders. Loutitia's nephew, Lyman Thornton, was having difficulty keeping up with his aunt. The leanly fit gentleman trailed a full three feet behind the red-faced, panting woman.

With her flowing nightgown and billowing robe sailing out behind her, she resembled a ship being pushed by a full gale. "Miss Step, here you are at last. We've been looking all over for you." Loutitia barely stopped before running into Emma. "Where on earth were you?"

"I was—"

"Oh, never mind!" the woman shrieked. "It's gone. It's all gone!" She dabbed at her eyes with a grimy handkerchief. "The dreadful fire has destroyed everything. Oh, what will become of me?"

"Since you were already planning on closing the school, its loss can't be that painful."

The callous remark came from Loutitia's nephew. Unlike the people milling about, Lyman Thornton was dressed in something other than sleeping apparel. His coat, shirt and trousers showed no evidence of soot or water stains. Evidently, the owner of Denver's largest hotel hadn't seen the necessity of assisting the water brigade.

"But I intended on taking my furnishings," she wailed. "Oh, my beautiful French bed, my lamps, my armoire—" Her voice broke on that last treasured possession. "My armoire is ashes."

The older woman sobbed into her handkerchief, as heartbroken as if listing the names of her own children who had perished in the fire.

Her nephew remained coolly unaffected. "Come now, Loutitia, the insurance will cover our losses. And, as the

French haven't stopped making furniture, I'll see you get another ostentatious bed to take to when a fit of the vapors strikes.''

Miss Loutitia raised her damp face from the hankie. ''And a new armoire, too? Do you promise?''

''Whatever you want,'' he said negligently. Emma noticed that his wavy brown hair was neatly combed. The only indication that he'd dressed in haste was his open shirt collar.

Loutitia blew her nose. ''Oh, I don't know how you can be so inhumanly calm.''

''Practice, dear Aunt, practice.''

''That and the fact *you* didn't lose anything in the blaze,'' she sniffed. ''Goodness, you planned on tearing down the building to make room for that new hotel you've been talking about ever since you informed me Hempshire Academy could no longer remain in business.'' Loutitia took a hiccupy breath as she turned her attention to Emma. ''We were afraid you didn't make it out alive. I guess I shouldn't chide Lyman for always being so calm. He certainly wasn't, my dear, when it appeared you'd been trapped inside.''

Emma was aware of Lyman Thornton's regard. During the few weeks she worked for his aunt, she'd wondered what she'd done to spark his curiosity. Much to her consternation, he'd developed the unsettling habit of standing in the background and observing her. Rarely did he take the opportunity to engage her in conversation. He seemed content just to watch her. She didn't know what to make of him. Because he was wealthy, smoothly handsome and a pillar of the community, she knew his interest wasn't of a personal nature.

''As you can see, I'm fine.'' Emma looked toward the fire. It amazed her that in a matter of minutes it could recede from an inferno to the smoldering hiss of dying flames. The morning sun came out, banishing the fog. As the smoke settled, a blackened ruin stood in place of the academy. ''Did everyone make it out safely?''

It was a question she should have asked sooner. She visualized the faces of her students and co-workers, realizing she'd delayed voicing it because she didn't know if she could bear the answer.

A look of despair welled up in Loutitia's puffy eyes. "I'm afraid we lost the Cade girl...."

"Courtney's all right," Emma said quickly, wanting to spare Loutitia an extra moment of grief. "She's at her uncle's house."

"Thank God!" More tears streamed from the headmistress. "Of all the students to have lost... I was terrified when Mr. Cade found out, he would... Well, there's no telling what a man like that might do."

It was at that juncture that Emma saw Gideon Cade standing behind the older woman. Flames every bit as deadly as those that had lapped at the academy smoldered in his angry gaze.

"It was horrible to be awakened by the shouting and screaming," Loutitia continued. "Smoke was everywhere. I thought I was going to die. It was..." She dissolved into more sobs.

"Come, it's time I take you home," Thornton said.

"My home's burned to the ground!" she cried pitifully.

"You were planning on living with me after the academy closed," her nephew reminded her.

She sighed. "I know, but it wasn't supposed to be like this."

"Just a moment, Miss Hempshire."

Emma watched Jayne Stoneworthy, Loutitia and Lyman Thornton turn in unison toward Gideon Cade. That he towered above the women, and even Loutitia's nephew, was probably something Cade took for granted.

"Uh, yes, Mr. Cade?" Loutitia inquired timidly.

"Are you certain everyone is accounted for?"

She nodded. "Yes, Miss Stoneworthy and I tallied the number of teachers and students before they left for the various hotels that agreed to take them in for the night. Everyone made it out safely."

"Do you know how the fire started?"

Her plump hands fluttered uselessly. "I have no idea."

"We'll probably never find out," Lyman Thornton interjected. "A candle could have been set too close to the draperies, a log in one of the fireplaces could have shot a spark that caught, a lamp could have tipped over—any number of things could have happened."

"I'm just grateful no lives were lost." Loutitia wiped her eyes with the twisted handkerchief. "It's bad enough my armoire was destroyed."

"Yes, Aunt, tonight has been a terrible ordeal for you."

"I'm really not sure I'm going to be able to recover." Loutitia looked helplessly at her nephew.

"I'll take you home now." He glanced at Emma. "Naturally, you'll be joining us."

Until that very moment, Emma had given no thought about where she would sleep. Nevertheless, his assumption startled her. "It's very kind of you to offer, but I imagine I'll stay with the other teachers at one of the hotels."

It was only as she spoke that the dire nature of her plight struck Emma. She had no money, no clothes, and nowhere to go. A trunk being dropped on her head couldn't have struck with greater impact.

At the age of twenty-four, she was stranded in a strange city where she'd lived a few weeks, out of work and destitute.

Chapter Five

Emma Step brushed a lock of hair from her cheek. Throughout their early-morning encounter, Gideon had watched a myriad of emotions cross the schoolmistress's mobile features. For the first time since he'd met her, fear touched her gaze. Her vulnerability aroused protective instincts he was chagrined to discover he possessed.

"Don't worry about imposing upon us," Lyman Thornton persisted. "Having you in our home is the least we can do. Right, Aunt Loutitia?"

"Certainly you're welcome to stay the night, dear."

"It's already morning," Lyman corrected. "You'll be more comfortable with us than at one of the hotels. It's bound to take time to reestablish yourself here, Miss Step. You're welcome to remain our guest for as long as you wish," he added persuasively.

Gideon had never cared for Lyman Thornton. Like the majority of Denver residents, he was an eastern transplant. They'd never conducted any business transactions, but their paths had crossed more than once socially. The man projected a snobbish attitude that grated on Gideon's nerves. The irony didn't escape him that Emma had charged him with the same fault. Thornton's suggestion that she stay in his home indefinitely pushed Gideon's passive dislike to active hostility.

He had no intention of letting Thornton stampede her into

moving in with him. Especially when, considering Loutitia Hempshire's flightiness, the older woman would be a washout as a chaperone. Judging from Miss Step's pallor, and the way she stood huddled in her shabby cloak, she was in no condition to make decisions for herself.

It shouldn't have mattered to Gideon what happened to Courtney's teacher. He frowned. Since the academy no longer existed, the woman was his niece's *former* teacher. Not even the flimsiest connection existed between them. No argument could be put forth that she was his responsibility.

And yet, he found himself unable to abandon her to Thornton's suspect hospitality. Something had passed between the queerly appealing woman and himself. Her earnest, prickly, damnably intriguing manner had nudged him to a peculiar awareness that wouldn't let him walk away from her.

"Miss Step appreciates your offer, Thornton." *Complications*... Knowing he was inviting a swarm of them into his organized household wasn't enough to nail his lips shut. "But she's decided to stay with my niece and me."

Miss Step's head came up. Some of the dullness faded from her eyes. "I certainly have—"

Since he was fairly certain he wasn't going to like what she had to say on the matter, he silenced her by sweeping her into his arms.

"Oh!"

The startled gasp had to be less of a protest than the one she'd been about to utter. He noticed again how light she was. A robust breeze could have blown her into Kansas.

She attempted to squirm free. "Now just a minute..."

"She hurt her foot earlier this evening," he informed the clearly shocked group. "She'll be able to recover more quickly at my place."

It didn't matter that his explanation made no sense. People rarely challenged his decisions.

Proving there was an exception to every rule, Thornton spoke. "I don't think Miss Step appreciates being manhandled. As for her foot—"

"Terrible accident," Gideon interjected. "The pain makes it difficult for her to speak."

"I can talk perfectly—"

Gideon patted the back of her head. "You don't have to thank me."

"Mmmph..."

With her cheek pressed against his chest, her objection emerged as a muffled squeak.

Suspicion clouded Thornton's hostile expression. "If she injured her foot, a doctor should examine it."

"Good idea," Gideon responded. "If it isn't better by morning, we'll send for one."

Miss Step ceased her efforts to free herself. He waited a half second for her to launch a verbal battle, demanding he release her. None was forthcoming. "Well, it's getting late. We'd best be on our way."

Gideon strode toward his carriage. Hennesy hadn't returned. He'd probably joined the bucket brigade dousing the last of the smoldering wreckage that had been the academy. Smoke, and the promise of more rain, ripened the morning air. The driver's help wouldn't be needed much longer.

Gideon jerked open the carriage door. Emma Step remained a stiff and unyielding package. Even though she wasn't struggling to free herself, she still refused to put her arms around his neck. If that was all the form her rebellion took, he counted himself lucky. He wouldn't have been surprised to hear her yell for help, rather than allow him to carry her anywhere. Maybe the puny blow she'd delivered to his jaw had siphoned some of her spunkiness.

Taking care not to jostle her foot, he deposited her inside the carriage. Her lips were compressed into a tight line. There was a defiant gleam in her eyes as she glared straight ahead, refusing to acknowledge him or his considerate gesture. Damned female was too stubborn for her own good, that much was obvious. It irritated him that she didn't seem to realize how fortunate she was that he'd taken her under his wing.

If the gray gown she wore was any indication of the quality

of her clothing that had been burned, Gideon was ready to declare the fire a community service. He remembered the surge of anger he'd experienced when he removed the miserably constructed walking slipper from her injured foot. In the split second when he first saw the newspaper she'd used to add a layer of protection to the worn sole, he'd tried to dull his sense of outrage with a quip about her putting the negative editorials printed about him to good use.

Then he'd noticed the proud tilt of her chin so at odds with the look of hot embarrassment flashing in her eyes. At that point, he'd wanted to pitch both her shoes in the hearth. It hadn't mattered that she was a stranger to him. He'd been struck by the bizarre urge to buy her several pairs of shoes, and some new stockings—ones with pretty bits of lace instead of neatly darned patches. While he was at it, he'd make sure she had a pair of pantalets that didn't look as if they'd been fashioned when Martha Washington was First Lady.

He ducked his head inside the carriage. ''The last two times I've asked you to wait for me, you've struck out on your own.''

He wanted her to know he'd kept count of her mutinies.

She stared straight ahead. He discovered he didn't like being treated as if he were invisible. ''I'm getting Hennesy. You *will* be here when I return.''

She maintained her silence.

''I'm not leaving until you promise to do as I say.''

More silence.

''Stop frowning. You've got enough wrinkles as it is.''

As he figured, that had her head pivoting toward him.

''You are the rudest, the nastiest, the most vile man whom it has ever been my misfortune to meet.''

''I just said that so you would pay attention. You don't have any wrinkles.'' If she owned a mirror, she would know that.

''Well, you've succeeded. You definitely have my attention.''

Probably the same kind of dangerous attention Delilah had directed to Samson before she sheared him like a sheep.

"Look, we both know I could stand here for hours telling you how lovely you are."

Her eyes narrowed. He wondered why he should be surprised. Whereas most women turned to warm honey when they received a compliment, Emma January Step imitated a blast of arctic air.

"Do I appear to be an imbecile?"

There was only one safe answer. "No."

"Then, once and for all, cease your remarks about my appearance!"

Obviously the night's events had caught up with her. Rational thought was beyond her. He decided to employ a different tactic.

"Be reasonable. You've been up all night, and a hell of a night it's been—what with Courtney running away, you hurting your foot and the academy burning down. Why don't we call a truce? After you've had some rest and taken stock of your situation, I'll deliver you wherever you want to go."

From the slight thawing of her formerly frigid gaze, he sensed he was making headway.

It occurred to him that life would be a lot easier if he and Emma were from an earlier period of time. Maybe the Dark Ages. Back then, if a man chanced upon a woman as damnably intriguing as she was, he could carry her off to his castle, declare her his possession and then go about the business of organizing his next battle.

There was a lot to be said for simpler times. But then, the chances were that a woman as sharp-tongued as Emma would have been burned at the stake before she reached her eighteenth birthday. Back then, people hadn't taken kindly to witches, even if they shared an uncanny resemblance to more angelic beings. He let go of the image of her in a tower bedchamber reluctantly.

"When Courtney wakes, up, she'll be devastated about the school being destroyed," he continued. "I know she loved it there."

He took shameless advantage of the tender sensibilities

Emma had evidenced when she believed Courtney was wandering Denver's streets.

"The fire will come as a shock." A pensive expression claimed Emma's features. "I do care about your niece, Mr. Cade."

"Gideon," he corrected, suspecting it would be a while before she felt comfortable calling him by his given name—more than the couple of days she probably envisioned staying in his home. "Courtney kept most of her belongings in her room at the academy, Emma."

He remembered the wagonload of girlish clothes and assorted possessions Hennesy had transported from Courtney's upstairs bedchamber to the school. Gideon's conscience stirred. His niece really would be devastated that her things had been destroyed. He recalled one photograph, in particular, that of her parents holding her when she was a baby. Locked in his memory was the image of Courtney carrying the framed picture when her former governess had accompanied her to the academy. Where before his motives for having Emma stay with him had been vague, Gideon acknowledged she would be better suited than he to console his niece.

"Ask me."

He looked into Miss Step's otherworldly eyes and decided clarity was needed. "What?"

"Ask me if I'll accept your invitation for shelter." ·

Judging from her pallor, her own losses weighed heavily on her thoughts. Nevertheless, she was apparently considering Courtney's needs. He admired the woman's generous spirit and the resurgence of her natural feistiness.

"Please come home with me—for my niece's benefit?"

And mine. I'm not done finding out who you are, Emma.

As if trying to divine the motive for his persistence, she studied him intently. Since he lacked the answer himself, he didn't object to her scrutiny.

"I'll come under one condition."

That he never put his hands on her again? He didn't delude himself into believing there was a chance on this good earth that he would let her disappear from his life before discovering how the inside of her mouth tasted. He was betting on berries. The tart kind that had a man reaching for more.

"What's the condition?"

She gestured, pointing beyond the open carriage door. "Do you see that woman over there?"

He looked to where Lyman Thornton still stood, staring at them. A slender woman of medium height, wearing a soot-stained robe, had just turned from him and his aunt.

"Yes."

"That's Jayne Stoneworthy, an acquaintance of mine. I want you to invite her to stay at your home, also."

Her hellhound would probably be next, Gideon thought, dourly. Evidently, Emma January Step was a collector of lost souls. The thought of establishing a home for unattached females held no appeal, but he'd learned long ago that success sprang from consolidating victories as they materialized. The lesser issues could be debated later. "Consider it done."

Gideon Cade had scarcely agreed to her impetuous request before he turned from her, striding purposefully toward Jayne's retreating figure. Emma leaned wearily against the carriage seat. Every instinct she possessed told her that now was the opportunity to escape Mr. Cade's domineering company. The only problem was that she wasn't sure what would fill the void of his bullying tactics.

She was too exhausted and overwhelmed to go tramping about town, looking for a hotel to take her in. Nor would such a trek be beneficial to her battered toes. She could have accepted Lyman Thornton's offer of shelter, but something about the man disturbed her. Though what could be more disturbing than trading insults with Courtney's uncle remained a mystery.

Thornton, a hotel, or Gideon Cade? She tried to consider her limited options logically. Thornton was creepy—not logical, but reason enough to avoid him. If she went to a hotel, they would expect her to begin paying almost immediately for her lodging. She had no money. Gideon Cade was so supremely arrogant, he invited fantasies of insurrection. The vote wasn't even close. What did it say about her that she preferred arrogance to creepiness?

She surrendered to a full body yawn. Gideon Cade had another asset that swung her decision in his favor. In the short time since she came to know his niece, the girl had come to mean a great deal to her. Something about Courtney's quiet but inherently cheerful disposition had drawn Emma to her.

Emma's gaze drifted to what was left of the academy—a charred mass of rubble. The building looked as if it had been struck by several cannon blasts. A lump swelled in her throat. She'd seen dark times before, she reminded herself, remembering when the orphanage she grew up in had "graduated" her to independence. It had been a frightening experience to leave the Burnby Heartshorn Foundling Home, but she'd done it.

The difference between then and now was that the staff had arranged several interviews for her. That was how she'd come to be employed as a companion to Beatrice Kenswick. That position had provided free room and board. The money she earned had financed additional classes at a secondary school where she became certified to teach. From there she'd become an instructor at Reverend Wade's Fundamentalist School of Higher Learning.

Looking back, Emma could see quite clearly how she'd come to be where she was today. When she looked ahead, though, she saw only a hazy blur of nothingness.

Emma watched Mr. Cade catch up with Jayne Stoneworthy and engage her in conversation.

He'd urged her to called him Gideon.... She couldn't, of course. It would be too personal a liberty.

As he escorted her friend toward the carriage, Emma was struck by Jayne Stoneworthy's graceful beauty. Mr. Cade had suffered no compunctions about emphasizing her own plainness with his exaggerated compliments, but Jayne was lovely enough to justify such flattery.

Their burly driver, Hennesy, joined Mr. Cade and Jayne as they proceeded to the carriage. Emma scooted across the seat to make room for her friend as Courtney's uncle assisted her inside. It would be a relief riding back to Mr. Cade's home without trying to outmaneuver his entirely-too-familiar hands.

"Here's your friend." With an economy of motion, he climbed into the carriage and sat across from them. His long legs neatly bisected the distance between herself and Jayne. "She seems, however, to have her own idea about where she plans on spending the next few hours." The carriage lurched forward.

Jayne patted her arm. "Emma, it's sweet for you to be worried about my welfare, considering your own desperate circumstances."

Emma tried not to flinch at her friend's use of the word *desperate*. Perhaps it was foolish at this point to try to preserve a modicum of dignity where Gideon Cade was concerned, but the thought of him pitying her stung the tattered remnants of her pride.

"I wouldn't call my situation desperate," Emma protested firmly.

Jayne gathered Emma's hands into hers. "I wish there was some way I could hire you to teach at my school!"

Emma briefly closed her eyes. Good grief, it appeared that every aspect of her private life was to be trotted out for Gideon Cade's contemplation. "You've already explained that—"

"I know I have." Jayne interrupted Emma, foiling her plan to change the subject. "But the fire changed things. Goodness, most of my possessions were already moved into the new school building, but you've lost everything."

"I'm aware of that, but—"

"You can't go through this alone." Jayne worried her bottom lip. "I know I told you that I couldn't afford to pay you a large enough salary to live on. That's why the instructors I've hired are married women. If I put my mind to it though, I can find the extra money needed to secure a place for you on my staff."

Emma was painfully conscious of Gideon Cade's speculative gaze as he listened to Jayne. "I won't trade on our brief friendship. Besides, your own situation is too precarious to start taking in charity cases."

"Oh, Emma, I have to do something." Tears filled her fellow teacher's eyes. "No matter what happens, I want you to know you have a place with me."

"I'll be fine."

"But what will you do? Where will you go?" Jayne wiped her eyes. "You don't have any family to help you," she continued, her voice choked with emotion. "You're totally alone in the world."

Emma refused to meet Mr. Cade's stare. It was one thing to receive Jayne's genuine compassion, another to endure his pity.

"Nonsense. I have you for a friend. Miss Hempshire will refer me to another employer, and…and…"

And what? Should she add Duncan, stray mongrel and all-round rogue mutt, to her diminished list of worldly assets?

"I have nothing to offer but room and board for your labors, Emma. If you can accept that, you're hired. Don't worry about the loss of your clothes. I'm a little taller than you, but we can take up my hems. As for your other possessions, I'll loan you enough money to get by until…well, until the school begins producing an income."

At Jayne's generosity, a feeling of expanding warmth filled Emma's chest. But her friend was trying to get a fledgling business started. Emma knew the offer of a loan, along with room and board, would be too great a burden to manage.

Emma blinked back threatening tears. She couldn't jeopardize Jayne's chance for success. "You're too generous for your own good. We both know the charity you're offering would put too great a strain on your resources."

"It's not charity," Jayne said hastily. "You're a wonderful teacher! I've wanted you on my staff from the beginning, just as I wanted you for a partner. All the fire did was…hasten things a bit."

In light of how briefly they'd known each other, Jayne's loyalty was touching. The carriage came to a halt in front of the two-story building Jayne had bought and was having refurbished. "Are you certain the place is fit for you to spend the night? I thought the workmen had barely begun."

"Things are progressing faster than I expected. The bar counter didn't have to be torn down, after all. The last thing Denver might need is another saloon, but there's one going up several blocks from here. The owner heard about the changes I was making to the 'Wet Beaver' and paid me twenty dollars for the bar."

Gideon Cade make a choking sound. Emma glanced at him. "Are you okay?"

He cleared his throat as he opened the carriage door. "I'm fine."

"You're welcome to stay with me," Jayne repeated as she slid toward the open door. "Only one bedroom has been finished, but we can share it. The bed is big enough for both of us."

Emma's cheeks warmed. Gideon Cade was certainly getting an earful about every aspect of her life, along with her prospects. "Uh, I'll be in touch with you and let you know my plans."

"I'm serious, Emma. You can count on my help."

"I know." That strange warm feeling unfurled in Emma's chest again. Unaccustomed to having her welfare considered by others, she was profoundly touched by Jayne's consideration.

Was this how it felt to be part of a family, as if a powerful thread were connecting one to others?

She watched Mr. Cade walk Jayne to the tavern. The hinged doors had already been replaced by two conventional portals. It didn't escape her notice that he played the role of a gentleman easily when dealing with her friend. Emma tried and failed to recall a single breach of decorum on his part while the teacher had been in his carriage. Perhaps he reserved his especially nasty behavior for women who traveled in the company of stray dogs.

She was reviewing that dampening thought when he returned. Why had he spent so much of the evening picking on her? She was about to ask when, instead of taking the opposite seat, he sat down next to her. His muscular leg took up residence intimately against her, and the question went flying.

"Do the words *déjà vu* have any meaning to you?"

"French for 'a sense of familiarity,'" he answered obligingly.

"*I* know what it means. I wondered if you did." She tugged on her skirts. "Scoot over, you're practically on top of me."

"Don't be so prickly, Emma."

Anyone overhearing them would think *she* was the one being difficult. "I'm only asking you to give me breathing room."

"You've got plenty of room," he contradicted smoothly. "How long have you and Miss Stoneworthy known each other?"

It was useless to try to budge him with the physical force at her disposal. "Six months."

"How did you meet?"

"For someone who doesn't approve of newspaper journalists, you ask a lot of questions."

"Humor me. I'm curious."

The ironic tone that tinged his request was impossible to overlook. "We met when Miss Loutitia was interviewing applicants for the academy."

"In Philadelphia?"

The man had a mind like a trap. "That's right."

"You've made quite an impression upon her."

"Why do you say that?"

"It isn't every day one has an acquaintance offer to bankrupt herself for the sake of friendship."

"I think you're overstating it a bit," Emma objected.

"Not at all. I was able to surmise a great deal about Miss Stoneworthy and her resources from your discussion. It's obvious she barely has the means to keep her new business afloat. If your resolve had faltered and you'd accepted her charity, you would have sunk her dreams of success beneath a sea of red ink."

Emma wished he hadn't said that. About now, her resolve

was weakening. Accepting Jayne's offer seemed the only way out of her present dilemma. Yet, according to Mr. Cade, doing so would spell doom for the teacher.

"You heard me decline her assistance," Emma muttered grumpily, wishing she could ignore the particulars of her dire situation.

"To have done anything else would have been extremely selfish on your part," he observed with maddening heartiness.

Emma didn't think she could feel any lower. She tugged futilely once more against her skirts, gave up and closed her eyes. Maybe if she pretended to fall asleep, he would keep his pithy observations to himself.

"We're almost home, Emma. Things will look better after you've gotten some rest."

Behind her closed eyelids, she felt the burning moisture of tears she wouldn't permit herself to shed. *Home…*

Only a few minutes elapsed before the carriage halted again. The wheels had barely stopped turning before Mr. Cade opened the door and alighted to the ground. She slid closer to the exit, expecting him to offer his arm in assistance.

When he leaned in and reached for her with outstretched hands, she decided the time had come for one of the Western "showdowns" she'd read about. Courtney's uncle was going to find out where his body ended and hers began.

"Hold it right there, Gideon Cade."

Chapter Six

"What's wrong?"

She slapped at him. "You've gotten the mistaken notion you can put your hands on me any time the fancy strikes you."

Leaning as he was into the carriage, she was in the unusual position of meeting him at eye level.

"And you have a problem with that?"

"Of course. The proper way to assist a lady from a carriage is—"

He seized her waist and lifted her from her seat. While she couldn't help being somewhat impressed by the raw physical strength at his command, his continued barbarous handling incensed her.

After a brief and utterly fruitless struggle, he held her suspended above the ground. "This is hardly the time or place for a lesson on manners, Emma."

"Are you going to put me down?"

"I guess I'll have to—sooner or later."

Her heartbeat skittered. "I've been walking for as long as I can remember. I'm capable of doing so with a few bruised toes."

"Is that your prissy way of telling me to behave myself?"

It would have been so satisfying to rough him up. Pity she didn't have Johnny McGuire's right hook. Her fellow orphan had been able to make quite a career for himself in the East as a pugilist. Had *he* taken a poke at Mr. Cade's jaw, the freighting tycoon wouldn't be so full of himself.

"I resent being called prissy when I'm nothing of the sort."

"I stand corrected."

She nodded in satisfaction, pleased that she'd gotten him to reassess her. As he carried her up the flagstone path to his residence, though, she realized his easy surrender had not resulted in him putting her down.

Broadbent must have observed their arrival through a window, because he opened the door as Gideon reached the front step.

"Good morning, sir."

"Good morning, Broadbent."

"Good morning, Miss Step."

Oh, really, both men's deadpan expressions were too much. "Good morning, Broadbent."

"Emma will be staying with us, Broadbent. She'll be using the third-story bedchamber at the end of the hall."

"Indeed, sir?"

"If she isn't already up, please awaken Mrs. Foster. Emma will want to avail herself of a bath, of course."

Broadbent nodded sagely. "Of course."

"Mrs. Graves will need to send a breakfast tray up, as well."

"As you wish, sir."

"Uncle Cade, what are you doing up so early?"

At the sound of Courtney's voice, Emma looked to the top of the stairs, where the young woman's rose-colored skirts drifted into view.

"Despite my best efforts, sleep somehow eluded me last night," Gideon responded dryly.

Emma's stomach flipped over. She attributed the peculiar reaction to the nearness of Mr. Cade's deep voice.

"I thought I heard—" Courtney broke off when her descent brought her within sight of her uncle carrying her schoolmistress.

"Good grief, is that you, Miss Step?"

Emma rolled her eyes. "Yes, it is."

What she wouldn't have given for some good old-fashioned decorum on Gideon Cade's part. Since any tussle would probably result in her landing in an unseemly heap on the stairs, however, she folded her hands and pasted a resigned smile on her lips.

Courtney's blue eyes filled with obvious concern. "What's happened to you? Are you hurt? You look dreadful!"

From her student's dramatic reaction, Emma assumed she looked as if she'd been run over by a team of horses.

"Miss Step will answer your questions after she's been taken care of," Mr. Cade announced calmly, passing his niece on the stairs.

Taken care of? Emma told herself that it was only her overactive imagination that lent a sinister tone to his words.

"But—"

"For now, your instructor needs a bath, food and some rest. You may keep her company and have your questions answered after that."

"I'm fine, Courtney," Emma called out as Gideon toted her up a second flight of stairs. "Your uncle is carrying me because he's a…"

The word *fool* hovered on her lips. Looking up from her position in his arms, she had a clear view of his darkly bristled jaw. For reasons of self-preservation, she searched for another term.

"A…*what?*" Courtney hollered up.

"A worrywart," Emma answered, putting her survival ahead of a strict need for honesty.

They passed several closed doorways. This ridiculous journey had to end soon. That thought had scarcely formed before Gideon Cade reached the last ivory-colored door. True to form, he didn't stand her on her feet to gain admittance to the room.

She decided it was perfectly natural that her musings drifted to brides, grooms, and the social tradition of being carried across the threshold. Since she never expected to marry, this was probably as close as she'd get to experiencing the ancient custom. Which was just as well, she reasoned. If she should ever be obliged to be carried by someone else, it would be impossible not to remember Gideon Cade's strong arms. Despite his long list of imperfections, there probably wasn't another man alive who could compete with his indelible memory.

He set her on the soft mattress of a canopy bed that filled much of the chamber. The pale green counterpane was made of silk.

An awkward silence ensued. She would rather have bitten her tongue off than thank him for lugging her about as if she were an invalid. Still, he had offered her this beautiful room, food and a roof over her head for a couple of days. She glanced down at her clenched hands. She hated being beholden to anyone. Whether provided by a handsome robber baron or by a cherished friend, charity tasted just as bitter. Unfortunately, a strongly developed Christian conscience prevented her keeping silent. She peeked at him through her lashes.

Look at him standing there. A pool of sunlight poured through white lace curtains. Despite the illusion of being framed in a golden halo, he bore no angelic likeness. His black shoes were planted firmly on a cream-colored oval rug, and his hands were pushed into his pockets. He studied her through dark and inscrutable eyes. While the early-morning events hadn't made a dent in his autocratic bearing, she felt as if she now bore an unmistakable similarity to Duncan.

She opened her mouth to say thank-you and end Gideon Cade's uncomfortably assessing gaze. A huge yawn took her by surprise.

She put her hand over her lips. "Excuse me. I seem to be a bit tired, after all."

"Let me get this straight—you have no family," he began without preamble.

Emma sighed. "I knew you were listening to everything Jayne said."

"We were in the same carriage. It's not as if I was eaves-dropping."

"Still, it's extremely rude to bring the matter up. The polite thing would be to ignore what you overheard."

He rocked back and forth on the balls of his feet. "How long have you had this unnatural preoccupation with social nicety?"

"I'm sure I don't know what you mean."

"Then let me make myself clear. I grew up on the Boston docks. Due to a lot of hard work and some luck, I was able to accumulate a lot of money."

"What has that got to do with anything?" Other than that he took every opportunity he could to brag about himself.

"I'm not finished. When I began rubbing elbows with members of polite society, I discovered many people use their knowledge of etiquette to subtly insult those without privileged beginnings."

"That can be very annoying," she observed, wondering how anyone in his right mind would seek to intimidate Gideon Cade about a lack of social polish. He certainly couldn't think she was doing that. In her case, it was a matter of trying to keep him from rolling over her like a runaway locomotive racing downhill on greased tracks.

"Right here and right now, I want your promise you won't bring up the subject of manners again."

"*Never?*" Surely it wasn't wise to agree. After all, Courtney's uncle had demonstrated an alarming tendency to impose his will upon anyone who crossed his path.

He shook his head. "I find it tedious. You have no desire to be tedious, do you, Emma?"

"Well, no, but—"

"Then you agree?"

He was pushy beyond measure. But she was dirty, and there had been talk of a bath. She was also hungry and thirsty. He'd said something about a tray being brought to her room. The mattress beneath her felt incredibly soft and accommodating. All things considered, it wouldn't hurt to humor

Courtney's uncle. And, anyway, theirs was to be a brief association.

"All right."

"There are consequences for breaking promises, Emma."

Her eyes narrowed. "You sound as if you're threatening me."

His dark eyes gleamed. "It's always nice to be understood."

"You really hate hearing about etiquette, don't you?"

"There are few topics that annoy me more."

"Uh, well, you have my word."

"Good."

Why did she feel as if she'd just bargained away a portion of her independence to the devil?

"If you have an objection to something I say or do, it's perfectly all right for you to state it."

"How magnanimous," she muttered, wondering where this odd conversation was headed.

"As long as your objections are based on something other than 'Oh, Mr. Cade, you're a mannerless beast.'"

She took strong exception to his shrill impersonation of her voice. "There's no need to beat the matter into the ground."

"Now then, is it true you have no family?"

The question reminded her why she despised chess. She absolutely loathed the point in the game when her opponent would say, "Checkmate." Even when someone as nice as Jayne Stoneworthy said it, Emma wanted to tip the board over.

"Yes, I am without family."

His rough-cut features softened. "For how long?"

"I cannot abide being pitied," she stated firmly.

"Too bad. How long have you been on your own in the world, Emma?"

"For about as long as I can remember." She made her answer cold and clinical.

"I'm not going to back off until I find out what I want to know."

"And, of course, you expect to get your way!" she cried out in frustration.

"I do."

"Just because you're a man and bigger than I am."

"That's the way it is."

"And it doesn't matter that you have no right to pry into the personal aspects of my life, and offering me temporary shelter doesn't give you permission to go poking and prodding where you have no business?"

"When a man gets to be my age, he learns to reach out and take what's important to him."

Emma studied him in consternation. What did he mean about reaching out and taking? Surely he wasn't referring to her.

"Ask your questions and be done with them," she said, willing to do almost anything at this point to get him out of the bedchamber.

"Was everything you owned lost in the fire?"

"Yes." The word came out through gritted teeth.

"You have no present employment?"

She glared at him, hoping to silently convey her contempt for his bullying tactics. "No."

"You have no money, no resources?"

The tears she'd been fighting all evening pricked her eyes. "No."

"Why did you come back here with me, Emma?"

That question so startled her that the pressure of imminent tears lessened. "What?"

"Why are you in my house, in that bed?"

"You know why," she shot back, her voice trembling. "You...you virtually kidnapped me."

"That's not good enough."

"Not *good* enough?" she repeated, her temper jumping to new heights.

"You and I both know if you had called out, a dozen or so men would have raced to your assistance. But you didn't ask for help. You had three other choices of where to be right now—a hotel, Lyman Thornton's, or Miss Stoneworthy's place.''

"How kind of you to list them." She *was* tempted to call him a mannerless beast, but his warning about breaking her promise was fresh in her mind.

"So, why are you here?"

"Because your invitation sounded the best!"

"And why is that?" he drawled, in a tone that set her teeth on edge.

"Because if I'd gone to a hotel, they would have expected me to start paying almost immediately for my lodging. If I'd accepted Jayne's kindness, I would have been a burden."

"Why not Thornton?"

Her tormentor's darkly challengingly stare made the fine hairs at the nape of Emma's neck rise. "I...I don't know."

"And, if you did know?" Gideon pressed.

The man was demented. How she could know what she didn't know? "I suppose he makes me...uneasy."

"And I make you feel safe and secure?"

"Hardly."

His eyes radiated cynicism. "Then why are you here?"

"I came with you because I didn't think you would expect me to pay for my room, my presence here would impose no hardship, and, when the time came to leave, my general loathing of you and everything you stand for would make it easy to walk away."

He accepted her bone-deep insult with equanimity. The man really was an enigma.

"Don't you feel better for getting that off your chest?"

That she did said remarkably little for her character.

"I believe you, Emma."

Surprise washed through her. "Why would you have doubted me?"

"I might have been clinging to the vain hope you had an ulterior motive for accepting my hospitality."

"What possible motive did you think I had?"

"Hmm, let's see..." His gaze performed a leisurely inspection of her bedraggled person. "Well, there was always the possibility you might want to trade the use of your delectable body for a new wardrobe, some hard cash and plush living conditions.''

Emma's corset seemed to have instantly shrunk. She couldn't get a decent gulp of air to her lungs. And, from the heat flaming across her cheeks, she knew her face must be scarlet.

"It's not very flattering that the thought never entered your mind.'' He sounded disgruntled.

"But why should I have thought that you'd want to—" She swallowed. Her mind was suddenly filled with images of what he'd been thinking she was capable of doing. Kissing him. Letting him kiss her. And surely much more, though she wasn't precisely sure what that "more" entailed. She suspected disrobing would be involved.

"You can't even say the words, can you?"

She didn't appreciate his mocking tone. Who was he to make fun of her? Only a thorough cad would be amused by her innocence.

Wrapping herself in a cloak of self-righteousness, she straightened as best she could on the soft mattress. "There are some words a—" Having been about to say "lady," she broke off and regathered her thoughts. She didn't want to reintroduce the subject of manners or decency. Clearly, the man was morally bankrupt. "There are some words *I* choose not to pronounce.''

"Too bad. I think I'd like the sound of some of those words coming out of your mouth.''

There was a discreet knock at the door. Emma wanted to cheer.

"That's probably the water for your bath.''

His guess proved correct, and another remarkable interlude with Gideon Cade concluded. A soak in a steamy tub of water, followed by a tray of breakfast dishes and the luxurious feeling of climbing between lavender-scented sheets occurred in well-ordered succession. Blessedly, she was too tired to worry about her circumstances, and surrendered easily to sleep.

* * *

Emma awoke to a darkened bedchamber. While she slept, someone had thoughtfully drawn the blue velvet draperies across the lace curtains. She stretched into the accommodating softness of the feather mattress, noticing how strangely invigorating it was to feel the friction of her skin being caressed by silken sheets. Goodness, who would have guessed that sleeping in the nude would afford such sensual stimulation?

She rolled onto her stomach and scrunched her head beneath the pillow. She didn't want to get up. When she did, she would have to deal with the hopelessness of her present situation. The only clothing she had to her name was no doubt being laundered and would shortly be returned to her. When she was again properly attired, she would be obliged to find someone who would offer her a means of employment.

Perhaps she could find a teaching position at a public school. She had impeccable references, and Denver boasted a rising child population. Despite Gideon's aspersions regarding her advanced age, she had her health. Rather than let the future terrify her, she ought to look at it as an adventure. She didn't need anyone's help. She was perfectly capable of taking care of herself.

Rolling over again, she sat up and pushed her still-damp hair back from her eyes.

"So you decided to join the world of the living."

The deep masculine voice emerged from one of the bedchamber's darkened corners.

Emma yelped and jerked the covers from her waist to her throat.

"Relax, it's only me."

With her heart hammering in her eardrums, she gaze swung toward Gideon Cade. He sat in a tall wingback chair six feet from her. She had no difficulty making out his watchful expression, which meant he'd probably had no difficulty observing her bared bosom. No wonder he'd ordered her to cease all references to mannerly behavior. Considering his appalling disregard for social rules, that would be all they ever discussed.

"*Only* you?'' she said, mimicking him. "How foolish to be alarmed then.''

"I didn't see that much, Emma. There's no reason to be embarrassed.''

"I'm not embarrassed.'' It was only a small lie. "Nor am I surprised.''

"Good, then there's no need to waste time with an outburst of maidenly horror just because I slipped into your bedchamber.''

"Heaven forbid I should waste your valuable time,'' she agreed dourly.

"I'm here to present a solution to your problems.'' He lounged in the chair with one leg crossed at the ankle, his pose one of negligent nonchalance.

Hope stirred. "Do you know someone who's looking for a teacher?''

"Not exactly. Your labors would be in a different direction.''

"I suppose I can't afford to be choosy,'' she mused thoughtfully. "At this point, I'm desperate enough to accept any kind of work.''

"The work I'm thinking of would be extremely... pleasant.''

It was shamefully improper to conduct this conversation with Gideon in a bedchamber, let alone without her having a stitch of clothing on. Yet he didn't seem to be the least bit affected by the shocking impropriety he'd initiated. She was vaguely insulted by his indifferent attitude. Not that she wanted him to force himself upon her, but still, it would have been vastly satisfying for him to excuse himself until he could assert control over the manly lusts her close proximity incited.

"Are you interested?''

His question made her realize her thoughts had drifted. "In pleasant employment?''

"Very pleasant.''

"I'd be a fool not to be. What exactly would I be doing?''

"Acting as a...companion.''

She considered that. "Are you referring to traveling with

an older woman, or serving as a chaperone for someone younger?''

"Some travel might be involved, but your employer would be a man.''

Emma frowned. "I would be caring for an older gentleman?''

Gideon cleared his throat. "Just eight years older.''

"I don't understand. Is he incapacitated in some way? Does he require a nurse?''

"He's in perfect health.''

Emma was at a loss. "Then why on earth would he require my services?''

"Has anyone ever told you that you're extremely naive?''

Her patience began to wear thin. "Maybe once or twice, but what has that to do with anything?''

"Emma, I'm trying to tactfully ask you if you'd be interested in changing careers.''

"And I've already said I'll work outside the teaching profession.''

"The work I'm suggesting is becoming a...er...I believe the European word is *courtesan*. Do you know what that means?''

The blush that swept across her succeeded in blistering the tips of her ears, her toes, and everything in between. "Of course I know what it means! You're suggesting that I become a kept woman!''

"All women are kept—either by their fathers, family or husbands,'' he responded with maddening calm.

"That's untrue. I've managed on my own, without the benefit of a family *or* a man caring for me.''

"Until now,'' Gideon observed in that same quiet tone.

"Including now,'' she corrected swiftly. "I should have known your invitation to stay here carried strings.''

"Very nice strings,'' he murmured. "Think about it, Emma. You would have lovely clothes, a carriage at your disposal, and your own private residence. Life would cease to be a struggle.''

"We've already had this conversation. I told you I wasn't interested in becoming any man's mistress."

"You told me you hadn't accepted my invitation with that thought in mind. We were interrupted before I got to the part of trying to corrupt your pure intentions."

"Good grief, you do have a low opinion of me."

"On the contrary, I admire you."

Dazed, she shook her head. "I don't see how you could have missed the fact that only an idiot would agree to become some man's...toy."

He leaned forward. "I'm not talking about *some* man. I'm talking about me, and you wouldn't be—"

"*You?*" she gasped.

"Hell, yes, me. Who did you think I was talking about?"

She rubbed her forehead. "I thought you were trying to...er...hire me for one of your friends."

He uncurled to his full, dauntingly impressive height.

"Where on earth would you get an idea like that?" he fairly roared, as if he were the injured party.

"Stop yelling. It was an honest mistake. It isn't as if you've acted as if you...liked me."

He took two steps forward. She pulled the covers higher.

"Oh, I like you. I like you a lot."

She sucked in her breath. A mouthful of blanket came with it, and she was forced to lower the covers to be able to speak. "Thank you. But I can assure you the feeling isn't mutual."

"How do you know? You just met me. Sometimes it takes a while for people to warm up to each other."

Warm up? She couldn't have felt any hotter than if she were being turned on a spit over a blazing hearth.

"Don't take another step toward me," she commanded firmly. "I'm not interested in any of your hanky-panky."

"Before turning it down, maybe you should wait and see how you like it."

Even though her eyes had adjusted to the room's semi-darkness, there seemed more shadow than substance to the man towering above her. "Would you force yourself upon a defenseless woman?"

"Force will never be an issue between us, and I'd hardly call you defenseless, Emma."

"Ha! That's easy to say, when you're the size of a pachyderm."

Her words didn't appear to dent his thick hide. He closed the distance between them and sat down. The mattress dipped heavily. She scrambled to put additional space between them.

"Hold on, where are you going?"

His arm came around her shoulders, and he trapped her against his side. The material of his coat sleeve rubbed against her naked back. She stilled. In the quiet bedchamber, her breathing was loud and shallow.

"I didn't think you would sink so low as to assault a guest in your home." And she hadn't believed that of him. At the discovery of how badly she'd misjudged his character, fear grew apace with her disillusionment.

"Dammit, I'm not going to assault you," he growled huskily. "Just give me five minutes to show you how enjoyable I can make it."

His breath feathered across her hair. She remained transfixed in his half embrace. A diabolical lethargy invaded her limbs. She felt the gentle stroke of his fingers upon her bare shoulder.

"Mr. Cade—"

"Gideon." He raised his other hand, and a lone fingertip caressed her cheek.

She shivered. "Gideon, I want you to let me go."

He nestled his face in the curve that joined neck to shoulder and inhaled deeply. "You smell so good, so womanly."

He smelled of tonic water, tobacco, and something powerfully male. "This has gone far enough."

"A kiss, Emma January Step. You wouldn't be so cruel as to deny me a kiss…"

He shifted his position so that he was leaning over her, pressing her down toward the mattress. There was nothing violent or brutal about his trespass. On the contrary, there was a timeless gentleness, an inevitable persuasiveness, to the slight pressure he exerted.

Her hands came up to push him away.

He hesitated above her. She sensed his gathering determination. A need she didn't recognize, had never seen before in any man's face, sharpened features that were shadowed but still visible. In the pit of her stomach she felt a shuddering tremor.

"Will you let me keep you?" His lips brushed her forehead. "Will you let me care for you and protect you?"

Her senses swam. A part of her that seemed both alien and familiar surged to life. She wasn't sure if she was pushing him away or pulling him to her.

"I can take care of myself." Her answer poured out slowly, from within that part of her soul which had been forged by the terrible aloneness she'd known all her life.

With the words came an increased resolve to resist this devil-man's seduction. And it was seduction, she thought, for the first time comprehending how a rational woman could be led astray by yearnings and the man who could arouse those yearnings to a fever pitch.

As if carved from the granite mountains encircling Denver, his body went rigid. "I was hoping for a different response."

With every particle of willpower she possessed, she shoved against his broad chest. At the same time, a liquid pulse throbbed between her thighs. The desire to rub herself against him became as intense as her need for independence. She held her breath, wondering which need would prevail.

"I'll take the kiss, Emma."

Again his position shifted. He lay now completely on top of her. His lips found hers. And, oh... No amount of will could keep her mouth from opening to him. Waves of delicious heat flowed through her. The slick abrasion of his tongue seeking entry undid the last of her resistance. Her arms twined around his neck, her hips moved beneath a hardness that further inflamed her senses.

Deeper the kiss went, until it seemed there was nothing else to focus on. For a few moments, there was just the darkness, the man, and the aching pleasure-pain he created within her.

The palm of his hand came into contact with the tip of her breast.

"Ooh!"

"Easy, honey. I'm not going to hurt you...."

Suddenly there was too much of everything, too much sensation, too much need, too much man. She tried to wrench free, but the twisted blankets and her tangled hair conspired to trap her.

"Whoa, easy. We're going to take it slow. There's all the time—"

The slap rang out with satisfying loudness and sufficient force to snap Gideon's head back. Her palm didn't sting quite so much as her outrage. He'd said something about wanting a kiss, but he'd tried to take far more.

"Go ahead, hit me back!"

"Believe me, I'd like to."

That made her pause in midshove. This wasn't the first time she'd thought him capable of striking a woman. "Get off me."

"I will. Give me a minute."

"Your time has run out, Gideon Cade."

"Maybe it has, but I'm hard and hurting. Do us both a favor and hold still."

"Holding still was how I got into this mess. The minute you tried to kiss me, I should have screamed my head off."

"Why didn't you?"

"I..." Why hadn't she? Because he'd employed some kind of black magic to stupefy her, but she certainly couldn't tell him that. He might use it again. "I thought I could spare one kiss. I didn't think it would lead to you...um...losing control."

"With you naked under those covers?" he asked, his skepticism obvious. "You don't know much about men."

"There doesn't appear to be all that much to know. Are you ready to get off?"

"Don't nag, I'm moving."

And he did so, with what she thought was highly suspect sluggishness, as his body molded itself into hers.

She sat up, using the covers as a shield. "If you'll have my clothes returned to me, I'll leave at once."

He adjusted the front of his trousers. "That's going to be a problem."

She was sick to death of problems! "And why is that?"

"Because I had everything burned."

"What?"

"You heard me. That awful dress is ashes, as well as your mended stockings, whalebone corset, pantalets, chemise, garters and shoes."

Which was everything that separated her from nakedness.

"Am I supposed to wander Denver's streets wrapped in a blanket while seeking employment?"

"Now there's an interesting picture."

"You had no right to burn my things!"

"Consider it fate. If you'd been where you belonged when the academy caught fire, they would have been destroyed."

"Do you think you're funny?"

"Sometimes."

"I think you have a rotten sense of humor!"

"That hurts, Emma."

"Ooh!" She hurled a pillow at him. Naturally, he eluded its lethal trajectory by ducking.

"Calm down. I've already sent for a seamstress to take your measurements. She'll be bringing some ready-made dresses and all the underpinnings. Denver's citizens are going to be deprived of the scintillating sight of you traipsing around town in a sheet."

"And how am I going to pay for everything?"

"With the wages from your new job, of course."

"But I don't have a job!" she cried in exasperation.

"Of course you do. You're working for me."

Chapter Seven

"**Y**ou're either conveniently deaf or crazy. In case you didn't notice, Mr. Cade—"

"Gideon."

"*Gideon,* I turned down your revolting offer. Nothing on earth could induce me to become your mistress."

"Yeah, I could tell how much you hated being kissed."

Emma could think of nothing sufficiently scathing to say to the nasty observation. She'd acted shamelessly, throwing her arms around his neck and drawing him closer. Goodness, she'd devoured him as if he were a wedge of warm apple pie and she meant to lick the plate clean. And, he knew it. His smug expression pricked her feminine ire.

"Being kissed wasn't a hardship. It's the man I found objectionable."

As if kissing were a normal happenstance! Gideon Cade was the first man to ever place his lips against hers. She wished he would leave her in peace so that she could affix the cataclysmic event in her memory.

"Your objection is duly noted. The kiss will not be repeated."

She told herself she was thrilled by the news.

"The only matter of business remaining to be discussed is your wages." A distinct coolness shaped his words. "I'll leave the specific details of your duties to your own discretion.''

''You're not making any sense.''

''For a teacher, you have difficulty concentrating. I've hired you to instruct Courtney until she can be enrolled at another finishing school that meets my standards.''

Emma inhaled sharply. ''Aren't you overlooking something?''

''What's that?''

''I haven't agreed to accept the position.''

He raised an eyebrow. ''Am I to believe that sitting naked under a blanket you don't own, in a house that at best is only a temporary shelter, you intend to refuse an *honorable* offer of employment?''

His tone implied that only a dimwit would commit such an act of unmitigated folly. Unfortunately, he was right.

''There's the matter of my salary to be discussed.'' It was a challenge to keep her voice from trembling, when she was overcome with gratitude at his gesture. It astonished her that a black sheep such as Gideon Cade was capable of such kindness. Had anyone other than Courtney's uncle rescued her from the terrible uncertainties yawning about her on all sides, she would have sobbed out her thankfulness.

Instead, she forced her expression to remain neutral. ''I believe that sixty dollars a month would be fair wages.''

It was an exorbitant amount. She anticipated some keen bargaining on his part to negotiate the figure downward.

''With room and board included beyond that,'' he replied.

Prepared to have her overinflated proposal scoffed at, she looked at him in amazement. Good grief, what kind of robber baron was he?

''Naturally,'' she said.

''As to the matter of the sums I'll be advancing you—''

She rushed in to express her opinion about the sensitive issue. ''Uh, Mr. Cade—''

''Gideon.''

''Gideon, I'm really not comfortable accepting articles of clothing from you. I mean…er…I don't want there to be any misunderstanding between us that the position I'm accepting is that of Courtney's teacher and not your...ah...companion.''

"There will be no misunderstanding."

Was she naive to believe she would be safe living in this man's house? Who was to say that late one night he might not invade her bedchamber and force himself upon her? It was possible that her urgent need for employment was blinding her to the inherent dangers of sharing the same domicile with a man who'd made improper advances.

"It's ridiculous for you to be concerned about me having my way with you, Emma."

Her misgivings must have shown on her face, for him to have guessed so accurately what she was thinking. "In light of your earlier advances, I think my concerns are justified."

"You're overlooking the fact that were I the kind of man to take advantage of you against your will, we would at this moment both be naked beneath the covers."

Another hot wave of self-consciousness swept through her.

"Be at peace, Emma," he said quietly. "As Courtney's teacher, you are the last woman I would involve in a personal liaison. I consider the welfare of my late brother's daughter a sacred trust, and would do nothing to damage her innocence. Nor would I make her home a place of speculation or gossip."

There was something so innately honest about his blunt reassurance that Emma's suspicions eased.

"As for the purchase of your clothing, use your head. You can't go around wearing a sheet. The dressmaker will be here for Courtney's benefit. Remember, she also lost her entire wardrobe in the fire."

"I hadn't thought of that." Both she and her student were in dire need of everything from chemises and pantalets to stockings and everything else a lady wore beneath her dress. As used as she was to budgeting her meager resources, she was painfully aware of how costly it would be to purchase only the necessities.

"To make things easier on your puritan ethics," he said,

forging on, "I'll advance your first month's wages. Is that acceptable?"

She nodded. Struck by the astonishing change in Gideon's demeanor, she could scarcely believe that this cold, self-contained man had pushed her against the mattress and breathed fire into her.

Within minutes of their meeting, she recalled, she'd thought there were secret complexities to him. Now she was certain. Nothing she'd read or heard about Gideon Cade, millionaire freighting tycoon and suspected leader of the Vigilantes, a gang of cutthroats, portrayed his true character.

As he turned to leave the bedchamber, another thought lingered. In his own way, she suspected, he was just as alone and isolated from the company of others as she was.

There was no doubt about it, Gideon thought as he stalked into his library. He'd made a gold ass of himself. He poured himself a bracing tumbler of brandy, drinking absently as he paced.

What had he been thinking to try such a heavy-handed seduction attempt on Emma Step? That was it, of course. He hadn't been thinking. He'd allowed himself to be caught up in his unexpectedly strong attraction to her, disregarding anything as relevant as sense. It infuriated him that within a few hours, one pint-size female could derail his well-ordered approach to life.

Damnation, he'd come within seconds of stripping the bedcovers from her. He didn't think she had any idea what a close call it had been. That was part of what galled him. When he leaned her back against the mattress, he'd felt her resistance melt. She'd been all softness and feminine need. She'd surrendered her mouth completely. As he took his leisurely taste of her, he'd been aware of her hands around his neck, pulling him closer. His tongue had met no resistance. He'd probed, thrust and explored at will. She'd made little clutching sounds deep in her throat and moved her hips restlessly beneath him.

Gideon took another drink, scowling when he noticed the

fine trembling of his hand. He'd trembled when he touched her satin breasts. When his fingertips brushed her hard nipples, he'd expected to taste them, also. At the very moment he was reaching for the front of his trousers to free himself to take her, she'd jerked away as if repelled. In one blinding moment of need, he'd almost ignored her wishes. There was a point when a man couldn't subdue the loosened beast. As he'd lost himself in her sweet, moist mouth, he'd wanted to lose himself in the pulsing wet heat of her womanly core. He knew she would have tasted just as deliciously feminine there.

From her shyly earnest response, he gauged Emma did not have much experience with men or, for that matter, with the powerful needs of her own body. The temptation to be the man who awakened her to the delights of lovemaking unleashed a hot coil of desire.

Gideon drank slowly, scarcely noting the brandy's potency. He'd never considered himself dishonorable. Yet what kind of man would take advantage of someone as vulnerable as Emma? As he'd watched her slowly awaken in the darkened bedchamber, the ethical side of his nature had been taken prisoner by the womanly body housing the soul, intelligence and spirit of his niece's schoolmistress.

When she sat up, her breasts bared for his personal perusal, his breath had locked in his throat. Despite being bathed in the room's muted gray light, her naked flesh had seemed to glow. Then she'd pushed back her damp and tangled hair. The unconscious action had lifted her breasts to further prominence. He didn't know how he'd managed to remain seated while calmly offering her the position of his mistress. And even then, when he thought he'd been crystal-clear about what he wanted from her, her own naiveté had blinded her to his base intentions.

Gideon shook his head. Her maddening innocence had forced him to be as direct as a bullet. Then she'd turned him down, but not before insulting them both by claiming she thought he'd been trying to acquire her services for another man. That was when his control had snapped.

He tried not to flinch under the harsh light of self-examination, but his lust and his attempt to seduce the stalwart Emma Step reproached him. Dammit, he had nothing to feel guilty about. He'd offered her a straightforward proposition, and she'd thrown it back in his face. He'd gotten the kiss he craved and, along with it, the memory, burned into him, of how her soft breasts felt cradled in his palms.

Her skin had smelled of soap, lavender and woman. He couldn't recall any expensive French perfume ever being so arousing. Her well-scrubbed face had seemed more lovely than any enhanced with paints or blushes. Even her hair, hanging in damp clumps to her shoulders, had beckoned him, mysteriously becoming a part of her feminine allure. It stunned him to realize that, with the right woman, soap and water could be a powerful aphrodisiac. But she wasn't the right woman, he reminded himself. She was the most *wrong* woman who'd ever strolled through his life.

The matter was settled. He'd hired her to tutor Courtney. He and the schoolmistress would have a strictly business arrangement. During the months she lived in his home, he would treat her with the distant cordiality and respect he showed all his employees.

There was a discreet knock at the library door.

"Come in."

Broadbent poked his homely head into the room. "This message arrived a few minutes ago."

Gideon set his glass on the desk and strode to the doorway. From his butler's neutral expression, Gideon assumed either Hunter or Burke was contacting him. He removed the note from the sealed envelope with his name on it to the sound of the library door being firmly shut.

4:00 p.m. Walker's.

Though someone else might not have understood the note's terse instructions, Gideon did. A meeting of the Guardsmen would be conducted at Nat Walker's cabin.

As nothing else could have, the message reminded Gideon of several things. He didn't have time to lose his head over some peculiar woman fate had temporarily dropped into his world. He was on a mission to track down his brother and sister-in-law's killers. He'd promised retribution for the murdering bastards who'd taken his niece's parents from her. Until Jonathan and Cynthia had been avenged, he refused to slack off his quest. As a Guardsman, he'd made promises to Hunter and Burke to join them in ridding the area of rustlers, claim jumpers, and the other murdering thieves who preyed on those weaker than themselves.

Those were his priorities, that and his determination to become so damned rich that Courtney would be set for the rest of her life. That was why he got up each morning. He plucked a match from its cut-glass container and flicked his thumbnail across the sulfurous head. The yellow flame wavered, then burned brighter. He held a corner of the note to the burning match tip. The paper immediately caught. He dropped it into an ashtray and watched it reduced to a curling black ribbon.

His gaze drifted from the ashtray to the almost empty tumbler of brandy. He reminded himself of something else. Unlike his father, he did not use alcohol as a crutch to see him through life's darker passages.

As he turned away from his desk to leave the library, it occurred to him that in a frighteningly short span of time, Emma Step had made him forget some pretty basic truths about himself.

He didn't seduce innocent females dependent upon him for their livelihood.

He had no time or inclination to involve himself with a woman who surely deserved more than a casual tussle in bed.

His bodily appetites didn't control him; he controlled them.

And, most important, he didn't deviate from a path once he'd committed himself to it. He took the stairs to his bedchamber two at a time. For four years he'd been trying to find the men who gunned down Jonathan and Cynthia. Nothing and no one was going to further delay the justice he intended to personally inflict upon the murdering cowards.

His only regret was that they could die only once.

* * *

Courtney pirouetted before her bedchamber's cheval mirror, holding out the skirts of her new pink shirtwaist. "Miss Step, I feel awful about the fire and all, but I'm so happy you're staying here."

Emma smiled, warmed by the sincerity in her student's voice. They had just finished one of the most pleasantly amazing interludes of Emma's life. True to his promise, Gideon had sent a dressmaker to his residence. Miriam Goodwin had arrived with a multitude of parcels in tow and a high level of enthusiasm for her assigned task of outfitting two women from the skin out.

It had taken the better part of an afternoon, but ready-made dresses had been fitted and sewn, and other gowns had been ordered. More than a bit overwhelmed by the experience, Emma was chagrined to discover when they settled up that she'd spent her entire first month's wages on clothing. She'd tried to chastise herself for her overspending, but it had felt so wonderful to have pretty new undergarments and colorful dresses that she couldn't summon the necessary guilt needed to spoil the pleasurable afternoon she'd shared with Courtney. There would be time enough to return to her miserly ways.

"I'm glad, too, that your uncle hired me to be your tutor."

"I wish he'd hired you permanently." Courtney continued to swirl about the room, clearly enchanted by the airy sway of her skirts.

At the word, *permanent,* Emma was reminded how brief her stint as tutor might be. Her pleasure over her purchases ebbed quickly. "I'm hoping I shall be your instructor for at least six months."

Courtney took her skirts in one hand and executed a surprisingly graceful descent into a nearby chair. "Did Uncle Gideon happen to mention how long it would be?"

Emma's spirits sank. "No. He just said I was to oversee your studies until he found another institution for you to attend."

The sixty dollars Emma had squandered for a new wardrobe suddenly seemed a fortune. With considerably less grace than her student had demonstrated, Emma plunked down on a chair. How could she have gotten so carried away buying cloths? She'd left herself without coin until Gideon paid her second month's wages.

"I wonder when Jayne Stoneworthy's school will open."

"I'm not certain, but I know she's working very hard."

Emma made a quick decision to cancel the additional gowns she'd ordered. The three ready-made dresses she'd bought were sufficient for her needs.

"As far as I'm concerned, she can take her time. I like having you all to myself."

Emma appreciated Courtney's loyalty, but she doubted her uncle shared his niece's sentiments.

"And I like having you all to myself," Emma returned sincerely, even though preoccupied with finances. Suddenly it had become imperative that she make a mad dash to Miriam Goodwin's store and cancel her order.

"I really like that shade of green on you." Courtney tipped her head consideringly, her delicate brow furled. "Would you call it a moss color?"

Emma glanced down at the linen material trimmed with white lace. "That's a good way to describe it."

"It's a beautiful shade on you. I never noticed before, but your hair has reddish highlights, and your eyes aren't just plain gray. They're sort of a luminous silver color."

Not used to being stared at so intently or complimented so lavishly, Emma felt her face grown warm. "You're a kind-hearted girl, Courtney. But, if anyone should be receiving compliments, it's you. With your black hair and blue eyes, you put me in mind of a fairy-tale princess."

The girl blushed prettily. Gideon Cade was going to have his hands full keeping would-be suitors from overrunning his mansion when his adorable niece became a part of Denver's social whirl.

"Let's take a stroll with our new parasols and show the world how good we both look," Courtney suggested with engaging enthusiasm.

"That sounds enjoyable, but I've an urgent errand."

"What errand is that?"

I've got to stop Miriam Goodwin from taking one snip of her shears into the fabric I ordered! Since she didn't wish to burden Courtney with her money concerns, Emma bit back the frazzled explanation.

"I need to discuss my purchase with Miss Goodwin," she limited herself to saying.

"Oh, that's a capital idea. Have you decided to buy the lavender material so she can sew that evening gown design she showed you?"

"Not exactly," Emma hedged, "but I do need to talk with her before I do anything else this afternoon."

"Let's have Broadbent order the carriage for us, then."

Emma was grateful for her student's generous disposition, but she didn't wish for Courtney to overhear her canceling her order with the dressmaker. There didn't seem a tactful way of declining the girl's company, though.

If only she hadn't gotten carried away by the sight of all those beautiful fabrics and dress designs. Emma wanted to blame Miss Goodwin and her beguiling manner of describing her gowns for making her lose track of her common sense. But one had to assume responsibility for one's own actions, even when foolhardy.

"Come on, let's go downstairs and have the carriage sent around."

Emma gave up trying to separate herself from her student. The best she could hope for was a private moment with the seamstress. But, no matter what, she had to cancel her order.

They located Broadbent in the kitchen. He and a large, lushly padded middle-aged woman called Mrs. Graves were in the midst of a heated debate.

"It's my kitchen, Mr. Broadbent, and no dirty, flea-bitten mutt has any right inside it."

The cook folded her huge arms across her wide, matronly bosom and glared at the red-faced butler.

"Mr. Cade told me to make sure the dog was fed."

"Then feed him outside. He's not putting one muddy paw in here."

"Be reasonable, Mrs. Graves. If we put his food outdoors, we'll be inviting every stray dog in Denver into the yard."

She squared shoulders almost as wide as the butler's. "That's your problem."

"What dog are you talking about?" Courtney asked as she looked about the kitchen.

"That ugly-looking demon on the other side of that window. Look at him, drooling over himself like some toothless old man."

Emma's gaze went to the low window that bordered one of the room's stone walls. Sure enough, there was Duncan, staring intently into the kitchen.

"Look, Miss Step, it's the dog that's been hanging around the academy. What on earth is he doing here?"

"That's what I'm asking," Mrs. Graves said sharply. "The mutt's got no business having the run of a nice neighborhood like ours. It's as clear as the mud caked between his paws that he belongs to no one, and that's because no one will have him."

Recalling Duncan's fearless defense on her behalf, Emma couldn't stand by and hear his noble character defamed.

"Actually, Mrs. Graves, he belongs to me." Emma heard the explanation leave her mouth and, despite the cook's horrified expression, had no desire to retract it. "I admit he looks a bit under the weather, but after a thorough scrubbing, he...well, he'll look almost civilized."

There was no point trying to oversell Duncan. The cook appeared to be an intelligent woman, and only a pea-brain would attribute any stellar qualities to the mongrel. It was a pity the animal's admirable character was in no way reflected in his disreputable appearance.

"Well, he ain't putting a paw in my kitchen until he's been washed."

"Well then," Courtney said, unbuttoning the cuffs of her new dress, "I say we all pitch in and give him a bath."

The cook relaxed her militant stance and turned to the stove, where an empty pot suddenly needed rattling. "I've got a supper to fix, missy."

Broadbent straightened and edged past Courtney. "Naturally, I would be happy to assist, but I've pressing duties that require my attention."

"I guess that leaves you and me to get the job done," Courtney said with the kind of good cheer that could occasionally grate on one's ears.

"Let's give him his bath after we visit Miss Goodwin's."

"But, Miss Step, he looks so pitiful out there. I bet he's starving, and you heard Mrs. Graves. He'll get no food until he looks like a gentleman instead of a tramp."

Emma scowled at the cook's wide back. Oblivious to her dark thoughts, the woman reached for another empty pot.

"I really need to have a discussion with Miss Goodwin," Emma said, feeling desperate.

"You will." Courtney took her arm and tugged her to the side door. "We'll give Duncan the quickest bath he's ever had."

As Emma allowed herself to be led outside, she thought it was distinctly possible that his forthcoming scrubbing would be Duncan's *only* encounter with soap and water.

As it turned out, the "quickest" bath was fraught with inherent impediments, not the least of which was the dog's determination to stay out of the wooden washtub Mrs. Graves donated to the cause. Emma knew she outweighed the ill-tempered beast, and yet it required both her and Courtney's dedicated efforts, along with a good portion of time, to get him into the sudsy water. When they'd actually accomplished that major milestone, both she and her student were spattered with suds. And while they'd pushed up their sleeves and appropriated aprons from the housekeeping staff, they were still generously drenched.

As Emma balefully surveyed the black dog standing up to his scarred nose in bubbles, she decided it had been his intention to soak them. No doubt he felt entitled to his revenge, but she judged him to be a spiteful wretch.

"Uh, Miss Step, I think you might be scrubbing a tad too hard. That looked like a piece of fur you rubbed off his back."

"You heard Mrs. Graves," Emma muttered through gritted teeth. "She's not letting him in her kitchen until she pronounces him clean."

"Knowing Mrs. Graves, she'll be sending us out to buy some doggy clothes to make him decent if we return him hairless."

Emma looked up and blew a lilac-scented soap bubble off the tip of her nose. "I promise to ease off on the scrubbing, if you agree not to dump any more bath crystals into the water."

Courtney's gay laughter rang out. "That's not fair. You know I didn't mean to pour so much in. If Duncan hadn't tried to jump out at the exact moment I was trying to make his bath smell better, I would never have lost my grip on the decanter."

Despite her grumpy mood, Emma smiled. "You'd already put enough in before we even got him close to the tub. It was probably the sight of all those foamy bubbles that had him running the other way."

"You just wanted to be coaxed," Courtney crooned, "didn't you, Duncan?"

The dog refrained from commenting. Judging from his stoic expression, he'd resigned himself to being at the mercy of two demented humans. Emma just hoped he wouldn't throw himself into the first mud puddle he saw to reassert control over his own doggy destiny.

"It's really an odd coincidence you named him Duncan."

"Actually, Broadbent christened him."

Courtney paused, her washcloth poised in back of the dog's twitching ears. "I can't believe he would do that."

Emma recalled the cryptic look the two men had exchanged when the butler first pronounced the name. "Well, he did."

"When I was a little girl, my father told me a very sad story about a dog named Duncan."

Even though Emma suspected Gideon Cade would strenuously object to having any part of his personal life revealed to someone outside his family, there was no way she could subdue her curiosity. Besides, Gideon had forfeited his rights to privacy when he invited her to become his mistress.

"If it's too sad, you might not want to tell it." There, she'd tried to discourage the girl from sharing the story.

"It happened a long time ago, when my daddy was a little boy. Grandma Cade had died—that was my father's and Uncle Gideon's mother. Grandpa Cade was sick, too, and couldn't take care of his sons. So it turned out that, even though Uncle Gideon was only fourteen, he had to work to support his little brother and his father."

Emma remembered Gideon's terse explanation about his distaste for discussions of manners. He'd said he'd grown up on the Boston docks. He hadn't mentioned anything about having an ailing father and younger brother to care for.

"From what father said, they lived in a pretty rough part of town. They had a room over a run-down tavern. Since Grandpa wasn't well enough to work, it was his job to care for Daddy while Uncle Gideon loaded and unloaded cargo in Boston Harbor."

Emma's heart twisted. What a grueling life for a young boy.

"One night Gideon came home from the docks carrying a black puppy. Father was six, and absolutely thrilled by the new addition to their family. Grandpa thought it was foolish to add one more mouth to feed. But Uncle Gideon said the puppy was for Daddy, and that was that."

Emma tried to imagine Gideon Cade as a hardworking yet sentimental young man. The image wouldn't appear. Oh, she could visualize him putting his wide back to use, struggling under loads heavy enough to bring a grown man to his knees. But, no matter how hard she tried, she couldn't see him bringing a puppy home for a little brother.

"Father named the dog Duncan, in honor of our Scottish heritage."

"Scottish?" Emma asked, surprised. She'd thought Scots were generally fair-haired and ruddy-complected.

"Our family name used to be McCade, but it got shortened before Grandpa was born. Daddy said we were descendants from an old, respected clan that had fallen on hard times. Our ancestors came to America to find a better life. To hear Father talk about the McCades, they were a fierce band of 'black' warrior Scots who laid claim to a remote, high mountain valley in the most northern part of Scotland.''

That was something Emma could picture. Gideon Cade with a shoulder-length mass of tangled hair and a black beard, dashing about the Scottish Highlands, bare-chested and wearing a kilt while brandishing a sword to terrify any unsuspecting visitor who strayed into his self-proclaimed kingdom.

"Things went smoothly for almost a year. Even with the extra mouth to feed, there was sufficient food.'' Even though the story had come to her secondhand, Courtney's blue eyes filled with nostalgia. Gradually her expression sobered. "Then, one December night, Uncle Gideon came home to disaster. Grandpa had gone somewhere and left Daddy alone. The fire in the hearth had gone out, and the tiny apartment was freezing. Daddy was sick and couldn't stop coughing. No one knew it back then, but he had tuberculosis.''

"Was that why your family came to Denver?'' From what Emma had learned during her short time here, a lot of Easterners, especially with lung problems, came to the area in hopes of the "Denver Cure.''

Courtney nodded. Emma noticed that the girl's fingers trembled as they continued to rub the blue washcloth over Duncan's wet fur.

"All Uncle Gideon was thinking about was finding a doctor to help father. Daddy said Uncle Gideon wrapped him in a blanket and carried him from place to place until he finally found a physician who agreed to examine him. Father ended up spending three weeks in a hospital.''

"What happened to your grandfather?''

"He died that night. According to Daddy, Grandpa sometimes drank too much for his own good. I guess when he got to missing Grandma, the liquor was the only thing that comforted him. He must have gotten befuddled, because he never made it home. The authorities found his body in a back alley behind a tavern. He'd frozen to death.''

"How horrible."

"I know. Father said Uncle Gideon blamed himself for not spending the rest of the night searching the streets for Grandpa."

Emma thought of the long hours of backbreaking toil Gideon must have put in before he came home to find his brother alone and deathly ill. "Surely your uncle's first responsibility was to a brother too young to care for himself."

"I think so, too. But Uncle Gideon always acts as if he should be able to accomplish all things—you know, handle several businesses, and at the same time make every aspect of his life proceed smoothly."

Since Emma had previously thought of him as a tyrannical overlord and oppressor of the weak, it required a stretch of the imagination to perceive him as a sympathetic and heroic figure.

"When Daddy was in the hospital, he was burning up with fever. He kept calling for Duncan and Grandpa."

"How hard that must have been for your uncle."

"I guess it took several days for him to discover what happened to the dog. It turned out that Grandpa had sold Duncan to a tavernkeeper who planned on using him as a watchdog. Some of the patrons thought it was great sport to get him sloshed on ale and observe his antics. But things got out of hand when someone tried to force a lighted cigar down the dog's throat, and was bitten."

"Served him right," Emma muttered.

"Evidently no one else saw it that way. The man pulled out a derringer and shot poor Duncan dead on the spot."

"Only a thoroughly despicable person would do such a thing."

"Anyway, it just so happened that Broadbent entered the tavern shortly after the shooting. In those days, he worked alongside Uncle Gideon on the docks. He'd been to the apartment many times, and recognized poor dead Duncan. Daddy said he buried the dog and then told Uncle Gideon what had happened. Then, in less than a fortnight, there was some kind of accident on board one of the ships, and Broadbent's arm was badly injured. Uncle Gideon let him move in until it could heal. Broadbent did such a good job taking care of Daddy and the apartment that Uncle Gideon decided to pay him for his services. It turned out years before Broadbent had been in training to become a butler. Isn't that an amazing story?"

Emma was forced to agree. "It's astonishing how seemingly unrelated incidents can interweave people's lives together."

Chapter Eight

"It just doesn't feel right." Burke Youngblood, owner and president of Denver's largest bank, said in frustration. "A band of robbers new to the area shouldn't have known to hit a stage that's never carried a shipment of gold before."

Gideon looked across the scarred table to where Burke and cattle baron Hunter Moran sat. Their expressions were as somber as Nat Walker's as he stood at the cookstove, pouring himself more of the black sludge that passed for coffee in his mountain shack.

Nat returned the dented pot to the stove. "One thing's sure, the murdering thieves know how to cover their tracks."

"Someone with a lot of money must be backing them," Burke pointed out. "We haven't heard of a single newly minted gold coin being circulated within a two-hundred-mile radius."

"I agree," Gideon said. "Only one thing would prevent the robbers from dipping into that gold stash."

"They must have gotten enough money up front to tide them over for a while," Hunter said, finishing the thought.

Gideon drummed his fingers on the table. "They had to be tipped off that the stage was carrying the gold."

Burke nodded bleakly. "I don't want to agree with you, but the evidence points to it being someone at the bank. I would have sworn I could trust the men working for me. Only three of them knew the particulars about that shipment, and they've been with me for years.''

Hunter pushed back his chair and stood. ''Someone connected with the stage line could have let the information drop that there would be an extra guard on the Denver-to-Boulder run.''

''The extra guard would be a tip-off that the stage was carrying more than its usual group of assorted travelers,'' Gideon agreed.

Burke thoughtfully rubbed his fingertip along the side of his mug of untouched coffee. ''The presence of an extra guard could have indicated there was something worth stealing, but we're talking about twenty-five thousand dollars. A shipment of that size hasn't left Denver in months.''

''They didn't just stop the stage and demand the strongbox,'' Nat said. ''They surrounded the coach, bullets flying. The sheriff thinks the driver and half the passengers were already dead before the team was run to the ground.''

''And the rest of the travelers were murdered in cold blood,'' Hunter said hollowly, ''including that family from Tucson.''

That was the worst of it, Gideon silently concurred. The thieves had shot to death a pregnant woman and her young son. The heartless brutality of the attack was eerily similar to the way his brother and sister-in-law had been killed four years ago.

''I know this hits close to home,'' Hunter continued, shoving a hand through his thick crop of dark hair. ''Your brother and his wife were gunned down just as viciously the night they took your buggy home from my place.''

Burke shifted. ''I was thinking the same thing. The men who attacked your brother showed the same callous disregard for life as the robbers who ran down the stage.''

Gideon had a choice. He could rewalk that road of grief, or he could focus on catching the animals who'd killed Jonathan and Cynthia. He didn't think twice about choosing the latter.

''Maybe the killers cleared out after those murders,'' Hunter suggested. "They could have moved to greener pastures for a while. It was after the killings that we organized the Guardsmen."

"Everything was going wrong at once," Burke recalled. "Your cattle were being rustled in droves, Hunter."

"And I was having a tough time protecting the gold shipments coming down from the mines." Gideon stared at Burke. "You had your hands full maintaining security at the bank."

"It was a bad time, all right," Hunter agreed, "and the sheriff couldn't have caught the devil at a Baptist revival."

Nat Walker, Hunter's foreman, smiled briefly at the jest, but his eyes remained somber. "We've come a long way from those black times, but I've got a feeling things might be taking a turn for the worse."

"You think there's going to be more trouble?" Burke asked.

Nat nodded. "Trouble's already here. Rustlers are at it again."

Gideon turned to Hunter. "When did they start back up?"

"A couple of weeks ago." Anger smoldered in the rancher's dark eyes. "The losses are starting to add up."

"What have you done about it?" Gideon asked.

"Put men on double shifts till we hire more cowpunchers to ride watch."

Nat drained his mug of sludge and slammed it on the table. "There's something peculiar about the sudden boldness of these crimes. We've got a new sheriff who's supposed to be one tough hombre, but—"

"But he hasn't managed to do more than round up the town's drunks since he was sworn in," Hunter cut in derisively.

"I notice he and Lyman Thornton seem to be good friends," Burke observed thoughtfully.

"Sheriff Beckman has friends in high places," Gideon said in disgust. "Dilicar's newspaper can't say enough good things about him."

"Looks like the Guardsmen will be picking up the slack,"

Hunter announced. "I plan on hiring a bigger crew to protect my cattle."

Burke shoved aside his cold coffee. "I'm bringing in more armed guards to provide increased security for the bank's patrons."

"And I'll add more men to ride shotgun for the mule trains and freight cars transporting the gold from the mines."

"It looks as if the cost of doing business in Denver just went up for all of us," Hunter observed with bitter irony.

It occurred to Gideon that, for the next few months, at least, his attention would be focused solely on the Guardsmen. He decided to look at it as a blessing in disguise. With his mind on life and death issues, it would be easier to keep his hands off Emma Step.

"You know," Hunter muttered, "life was a lot simpler when I was seventeen, and the only thing on my mind was Saturday night and the good-time gals who used to hang out at the Wet Beaver."

Nat's cabin suddenly filled with the sounds of sympathetic male laughter. Gideon recalled Emma and her friend's innocent reference to the brothel. That the two straightlaced women had no idea of the crude meaning behind the former establishment's name was obvious.

"I heard the Beave shut down, boss," Nat said good-naturedly. "I guess when they lost you as a steady customer, they went out of business."

"When a man passes a certain age, he starts thinking with more than his privates."

"I wouldn't know about that," Nat said slyly. "Some of my best thinking comes from south of the border, if you get my drift."

More appreciative chuckles followed the earthy observation.

"Well, my randy friend, you'll find when you reach thirty, the thought of finding a good woman to settle down with and raise a family isn't as repulsive as it once was."

Nat shuddered dramatically. "Boss, don't tell me one of the richest bachelors this side of the Missouri is thinking about letting himself get hog-tied by some honey-mouthed virgin who'll put a ring through your nose and keep you dancing to her tune for the rest of your life!''

"That's your problem, Nat," Hunter responded, clearly amused by his foreman's low opinion of matrimony. "You're a natural-born pessimist."

Nat snorted. "I'm not the only one who recognizes what a black trap it is for a man to get roped into marriage. I'll wager Burke and Gideon would rather serve a stretch in prison than be leg-shackled to the same woman for the rest of their lives."

As if wanting no part of the conversation, Burke raised his hands. "Consider me an innocent bystander. My brother, Logan, appears to be happily married to a Bostonian bluestocking who's turned his life upside down. Most of the time he walks around with a moronic grin on his face—which can be damned irritating for anyone wanting to have a serious discussion with him. On one hand, he's obviously happier than he's ever been. On the other, he's so besotted with his wife it's almost painful to be around him."

"That won't last long." Nat laughed. "A few months from now, he'll be singing a different tune."

"It's been a couple years already," Burke said drolly. "His tune hasn't changed. If anything, it's gotten louder and more annoying. There's just something about a man who acts as if he's got paradise in his hip pocket that puts a strain on everyone else."

"What about you, Gideon?" Hunter asked. "Have you thought about the kind of woman you might eventually marry?"

Gideon's earlier amusement with the topic died a quick death. "I have no intention of marrying."

"Oh, so we've got another woman-hater in our midst."

"I don't hate women." Both Nat and Gideon spoke the comment in unison.

"Yeah, of course not." Hunter snickered. "You just expect to pay for your pleasures and then go to sleep alone in your own bed."

"It works for me," Nat said, walking over to his cot and stretching out. "Beats having some female nagging about all my supposed shortcomings."

"What do you mean, 'supposed'?" Hunter shot back. "There isn't a civilized female in America who wouldn't expect you to patch that hole in your roof and fix up this shack you call home."

Nat looked around the one-room cabin. "Everything's just the way I want it. There's not one thing I'd change. Besides, I got plenty of pots to catch any rainwater that falls my way."

Even Gideon had to smile at that statement. "You mean the squirrels could keep living in those old coveralls you've got hanging on your porch?"

"That pile of whiskey bottles in the corner does add a certain charm," Burke said, joining the fun. "And think how much time you'd save the lady by having her sleep directly on that old mattress. She'd never have to slave over a boiling kettle of soap, washing the bedding."

"Yeah, and since you eat beans for breakfast, lunch and supper, she'd be spared the trouble of trying to find recipes to please you." Hunter allowed himself a good laugh before continuing. "Of course, she'd have to get used to sleeping with the windows open even in December, because those beans you favor so highly don't seem to favor you, Nat."

At the foreman's offended expression, all three men broke into laughter.

"Well, I never claimed to be no housekeeper," he said, jumping up from his cot and wading into the pile of whiskey bottles. "Unlike you dandies, I don't have high-priced servants working for me." He started pitching the glass containers through an open window. "But now that I know how disgusting you find my place, I'll spruce things up."

There was something so incongruous about watching the tall, lanky foreman become upset when the dismal nature of his abode was brought to his attention that none of his guests could stop laughing.

Nat kept hurling the empty bottles outside. An outraged animal shriek reverberated through the cabin. The foreman froze in midthrow. Hunter went to the window and looked outside before turning to his red-faced wrangler.

"Well, Nat, it appears you just solved your problem about those pesky squirrels. They're leaving."

"Ah, hell, I was attached to those fellers." Nat lowered his arm.

"I'm sure if you leave the coveralls where they are, you'll find yourself with more company," Burke said consolingly.

"Yeah, I heard about a family of skunks who've been knocking on doors, looking for a place to live," Hunter said brightly. "If you promise to cut back on those beans, they might be willing to stay here."

Even Nat chuckled at that well-aimed barb.

"I think that pink ribbon is the perfect touch, don't you, Miss Step?"

If Emma hadn't known for a fact that the freshly scrubbed and perfectly combed dog standing in front of them was Duncan, the disreputable hellhound from Denver's back streets, she wouldn't have believed it. "Even without the bow, he looks like one of those pedigreed champions you see being walked Sunday afternoons on Twitchell Avenue."

Courtney knelt down and threw her arms around his neck. Even his personality seemed to have undergone a significant change as he licked the young woman's cheeks. "Ugh— you've still got dog breath."

Emma laughed. "Forget it, we're not going to scrub his teeth."

"Why not? I'm sure human tooth powder would work just as well on him as it does us."

"Perhaps so, but I'm not willing to donate my new toothbrush to the cause, are you?"

The girl wrinkled her nose. "Well, maybe not my very own *personal* one, but I bet we can find another laying about somewhere."

"Another what?"

At the sound of Gideon Cade's voice, both Emma and

Courtney turned toward the side door he'd just stepped through.

The sight of her student's uncle dressed in rough Western clothing did something peculiar to Emma's stomach. Goodness, who would have believed how masculine and dashing a pair of snug-fitting denim trousers and a black shirt could make a man appear? The leather vest seemed to make his shoulders look even wider, and the gun belt strapped to his lean hips emphasized his powerful thighs and…that manly portion of his anatomy residing betwixt them.

"Uncle Gideon, you're just in time to tell us what a wonderful job we did cleaning Duncan. You won't believe how hard it was to get him to cooperate with being bathed."

"On the contrary." His thorough gaze seared itself into Emma's awareness. "I can see that both of you must have thrown yourselves wholeheartedly into the project."

Emma glanced at her wet apron. Liberal numbers of black dog hairs covered it, along with large, grimy smears and a couple of grass stains from the tussle she'd had getting Duncan back into the tub after a grievously stupid cat entered the yard. She could feel strands of hair hanging around her face, and from the tight, hot feeling stretching across her cheeks, she suspected she'd become sunburned from being outside all afternoon.

"But it was all worth it," Courtney said exuberantly. "Even Miss Step pronounced him perfect."

"If Miss Step says he's perfect, then he must be. I've observed your teacher maintains high standards in all aspects of her life."

She knew the flush she felt spreading across her cheeks had nothing to do with the sun. Darned if Gideon Cade didn't have an annoying habit of making her feel self-conscious.

"Isn't she wonderful?" Courtney demanded with enough enthusiasm to make Emma wince. Clearly, the girl hadn't yet learned the subtle nuances of adult sarcasm. "I told you she was magnificent when I came home last night, but you didn't believe me."

"How could I?" he inquired. "Until one actually meets

Miss Step, one can have no idea how truly remarkable she is.''

Continuing to remain oblivious to her uncle's rude brand of irony, Courtney beamed. "Exactly. And now I have her to myself as my very own personal instructor. Oh, Uncle Gideon, thank you!''

With that, the girl let go of the pink ribbon she'd secured around Duncan's neck and launched herself into her uncle's arms for a spontaneous hug. Clearly, Gideon was caught off guard, but he braced his feet apart and allowed himself to be squeezed as if he were an oversize pillow. Emma noticed that his hug was only a faint replica of the vigorous embrace his niece bestowed upon him. It shouldn't have made her heart twist that the man evidently didn't know how to respond to Courtney's uninhibited burst of affection, but his reserved reaction provoked a wholly unwelcome pang of tenderness within Emma.

When the side door opened again, she was more than willing to shake away the disturbing feeling.

"Sir, if the ladies have finished their ministrations on Duncan's behalf, Mrs. Graves is prepared to reward their labors with a pot-roast dinner that would make Saint Peter abandon his post at the pearly gates.''

"Dinner?" Emma asked, tugging at the confining strings of her apron. "Oh, my goodness, what time is it?''

"About six,'' Gideon answered, eyeing with obvious fascination her efforts to gain her freedom from the uncooperative apron.

"Six! Oh, no, I hope I'm not too late.'' When she'd finally wrestled the garment from her, she let it fall to the lawn and began rolling down her sleeves. "Broadbent, would you please have the carriage sent around? I have an urgent errand to run.''

"But dinner is ready,'' he said, as if that minor fact were more important than stopping Miss Goodwin from bankrupting her.

"I know, and I'm sure Mrs. Graves has outdone herself, but I have some very important business to conduct. Now.''

Broadbent's gaze went to his employer. "Sir, you know how Mrs. Graves is about serving her meals on time."

"A termagant," he replied matter-of-factly.

"Oh, Miss Step, in our struggle to bathe Duncan, I forgot about going to Miss Goodwin's shop," Courtney said apologetically. "Since it's gotten so late, why don't we go tomorrow?"

The question was so reasonable, Emma wanted to cry. Because she hated revealing what an addlepated ninny she'd been in mismanaging her finances, there was no way to explain her desperate need to visit the dressmaker.

"Have the carriage sent around, Broadbent."

At Gideon's even-voiced command, Emma was tempted to imitate Courtney and throw her arms around him in a ferocious hug of gratitude. Luckily, common sense prevailed before she made an even greater fool of herself.

"As you wish, sir. I'll see if I can persuade Mrs. Graves to keep a plate of food warm for when Miss Step returns."

"Have her prepare two. I'll be accompanying Miss Step on her errand."

"That's not necessary," she said hastily.

"Oh, but it is," he countered lightly. "By the way, how is your foot?"

Her foot? What foot?

"Are you still limping?" he prompted patiently.

She wriggled her toes in the new shoe that graced her right foot. A familiar pain shot upward. "Uh, I'm not fully recovered." She stepped back. "But I certainly don't need to be carried."

He rubbed his hands together. "I have a very strong back, and I'm more than willing to oblige."

She'd just bet he did. Luckily, she had no need of it. "I'm perfectly capable of moving about under my own steam."

The carriage arrived outside the yard, sparing the need for further debate. She took off toward the gate.

"You *are* in a rush." Despite her head start, Gideon reached the wrought-iron gate before her and opened it. "Allow me."

She gritted her teeth. His exaggerated politeness when she was in such a frightful hurry was more than she could tolerate. "Thank you."

Naturally, she had to wait for him to open the carriage door and assist her inside. Nor was her sense of haste appeased by their team's sedate pace as they proceeded toward the business section of town.

"I should think your horses could go faster," she suggested, with what she hoped was casual interest.

"I'm sure they can."

He sat on the seat across from her, with his arms folded and a look of heightened curiosity flickering in his dark eyes.

"Well?"

"Well, what?" he drawled.

"Why don't you tell the driver you want to go faster?"

"It's only a ten-minute drive," he pointed out with maddening reasonableness.

"It's already after six, and she said that was when she closed."

"Then it appears you should have done as Courtney suggested and rescheduled your visit for tomorrow morning."

"But she also told us that she does most of her sewing in her apartment over the shop during the evenings."

Gideon shook his head. "Are you always so impatient when it comes to increasing an order? It's not as if one night is going to make much difference one way or the other."

"*Increasing* my order?" Emma asked, startled by his misconception about why she was in such a hurry to speak with Miss Goodwin.

"Even though I prefer seeing you dressed in something more flattering than that atrocious rag you were wearing last night, there is something to be said on behalf of Mrs. Graves's pot roast."

"It was your idea to accompany me."

"A new element of lawlessness has invaded Denver. I didn't like the idea of sending you out alone. There's no telling what kind of trouble you might embroil yourself in."

"I should think you could trust your own driver to deliver me safely to my destination."

"Hennesy's all right, but even a good man occasionally needs support."

Gideon had an answer for everything. "I just wish he would hurry."

"You still haven't told me why you're in such an all-fired rush to talk to a seamstress."

Emma knew she was flushing again. "It's a private matter. I just need a couple of minutes alone with her."

His gaze roved over her speculatively. "Did she mismeasure something important?"

"No."

"Did she coerce you into buying something that doesn't agree with your own personal taste?"

Close, but no prize. "No."

"Did she fail to add the bill correctly?"

"Is there any way I can get you to drop this subject?"

"I suppose if you threw yourself into my arms and forced me at gunpoint to accept your kisses, I might be sidetracked."

"You're the one with a pistol strapped to his hip."

"You could always wrestle it from me."

"You must have been in the sun too long without a hat, to think I'd do something so crazy."

"I wore a fine black felt Stetson every moment I was outside."

What would he do if she did try to wrestle his gun free? Before he'd desist plaguing her, she would probably be obliged to shoot him. On the bright side, the sound of the gunshot might hurry the horses.

"That shade of green is most becoming on you, Emma."

If he knew the dark turn her thoughts had taken, he wouldn't be so free with his compliments. "Thank you."

"It makes you look years younger," he added, spoiling the foolish pleasure she'd taken at his praise.

"How kind of you to point that out." She folded her arms and tapped her foot against the carriage floor. "For someone of your advanced years, you seem awfully preoccupied with *my* age.''

He didn't appear offended by her snide remark, which disappointed her considerably.

"How do you know how old I am?" he asked, his lips curved in an infuriatingly complacent smile.

"I did the math."

"What math is that?"

"When you offered me the position of being your…companion, you stated the man I would be working for was eight years older than I am. That means you must be thirty-two."

"And you consider that old?" he inquired mildly.

"Well, it's certainly much older than I am. I daresay you are on the downhill slide of life, sir."

"You have a cruel streak to your nature, Emma."

She shifted uncomfortably. If her words were cruel, it was because he'd driven her to speak them in order to prevent him harping on about her age. "Perhaps I was letting you know I don't appreciate your constant references to how old I am."

"I see. At twenty-four, you're beginning to feel sensitive about your advancing years."

Her hands clenched. At times, the man could be obnoxious beyond measure. "Now that we've brought the matter into the open, I trust you will cease making disparaging remarks such as that about my age."

"It's probably because you're a spinster," he said, with stunning disregard for her stated wishes about such tactless comments. "No doubt if you had a husband and a couple of children, you would be more comfortable with each approaching birthday."

"Nevertheless, in comparison to your own august age, I'm but a mere infant," she stated coolly.

Instead of being properly put in his place, he laughed at her. Emma's fingers itched to go for his gun.

"You really need to lighten up, Emma. Life's too short to be so tightly wound."

"Ha! As if you have any right to talk about me being too tightly wound. Sir, allow me to point out that upon most occasions you come across with all the warmth and cordiality of a fireplace poker!"

"Things are different for men," he responded, with such good cheer that the thought of shooting him no longer seemed out of the question. "When I observe that a woman your age should realize that, I'm not implying that you're an old crone on the verge of quitting life. I'm merely crediting you with intelligence beyond that of a giggling schoolgirl."

Did he think that made her feel better?

"Women are encouraged to be warm, soft creatures of compassion and tenderness," he continued. "Men are supposed to be cool-headed, hardworking and logical."

"Women can be just as coolheaded, hardworking and logical."

"But they shouldn't have to be," he argued. "With proper guidance from a husband, father or male relative, a woman can yield to her softer tendencies."

"Even you can't believe such tripe."

For the first time during their discussion, a hint of heat entered his dark eyes. "There might be an occasional sharp-tongued female who needs firmer handling, but by and large I would say most women are softhearted creatures who benefit from the company of wise and generous men."

"Why try to dress up your positively medieval beliefs with words that camouflage what you truly mean?"

"Am I to assume you're prepared to tell me what I do mean?"

"Naturally. When you refer to a sharp-tongued female, you mean a woman who thinks for herself. When you pronounce someone of my gender as being softhearted, she could more accurately be termed *softheaded*. And last but not least, your 'wise' and 'generous' husband or male family member often is *not* a gentle guide, but instead a tyrant who uses his authority to keep a woman under his domineering thumb, lest she find out that she's fully capable of making her own decisions in life."

"That is a very cynical view, Emma."

"That depends on whether a person lives their life with or without skirts."

"Are you saying you don't believe in the sanctity of matrimony?"

"You're a fine one to bring up the subject of marriage, after trying to compromise me with a sordid invitation to become a kept woman."

His lips thinned, and his eyes glowed hotter. Good—she was tired of his casual attitude. "I would hardly call my offer to take upon my shoulders all your worldly cares, *sordid*."

"Of course you wouldn't. Being a man, you disguise all less-than-sterling behavior with prattlings about generous rewards."

"That's overstating it considerably," he muttered coldly.

"I think not," she retorted. "Unless my ears deceived me, you were more than ready to claim my virginity in exchange for that *generosity*."

"I believe a woman's virginity has been overrated through the ages."

"Of course you do. A man incapable of feeling true love has to tell himself a chaste woman is of no more value than a harlot."

"You're a harsh judge, Emma."

"Not I," she protested. "I believe in live-and-let-live. But when it comes to my own life, there are standards I will never compromise."

"Little Miss Purity… Tell me, does being a saint ever become a burden, or do you enjoy preaching?"

Knowing that she'd finally goaded him beyond his usually rigid control compensated for the insult. "I rarely preach. Goodness, as I reflect upon it, you're probably the first person I've ever had to…er…chastise. Believe me, it's not a task to be relished, but unfortunately I seem to be the only one with enough grit to point out your vast reservoir of shortcomings."

"Isn't there something in the Scriptures about casting the beam out of your own eye before tackling the mote in someone else's?"

"I have perfect vision." She blinked her lashes at him. "Nothing is blocking my view."

"Not even a wall of self-righteousness?"

"Don't be mean-spirited, Gideon. Everyone is capable of improving themselves. I daresay that should you ever truly fall in love with a decent woman and marry her, you would cheerfully abandon your archaic beliefs about women being subject to men."

"My *archaic beliefs,* as you call them, happen to be irreversible."

"Well then, may your bachelorhood last your entire mortal life."

"Better bachelorhood than spinsterhood."

"Why would you think that?"

"Whereas men become more seasoned with age, women tend to shrivel."

"That's just another one of your outmoded prejudices." Was that how he thought of her, as shriveling like an empty corn husk with the passage of time? "Women are like roses," she observed, wondering why she was wasting her breath trying to dissuade Gideon from his shallow male views. "As they mature, they become fuller and more lush."

"Then, one morning, you wake up and all the petals have fallen off and blown away. All you're left with is a thorny stem that, if carelessly handled, can slash your skin to ribbons."

"Oh, really, what a ridiculous analogy!"

"You're the one who presented it. I took it to its natural conclusion."

She glared at him. "Do you really think men are superior to women?"

"Only in size, strength, endurance, quick reflexes and our keen reasoning ability."

"I'm surprised your list isn't longer!"

"I forgot to add that we don't suffer from timidity, uncontrollable emotions and a total lack of logical deduction."

"That being the case, I'm surprised you'd want a woman for *any* purpose."

A thoroughly smug smile twisted his lips. "From our little interlude earlier today, we both know what purpose is satisfied when a woman gives herself to a man. Mutual pleasure."

Emma's womb clenched, releasing a spasm of tremors. "Even in that regard, you insist on saying a woman gives herself to the man. Did it ever occur to you that a man could give himself to a woman?"

He leaned forward, planting his elbows on his knees. "It will no doubt shock you that the idea of giving myself to you is extremely stimulating. Had you accepted my original offer, it was my intention to bury myself so deeply in your sweet core that you would be left to wonder how you ever survived without having me there."

The carriage came to a stop at the precise moment his gritty voice ground to a halt. To save her life, she couldn't think of a fit reply to his carnally evocative description.

"It appears we've arrived," he observed.

She nodded weakly.

"Control your impatience, and remain seated long enough for me to assist you from the carriage."

She nodded again, wondering how he could possibly think she was capable of summoning sufficient strength to make any movement.

Chapter Nine

As Emma had feared, the downstairs lamps were extinguished in Miss Goodwin's shop. By craning her neck, however, she saw the upper floor room was lighted. An outside flight of stairs led to the private residence.

"Should you permit, I will escort you up those steps,"

"Sorry, this weak-brained, physically inferior female feels quite capable of taxing herself well beyond her pitiful limitations and actually walking up those stairs unassisted."

"What a charming creature you are when left to your own wits."

She stopped and looked over her shoulder. Even though he was one step behind her, she could feel him breathing down her neck. Really, the man needed to learn to back off. "Aren't you grateful I didn't agree to become your paramour? Think how disagreeable it would have been to be forced to endure my company on a long-term basis."

"Some challenges make the effort to achieve them far from disagreeable."

"You're doing it again, bending the truth to fit your own demented thinking. Why can't you admit we don't suit, and it was foolishness on your part to believe otherwise?"

"Only a cad would tell a lady he'd made such a mistake."

"That's another point of contention. I maintain only a cad would seek to compromise a lady in distress."

"Are you suggesting that, if I'd been reckless enough after a few hours of acquaintance to propose marriage, you would have accepted?"

This time, his insult struck home with such force that Emma almost staggered. "I'm well aware that a man such as yourself would consider a woman like me too far beneath him socially to ever consider marrying her. What hurts is that, while you deem me unworthy to become someone's lawfully wedded wife, you've no scruples against defiling the only gift of value I am capable of giving a would-be husband. My virtue."

He reached out in the semidarkness and took her arm. "You don't comprehend your true worth."

"Under the circumstances, I find it difficult to believe you feel I'm worth anything at all."

"Forget the circumstances. Believe me when I say that I've never considered myself husband material. For as far back as I can remember, I've been responsible for others. The thought of burdening myself with a wife is a fate I've sought to spare myself."

"That's a wise decision." She shook off his hand. "I can't imagine any woman wanting to be considered a burden by her husband."

She turned and proceeded the rest of the way up the stairs. Miriam Goodwin answered her door after the fourth knock. She had a pair of shears in her hand. Not a good sign.

"Miss Step, what are you doing here?"

Emma squared her shoulders and entered the cheerfully decorated room. Evidently, Miss Goodwin was skilled at doing more with fabric than sewing clothes. A luxurious green-and-pink flowered material covered an upholstered sofa and chair. The room's curtains were made from a softer shade of green with narrow white stripes. A patchwork combination of fabrics had been used to make pillows and lampshades. Emma felt as if she'd invaded a cozy nest.

"I'm sorry to intrude after you've closed the shop, but there's a matter of grave importance I need to discuss with you."

Gideon closed the door behind him and crowded so close to her, she had no choice but to move farther into the room.

Miss Goodwin's attention went immediately to Gideon. "Mr. Cade, was there something amiss with your niece's purchase?"

Emma felt guilty for the concern filling the seamstress's gaze.

"Courtney's pleased with her selections. It appears, however, that Miss Step is not altogether satisfied with her transaction."

Emma flushed. "If I could just have a moment alone with you, I'll explain what the difficulty is."

Miss Goodwin glanced around what was obviously a one-room apartment. "I suppose we could go to the store to discuss your order."

"Nonsense, Miss Step doesn't expect you to reopen your shop."

Emma wanted to gnash her teeth at Gideon's attack of thoughtfulness. She hated having to swallow her pride one more time in front of him, but there appeared no help for it. In the interest of financial survival, the dressmaker had to be stopped from filling the order.

"This will only take a moment. I...uh...this is embarrassing to admit, but I'm afraid I must cancel the rest of my order."

Emma was aware of Miss Goodwin's puzzled contemplation and Gideon's interested gaze. Well, it was better to suffer a few minutes of humiliation than to find oneself living on the streets.

"I don't understand, I thought you were pleased with my designs."

Emma knew her cheeks were scarlet. Good grief, she'd blushed more in the past twenty-four hours than in all the previous years of her life combined. "Your designs are excellent."

"I assure you my prices are more than fair."

"Uh, well, actually cost is a factor. I'm afraid I got a bit carried away this afternoon. I've reconsidered the amount I've spent and realize I was...er...hasty in my expenditures.''

Miss Goodwin continued to stare at her as if she were speaking a foreign language. Was she going to be forced to come right out and say she was on the verge of becoming unemployed and there were more important considerations than a new wardrobe? How would the attractive seamstress react if Emma blurted out, I need food and a roof over my head more than I need beautifully tailored dresses?

"Is there a problem with Miss Step canceling her order?"

"No, of course not," the dressmaker assured him.

"You haven't cut any of the fabric, have you?" Emma's conscience became relentless at the realization that Miss Goodwin had accepted her order in good faith and had probably already mentally banked the money due her. It wasn't the businesswoman's fault that, in a moment of weakness, Emma had contracted to spend funds she couldn't afford. "I'll certainly pay for the cost of any material you might have already cut."

Miss Goodwin glanced down at the scissors she held and thrust them behind her. "That won't be necessary. I understand people sometimes change their minds about purchases. This certainly isn't the first time such a thing has happened, and it won't be the last."

Emma felt terrible. "I'm sorry for any inconvenience I've caused you. You do beautiful work, and when things are more...settled for me, I promise I'll return to your shop."

The seamstress smiled thinly. Emma felt even worse. Clearly the loss of this sale was of significance to the woman.

"I look forward to it."

An awkward silence grew while Emma sought another way to apologize.

"We regret intruding upon your evening, Miss Goodwin," Gideon said, breaking the uncomfortable quiet that had claimed the apartment.

He turned to the door and opened it. Emma had no choice but to precede him through it. She was greeted by a cooling breeze and deepening darkness. A cloud of depression hung over her at having disappointed the dressmaker about the anticipated revenue from the sale.

Gideon failed to join her on the upper landing. Instead, he leaned out the door. "I have something to discuss with Miss Goodwin. Don't even think about walking down these stairs alone."

"You just live to bark out orders, don't you?" Inciting Gideon to anger was preferable to the pall hanging over her.

He flashed her a sudden smile. "I never bark, Emma. I find the occasional growl or howl much more satisfying."

How could she argue with a man who spoke gibberish?

He shut the door in her face. She was left with a strangely unsettled feeling. It was as if the blood rippling through her had been stirred up for a strenuous burst of activity and she'd just been sent to bed. Alone.

Less than a minute passed before Gideon rejoined her. His strong fingers curved proprietary around her upper arm. "Come along, we've waited long enough for some of Mrs. Graves's succulent pot roast."

Nary a creak or groan sounded from the wooden treads they traversed. Emma wanted to point out that the stairs had obviously been built securely, and she didn't need Gideon's hand wrapped around her arm. Nor was there necessity for him to stand so close.

Her curiosity, however, proved stronger than the urge to engage him in battle. "What did you say to Miss Goodwin?"

"Nothing important," he replied smoothly.

No one she'd ever encountered could make her so furious in so few words. "Is that your way of telling me to mind my own business?"

They stepped to the boardwalk. "Do you realize how childish it is to take every remark personally?"

"I realize how annoying it is to ask a question and have it ignored."

He urged her toward the waiting carriage while bending his head toward her ear. "Your present behavior exemplifies the one female trait that makes the thought of marriage so repugnant."

She faltered, but was carried along in his aggressive masculine wake. "And, pray tell, what trait is that?"

He jerked open the carriage door. "You nag."

His low-voiced growl resonated through her. "And you, sir, *do* growl, as uncouthly as a dog hoarding a bone."

He lifted her into the carriage and called out instructions for Hennesy to take them home.

Before Emma could arrange her skirts, Gideon was seated across from her. "You should hear me howl."

Because she didn't trust his faintly predatory look, which the carriage lamp revealed in its yellowish glow, she choked down the question about what it took to make him howl. She merely folded her arms and frowned.

"Try smiling instead of scowling."

"Ha! As if you deserved a smile."

"If we got only what we deserved, life would be very bleak."

She pursed her lips and said nothing. In their short acquaintance, she'd discovered that, when Gideon waxed philosophical, he somehow managed to outmaneuver her superior intellect.

"I merely increased Courtney's order."

At first, his terse statement made no sense. Then Emma realized he was answering her question about what he'd discussed with Miss Goodwin. It took a moment to assimilate his clearly grudging explanation. Obviously he'd experienced feelings similar to her own about the seamstress being distressed by the cancellation, and he'd resolved the matter by increasing Courtney's order. Emma swallowed. "That was very generous. Thank you for showing such consideration. You have no idea how bad I felt at having to cancel my order."

Apparently, her praise was the last thing he wished to hear. His eyebrows converged, and his lips twisted into a grimace. Even with the meager light provided, she could see a hint of red tingeing his lean cheeks. Goodness, Gideon accepted a compliment with the same forbearance with which Duncan had endured his descent into a tub of foamy bathwater.

He cleared his throat. "Yes, well, it occurred to me Courtney could always use more clothes."

Emma felt a tug of reluctant affection toward Gideon. She didn't know which touched her more, his concern for Miss Goodwin's financial situation or his unfailing generosity to his niece.

"You know," she said softly, "for a robber baron, you're not so tough, after all."

His expression darkened. "Perhaps I was too hasty in making any discussion of manners off-limits. You could benefit from a lecture on politeness."

She couldn't help smiling at his disgruntled attitude. "We'd have to drive all over Denver to find someone qualified to present the lecture."

He didn't return her smile. "Fair is fair, Emma. I answered your question about what I said to Miss Goodwin. Now you're obligated to tell me why you canceled your order."

She felt her smile fade. "Uh, well, actually, that's a bit personal."

"After nagging me relentlessly to satisfy your own prying interest, you can't possibly expect me to let you weasel out of appeasing my curiosity."

He was never more obnoxious than when he was being reasonable. She knew it was childish, but she wished she could let out a little of her pent-up frustration by hitting him again.

As if he'd read her the militant nature of her thoughts, a cautionary look flashed in his eyes. She had the feeling she'd been fortunate in how he reacted to her previous assaults upon his person. She sensed that he'd accepted his own provocative behavior in the altercations. Now, however, she suspected she would not be let off so lightly. Retaliation would surely follow an act of aggression on her part. A thrill of excitement raced through her, and she considered giving in to her violent inclinations. She sighed. Just because she detested revealing her innermost secrets to Gideon Cade didn't justify her acting like a demented wild woman. No, it was better to sacrifice a bit of pride and get this unpleasant exchange over with.

"I told Miss Goodwin the truth. I got carried away with all the beautiful things she showed us. I spent the first month's wages you advanced me."

"Considering the only thing separating you from nakedness was a borrowed sheet, that can hardly be called overspending."

She flushed. "Since my employment with you is going to be of short duration, my expenditure was an extravagant act of foolishness."

His eyes darkened in grave consideration. "How long do you imagine you'll be working for me?"

"When you told me you wanted me to become Courtney's private tutor, you indicated you would seek another school for her to attend. That could take less than a couple of weeks."

"I believe I said the institution would have to meet my standards."

"There are many excellent schools for young ladies." She didn't add that, with his vast fortune, money would be no obstacle.

"I have extremely high standards."

"That doesn't exactly surprise me. Even so, it won't take long to locate a learning facility for Courtney. As you're already aware, Jayne Stoneworthy is establishing a wonderful school here in Denver."

"I hardly envision sending Courtney to a place formerly called the Wet Beaver," he said dourly.

"Goodness, what has that to do with anything?"

"I'm a conservative and somewhat traditional man."

She blinked at him. "I don't mean to sound unkind, but those are the last two adjectives I would apply to you."

"Nevertheless, I have no intention of having my niece enter a building previously used as a brothel."

"But…" In midprotest, the full import of his statement registered.

"The Wet Beaver was a saloon, not a…um…one of those places," she finished weakly.

"I'm going to make several things clear. I won't permit

my niece to enter an establishment that's been used as a saloon. The term *wet beaver* is extremely vulgar. And as I once availed myself of one of its 'girls,' I can damned well attest I got exactly what I paid for—one hour of carnal relief.''

Emma knew her mouth gaped open. She couldn't summon the strength to shut it. Gideon's shocking disclosure electrified her brain. Surely being struck by lightning couldn't have flustered her to any greater degree.

''I have no intention of embarrassing you more than I've already been forced to do. I find no pleasure in informing you that your friend's business is doomed to failure. And believe me when I say that telling you I once entered such an establishment demolishes my pride.''

''Jayne has no idea the building was anything other than an obscure tavern that fell upon hard times,'' Emma murmured, forcing herself not to think of Gideon kissing and caressing a prostitute. ''Jayne assumed it was a little-known business that had only a few regular customers. With its old sign gone, a fresh coat of paint and fashionably redecorated rooms, she expects people to view it as an entirely new building.''

''The place was one of the most notorious bawdy houses in Denver. No father will send his daughter there.''

''Poor Jayne! When she finds out the truth, it's going to devastate her. She's put all her savings into the project. I'm afraid she's going to lose everything.''

''Women are not designed to run their own businesses. It's unfortunate none of you seem to realize that.''

Emma scrubbed away the tears she felt welling up in her eyes. ''What a typically stupid male thing to say.''

''You've got a brain—use it. Look what happened when Miss Loutitia tried to manage the academy.''

''She ran it successfully for many years.''

''Ran it into the ground,'' he observed coldly. ''Only a few minutes ago, we watched Miss Goodwin become overly emotional about the loss of a sale. It's obvious she's on very thin ice, financially speaking.''

"I disagree. I thought she handled herself very professionally."

"She was about to burst into tears, and you know it. That's why you were so grateful I increased Courtney's order."

Emma glared at him. She was tired of the sneaky way he twisted things so that he appeared to always be right. "Bad luck happens to men, as well as women. Look at the previous owners of the...um...drenched, wood-chomping animal-named establishment Jayne bought. Men ran that, and it still failed."

Gideon threw back his head and laughed. For some incomprehensible reason, the sound of his unrestrained humor almost made her smile. Nevertheless, she managed to school her features. "I don't see what's so funny."

He shook his head in amused reflection. "How about the phrase *drenched, wood-chomping animal?*"

"After your cryptic allusions to the vulgar definition of what seems an entirely unoffensive name, I'm hardly likely to repeat it."

"Good heavens, you mean you're going to listen to reason?"

"You are a vile bully."

"Do you usually resort to name-calling when you're upset?"

"Sometimes I become violent."

Instead of appearing the least bit intimidated, he grinned openly. "So I've noticed, Miss Emma January Step. I've also observed that, because you loathe to lose an argument, you never give up. As long as you have breath in your body, you refuse to yield any debate."

She raised her chin. "I intend to take that as a compliment."

"I meant it as such."

The carriage came to a halt. Emma slid closer to the door. She was more than ready to escape Gideon's disturbing company.

"There's a couple of other things I need to make clear to you."

Having no idea what those things would be, she braced herself.

"Courtney is so ecstatic at having you to herself that I'm not in a rush to send her off to another school. It may very well be that you'll go from being her tutor to becoming her chaperone and companion. I see no reason for that arrangement to change before she becomes a married woman. I foresee you being in my employ for several years. When the time comes for you to seek a new position, you can count on receiving the equivalent of one year's wages as a severance fee."

She was so overwhelmed by his astonishing generosity that she was unable to hold back the tears she felt brimming again in her eyes. "I hardly know how to thank you."

His mouth curved ruefully. "That's a shame."

In her euphoric state, she overlooked the suggestive remark. "I want you to know that I'll pour my heart and soul into being Courtney's tutor."

"I have no doubt of that."

"And...and..." She broke off, brushed back the tears and sniffed.

"And?" he prompted.

"I'll assist your household in any way you deem necessary."

"Does that mean you're willing to muck out the stables, press my shirts and bath Duncan on a regular basis?"

She poked lightly at his shoulder. "Is there no way you'll accept my gratitude for your incredible kindness?"

A sudden burst of raw energy seemed to radiate from his gaze. "That's a subject we would be wise to avoid."

"Thank you, Gideon," she said sincerely.

"And thank you, Emma."

"For what?" she asked in surprise.

"For not flying into an entirely useless fury of feminine outrage when you receive the dresses you ordered from Miss Goodwin."

"*What?*"

"I found myself unable break the lady's heart by allowing you to renege on your agreement."

"But you said you increased Courtney's order!"

"I did, as well as assuring Miss Goodwin there was no reason to cancel the items you'd requested."

"But—"

"Come now, Emma, show me the stouthearted woman I know you to be and bravely accept the pleasant turn of events fate has dealt you."

"Now you're calling yourself *fate?*"

There was a ferocious pounding on the carriage door. "Are you going to stay in there all night jabbering?"

Gideon unlatched the door and pushed it open. "Mind your manners, Hennesy. Miss Step hardly ever jabbers."

The next thing she knew, Emma was staring at the back of Gideon's head as he vaulted from the carriage with a natural grace that made her stomach tingle. She was put in mind of a beautiful panther she'd once seen in Philadelphia, at the only circus she ever attended.

The animal trainer had positioned himself in a steel cage where, at different times, he cracked his commanding whip over the backs of lions and tigers who sluggishly yielded to his authority. The last wild cat to enter the cage had been a black panther with slitted green eyes and a dangerous aura of power radiating from the muscles that rippled beneath his sleek, black fur. When the trainer snapped the snakelike whip at the predator, he'd turned on him. His ferocious snarl had been accompanied by a vicious swipe of lethal claws. The panther had rejected being controlled by either the whip or the puny human trying to urge him to the highest red barrel.

The performance had ended with the jungle cat ignoring the script and the trainer. As the proud animal padded into the smaller cage prepared for him, Emma had released a sigh of relief. She had the feeling the panther had let the trainer off lightly. Had the cat been in a mood to do so, she could have visualized him sinking his teeth into the man and making a meal of him.

"Now's not a good time to dawdle, Emma. I'm starving,

and the thought of sinking my teeth into Mrs. Graves's pot roast has me salivating.''

Emma slipped her palm into Gideon's strong hand. The friction of his calloused skin against her smoother flesh felt strangely right. She stepped to the ground and reminded herself that he had no claws. It was foolish to frighten herself with images of a wild predator escaping its cage.

Her gaze dropped to his narrow hips and the low-slung gun belt strapped there. Of course, modern man had no need of primitive fangs and claws. Civilization had provided him with a variety of lethal weapons with which to control his world.

She shivered.

Gideon's arm came around her shoulders. ''You should have worn a shawl. I hoped you ordered yourself a new cloak from Miss Goodwin. I had them burn that pitiful rag you wore last night.''

Emma tried to push aside the unreasoning fear that came upon her. Gideon Cade was an arrogant, dictatorial man of incredible wealth. And, though he was oftentimes insensitive and abrasive, he could also be generous and thoughtful. There was no reason to be afraid. Despite their bumpy beginning, she knew in the deepest, wisest part of her woman's soul that he would never physically hurt her.

Even that private inner knowledge didn't banish the feeling that it was within his power to cause her great pain. She touched her fingers to her forehead. Clearly, she was becoming light-headed from lack of food.

Chapter Ten

Emma placed her forefinger against a thin strip of blue on the large globe she'd borrowed from Gideon's study. "As you can see, the English Channel is quite narrow—only thirty-five miles wide at its farthest point. When the Norman Conquest began in 1066, the distance represented no serious obstacle to the French invaders."

"How exciting it must have been! Knights in shining armor, sword fights, archers, and lovely princesses in castle towers being carried off by chivalrous warriors." Courtney sighed dramatically. "I wish I'd been alive when there were dashing knights climbing castle bowers."

Emma smiled at the girl's romantic view of the Middle Ages. "You're assuming you would have been a princess?"

"Of course." She laughed and tossed thick dark curls. "I would have worn sparkling gowns both day and night. My father's soldiers would have willingly given their lives before letting someone speak an unkind word to me. I would have walked on rose petals and wrapped myself in lush ermine pelts. When my father's castle was laid siege to, a mighty knight would have come to our rescue. After defeating our vile enemies, he would have knelt before my father, pledged his loyalty and humbly supplicated my hand in marriage."

"Would you have accepted?" Emma inquired, helplessly enthralled by the far-fetched tale.

"Not at first. No self-respecting princess gives herself to the first handsome knight who comes along."

"I don't know if that would have been wise. There probably wasn't an excess number of handsome knights, even back then."

"This knight wouldn't have given up. He would have courted me."

"I see."

"He would have slipped into my private garden to woo me."

"I'm not sure a father would approve of such behavior."

"My rogue knight would have rained passionate kisses upon my hands," Courtney continued, undaunted by anything that might spoil her rosy view of the past. "They did that back then, you know."

"Kissed hands?"

"Oh, yes." Her expression remained dreamy. "Though he would have been content just to brush his lips against the hem of my gown."

"Naturally," Emma said dryly.

"He would have whispered tender words of love, given me jewels and offered to be my champion in a joust. The winner would become my husband."

"Naturally, your garden knight would be the victor," Emma surmised.

"He would have, if the other knight had fought fairly," Courtney explained with a flourish of dramatic anguish, "but alas it wasn't so."

"*Alas?*"

"No, my brave and beautiful warrior was pierced in his side."

"I should have thought armor would prevent that kind of mishap."

"The swine who challenged him ordered a hireling to weaken the links."

"It seems a shame for you to end up with the villain," Emma observed, captivated by Courtney's talent for story-telling.

"My feelings exactly." Courtney squared her shoulders. "I wouldn't have been a fainthearted princess."

"Never," Emma agreed.

"There's no way I would have sat passively by, weeping while my beloved knight bled to death."

"What would you have done?"

"Dashed to him and, heedless of the cost of my beautiful gown, I would have pressed the material to his side to stanch the flow of blood."

"How noble."

Courtney nodded cheerfully. "And brave."

"Why brave?"

"Because when the dastardly knight saw me kneeling beside my beloved, he would have flown into a rage and charged at me with a drawn sword."

"Oh, dear, do you die in this story?"

Courtney blinked in surprise. "That could never happen. True love always triumphs."

"Tell that to Romeo and Juliet."

"Everyone knows Shakespeare was entirely too gloomy about such matters. My valiant knight would have opened his eyes, wanting to enter paradise while gazing upon my cherished face. He would have seen his cravenly opponent about to stab me, and a miraculous burst of strength would have coursed through him, enabling him to raise his own sword one more time and dispatch the most wicked knight in all Christendom to an eternity of fiery brimstone."

Emma clapped enthusiastically. "Bravo, Courtney, that was *splendid*."

Another burst of applause sounded in the doorway. Startled, Emma spun around. Larger than life, stood Gideon Cade, one shoulder propped negligently against the door frame.

Surprised at seeing him in the upstairs bedchamber that had been turned into a schoolroom, complete with two desks, bookcases and a chalkboard, Emma felt both shy and awkward. Since the evening they returned from Miss Goodwin's shop, several weeks ago, they'd exchanged only the most banal of pleasantries when their paths chanced to cross in the large house.

She'd decided she must have imagined the intimacies that transpired during the first thirty-six hours of their acquaintance. Telling herself that, however, had no discernible effect in curbing her heart's rhythm or uncoiling the knot squeezing her stomach.

"Uncle Gideon, how long have you been standing there?" Courtney demanded, a rosy blush brightening her cheeks.

That's exactly what I'd like to know, Emma thought, embarrassed that she and her student had been caught in such foolery.

He straightened and stepped into the schoolroom. "Long enough to receive a history lesson, the likes of which I've never heard before."

Emma knew her cheeks were as pink as her student's.

"It wasn't a history lesson," Courtney explained, before being overcome by giggles. "I was merely telling Miss Step it would have been much more exciting to live in the Middle Ages than now."

"There's no doubt we're related." His eyes sparkled with unusual warmth. "I've always been partial to the idea of riding one of those powerful warhorses and having a six-foot sword."

"Oh, honestly, Courtney believes she would have been a princess, and you think you would have been a knight. The odds are far greater you would be serfs and endure a lifetime of excruciating hardship."

Neither Courtney nor her uncle seemed to take offense at the logical observation, which should have pricked the bubble of their fantasy. They just smiled at her as if she were a hundred-year-old woman who needed humoring.

"She doesn't understand that, if it were possible to go back in time, we wouldn't end up as mere peasants."

"Impossible," Gideon concurred, a grin tugging at his mouth.

"And you really would have preferred living back then?" Emma asked skeptically.

Both Courtney and her uncle nodded.

Emma threw up her hands. "I'm sure you wouldn't have considered the bubonic plague anything more than a mild inconvenience. The Norman Conquest would have been jolly sport. And the lack of running water and indoor plumbing would have been quaintly charming."

Gideon waved his arm, as if brushing aside trivialities. "If we'd lived then, those things would have been accepted as a part of life."

"Like not bathing, having head lice and a colony of fleas constantly crawling over you."

"Ugh—leave us some romantic illusions," Courtney protested.

"You'll have to excuse Miss Step," Gideon interjected mildly. "If she believes all young lovers end up like Romeo and Juliet, it stands to reason her soul isn't of a romantic nature."

"We'll leave the nature of my soul out of this discussion, if you don't mind." She noticed that whenever Gideon and she passed on the stairs or in a hallway, he called her Emma. If his niece or any of the servants was present, he referred to her as Miss Step.

Courtney laughed, circled the desk and embraced Emma in a fierce hug. "We're just teasing, right, Uncle Gideon?"

Emma would have liked to study his expression, but her field of vision was suddenly filled with a swath of black, curly hair.

"Naturally we're joking," drawled the deep masculine voice.

When Courtney's hug ended, she turned toward her uncle. "It's been ages since we've seen you. When we wake up in the morning, you've already ridden out to the mines, and you don't return before we're in bed. I was beginning to think I'd imagined having a handsome uncle taking care of me."

A frown drifted across his face. "No matter where I am or what I'm doing, I'll always take care of you, Courtney. Even if I have the bad luck to get myself killed, your future is protected. There's no reason for you to ever feel threatened or fearful."

"Don't talk about being killed," Courtney begged, her rosy complexion suddenly bleached of color. "I couldn't bear it if anything happened to you."

This time it was Gideon who reached for his niece. He drew her to him. "Haven't you been reading the papers? I'm too ornery to die."

It was difficult for Emma to swallow past the thickness in her throat. The sight of the tall man dressed entirely in black, with a mean-looking pistol strapped to his side, tenderly soothing a trembling girl in a ruffled blue gown, was incredibly moving. She could almost envision him as a powerful knight protecting a princess from the brutal forces of an unmerciful world.

"Now dry your pretty eyes," he ordered softly, stepping back and loosening the ebony-colored neckerchief knotted at his throat. "Medieval princesses rarely have reason to cry."

He dabbed lightly at the fragile tears with his big hand. So tender was the moment that Emma felt in dire need of a handkerchief herself. The poignant interlude ended abruptly, however, when Courtney helped herself to the black cloth and blew her nose.

Gideon chuckled. "Don't bother returning that before Mrs. Foster has the opportunity to put it through the laundry."

Courtney giggled self-consciously. "I'm sorry for falling apart. I don't know what's the matter with me."

Emma knew what was wrong. During the weeks following the ambush, robbery and murders of a group of travelers taking the stage from Denver to Boulder, the newspapers had used their venomous ink to blame Gideon for the "Massacre of the Innocent" as the heinous crime was now called. They claimed that as the freighting king of Denver it was his responsibility to see that all gold leaving the city was properly guarded. Never mind that he'd made sure the ore arrived safely at the bank where it had been minted into coins and he had no connection with the stage line. The citizenry had been whipped into an angry frenzy by the press. One newspaper had been more vicious than all the others combined in its relentless attacks upon Gideon. Unfortunately, it was the town's most widely circulated daily paper.

"Honey, that's the great thing about being born female. You never have to apologize when your emotions get away from you."

It was the first time Emma had heard Gideon address his niece by anything other than her given name. His deep voice textured the endearment with a tenderness Emma never would have believed him capable of expressing. As she reflected upon the complex nature of the rugged, arrogant, gun-toting man, she concluded that his nature was a study in contrasts. He could be both gentle and cruel, wild and subdued, passionate and cold, stubborn and yielding. Both direct and subtle. It disturbed her that each turn his character took exerted a compelling tug upon her sensibilities. It was as if he possessed an invisible force that enabled him to draw her. But surely the Creator would not endow a mortal with such unfair powers.

When her thoughts strayed to how it felt to have his mouth on hers, she slammed the lid shut on the unsettling memories and the inner restlessness they sparked. She jerked herself to the present, where Gideon was suggesting Courtney go downstairs for lunch.

"Are you eating with us?"

He shook his head in obvious regret at having to disappoint his niece. "I'm afraid not. I dropped in on your history lesson to say a quick hello before I left again."

"How long are you going to be gone this time?"

"Probably a week."

"A *whole* seven days?" she cried, clearly dismayed.

"Maybe not that long," he answered vaguely.

"Well, spit. What's the good of having an uncle if I never see him?"

"Courtney," Emma chided, embarrassed that her pupil would use such common language in Gideon's presence. It required no stretch of Emma's imagination to visualize him cutting her wages because of poor teaching practices. "I've never heard you use that word before."

"What word?" she asked mischievously.

"You know very well, young lady," Gideon answered. The grin tugging at his lips, however, spoiled any effect his reprimand might have had. "Apologize to Miss Step for embarrassing her. Then run downstairs to lunch."

"How did I embarrass her?" Courtney demanded.

"She's your tutor. Everything you say and do reflects on her."

Courtney looked stricken. "I'm sorry, Miss Step!"

Distracted as she was by Gideon's perceptiveness and the conciseness of his statement, it took a moment before Emma could clear her thoughts and reassure her student no serious harm had been done.

"It was hardly a major transgression, Courtney. I do hope you'll be more careful in the future, however."

"I will! I promise!" With those pledges, the girl turned and bolted from the room.

The next sound they heard was the rapid thud of her footsteps as she apparently ran down the staircase.

Gideon stared thoughtfully at the open doorway. "She's changing. It's been a long time since I've seen her so...so full of life."

"I've noticed the same thing." Emma hoped he felt, as she did, that Courtney's newfound exuberance indicated she was growing more confident. "When I first met her at the academy, she kept herself isolated from the other students. There was a reserve about her that seemed to discourage the girls from getting to know her."

Gideon pinned her with his somber gaze. "No one could say that was the case now."

Emma stiffened. "You don't approve of the change?"

"When my brother and sister-in-law were alive, Courtney never walked where she wanted to go. She had a pair of dancing feet that seemed to propel her across a room. The thing I remember most about visiting my brother's house was the sound of Courtney's sweet laughter."

Emma's heart trembled at the pent-up pain in Gideon's description. "It sounds as if she was well loved."

"She was. Everyone doted on her."

"Even you?" she guessed gently.

"Especially me." His gaze was that of a man who'd glimpsed heaven but hadn't been allowed through its gates. "Four years ago, when her parents were murdered, Courtney withdrew into a world of silence."

"Her mother and father were *murdered?*" Emma repeated numbly, having had no idea that such a horrific event had occurred.

"You didn't know? I thought she might have confided in you."

Emma shook her head. "She never once hinted something so devastating had happened."

"Since you're the first person who's been able to slip past the defensive walls she's erected, I assumed she'd told you."

"I wish she had."

"When she rushed home in the middle of the night all those weeks ago, asking me to lend money to the Hempshire Academy, she seemed like the animated girl she'd once been. Every other word she spoke was about you and what a wonderful teacher you were."

"You didn't act very impressed by her description," Emma couldn't help pointing out.

"Don't push it, Emma. You know I had every right to be angry that she'd slipped away unnoticed."

"So you did."

Gideon's gaze darkened. "I failed my brother and his wife, but I have no intention of failing their daughter. This time I'm going to get it right."

"This time?" she prompted gently.

"I thought things were on track before," Gideon said, looking at an inner vista that was closed to Emma. "I believed the pain from our past was behind us. Jonathan had grown up sickly. The doctors said that continuing to live in the East would kill him. I was the one who coerced him and his new bride to move to Denver. The doctors claimed the high altitude and dry air would prolong his life.''

''Hundreds of others have done the same thing with amazing results.''

Gideon raked his fingers through his hair. ''That's how it seemed for Jonathan. He'd been diagnosed with tuberculosis, but after settling here, he steadily improved. It was as if the streams washing down the mountains surrounding Denver possessed the same mystical healing benefits as holy water. With each passing week, my brother became more robust. The incessant coughing ceased, and he developed increased stamina. It was the miracle for which we'd prayed. Before our eyes, Jonathan was becoming a new man.''

Emma recalled Courtney saying that Gideon had been responsible for his brother from his early childhood. ''That must have made you very happy.''

One side of his mouth twisted downward. ''Hell, yes, I was happy. I was so happy I got drunk on the mistaken notion I'd saved his life by insisting he come west with me. I was so damned happy, I figured I had the world by the tail. I thought I was invincible. All my decisions were enshrined in my gold-plated confidence that *I* knew what was best. The Bible says, 'Pride cometh before the fall.' I learned the truth of that the hard way.''

''You...you can't possibly blame yourself for the murders.''

''Can't I?''

She'd never heard his tone be so self-condemning. She rested her fingertips against his black sleeve. ''I don't know the circumstances of how they died, but I know you didn't contribute to their deaths.''

The focus of his eyes drifted to where she touched him. The tingling scrape of déjà vu caused a crop of goose bumps to spring up on her skin. The first night she met him, she'd touched his arm in this same way. It alarmed her that she couldn't control the reckless need to comfort this man.

He laid a wide palm over her hand and stared deeply into her eyes. The impact of his gaze and the calloused warmth surging through the points where their flesh met generated a pulsing vibration. She swayed toward him.

He lightly squeezed her fingers, then removed his hand. In doing so, he freed his arm from her touch and gently returned her hand to her side.

"I'd finished blasting a way through the mountains to the mines. The track was laid for the two rail spurs I'd decided to build. There had been a dozen or so threats on my life, even a couple of attempts."

"That's horrible!"

"At the time, I scarcely gave the incidents a second thought. Remember, I considered myself invincible. I just went on my merry way, making plans and working to make them a reality. Then, one fine night, Jonathan, Cynthia and I happened to be at the same party. Hunter Moran's foreman was getting married, and everyone within a hundred miles was invited to the celebration."

It hurt to hear the barrenness in Gideon's voice. She didn't make the mistake, though, of reaching out again to try and console him.

He paused, as if collecting his thoughts. "My brother and his wife had ridden a surrey out to the ranch. I'd brought a couple of friends in my carriage. We were loaded down with presents from people who couldn't make it out. When it came time to leave, Jonathan discovered one of the surrey's wheels had cracked. Since I was well past drunk and had already planned on spending the night at Hunter's, I told my brother to take the carriage."

Emma's mouth was dry. She suspected the story's violent conclusion was close. "Under the circumstances, that was a reasonable thing to do."

Gideon laughed harshly. She didn't think she'd ever heard such a bitterly jarring sound.

"Reasonable? You're forgetting there had been threats and a couple of attacks. Someone clearly wanted me dead, and I witlessly offered *my* carriage to Jonathan and his wife. Whoever had been gunning for me obviously thought I would be its passenger."

Gideon paused again and scrubbed his palm across his face. "Whoever he was, he didn't act alone. The carriage was riddled with bullets from three different guns. So were the driver, my brother and his wife."

There was no strength in Emma's legs to support her. She had to sit before she collapsed. She claimed the chair next to her desk and bowed her head. "I'm sorry."

She couldn't remember ever feeling so inadequate. But the words of comfort she longed to offer didn't appear to exist in her vocabulary.

"For the first few days—"

She looked up. "Yes?"

He cleared his throat and took another swipe at his reddened eyes. "For the first few days afterward...I couldn't get it through my head there was no way to go back and change what had happened. I must have been close to crazy, but I kept thinking there had to be a way I could fix things. There had to be a way I could give Courtney back her parents. When I finally came to my senses and realized there was no way on earth or in the heavens to alter the past, the only thought that offered any relief was that I would track down the murderers and see them all hang."

"I can see how revenge—"

"Not revenge," he corrected swiftly, "I want justice."

Cade's justice... It would be delivered with a cold finality immune to any pleas for clemency—not that the murderers deserved mercy, but she perceived the high emotional toll his quest for justice had taken upon Gideon over the past four years. "The killers weren't apprehended?"

Another soulless burst of laughter bruised her ears. "They vanished off the face of the earth. We haven't had any luck finding them."

"We?"

Gideon's expression became shuttered. "Myself and the authorities."

Emma relaxed. She'd feared he was referring to the vigilantes. "Have you thought about enlisting the aid of the Guardsmen?"

"So, even though you aren't impressed by overly romantic yarns about the Middle Ages, you still believe in fairy tales?"

"The Guardsmen are real, I just know it."

"And how am I supposed to contact them? With smoke signals?"

"How long has it been since you read a newspaper? Almost every day they publish letters from people requesting help from the Guardsmen."

"So that's how it's done."

Everyone living in Denver knew that was the case. She regarded him pensively, feeling that he was playing another game of cat and mouse with her. "Have you considered how similar Jonathan and Cynthia's murders were to those of the passengers killed by the thieves who robbed the stage?"

An almost tangible aura of menace gathered around him. The dangerous energy he radiated reminded her of violently churning storm clouds. "The similarity definitely caught my attention."

She licked her lips. With the lethal weapon strapped to his side, and dressed in black as he was, he looked like the personification of death—in the guise of a gunslinger.

"Be careful." The cautionary advice flew uncensored from her heart.

In two strides, he closed the distance separating them.

"I didn't pour out my guts so you could offer a motherly warning and pat my arm."

Chapter Eleven

Stung by Gideon's unexpected harshness, Emma started to rise from her chair. She refused to let him use his superior height to intimidate her.

He placed his hands on her shoulders and exerted the necessary pressure to keep her seated. "I'm not done talking to you."

He was her employer, she reminded herself. Nevertheless, it took all her willpower not to kick his shin. Hoping to curb her hurt anger, she took several deep breaths. The only thing that kept her from striking out with her foot was the painful memory of her battered toes when she'd banged into that chair. His bones were probably just as solid as his stony heart, and surely that was harder than mere oak.

Two things became inescapably clear. She no longer found anything about his complex nature the least bit appealing, and he didn't deserve one particle of her compassion or sympathy. In fact, his only redeeming quality was his growing ability to reach out to Courtney. Oh, and perhaps the generous way he treated his servants. Then there was his kindness to the dressmaker.... Bah, those measly virtues couldn't compensate for his inhuman conduct.

One final truth emerged from her swirling thoughts. Gideon did not deserve to be desired. She resolved then and there to squash the lamentable weakness each night that compelled her to relive those tempestuous moments when his tongue had burned the inside of her mouth.

"I would appreciate you finishing whatever else you have to say."

Getting that spineless statement past her stiff lips clawed more deeply into her small reserve of remaining dignity. She could almost feel her pride leaking from the new holes he'd gouged in her heart.

"Emma..." He hunkered down and brought his grim face to eye level with hers. "Stop it. I can almost see you curling up inside yourself. You look like a daffodil shriveling under a scorching sun."

She looked directly into his solemn eyes. "I will endeavor not to resemble a shrinking violet."

"Daffodil," he corrected huskily. "That yellow dress looks as soft and fragile as the petals of a freshly blooming daffodil."

She swallowed. *Tender and cruel...*

"Please finish what you have to say," she said hoarsely.

"I'm sorry."

Direct and subtle...

"For what?" He'd only been acting true to his unpredictable nature. Such behavior was probably instinctive with a man of turbulent moods.

A spark of primitive anger ignited his gaze. *Wild and subdued...*

"Dammit, Emma. This isn't easy for me. You're the first person with whom I've discussed the murders in years. I'm feeling raw and frustrated. I don't want, nor am I entitled to, your compassion. I intend to sharpen the edge of the guilt burning inside me and use that honed sword to send those murdering bastards to hell."

Passionate and cold... "That's where God's justice will send them."

"I don't want them living on the same earth with me. I don't want them breathing, feeding their bellies or enjoying a second's pleasure. They don't deserve to live. Until I know they're dead and buried, I'll be hunting them."

"Yes, I can see that you will."

"I told you about the murders for two reasons."

She wanted to look away from the glow of hatred illuminating his eyes, but she was trapped by the lapping force of his smoldering need for revenge.

"I've started receiving death threats again, and—"

"Oh, God."

"Don't panic. I'm too tough to be killed. What concerns me is you and Courtney have gotten into the habit of walking Duncan through the neighborhood and taking afternoon carriage rides."

Emma raised a hand to her throat. "They seemed harmless pastimes."

"Under normal circumstances, there would be no problem. Now that I'm receiving those nasty little notes again, though, I'm not taking chances with other people's lives, especially yours and Courtney's. I know how it is to feel cooped up, but from now on neither you nor my niece will leave this house unless you're escorted by one of the guards I've hired."

"We'll be living like prisoners."

He grasped one of her hands and stood, causing her to rise, also. "I've thought about sending you and Courtney to Boston. I have friends there, and you would be able to move about more freely."

She wanted to shout that being separated from him would be torture. Recalling how furious she'd been at him moments before, she realized the change in her attitude was insane. "Courtney would miss you terribly."

"Her safety is more important than her feelings."

"Of course," Emma conceded hollowly.

"I can't shake the premonition that she might be an easier target in Boston. Here, I've got Broadbent and a dozen men I'd trust to ride through hell with me. They'll be guarding the house day and night. Nothing and no one will be able to get through them."

"Who will be guarding you?"

His expression softened. "I can take care of myself."

Sure you can. If a gang of murdering outlaws surrounds you, you'll demolish all twenty with one pistol. "Feeling invincible, are you?"

She felt him go still, and knew she'd struck at one of his most vulnerable points.

"I'm a lot smarter than I used to be, Emma. I don't count on happy endings anymore."

"All the more reason to hire bodyguards to protect *your* stubborn hide."

"Don't worry. Even with me dead, I've made sure you won't be out of a job. I've written a new will. The section guaranteeing you retain your position as Courtney's tutor after my death was drafted by two of the best lawyers in town. Until my niece becomes a married woman, you'll be in charge of her and this house. I even put in a provision that she can't be wed unless you approve of the groom."

The enormity of what he'd done staggered her. "But you hardly know me! To place me in control of Courtney's future happiness *and* this house is preposterous."

"One of my best friends is a banker. Burke Youngblood will help you administer the trust fund."

"You can't possibly be serious. You would never entrust a virtual stranger with such legal power over your estate. We've known each other for hardly more than a month and you've been away most of that time!"

"You make an indelible impression on a man, Emma."

"For goodness' sakes, don't joke about something this important."

"I'm deadly serious."

"You're seriously unbalanced!"

"Insult me all you want, but I've made up my mind. You're so damned honest and devoted to being the most conscientious teacher in America that I could search for a hundred years and never find someone else half as trustworthy to look after my niece's interests."

"But—"

"It's already settled."

"But—"

"You've hit a mountain that won't crumble because you would like it shoved aside. Besides, suppose I did get shot? As I lay bleeding to death, would you really want my last thoughts to be about what was going to happen to Courtney and who would be looking after her?"

"You said you could take care of yourself!"

"I'm pretty sure I can. If I'm right, the contents of my last will and testament won't ever become relevant to you."

The thought of him being killed made her knees buckle again.

When she tried to move toward the chair next to the desk, though, Gideon forestalled her retreat, gathering her hands into his. "While I'm gone, can I count on you to keep Courtney home?"

"I would never do anything to endanger her life."

"Good."

"Will it be all right for us to attend Sunday services?"

"I suppose you'll be safe at church, as long as you take Broadbent and at least ten of your bodyguards."

"How many did you hire?" she asked curiously.

"An even dozen."

The thought of what an unlikely group of worshipers they would make almost made her smile. "I'm not sure Broadbent or your men will enjoy Reverend Hobbly's sermons. He discourses at length upon the eternal consequences of drinking, gambling and associating with...uh...ladies of the evening."

Gideon's hold tightened. "Emma..."

Again she was trapped by the force of his unwavering gaze. "Yes?"

His head descended. He was going to kiss her again. She braced herself for the hot, steamy rush of the sensations that were about to engulf her. The knowing, remembering look in his eyes became too much. Her eyelids drifted shut. She could feel her lips softening, then parting. Just as she could feel his warm breath upon her mouth. Her stomach curled, and the tips of her breasts tightened. He separated her hands and lowered them to her sides. His hips crowded against her, generating a throbbing pulse of heat.

Her face tilted toward his, and her heart danced a strange, wild rhythm. The breaths she drew into her straining lungs were sharp and shallow. One moment passed, and then another. Why wasn't he already kissing her into a state of unconsciousness?

She hazarded a peek through her lashes. He raised his head and, as if to clear his senses, shook it. She felt him pull back from her.

No, her trembling body cried. Being denied what had surely been a promised ascent to paradise caused physical pain to her sensitized body. Her palms rested against his chest. She clutched his shirtfront. It was nip and tuck as to whether or not she was capable of releasing the black material. She discovered she did have some pride, after all. Carefully, as if both his shirt and her fingers were made from an incredibly fragile substance, she let the fabric slide through her fingertips. Several pleated wrinkles testified to the mauling she'd given him.

"We've struck our bargain, Emma. And, even though the odds make it more likely I'll die from frustration rather than a bullet, I refuse to violate our agreement." The ground out words sounded as if he'd crawled through barbed wire to deliver them.

Had she thought him stubborn *and* yielding? She couldn't believe how wrong she'd been. There was nothing yielding about Gideon Cade. Every bit of him—mind, heart and soul—was as hard as the thick ridge she'd felt pressing against her stomach.

"You have a visitor, Miss Step."

At Broadbent's announcement, Emma looked up from the lesson plan she was preparing in Gideon's study. Courtney was upstairs in the schoolroom, drawing a map of Europe from memory. Since she was required to define all national borders, capitals and major cities, mountain ranges and rivers, the exercise would take several hours.

"Has Miss Stoneworthy returned for another visit?" Jayne had dropped by several times, and upon each occasion she'd seemed more concerned and uneasy about being able to successfully open her school.

"Mr. Lyman Thornton is waiting for you in the parlor."

Emma jabbed the pen she'd been using into its inkwell. "What could he want to discuss with me?"

"He didn't disclose that information." Despite Broadbent's mild tone, interest flickered in his faded, bloodshot blue eyes.

She pushed back her chair. "I guess I have no choice but to find out."

"On the contrary, Miss Step, I can inform him you're too busy to see him and, in the future, you would appreciate the courtesy of him requesting an interview so you'll be able to make note of it in your appointment book."

"I couldn't do that. It would be impolite."

"Mr. Thornton arriving without an appointment is the greater breach of decorum. You're under no obligation to readjust your schedule to accommodate his social irresponsibility."

Emma stared at Broadbent in fascination. She no longer thought he looked like an oversize troll with the face of a gargoyle. Beneath his gruff exterior, his was a supportive nature. He also had one of the driest wits she'd ever been exposed to. And even though the nostrils of his blue-veined, pitted nose seemed to widen further with each passing day, she felt such growing affection for him that his battered countenance was rapidly becoming dear.

"I know what you've said is technically correct, but I'm really not comfortable being rude to anyone."

"I'll inform Mr. Thornton you will join him."

"Thank you, Broadbent."

"You're welcome, Miss Step."

He turned to leave. "Broadbent?"

"Yes?"

Emma nibbled her bottom lip. She'd lived most of her life without the companionship of others and had begun to weary of her isolation. The servants in Gideon's household were a congenial group, and in their own way seemed almost like a family. She summoned her courage, unsure of how she would feel at being rebuffed by the butler. "What is your given name?"

His busy eyebrows formed a vee. She had no idea what he was thinking as his protuberant eyes considered her.

"Elijah," he said after a lengthy pause.

"Did your mother name you after the Old Testament prophet?"

He nodded. "She wanted me and my brothers to follow the straight and narrow path."

"How many brothers did you have?"

"By the time she and my father finished fulfilling their procreative responsibilities, we numbered twelve."

"Twelve?"

"Adam, Noah, Jeremiah, Ezra, Enoch, Malachi, Joshua, Enos, Ezekiel, Isaiah and Abraham—including myself, that adds up to twelve."

"I'm surprised she didn't name any of you Moses."

"Moses was our mule."

"Did you have any sisters?"

"Eve, Sarah, Miriam, Rebekah and Rachel."

"That's seventeen children," Emma gasped in amazement. Goodness, she'd taught smaller schoolroom classes.

"My parents took the admonition to replenish the earth seriously."

"I can see that." It was scary to reach out for friendship. "The reason I asked about your given name is because I hoped that, whenever we chanced to be alone together, I might address you by that, instead of Broadbent, and you could call me Emma."

Again she found herself being contemplated solemnly. Gradually a brightening inner light softened his coarse features.

"I would be honored."

Warmth filled her chest. "We could be…friends, do you think?"

"The same thought has occurred to me…Emma."

"Uh, Elijah, I have another question."

"And that would be?"

"Has Mr. Cade recently increased your wages?"

Again the massive eyebrows knit above the servant's bulbous nose. "I'm not in a habit of discussing my salary with co-workers. But in answer to your extremely personal inquiry, he has enlarged the sum he pays me."

"By a dollar a week?"

Elijah's expression became rueful. "We must be better friends than I realized."

Emma flushed. "You probably think I'm forward, but on my first visit here, Mr. Cade implied your protection of his privacy ought to be rewarded. I agreed and suggested a raise in salary. I know it's impertinent to satisfy my curiosity, but I can't seem to help myself."

The butler chuckled. "So you're checking up on our employer to see that he not only kept his word, but was generous, as well?"

She nodded.

"Since I apparently have you to thank for my raise, I'll tell you the amount. You understand I expect this information to be kept confidential?"

"Absolutely."

"My wages have been augmented by twenty dollars a month."

Emma grinned. "You better give yourself credit for the increase. I never would have had the nerve to push for such a princely sum."

"Don't be modest. I've noticed a definite change in Mr. Cade since you've become a member of the staff. Believe me, he's mellowed."

"Considering all the challenges presently confronting him, I don't see how that's possible."

"Don't be overly concerned about our employer. He has a genius for getting out of tight spots. No villain will ever best him."

"You and Mr. Cade share the same opinion of his abilities."

"Then it's settled. As long as we're careful, there's nothing to worry about." The servant's face pinkened, and the fine blue veins mapping his skin became darker. "I'm glad you don't harbor any ill feelings about me not...er...ah... immediately admitting you that rainy night you showed up on our step. I'd been given strict orders not to disturb Mr. Cade again. He'd already gone the previous twenty-four hours without sleep. When I discovered it was Courtney pounding on the front door after he'd retired, I had no recourse but to awaken him. I would have preferred walking across burning coals rather than being obliged to disturb him again."

Emma patted his arm. "You were only doing your job. We just happened to be at cross-purposes."

"You're a kindly woman, Emma Step."

For some reason, the compliment brought tears to her eyes. "You're the kind one, Elijah."

He cleared his throat. The rumble sounded as if a freight train had thundered through the room. "I'll let Mr. Thornton know you'll see him."

"Oh! I forgot about him. I'll go directly to the parlor."

Elijah held up a palm. "Take your time, Emma. It does a man like Thornton good to cool his heels."

Chapter Twelve

When Emma stepped through the open parlor door, Lyman Thornton stood with his hands behind his back, gazing at the immense oil painting that hung above the hearth. Broadbent followed her into the room.

Emma joined their guest. "It's a lovely painting, isn't it?"

Every time she entered the parlor, she was captivated by the artist's rendition of an early-morning sky shot through with emerging shafts of sunlight illuminating a damp forest.

"It's dreary for my tastes." He turned and smiled warmly. "My attention was captured by the frame, overlaid in gold. Considering its size and weight, it must have cost Cade a small fortune."

"It probably did."

"Of course," he continued genially, "a man like Cade would never permit the consideration of cost to stop him from getting his hands on something he wanted—nor would he let other considerations get in his way."

What a rude innuendo. Emma was tempted to give Lyman Thornton a brief discourse on the proper attitude a guest should exhibit when visiting other people's homes. Recalling Gideon's reaction to such lectures, she decided men did not appreciate being reminded of the rules governing mannerly behavior.

"It's always been the painting that appealed to me." She

moved from the hearth to the settee and sat down, gesturing toward the maroon velvet chair positioned across the Oriental carpet. "Please, make yourself comfortable."

Disregarding her invitation to take the chair, Thornton sat down beside her on the sofa. "Thank you."

The sight of his cream-colored pant leg only inches from her green skirts made her uneasy. It wasn't the kind of edgy uneasiness laced with excitement that uncurled within her whenever Gideon was close. Despite Mr. Thornton's undeniable handsomeness, the overwhelming sensation he elicited from her was mild revulsion.

"Would you like tea or coffee?" she felt obligated to inquire.

He unbuttoned his jacket, which was also cream-colored and made from the same finely textured material as his trousers. Both his shirt and boots were pale beige. With his dark Western tie, he looked exactly like the rich and successful businessman he was. "I'll accept the civilized man's drink, tea."

She glanced at Broadbent. "Would you please bring us a tray?"

The butler didn't look happy about the request, but he nodded and left the parlor.

"Miss Step, allow me to say that amid all the expensive artwork, bric-a-brac and furnishings, you are the room's loveliest asset."

"Thank you." It took willpower not to laugh at the false observation.

"That shade of green is particularly attractive on you."

In an attempt to provide greater distance between them, she slid surreptitiously to her right. "Was there a particular matter you wished to discuss? I was surprised when I was informed you wished to see me."

"There are innumerable matters I wish to discuss with you, Miss—" He broke off and cocked his head, adopting an almost boyish expression. "May I address you by your first name?"

Whereas she'd been overjoyed to allow Elijah that privilege, she was reluctant to do so with Thornton. They scarcely knew each other. The bothersome thing was, there wasn't a polite way to refuse him.

"Uh, I suppose so."

Somehow he radiated even more good cheer. "Thank you...Emma. I've been looking forward to us becoming more than casual acquaintances."

"How is your aunt?" Uncomfortable with the degree of intimacy he seemed intent on establishing, she decided a change in subject was needed. "Has she found new furnishings to replace what was lost in the fire?"

A crease appeared between his pale eyebrows. "Loutitia is visiting relatives in New York. I'm certain, when she returns, a shipment of furniture will follow."

"I hope she finds a new armoire."

"I'm sure she will." He shrugged. "I plan to enjoy my peace and quiet while she's gone."

"In a few days, you'll be lonely for her company."

That was how she felt about Gideon. At first she'd been grateful for his absence, hoping it would provide her with the sense of perspective about him that she so urgently needed. As the days passed, however, she'd begun to miss him. If she wasn't careful, she would find herself pining for him. What a stupid waste of time and energy that would be!

"I find it hard to imagine missing Loutitia's high-pitched whinings."

"She's very devoted to you, Mr. Thornton."

He stunned Emma by reaching out, grasping her shoulders and gently shaking her. "Emma, I insist you call me Lyman. Surely our friendship has advanced to that level of closeness."

What friendship? As for closeness, he'd bridged the space on the settee she'd established. And yet it required more vinegar than she boasted to express her negative feelings outright. Surely, in a few more minutes, the man would be on his way, and this bizarre experience would be over.

As subtly as she could, she extricated herself from his unwelcome touch. Again she thought how differently she reacted when Gideon put his hands on her. Whenever his callused palm grazed her skin, assorted tremors and strange pulsing sensations flooded through her. Contact with Thornton's soft flesh caused her stomach to become queasy.

"All right, I'll call you…Lyman." His name sliding from her lips left a bad taste in her mouth.

He leaned forward, which caused his knees to nudge her skirts. She attempted to scoot farther away, but was stopped by the sofa's padded armrest. Refusing to allow good manners to hold her hostage for another second, she stood. He did likewise. Frustrated, she walked to the open doorway. "I wonder what's keeping Broadbent with our tea?"

"I'll be surprised if he shows up again. The man doesn't appear competent. I can't imagine why Cade keeps him."

He slipped his hands into his pockets and rocked back and forth on the balls of his feet. Evidently, the pose was common among men. She'd seen Gideon stand just that way. When he did, he never resembled a puffed-up toad.

"Mr. Cade is very satisfied with Broadbent's services."

"I don't doubt that, but it's obvious Cade's standards are low. I, however, don't tolerate slipshod behavior from my staff."

Emma's temper stirred. The more she was around Thornton, the more she disliked him. No amount of wealth could compensate for being a pompous bore. Did he think wearing fancy clothes and elaborately tooled boots made him better than everyone else? Although she'd often thought of Gideon as arrogant, he didn't have nearly the overblown opinion of himself that Thornton did.

"I find Broadbent to be a superior butler."

"Have you known many?"

"I once worked in a private residence as a companion for an older woman. While Higbee discharged his responsibilities admirably, he didn't possess Broadbent's intellect or his dedication to duty."

"You just haven't had the advantage of living in a well-run household."

"I must disagree with you. Mr. Cade's home runs quite smoothly."

"Considering he's away so much, that's remarkable."

"Remarkable but true," she said firmly.

"I've got to admit I'm curious about where Cade goes on these trips of his. It's difficult to imagine he spends all his time at the mines."

Thornton was obviously fishing for information. Luckily for Gideon's privacy, she had none. "I assume he goes wherever business takes him."

Thornton nodded as if she'd said something informative. "By the way, Emma, just what is it you do for Cade?"

A disagreeable element of speculation entered his eyes.

"I'm his niece's tutor."

He licked his lips. "*Are* you?"

"What else could I be? Courtney's a student in need of a teacher, and that's what I do for a living."

Unfortunately, her memory chose to remind her of Gideon's other, not-so-honorable offer. She felt her cheeks flame in self-consciousness. Was it her recollection of him joining her on the bed, lowering her to the mattress and branding her with a passionate, soul-consuming kiss that made Thornton's shiny lips and heated gaze reek of lewdness?

"I've always sensed you were capable of being more than a teacher."

She backed up instinctively. The spontaneous movement propelled her against something hard that clattered alarmingly. She jumped forward and spun around. "Oh, my goodness, I'm sorry, Broadbent!"

The butler's attention remained on the sliding silver teapot and the rattling floral-patterned cups and saucers. The creamer and sugar bowl collided. Emma wanted to help him get control of the shifting tray, but sensed that he was in the best position to regain its balance. In order to be of assistance, she lifted the teapot from the field of battle.

"Ow, that's hot!" She'd foolishly grabbed the elegant silver pot with both hands. Immediately she let go of its side and held the steaming server by its handle. It was much heavier than she'd anticipated and tipped dangerously. Several drops of scalding tea splashed on her skirts.

"Be careful, you clumsy oaf!"

At Thornton's bellow, Emma's head snapped up. "I'm doing my best!"

"Not you," Thornton corrected hastily. "I'm talking to that damned ox of a butler."

Before Emma could jump to Broadbent's defense, Thornton jerked a linen napkin from the tray. He wrapped the thick cloth around the teapot and took it from her. After Broadbent regained control of the runaway cups and saucers, he set the unwieldy tray on the cherrywood table in front of the settee.

Thornton slammed the silver pot down in its former resting place amid the china. Both cups bounced off the tray and struck the tabletop. There were two distinct cracks as the delicate handles broke off.

Emma winced. "Oh, dear, until now there weren't any casualties."

"Were you burned?" Thornton demanded.

She held her skirts out, aware of the growing heat in her palm. "No, the tea didn't soak through to my skin."

He snatched her left wrist. "I'm referring to your hand. It was reckless of you to assist this walking calamity you call a butler."

Broadbent shocked Emma by stepping in front of Thornton and thumping his beige shirt with a stout finger. "Keep a civil tongue in your head. Miss Step happens to be a lady of unsurpassed refinement and kindness."

"And we don't have a 'calamity' of a butler!" Emma added, trying to free her hand. "I bet Broadbent is a thousand times better than the man you have filling the same position at your residence."

Thornton pushed aside Broadbent's arm and held up her palm. "Emma, your skin is turning pink. It's obvious you've been burned."

When their visitor took the liberty of calling her by her first name, Broadbent's florid face twisted into a heavy scowl.

"Let me have a look at it," he said gruffly, reaching for Emma's wrist.

The two men tugged on her arm, each seemingly determined to claim sole possession of it.

"As you've already had an opportunity to examine the burn, I would appreciate you allowing Broadbent to have a look at it, Mr. Thornton."

His leonine head jerked up. His expression was one of puzzlement. "Are you angry with me, Emma?"

"I don't approve of your unkind words to Broadbent." She would have called him Elijah, but she knew doing so would make the servant uncomfortable.

"He's a butler!"

"What does that have to do with anything? He still has feelings."

"Feelings?"

"Yes." Emma decided she couldn't have shocked Loutitia's nephew more if she said Broadbent had ten wives.

With obvious reluctance, Thornton let her go. "He was right about one thing. You are a lady of unsurpassed refinement and kindness—with perhaps too much of the latter commodity for your own good. A firm rein needs to be exerted upon one's employees. They need to know their place."

"As I'm also an employee, I have no difficulty treating Broadbent as my equal—which he is."

Definite dissatisfaction simmered in Thornton's blue eyes. "This subject definitely needs more debate to put things in their proper perspective. Right now, however, your burn requires attention. Bring Miss Step a bowl of lard at once. We need to lather it over her skin."

"The burn needs attention, all right, but my mother always used cold water to numb the flesh and prevent blistering."

"We're sure your mother was a saint, Broadbent, but old wives' tales are hardly the basis for modern medicine."

The burn began to throb. Emma knew she hadn't hurt herself seriously, but she still wanted relief from the scorching band of tightness radiating from her palm. "I'll try both meth-

ods. For now I'll go to the kitchen and soak my hand in a
bowl of cool water. I'll apply the lard later.''

"Obviously, I can't force you to accept my advice.''
Thornton took her arm again and led her to the settee.
"There's no reason, however, for you to go the kitchen.
Broadbent can't object to bringing the bowl into the parlor.''

"But it would be much easier if I went there.''

"Easier for whom?''

She rested her elbow on her knee. "Broadbent, obviously.''

"Mr. Thornton has the right of it, Miss Step. I'll be back
before you know it.''

Loutitia's nephew joined Emma on the sofa. "I'll believe
that when I see it.''

She glared at him. Since his arrival, he'd done nothing but
belittle Elijah. And Thornton still hadn't explained the purpose for his visit. It was becoming an extremely demoralizing
day. She wondered how Courtney was coming with her map.

True to his word, Broadbent returned quickly with a tureen
of water. He must have had someone run to the icehouse,
because there were tiny chips of ice bobbing around her
dunked hand.

"This feels wonderful.'' It was cumbersome balancing the
oversize bowl on her knees, but the absence of heat more
than made up for the awkwardness.

Thornton stared disapprovingly at the water she'd splashed
on her skirts. "Lard would have been better.''

"You haven't told me the reason for your visit.'' Broadbent hovered in the background, probably as curious as she
to hear Thornton's answer.

"I've been busy since the academy burned. I'm in the
midst of building what will become Denver's tallest hotel. It
will be eight stories high.''

"That should be impressive.''

"Which is my intent.'' He looked over his shoulder and
frowned at Broadbent, who had begun rearranging figurines
on the mantel. "Why don't you stop eavesdropping and bring
us another tray with unbroken china. I'm parched.''

She wished she could order their obnoxious guest to leave.

Lyman Thornton, however, was one of Denver's leading cit izens. She had no idea how Gideon would react to her evic ing such a wealthy and powerful person from his house. Gid eon already had enough enemies. He didn't need another.

Emma's head began to throb. Maybe she should dip it i the tureen.

"I will return shortly with another tray," Broadbent sai with severe dignity as he cleared away the carnage from th table.

She wanted to tell the butler to take his time, but the soone Thornton drank his wretched tea, the sooner he would b gone.

When they were alone again, Loutitia's nephew settle more comfortably against the settee. "I'm here because I'n serious about us becoming friends. Actually, I'm hoping you'll be amenable to me escorting you to some of Denver' dining establishments and civic performances."

Could a burn cause a person to hallucinate? Surely sh hadn't heard him correctly. This dashing man-about-town whose photograph appeared frequently in the city's newspa pers, couldn't be asking her to keep company with him "Could you repeat that?"

He chuckled. "I know what you're thinking. You're a mer teacher, and I'm the richest man in Denver. How could I b interested in you?"

She'd been thinking exactly that, but resented his dismissa of her worth as a human being.

"To be truthful," he continued, clearly assuming sh shared his opinion on their vast difference in status, "the firs time I saw you, you took my breath away. You probabl aren't aware that I used to watch you whenever I caught sigh of you at the academy."

Maybe the same thing in Denver's water that miraculousl cured tuberculosis had a damaging effect upon one's vision Perhaps people who remained here for any length of tim suffered from deteriorating eyesight. That could explain wh she found Gideon's rugged features more attractive each tim she saw him. It would also explain why Elijah's pummeled-looking visage was becoming dear. Goodness, now that she reflected upon it, Duncan's appearance had improved dramatically since the night he followed her from the academy. Or had it? She blinked, trying to determine if her vision was blurred.

"Emma, you surprise me. I had no idea you were the kind of woman who batted her lashes at a man."

Thornton's purring tone froze those lashes in midblink. "Oh, but I wasn't—"

"I think you were." He chuckled again. "Relax. After our rocky start this afternoon, I appreciate a little encouragement."

She was rapidly growing to detest everything about him. "But—"

"Ah, here's Broadbent. You've certainly picked up your pace. Before you know it, you might turn into a respectable butler."

Emma tapped her foot. That Elijah didn't dump the entire tray and its contents on Thornton's lap said a lot for the butler's control.

Loutitia's nephew reached for the tall silver teapot and poured the steaming liquid into a cup. It was possible he wasn't as dense as he appeared. At least he knew better than to entrust a servant he'd insulted repeatedly to come near him with scalding tea.

"What took you so long the first time, Broadbent?" Thornton asked, helping himself to three spoonfuls of sugar.

Elijah handed Emma the cup he'd prepared for her. "An article in today's newspaper had the staff in a bit of an uproar."

Thornton poured himself a liberal helping of cream. "Well, don't keep us in suspense. What was the news that delayed our tea?"

"There was an account of a vigilante lynching that took place at Hunter Moran's ranch."

"Is that right?"

Emma didn't know how the man could be so casual, when

murder was being discussed. "Something has to be done about those dreadful vigilantes."

"I agree with you, Emma. Something definitely has to be done."

"I wish the Guardsmen could stop the vigilante killings."

"We're working on it."

Emma almost dropped her cup. "What do you mean? Are you connected with them?"

Thornton sipped from the dainty cup he held. "Excellent." His gaze settled on a plate of sugar cookies, and he reached for one. "Ah, these are still warm." He took a bite. "Umm, almost as good as those my cook bakes."

"I'll let Mrs. Graves know they met with your approval."

"Always thinking of others... I'm going to enjoy our association."

She was aware of Elijah's searching stare. "You were explaining your connection with the Guardsmen," she prompted him.

"You know, of course, those heroic champions act in secret." He blotted his lips with a napkin. "Their identities must be protected so they can perform their acts of bravery without retaliation."

Having abandoned any pretense of justifying his presence in the parlor, Elijah held a delicate green crystal vase while watching Thornton closely.

"I realize they're a secret organization," she acknowledged.

"Even so, people have begun to speculate about whom of Denver's citizens might be part of the group."

"I've heard some vague rumors."

"Have you come across a viable candidate whom you think could be affiliated with the organization?"

Elijah seemed to tense. Emma reflected. "I can't think of a soul."

"I'm disappointed. I thought you were more perceptive."

"Sorry to let you down," she grumbled.

"There's one thing I know for certain about you."

"What's that?" she asked warily.

"You're the kind of woman who can keep a confidence."

"Thank you." She wasn't convinced, but had no interest in challenging his assumption. The truth was, she'd never been told a secret, so she didn't know if she would be good at keeping one.

"I know it will go no farther when I tell you, I'm a Guardsman."

There was a soft explosion of shattering crystal. She glanced at Elijah. The fragile vase had slipped through his massive fingers and lay in broken pieces on the carpet.

"Oh, dear."

How disillusioning was life. That this inflated popinjay was one of the noble Guardsmen and her gun-toting panther stood accused by the newspapers of being the leader of the vicious Vigilantes seemed the cruelest blow. When she realized she'd thought of Gideon as hers, Emma became even more depressed.

Gideon would never allow himself to be possessed by any woman. Most likely he was incapable of loving. He had a terrible attitude toward marriage. If ever a man was destined to live his life alone, he was.

Chapter Thirteen

By Emma's count, more than a hundred gazes were trained on her and the two center pews she and her companions occupied. That was what came from being late to services. When they arrived, all but the first two rows had already been filled. She and her unconventional entourage had had no choice but to walk past the seated worshipers and sit at the front of the chapel. The oak pulpit loomed above them like Saint Peter guarding the pearly gates.

The church organist, a smidgen of a woman dressed in brown calico, her gray hair pulled into a marble-size bun, pounded and stomped the church's pump organ with all the vigor her aged limbs could command. Her lined face glowed with fervor as she wrestled a barrage of powerful notes from the polished mahogany instrument. The enthusiastic rendition of "Shall We Gather at the River" swelled inside the chapel.

Gideon's image materialized in Emma's thoughts. She knew her own weak character had conjured his likeness. After all, no matter what the setting, Gideon Cade was hardly the refined material from which heavenly visions were fashioned. Nor were her reflections of a lofty nature, for she was mentally comparing Gideon to the pump organ and herself to the organist. The rogue thought entered her mind that, if she were to attack him with such enthusiasm, she could wrest from him powerful notes that, while admittedly not divine in nature, could surely blow the roof off a church, or a bedchamber.

Definitely improper imaginings. She glanced to her right. Beside her sat Courtney, dressed in a pink gown with a white lace collar. Her uplifted face radiated sweet sincerity. The open hymnal on her lap, already turned to the song they shortly would be singing, was a reproach to Emma. When was she going to overcome her hopeless preoccupation with her employer?

His absence had again extended to several weeks. During that time, the papers had been filled with accounts of heroic deeds performed by the Guardsmen. They'd foiled a bank robbery and two attempts to steal gold being shipped by Gideon's freight wagons, and they'd captured more rustlers preying upon Hunter Moran's herds.

It disgusted her that, of the two entirely different groups of men, Lyman Thornton had managed to become a part of the elite Guardsmen, while the newspapers repeatedly hinted that Gideon was the suspected ringleader of the loathsome Vigilantes.

Courtney's lilting soprano mingled with the other worshipers' voices. The stirring words of "How Great Thou Art" returned Emma to the present. Elijah and most of the rest of the staff had elected to attend Reverend Horace Hobbly's Sunday-afternoon service—along with the twelve roughly dressed bodyguards who'd been assigned to keep Courtney safe. Their holstered guns were prominently visible.

Since Emma had long ago memorized the brief hymn, there was no need to open her songbook. The untrained male voices rising around her released a spate of notes completely unrelated to those produced by the organ. There was something touching about the men's awkward attempts to participate in the service. When they entered the building, each had removed his hat. Several had even combed their hair and shaved.

The organist ceased playing, and the chorister returned to her seat. Horace Hobbly stepped to the pulpit. Blessed with an overabundance of height and girth, the stern-faced minister silently sized up his congregation. His black hair was streaked with silver.

"Let us pray."

When he completed his solicitations on his flock's behalf, he opened his steely gray eyes and stared severely at the worshipers.

"I will not present my prepared text. Into our midst have come strangers whose souls would be better edified by a different sermon. Nevertheless, I pray our faithful followers will also heed my words, lest they plunge into that fiery pit prepared for all imbibers of demon alcohol, gamblers and fornicators."

Emma peeked surreptitiously at those seated close to her. Courtney appeared absorbed by the forthcoming message. The six bodyguards seated in their pew were grim-lipped. Lefty had returned his dusty, battered brown Stetson to his head and pulled it low over his eyes. Would any of her dour-faced protectors return next Sunday?

She had no doubt she could talk Nat Walker into accompanying her and Courtney again. Nat was the only one of Gideon's hired guns who looked as if he were enjoying himself. The moment they entered the chapel, his restless gaze had locked on Miriam Goodwin. Charmingly garbed in a green-and-yellow striped gown with muttonchop sleeves, the dressmaker looked crisp and fresh. She sat on one of the narrow benches to their right. Clearly returning Nat's interest, Miss Goodwin kept glancing at the tall, ruggedly handsome cowboy.

With a will of their own, Emma's thoughts gravitated once more to Gideon. She resented missing him so keenly, resented that he hadn't sent a single message to them. Though not in the form of letters, she wrote to him each day as she meticulously recorded Courtney's progress. It was probably a waste of time to do so. Most likely, he would never read the text of her lesson plans or her student's results. With all his business concerns, it was foolish to think she or Courtney ever crossed his mind. How discouraging that *he* had taken up permanent residence in her daily reflections. Even more disquieting was the admission that she wanted him to take her into his arms and kiss her. She yearned to be transported to that darkly passionate world where nothing existed save the power of his hard-angled body straining against her.

She feared she'd lost her reasoning ability where he was concerned. Even his cruelty the last time they'd been together couldn't break his unnatural hold upon her. If anything, the longer he was gone, the more she craved his company, his touch, his breath inside her...

That she could entertain such lascivious thoughts within a church indicated that she was in grave need of today's sermon.

Emma drifted upward through the wispy layers of sleep that cocooned her slumbering thoughts. She opened her eyes to a disoriented world of gray. The fading afterimages of an unremembered dream danced elusively at the edges of her consciousness. She struggled to comprehend what had nudged her to groggy wakefulness. The task proved futile, however, and her eyelids lowered. The drone of steadily falling rain lured her toward sleepy oblivion.

Several firm taps sounded against her bedchamber's windowpane. Emma sat up, recognizing that the imperious clicks were what had interrupted her rest. Someone was rapping at her window. Confused by the lingering tendrils of sleep that still embraced her, she pushed back the blankets and stood. The braided rug cushioned her bare feet. She fumbled in the murky shadows and managed to turn up the oil lamp on her bedside stand. A few steps took her from the warm comfort of the rug to the chilled hardwood floor.

When she reached the draperies and raised her arms to push the velvet material aside, her first coherent thought registered. Her room was on the second floor. One could only gain admittance to the outside terraces that circled the second and third stories from the inside. That meant whoever was on the other side of the glass was a household member. She didn't know what she expected to see when she parted the heavy curtains, but it wasn't Gideon Cade, rain-battered and scowling.

She stared at him blankly, wondering if she was caught in the thrall of a particularly vivid dream. While she pondered her state of wakefulness, Gideon's water-blurred image raised his fisted hand and rapped against the wetly beaded glass with his gloved knuckles. Pelting raindrops trampled the brim of his black Western hat over his glowering face. His thinned lips moved as he gestured toward the terrace door.

She caught only two words.

"Open...damned..."

His meaning was clear enough.

Her muddled reasoning suggested that she *was* probably dreaming. Curious to see what happened next, she unlatched the lock.

On a furious blast of wind, rain and man, Gideon burst through the doorway. She didn't get out of the way in time and was caught in the storm's path. A wall of drenched male shoved her backward. Powerful arms closed around her, swinging her at an angle to deflect his jarring impact.

"What—?"

Her unfinished question was swallowed up in an openmouthed kiss that sent tangled spirals of raw need coursing through her. At first cold and wet, his lips became hot and slick. The prickling rasp of stubble that encircled his demanding mouth scraped her face and, in some mysterious manner that defied logic, awakened that part of her pulled tightly to his groin. She stood on tiptoe and twisted her arms around his neck. His palms cupped her bottom as he positioned her more intimately against him.

Fire and water seemed to have snatched her into a wildly spinning vortex. Water poured off his broad shoulders and chest, wetting her arms and the rest of her, as he overwhelmed her on all sides. The first instant of cold shock turned to gathering waves of heat. Their bodies seemed to merge in a steamy vapor that, if unchecked, would melt them both.

Strands of his rainswept hair lay plastered against his neck. Beckoned to that new territory, she knocked off his hat. Her questing fingertips tangled in the lush pelt now available for her exploration. Her brazen aggressiveness seemed both alien and natural. It was as if she were the Emma she'd always been, only out of control. In that same moment, she was a new Emma, hungering for fulfillment.

Her mouth was hot and alive. And even though he claimed her with near-savage urgency, she couldn't get enough of him. His tongue entered, a bold conqueror, allowing no resistance. She wasn't of a mind to resist. She met each sleek stroke of his tongue with a counterstroke of her own.

As if locked in a primal struggle to mate through their pores, their bodies twisted against each other. Her flimsy sleeping gown and the thick barrier of his coat, shirt and trousers became abrasive impediments to some unknown pinnacle.

She tore her mouth from his. "Help me..."

She didn't know what she sought. An end to the pain? His naked flesh pressed against hers? She only knew she needed something desperately, and she needed it now.

Help me... She pressed wet kisses against his stubbled jaw and throat.

"I didn't come here for this."

Expelled on a ragged breath, the jerky words were an apology she didn't want.

"I don't care." She rubbed her breasts against his chest. His hands still cupped her bottom, and he rotated her against him.

"Ooh, that feels..." She closed her eyes. "...so...good."

"I know." He raised her hips.

The heightened contact made her cry out again.

"Damn, I've got to be out of my mind."

He took several steps toward the bed. Each time his booted foot struck the floor, a new series of rippling tremors radiated through her. He released his hold. She tumbled onto her tangled bedding. Her legs were open, as were her arms. She couldn't speak. She could only lie there, a quivering blob of desire, and watch as Gideon shucked off his coat.

She was glad she'd turned the lamp up. The sharply defined

muscles of his lean jaw and throat suggested that he was in as much pain as she. Good.

"I want to taste you."

The hurtful ache between her thighs made her want to rip off her nightgown. The shameless thought embarrassed her. What was she doing? Into what foreign place had she strayed, that such blatant desire could seize her?

She watched him jerk off his boots. In quick succession, his socks followed. Not taking his hot gaze from her, he tore off his shirt. Popped buttons flew as he exposed his broad, hair-roughened chest. Her suddenly dry mouth signaled the end of self-questioning. Firmly muscled and slightly tanned, his darkly furred torso seemed almost mythical in its perfection.

He sank one knee on the mattress and swung his other leg over her. His muscled thighs were long enough that he didn't touch her. As she stared at the triangle of space separating him for her, new tension built.

"Your eyes are as big as spinning lariats." His observation carried a husky thread of amusement.

Her gaze shot to his face. She found no amusement in his eyes, only a satisfying degree of smoldering intent. His hands drifted to his waist, and he unfastened his gun belt. She considered the long-barreled weapon inside its holster. The metal cylinder wasn't any harder than his manhood. Her cheeks flooded with heat. Even though she knew she would never share such an earthy reflection, it surprised her that she was capable of such carnal thoughts.

He leaned back and carefully draped the looped gun belt over a mahogany bedpost. His strong fingers went to the front closure of his trousers. He undid one button, then another. Curly black hairs appeared, joining the base of the tapering ebony arrow that plunged from his chest.

Despite her earlier bout of wantonness, she doubted she was ready to actually see that intimate part of him. Yet the decision seemed to have been taken from her hands, so to speak.

"That's probably enough for now." He adjusted himself

through the coarse denim fabric. "I don't want to give you more than you can handle."

The deliberate pause allowed time for second thoughts. Now that she knew she wasn't dreaming, it was up to her to stop Gideon from continuing.

He reached out and slowly untied the pink ribbon holding her bodice together. "The way you plastered yourself against me made your nightgown transparent. Look at yourself, see how beautiful you are."

His deep voice hypnotized her. Thoughts of protest splintered and blew away. She glanced down. The tips of her breasts were clearly defined against the sheer material.

"Let's get comfortable, honey."

Comfortable? Given the fact that they were in bed together, with him towering above her, what he suggested seemed unattainable.

He maneuvered himself between her legs. "I'm going to take time to make this good for you."

Mesmerized, she watched him raise her damp hem to her knees, then to the top of her thighs. The trailing fabric scraped lightly against her skin. When he reached the apex of her legs, she closed her eyes. It was inconceivable that she, Emma January Step, was going to let a man see that part of her. Goodness, it had never seemed proper for her own gaze to stray there.

"Open your eyes, sweetheart. I told you, I'm taking this slow. I won't push you further than you're ready to go." He chuckled softly, but there was no pleasure in the sound, only bitter acknowledgment. "I know I have no right to be here. I told myself I would just pass through your room to get inside the house.

"We both know I lied. Because I left without taking a key doesn't mean I couldn't have pounded on the door until Broadbent opened up. You're the reason I came home during our first rainstorm in months."

He inched closer, inexorably opening her more fully to him. From his raised angle, it was possible that he could indeed see the vulnerable area, across which a faint breeze drifted. He lowered his head. That movement brought the coarse fabric covering his groin directly against her.

The gentle friction was too much. "Ooh…"

"That's it, honey."

"Honey, sweetheart…" she murmured skeptically. "It's strange hearing those words from you."

"Funny, they feel right." His hands returned to her bodice.

She braced herself, thinking he was going to rip the flimsy material. He tugged the sheerly woven batiste fabric across her breasts. It was difficult to discern where the pleasure ended and the pain of wanting began.

He lowered himself so that his elbows supported his weight, and pressed his parted lips to the tip of one breast. She moaned. He stretched his long, powerful body over her. His fully aroused shaft moved with surprising gentleness in a rocking motion that made her want to weep at the steadily escalating need he loosened inside her.

He raised his head. His burning eyes scorched her. "I should forget the endearments and call you angel-woman."

"Angel-woman?"

That they should have this or any other conversation while he continued to rhythmically stroke her was the rawest kind of intimacy.

"That's how I see you, even when I'm utterly bewitched."

Her eyelids drifted shut as she concentrated on the wondrous tremors that rippled from his measured caress.

"You like what I'm doing, don't you?"

She ducked her face against his shoulder. "I… It's too…intense to talk about."

"Emma…" He stilled.

She thought she was going to die, had died. "Please, no matter what I say…I mean, even if it's the wrong thing…don't stop. I think I'll shatter if you stop before…"

"Before?"

"I don't know," she admitted honestly. "But you've done something to make me ache for more. There *is* more, isn't there?"

He slid his fingers into her hair, and exerted enough pressure that she was forced to look at him. "There's a world of *more*."

"I...I thought so."

"But even though I'm harder than I've ever been, I'm not about to steal your chastity."

"Haven't you already..." She cleared her throat. "I don't see how I can possibly be considered chaste after... Well, we *are* in bed together."

"I've still got my pants on."

His face was so close to hers, she felt his stubble shift against her cheek as he spoke. "And that makes a difference?"

"Yeah, baby, that's going to make the difference. I may have forced my way into your bedchamber in the middle of the night, but I'm not a big enough bastard to take complete advantage of you."

"I unlatched the door," she reminded him. Her fingers strayed to the satiny textured muscles that rippled along his upper arms and back.

"When I came barreling in and saw the lamplight spilling from behind you, it was like seeing you naked. A bomb seemed to explode inside me. All I wanted was to get my hands on you."

His admission made her womb clench. "And now you've changed your mind?"

He straightened, gathering her hands into his. "I'm slowing things down, so you know what is and what *isn't* going to happen in this bed."

"Is it your custom to lecture all your...uh...female companions?"

"The women I've lain with have been sophisticated enough to know what I wanted, and I've known exactly what they wanted." His voice was flat.

"I suppose that was mutual satisfaction, with no promises or strings attached." The knowledge that this magical adventure wasn't special to him hurt.

"Not exactly," he said harshly. "Whether it was in the

form of hard coin or pretty baubles, I traded money to enjoy their bodies.''

His callousness made her want to lash out at him. He'd bartered himself too cheaply.

He shuddered above her. "Aren't you going to tell me to get out?''

The question obviously came at great cost to his self-control.

"I know I should,'' she answered, "but I...can't.''

The confession left her feeling rawly exposed.

"This is what I'm going to do.'' With one movement, he jerked her gown over her head. She stared at him in shock. "I'm going to start with your breasts and drive us both a little crazy.''

His lips closed over a nipple. He sucked lightly, rasping the sensitive tip with his tongue. Powerful new sensations flooded through her. He moved to her other breast. Her fingers dug into the sheets. She had to hold on to something or be torn apart by the delicious spasms clutching her stomach.

"So beautiful, your breasts are so beautiful.''

She liked hearing his words of praise, but doubted there was anything remarkable about her bosom, unless it was the way his roving mouth made her flesh tingle.

His kisses became more voracious as he charted a new path of possession across her stomach and hips. She wanted to let go of the bedding and caress his arms and shoulders again, but her muscles wouldn't cooperate. She was bound by a new master that rendered her a prisoner of her building need for deliverance. *Surrender...* The word pounded in her head and heart and center.

His touch was everywhere. The burning trail of hot kisses reached the most private part of her. She thought he'd lost his mind, and tried to scoot free. He raised his head, his gaze locked with hers.

"It's all right. I'm going to make the hurting go away.''

She looked around wildly. There had to be some means of talking him back to sanity. "You can't... You're not going to put your mouth *there?*''

He smiled. Her stomach bucked. He looked like a savage conqueror from an earlier time, a despoiler of English maidens, a hedonist bent on sending his captive to…paradise, his fired gaze promised.

His warm breath fluttered against her exposed flesh, then went deeper. She wanted to shield herself, but it was too late. All she could see was his tangled black hair.

The tip of his tongue—it had to be that—probed gently. She bolted upright and cried out.

Again his gaze burned into her. "Did I hurt you?"

Hurt her? He'd all but destroyed her. Finding the power of speech beyond her, she shook her head.

"You've got to relax, honey. Ease yourself against your pillow."

The last thing she was capable of doing was *relaxing*.

"I know what I'm doing. Give yourself up to it. I can pleasure you without causing irreparable damage."

She didn't understand what he was saying, but his earthy invitation could not be ignored. His thumbs glided gently along her pulsing skin. She closed her eyes, then moaned. Soon she was sobbing for something that continued to remain out of reach. The rhythm of his plundering tongue quickened.

"I can't… I can't…"

He didn't stop, didn't slow his fierce pace.

She hung suspended between raging need and his promise. There was a split second of being nowhere, before Gideon's caress sent her careening over a waterfall of white pleasure. An explosion of fire and rain shot through her. Her womb contracted again and again. Eddies of pleasure settled in her nipples and loins, though, truth be told, she felt Gideon's magic everywhere—in her hands and feet, her arms and legs, even in her ears and lips.

On the arch of her foot… Emma's eyelids opened and she looked at him askance. He was kissing the sole of her foot.

"There can't be more," she hazarded, not sure she could handle it if he brought the extremity to a shattering pinnacle of pleasure.

His slumberous eyes glittered. "There's more, but you pretty much had what I'm going to give you tonight."

"Then what are you doing with my foot?"

He kissed her lightly, then released her ankle. "I've got you laid out in front of me without a stitch of clothing, I intend to do some investigating."

Now that Emma wasn't caught in the throes of a tidal wave of desire, her normal modesty returned. "This feels very…strange."

Still resembling a conquering warrior, he continued to look his fill at her. "Strange never looked so beautiful."

Embarrassed by his bold stare, she rolled onto her side and tugged at one of the trapped sheets.

"This is all the fun I'm allowing myself. Don't be stingy, Emma. I thought I'd come down slowly before I go." He ran a finger along her spine.

"You're leaving?"

It was ridiculous to be disappointed, but she knew that when he left her chamber, he would take the last fragments of this astounding interlude with him. The next time they greeted each other, it would be "Good day, Mr. Cade." And he would pronounce "Miss Step" in the same neutral way he did "Mrs. Graves" or "Mrs. Foster." She didn't think she could bear that.

He pressed a palm against her shoulder, easing her again onto her back. The corner of the sheet she'd pulled free to cover herself was sadly lacking. Instead of making another attempt to shield herself, she allowed him to touch her with his appreciative gaze.

Shameless… He'd made her shameless.

"I have to go. Not even my noble intentions will let me remain here without taking off my britches and sliding inside you."

They were only words, but they were spoken by Gideon, in roughened tones that stirred the inner fires he'd barely extinguished.

"I thought that's how it was done," she said, wondering

what it would feel like to have him inside her when the storm broke.

"Did you?"

"When you... When you did that thing with your mouth and my insides squeezed together, I—"

Shocked by her own bluntness, she broke off.

He ran the pad of his finger from her ankle to her knee and beyond. "Don't clam up." He revisited the tender area between her thighs, delicately inserting the tip of his middle finger.

"Are we starting over? I don't think that's a good idea."

He eased his way more deeply into her. "Don't you?"

Didn't she what? It was impossible to think coherently when those rippling sensations swam inside her. It took all her self-control not to push down against his daring touch.

He probed more intimately. "You were made for me."

His low-voiced words and clever fingers were exciting her again.

"I don't understand," she breathed in confusion.

"Understand what?"

"How you can bear to be aroused and not...uh..."

"It's my way of paying penance."

She trembled against his wondrous caress. "Penance?"

"For breaking my rule to keep my hands off you."

"You have more...control than I do."

"I have it till it's gone," he said cryptically.

The first tremor of release tingled through her. "I feel self-ish."

"Don't. I deserve whatever pain tonight causes me."

The magic grabbed her. Everything he made her feel was so new, so overpowering, she couldn't comprehend how to subdue its raw force.

"Gideon!"

He swallowed her cry.

Afterward, she curled into him. His arms came around her.

"Forget your penance." She rubbed her cheek against his chest. "I wanted you to kiss me. I...I liked the way you touched me. And I don't see how we can go back to the way it was before you did."

After a lifetime of isolation, her words of need took all her courage. The fear she faced in opening herself up to him, however, was less terrible than the aloneness that had pervaded her life.

He squeezed her to him. "Honey, you've got a body made for loving. The way I touched you... *Any* man could make you feel that way."

A slap in the face would have hurt less. Any man? He probably meant any *woman* could meet *his* needs.

"If I gave in to my inclinations and stole your innocence, where would that leave us?" he continued, apparently unaware of the pain he'd inflicted. "Right now, your body is humming with the newness of being with a man."

"This isn't new for you, is it?" She tried to slip from his embrace.

"You know the answer." His hold didn't ease. "I'm not letting you go, so you might as well stop trying to get away."

Knowing she couldn't break free, she resorted to goading him into releasing her. "I thought you said you were leaving."

"I will when we get a few things cleared up."

She crossed her arms over her breasts. "What's there to clear up? You invaded my bedchamber, forced yourself on me and then came to your senses. Everything is pretty straightforward."

"Emma—"

"You've probably done this with a thousand other women."

He rolled on top of her. "There haven't been a thousand."

"How do you know? Have you kept count?"

"No, my little termagant, but I'm not the rutting beast you think."

That was obvious. Despite the present provocation of having her naked beneath him, he seemed quite content to leave her...unbroached.

"I admit being completely in the wrong," he said through

gritted teeth. "But I'm not going to make Courtney's tutor my mistress."

Courtney's tutor... Of course, that was how he viewed her, not as a woman. She was his employee, nothing more. What had happened between them tonight wouldn't change that.

"I have no desire to become your mistress."

Liar, a rude inner voice whispered. But it wasn't a lie. She didn't want to become any man's kept woman, not even Gideon's. For down that path lay the ruination of all her dreams.

"Once I unpeel my body from yours, we won't have a problem."

She yawned, feigning indifference. "That shouldn't be difficult. It's time you made your grand exit."

"It would be a hell of a lot easier if I'd made my grand entrance."

There was no mistaking his meaning. "I've absolutely no sympathy for you."

"You're a hard woman, Emma. I don't want to leave you to your lonely bed."

If you would have stayed out of it, I wouldn't have known it was lonely! "I'm not afraid of the dark."

"Maybe you should be." He cupped her chin between his fingertips, forcing her to meet his gaze. "A person can get lost in the dark."

Even though the callous words he spoke earlier had hurt her terribly, the naked look of longing she saw in his eyes proved her undoing.

"What do you want?"

"You. In my arms. Until dawn."

"But—"

His lips closed over hers. "Just to hold you."

How could she resist both him and her own aching need to be held?

He didn't wait for a response before reaching across her. "I'll turn down the lamp, and we can share the darkness."

Chapter Fourteen

When Emma drifted awake in the darkened bedchamber, her cheek rested against Gideon's chest. Unable to resist, she stroked the lush carpet of hair that cushioned the pads of her fingertips. She hadn't understood before how a man could make a woman "fall." Now she did.

Other things had become clear. Due to Gideon's frankness about his body and its needs, she now grasped the puzzling details that had shrouded the mating ritual in mystery. The mechanics of making babies was also clear. One man, one woman. His seed, her womb. A miracle.

It was a splendid plan—if the man and the woman were married and that miraculous life could be born into a loving family.

"What are you thinking?"

Though softly voiced, Gideon's question thundered through her. She pressed her hand on her heart. "I didn't know you'd wakened."

"I was only half-asleep." He shifted so that her head rested on his upper arm. Snagging her wrist, he pressed her palm to his lips.

She sighed and snuggled closer. He'd done more than hold her during the past few hours. Under the cloak of darkness, she'd yielded to his enticements. Even though it frightened her how easily he could bend her to his will, she'd given him free rein of her body. He'd pleasured her, and tutored her hands in pleasuring him. When he buried his face in a pillow to smother his muffled shout of release, she'd thought of the church's pump organ. Had he not restrained himself, he could have surpassed it in volume.

"You didn't tell me what you were thinking."

She couldn't, of course. "Like you, I was just dozing."

"I know you too well. Your mind abounds with conjecture."

"After what you've done to me, I can't summon the strength to think."

Immediately she regretted her words. His lazy laugh penetrated places impossible to barricade.

"You enjoyed yourself."

A bone-deep blush burned her skin. "I...uh..." Stalling didn't add clarity to her thoughts. "There's no way to pretend you don't arouse me."

Humbling admissions were becoming a habit. How demoralizing.

"I can feel you blushing." He placed a large palm against her stomach. "Your skin is on fire."

"I've never been in this situation." Evidently, he needed reminding.

"I know, honey. Are you tender?"

Knowing what he meant, she blushed hotter. "Um, I'm okay."

"Do you want to fly again?"

She knew what that meant, too. "We're playing with fire."

"I can control it."

"Maybe I can't. You make me forget everything I believe in. Laying next to you like this is..."

"What?"

"Too much. I want to feel everything again."

"Is that so bad?"

"It's terrible! I'm shameless. I want to hand myself over to you and say, 'Here I am. Kiss me, kiss my breasts and any other part of me you have a mind to. Touch me, rub your hairy body against me. Open me up and fill me. And whatever happens, don't stop.'"

He buried his face in her stomach. Several moments of silence ticked by. His rigid body trembled.

"Then I'll forget the last of the rules," she whispered in the darkness. "If you don't do it first, I'll be the one pushing against you, saying anything to get you inside me."

He tore himself from her and rolled to the other side of the bed. "Enough... I'm not made from stone."

"Nor am I."

"When I entered your bedchamber and found my arms wrapped around you and my mouth on yours, I told myself we would share a few kisses. Then it was a few touches. And then I needed to taste more of you. I would stop after that. But I had to see you, and then..."

"Then it was just tonight. We would enjoy ourselves as far as I dared take us, till dawn. I would concentrate on pleasuring you. That would be my penance. When it was over, I would all but crawl from your bedchamber, without receiving my own release. Then it was anything and everything but penetration. I would hold your maidenhood sacred."

Emma's breaths came so rapidly they hurt her chest. "And now?"

"I'd sell my soul for all of you."

"But I can't sell mine," she said with growing conviction.

"Why do you say you *can't*, as if your soul isn't yours to do with as you please?"

As difficult as it was to discuss physical things with Gideon, baring her heart was harder. "I told you I grew up in an orphanage."

"Did they make you leave your soul at the door when you left?"

"I know you're joking, but in a way they did."

"How?"

"They taught us that most of our parents weren't dead, and we really weren't orphans."

"What were you?"

"Bastards." She'd never spoken the heinous word aloud. It tasted more bitter than any imagined poison.

"That's a harsh thing to tell a child."

"Harsh, but true. We were the babies of fallen women who'd broken the sixth commandment. We were the wages of sin, and must be on guard at all times not to follow in our parents' wicked footsteps."

"Children aren't responsible for their parents' transgressions."

"The rest of the world disagrees with you."

"The world's wrong. Whomever brought you to the orphanage when you were a baby was at fault. Not you. Never you."

The pressure of hot tears built. "I wasn't a baby. I was three years old when I was left at the foundling home."

Gideon sat up and reached for her. She didn't resist. "Do you remember anything about being taken there?"

Leaning against his shoulder, she pushed her memory back as far as it would go.

"Does it hurt to talk about it?"

"A little." The compassion she detected in his gritty voice penetrated a dark, lonely corner of her heart. "I've never discussed my childhood with anyone."

"Not even the other children?"

"Most the time we were too busy to talk."

"Busy?"

"There were bed linens to change, floors to mop and clothes to wash. We were forever folding stacks of laundry."

"Not when you were three."

"You would be surprised how much work a child can accomplish."

"Dammit, someone should have taken care of you, read you bedtime stories and pampered you."

"I can't even imagine such a life."

"And you weren't close to any of the other children?"

"Talking was discouraged. Our world revolved around keeping clean, eating, working and studying our lessons. When children started to get close, they would be separated."

"Why?"

"We were supposed to be independent."

"I can't believe you never made a friend."

"I was shy. I kept to myself. It was easier to stay out of trouble that way. Some children snitched on the rest of us."

He brushed his lips against her forehead. "It sounds as if you were in prison."

"In a way, I suppose I was. You know, there was one little boy, Johnny McGuire, who kind of looked after me."

"How old was he?"

"Seven."

"I hope he was big for his age," Gideon observed dryly.

"Actually, he was small, but Johnny knew how to defend himself. He threw the fastest punches. In fact—"

"Don't tell, little Johnny grew up to become 'the Dynamite Kid, Fighting Johnny McGuire.'"

"That's right. How did you know?"

"Lucky guess, and the memory of your fist flying at me in my carriage."

"I'd forgotten about that."

"My jaw still remembers. You pack quite a punch."

"I was aiming for your eye. I wanted desperately to blacken it."

"I was looking for a different kind of excitement."

"That's what earned you the blow."

"Getting back to your life at the orphanage, were you ever told about your past?"

"Not that I recall. I think when I first got there, I did remember a few things. Even when I was eight, there were blurry images of a woman's beautiful face smiling at me, laughing with a man.... It was like trying to see through smoke. After a while, I wasn't sure the faces were real. They could have been bits of forgotten dreams. When I was ten, I tried to make them appear, but I couldn't. They'd gotten lost somewhere along the way."

"There must have been a record of your arrival. Someone brought you there. What did they have to say for themselves?"

She shivered. "I was left at night."

"Alone?"

"I can remember that part of it. Someone was angry. A woman, I think. She was in a hurry. It was so cold. And dark. I was afraid."

"What happened next?"

"Nothing. I seemed to stand there forever. My teeth were chattering. I was crying. And the blanket she'd wrapped around me kept slipping off."

"Dammit, Emma, that's inexcusable. What time of year was it?"

"January."

"In Philadelphia, I recall you saying." His tone was as frigid as the night air that had blown about her. He tightened his hold. "It's a miracle you didn't freeze to death."

"That's what the policeman who found me said. It was foolish of me not to have knocked on the door. I wonder if the woman had told me to and I'd forgotten."

"What happened next?"

"The policeman took me inside. Soon I was surrounded by grown-ups. They undressed me and put me in a tub of warm water. There were lots of questions. The only thing I could tell them was my first name. They added the rest. 'January' because that was the month I was abandoned. 'Step' because that was where they'd found me."

He pulled her closer. "You shouldn't have had to go through that."

"When I was younger, I thought I was being punished." Tears slipped past the barrier of her clenched lashes. "Maybe I did something really bad, and they had to send me away.

"I used to wish there was some way to let them know that I would try harder to be good. If they would give me another chance, I would be...perfect. I would do everything they told me, and I would work really hard. All the time—if that was what it took for them to keep me. I wouldn't expect them to love me, of course. That would be asking too much. But..."

She couldn't go on. The jagged lump in her throat hurt too much.

He kissed her hair and wet cheeks. "Listen to me. You're the bravest, kindest, hardest-working woman I know. Nothing that happened was your fault. You *are* perfect. And I'd bet everything I own that you were a perfect child. Something most have gone terribly wrong in your parents' lives for them to lose you."

She shook her head. "Considering what's happened between us tonight, and the fact that we're in bed together, I'd say that's one wager you wouldn't win. Besides, I wasn't lost, I was given away."

He leaned over her, flattening her against him as he reached toward the bedside stand. It took a half second for her to realize he was turning up the lamp. "We've got a couple of things to settle."

As her eyes adjusted to the light, her gaze drifted across his magnificently formed body. She'd been right. It was overpowering to lie with him in a brightened room.

"I like how you look at me, Emma."

Guiltily she shifted the focus of her stare. Confronting his glittering eyes, however, did little to slow her racing heart. "Uh, you're the first bare-chested man I've seen."

"There's a lot more bare than my chest, and you've seen it."

So she had. "Why did you turn on the light?"

"I'll tell you in a minute." He twisted from the blanket and got out of bed. The lamp's light played over his ripping muscles.

She swallowed. It had never occurred to her that a man could be beautiful. There was no hint of modesty as he rounded the bed and reached for the trousers he'd discarded earlier.

He slid on his boots, but, there was no way he could be called decent without a shirt. Even after he put the garment on, a wide swath of his chest remained exposed. What would Mrs. Foster say when the garment showed up in the laundry without buttons?

He drew up a chair and sat down. "Emma, I took shameless advantage of your innocence tonight."

"I didn't put up much of a—"

"Hush. I want to get something off my chest."

Your shirt? "If you're going to apologize again, I—"

"I said, hush. Nothing you did tonight was your fault. I railroaded you every step of the way. As far as I'm concerned, you're as pure as an angel with golden-tipped wings."

"Now you're going too far."

"You were probably a disgustingly perfect child," he said, ignoring her protest. "I suspect you were conscientious beyond your years. Minutes after we met, you were lecturing me upon a multitude of subjects. The fact that I deserved to be lectured only shows how competent you are."

Was she supposed to feel complimented that he viewed her as a cross between a temperance crusader and a dowager aunt?

"Tonight happened because I went crazy and carried you along in my path. Even though an apology won't put things back the way they were, I'm apologizing. Somehow we're going to make it through this. I moved your room to the second floor so you wouldn't be such a damned temptation. If I ever try to enter your bedchamber again, you have my permission to shoot me."

Trembling, Emma glared at him. "I don't have a gun."

"Use mine."

She glanced at the bedpost where his gun belt still hung.

He leaned sideways and pulled it over the post. He must have sensed her mood. "The next time, Emma, not tonight."

"Pity."

He draped the holstered gun over his shoulder and plucked his coat from the floor. "Time will ease the tension between us. Eventually what happened will fade from our thoughts."

In a thousand years? "I'll be looking forward to the day."

"I'm glad you told me about your childhood, Emma."

His obvious sincerity punctured her escalating temper. She didn't want his compassion. She wanted him to be a beast all the way to his black heart so she could feel good about hating him.

"After everything you've been through, you need someone

special to love and care for you. The only thing on my mind is justice."

"Vengeance, you mean."

"Yeah, when I catch up with Jonathan's and Cynthia's killers, I'll be ready to squeeze all the agony I can from them. There's no way they're going to walk away without paying for what they did."

Why didn't he understand he was paying the greater price for his revenge? "Go and track them down. After you hang them, shoot them through with a hundred bullets."

"I'll be gone tomorrow. I want to make sure you understand nothing's changed between us. You still work for me, tutoring Courtney."

While Gideon was pursuing his prey, she would be pursuing new employment.

"Do you understand what I'm saying, Emma?"

"Of course—you're the boss and I'm not."

"Don't be flippant."

She rubbed her burning eyes. "I'm not. I'm just being conscientious and competent. That's what you admire about me."

"That and your smart mouth." He headed toward the terrace door.

"You're not thinking of climbing down? It's still raining. The railing is bound to be slippery. You're lucky you didn't break your neck coming up."

"I'm just retrieving my hat." He scooped it from the floor.

Remembering that she'd been the one to knock it off, she flushed. Then something totally abhorrent occurred. He stood before her with his stupidly battered hat plunked on his head, his buttonless shirt hanging loosely about him, his gun belt slung over his shoulder and his coat clamped under one arm. He looked as if he'd been swallowed up and spat from of one of those midwestern tornadoes she'd read about. All in all, he looked impossibly endearing.

You're outraged at him! There's nothing endearing about the scoundrel. Just because he has one pant leg tucked in his boot and the other cuff half way up his shin doesn't make him the least bit winsome. And the fact you know what he looks like beneath his rumpled clothes...

Oh, bother, she lost her train of thought.

He put his hand on the doorknob. "I've apologized. You don't have to worry about there being a repeat of what happened tonight. Are you going to be sensible?"

Sensible? Oh, yes, from now on that's exactly what she would be. "Let me add that to my list. Let's see, I'm agreeing to be conscientious, competent *and* sensible, right?"

"You have no intention of making this easy for us, do you?"

"On the contrary, I would say I've made things *too* easy."

"Have it your way, but there's one more thing I have to say."

Was he never going to leave?

"There will be a raise in your next paycheck."

A red haze clouded her vision. She bolted from the bed. The sheet came off before she reached him. It didn't matter. She shoved hard against his chest. Clearly caught by surprise, he stumbled back.

"Don't you dare give me a raise! I've never been so insulted in all my life! To think that you would try to pay me for—"

She broke off and socked him in the stomach. Unfortunately, his coat took the brunt of the impact. He closed his eyes. She must have hit him harder than she realized. Good.

"Emma, you're naked."

She tossed back her hair. "I refuse to be embarrassed. You had that coming."

"Yeah, I can see where you might feel that way. But the thing is, I'm apologizing for *almost* burying myself inside you and riding you to heaven. You stand there another minute with your sweet breasts bobbing and your tailfeathers flashing and I'll be apologizing for a lot more. But it won't change anything."

She knocked his hand off the doorknob and turned it herself. "You're a low-down, dirty polecat. Get out."

"Damn, now you're starting to talk like a cowboy."

"Get out!"

He planted a wet kiss on her shoulder. "Marry me, Emma."

"Ooh, you're the cruelest, meanest man alive!"

"Ssh, keep your voice down. The last thing we need is an audience."

She swung open the door and shoved him into the hall.

"Do you have any idea how vile you are?" It frustrated her to whisper.

"I'm beginning to get the idea."

"How could you lie in order to trick me into getting back into that bed with you?"

"I am not lying. Besides, it doesn't take trickery to get you to purr for me. I don't know why I've been so dead set against marriage, but now that I've thought about it, I think we could get along well."

She'd used the last of her control to subdue her voice. Nothing prevented her from brushing her fingertips against his groin. Sure enough, he was puffed up like a bullfrog. "I can tell what you're thinking with. Tomorrow a different part of your anatomy will be making your decisions."

"It's a safe bet I'll want you as badly tomorrow as I do now."

"How uncomfortable for you."

"I'm not going to change my mind. Marrying you is the only way I know to put myself out of my misery."

"Ooh! Why don't you pay some painted hussy to put you out of your misery?"

"Listen, you little—"

"Is something wrong?" Courtney's sleepy voice drifted from her room.

Emma quickly closed the door to her own bedchamber.

"No, honey. I got in a little late. Go back to sleep. I'll see you when you wake up."

There was a light tapping on the other side of Emma's door. She ignored it. Several moments of silence passed. The next thing she heard was Gideon's retreating footsteps. She bolted both the bedroom door and the one that led to the terrace before she returned to her mauled bed and cried herself to sleep.

Gideon pushed back his Stetson and squinted westward. A range of sharp-toothed granite mountains crouched above rolling hills forested with piñon, juniper and red cedar. The sinking sun ignited the jagged horizon with wide veins of crimson, gold and molten copper.

He dismounted Warrior. Despite his formidable name, the black quarter horse was an even-tempered gelding who ran hard and steady when pushed beyond his normal limits. Warrior possessed a giving heart and unflagging spirit—two essential attributes for a quarter horse, as well for as a man *or* woman.

His thoughts would have lingered on the woman who'd been torturing his mind and body the entire time they were apart, but five minutes ago he'd *re*resolved to eradicate Emma January Step from his mind. If a man wanted to stay alive in this untamed part of the country, he needed to keep focused on what he was doing. He drew in a gulp of cooling air. It felt good to finally overcome his fixation with Emma. A man could walk with his head high and his back straight when he took charge of his life.

He led his mount toward a clearing concealed by mountain mahogany and willows. A half-dozen horses were staked with trailing reins that scraped the ground. He hadn't gotten himself straightened out any too soon. After sharing tonight's watch, he would return home for a few days.

It was hard to believe that the all-consuming passion in his life had once been the creation of his freighting empire. After Jonathan and Cynthia's deaths, that passion had shifted. For the past four years, the burning force driving him had been the need to unearth the rock under which he would find the maggoty vermin who'd slain his brother and sister-in-law. Tonight, though, as he walked toward Jack Taggert's mine, a keen awareness of his surroundings mysteriously eased his craving for brutal justice.

The crisp air, the call of a chickadee and the tang of sage

being crushed beneath his boots brought a startling clarity to his thoughts. On a level of consciousness he'd never experienced before, he sensed the rhythmic beating of his heart and the life-sustaining blood pumping through his system. His heightened sensitivity alerted him to an emptiness somewhere in his chest.

A wily voice whispered that, if he abandoned his quest, the bleeding wound would close, and space for something rare and precious would expand within him. Mental images of Emma danced in his thoughts—as she'd been the night they met, dressed in drab clothing and dewed by the misting rain that preceded her arrival at his home. She'd reminded him of a flower, most plain, that had been left unprotected before the storm's full fury. Then there had been that mangy, rain-soaked hellhound, his scrawny body poised for the signal to go for Broadbent's throat.

It was after she soothed the beast, argued on Broadbent's behalf for a raise and revealed her anxiety about Courtney, while dispensing generous quantities of advice and brandy—*from his own liquor cabinet*—that the metamorphosis had occurred. Illuminated by a light within, the humble blossom had grown petals vibrant enough to out-dazzle a rainbow. He couldn't have been more captivated if an angel sprouted her heavenly wings in his presence.

Like restless fireflies, other images flashed, then dimmed. He remembered her outraged expression when he'd lowered her stocking and examined her injured foot. There was the time he'd found her up to her pretty elbows in soap bubbles as she and Courtney scrubbed Duncan.

Like tiny thorns protecting a baby rose, the innocent images he summoned dug deep into his serenity. Was he better off recalling earthier encounters? There was that brief glimpse he'd caught of her perfect breasts when she awakened from her nap. Whether it was ridiculous or not, he'd experienced a primal surge of possessiveness. He'd kissed her, offered her employment as his mistress and pretty much made an ass of himself.

The real insanity had occurred when he let his body talk

him into climbing to the second-story terrace during a rainstorm. That had been the ultimate lunacy.

Maybe he'd been sane when he came through the balcony doors. He couldn't remember. Prodded by a need that stunned him, he'd simply reached out and taken what he wanted. Emma had turned to molten wax in his arms. Her mouth had been hot and clinging, her hands as restless as his. When he touched her where no other man had ventured, he'd reveled in the knowledge that he was awakening her to shimmering heights she'd never scaled.

He closed his eyes. He'd tasted her, cherished her, to paradise.

He remembered the silky, golden hairs that skimmed her shins. A whore or society woman would be mortified for a man to view her limbs in their natural state. Emma's innocence protected her against such self-consciousness. The same fragile dusting of gold grazed her underarms and, more lushly, shielded the soft folds of her womanhood.

There had been a point when he thought he'd lost control. All he could think of was finishing what he'd started, the consequences be damned. Somehow, he'd scraped together the pieces of his honor and held back. He might not have taken her innocence with the stroke of his entry, but he'd tutored her trembling hands, showing her how to satisfy him.

He'd never lost control with a woman. He was a seasoned man of thirty-two and had no intention of allowing his appetites to rule him. He'd resuscitated a basic tenet he'd embraced decades earlier—one he'd never broken, until he crushed Emma against a soft mattress. Even when raw need clawed for deliverance, good women weren't for bedding and discarding.

No matter how he tried to deny it, he'd used her despicably.

She, dear, sweet Emma, had shared the sad tale of her childhood. His heart twisted at how unloved she'd been, and how brave. She might not know it, but she was still trying to be perfect. The painstaking outlines she'd made of Courtney's lesson plans showed an obsessive attention to minutiae.

He sensed she feared being lost in a world that had never

had a place for her. What had she said? "...I wasn't lost, was given away."

The simple words had made him want to put a fist throug[h] a wall. Something was terribly wrong when an innocent chil[d] was given away. He'd decided then and there to dig into he[r] past and exhume whatever records could be found about he[r] origins. If the news was grim, he would keep it to himsel[f]. She'd been hurt enough. Maybe, in some small way, tha[t] would repay for his trespass.

He'd been serious when he'd asked her to marry him. Tha[t] she doubted his sincerity had saved both their skins. A woma[n] like Emma needed the love of a God-fearing man, not some one with a rendezvous with revenge. But it wasn't reveng[e] that drove him. It was justice, and it was a burden he couldn'[t] put down until he carried it the full distance.

"How do you expect to keep an eye on Jack Taggert's dig[gings] when you're standing behind an eight-foot rock?"

Gideon drew his pistol and spun around with it cocked.

Jefferson Jones smiled broadly.

"Don't you know better than to sneak up on a man?"

The startling flash of Jefferson's white teeth contraste[d] against his dark clothing, his black skin and the thickenin[g] night. "I didn't sneak up on you. I walked over plain as day.[ ]

"You're lucky I didn't shoot you." Gideon reholstered hi[s] gun. "Where have you been?"

"Where have *I* been?" Jefferson tipped his head. "I coul[d] ask you the same question. How long have you been starin[g] at that rock anyway?"

"I wasn't staring at a damned rock."

"I reckon you could call it a boulder."

"Call it whatever you like. Why aren't you at your looko[ut] point?"

"I was headed there, feeling pretty good about standin[g] watch with a right smart fellow like you. I figured thing[s] would go without a hitch tonight, unless some thieving va[r-] mints are dumb enough to try and help themselves to Tag[-] gert's gold."

"I figured it the same way," Gideon said.

"Taggert and his cronies are tucked in his cabin, picking beans from their teeth and playing poker," Jefferson continued agreeably. "Al and George are in position to spot riders coming from the east and north. I'm set to do my part, and what do I find? Gideon Cade talking to an overgrown rock."

Despite his foul mood, Gideon's lips twitched. Jefferson's good humor was contagious. "I expect that's the story you'll spread."

Jefferson leaned closer and sniffed with exaggerated interest.

Gideon stiffened. "What the hell are you doing?"

"Just checking to see if you've been gargling whiskey."

Gideon scrubbed his palm over his face. He had no intention of admitting that a woman was behind his erratic behavior. Jefferson would be rolling around on the ground, convulsing in laughter.

"So what were you doing?"

"Thinking."

"Couldn't you have done that on the other side of that rock, so you would have a view of Taggert's cabin?"

"Speaking of which, we both better get our butts where they belong." Gideon pivoted and stepped forward, straight into the boulder.

Jefferson hooted.

"Hold it down, we're here to do a job."

"It's hard to keep my mind on business when you're acting so peculiar. If I didn't know better, I'd think some female had thrown a halter rope over you."

Gideon didn't like the sound of that. "You sound as if you've been doing a little tippling."

The grin flashed. "You're forgetting, I don't need liquor to cheer me up. I was born feeling good."

"Well, I was born avoiding entanglements with women."

"That's true," Jefferson agreed. "But I'm thinking things have changed."

"Nothing's changed," Gideon growled.

"I hear you've got a mighty pretty teacher living in your house."

Gideon's blood chilled. He'd always considered Jefferson Jones a likable acquaintance. The second he referred to Emma, though, Gideon wanted to plow his fist into his jaw. Control, Gideon reminded himself.

Control.

"My niece's instructor is a woman of exceptional character. It's my policy to respect my employee's privacy and keep their affairs confidential."

Immediately Gideon wanted to bite back the word *affairs.*

Jefferson chuckled again.

Gideon's hands fisted.

"I reckon what they say is true."

"And what do *they* say?" Gideon asked sharply.

"The man ain't been born who can't be lady-broke." Snickering, Jefferson disappeared into the night.

Gideon walked around the boulder and took up his guard position. Hunter, Burke and Nat, along with a couple dozen other men, were staked out at places across the valley. Usually, keeping watch was a boring way to occupy one's time, but they got lucky often enough to make the vigils worthwhile.

The memory of what he'd been thinking before Jefferson's arrival tried to sneak into Gideon's thoughts. He clenched his teeth. There was no way he would return to the masochistic hell of unfulfilled fantasies. That was one trap he wouldn't step into again.

The temptation to inflame his mind with images of Emma was harder to resist than ever. She'd become more than a habit. If he wasn't careful, she would grow into an addiction. He was better off remembering the times she'd aroused his anger. When nothing came to mind, he cursed his faulty memory. She'd done a dozen things to ignite his temper. Why couldn't he recall them?

Money... They'd gotten into a shouting match when she rejected the raise he wanted to give her. Considering the circumstances, she'd been right. She'd also been naked when she shoved him out her door. Emma naked. Now there was a memory to keep a man awake at night. And aroused.

Gideon groaned. He was letting her get to him again. His resolve hardened. He'd always prided himself on his self-discipline. Once his course was set, he did not deviate from it. He'd chosen his road. At times, the way was exhausting, but he thrived on challenges and wouldn't allow himself to be lured to another, easier path.

He reassured himself of the logic behind his actions. Emma was a part of his household because she was good for Courtney. He'd included her in his new will for the benefit of his niece. A woman of Emma's sound character could be trusted to protect Courtney's interests. How could he let base instinct override his niece's future welfare? That in settling Courtney's future he'd also secured Emma's was mere coincidence.

As long as he maintained a professional relationship with the teacher, he would be all right. No more fantasizing, or kissing or touching. He would keep his hands to himself. Both Emma and Courtney deserved to live in a home of solid moral character. Bricks and mortar didn't possess integrity. It was the people living in a house who imbued it with that attribute.

Suddenly everything became clear. All he had to do was keep his temper under control. He'd observed that anger jangled other, more visceral emotions. He would also benefit from maintaining a certain distance from her.

Feeling he'd regained his perspective, Gideon decided to make a sweep from this side of Taggert's place to the mine shaft located twenty yards away.

An explosion of gunfire roared through the silence. The barrage of bullets came from the north. That he would rather face flying bullets than deal with his feelings about Emma wasn't lost on Gideon as he tore off into the night toward George's position.

Chapter Fifteen

Several weeks after Gideon had swept into her bedchamber with the fury of a northern tempest, Emma entered the kitchen. The rich smells of brewed coffee, frying bacon and yeasty bread dough greeted her. Laced with those mouth-watering aromas were the subtler scents of cellar-ripened apples, vanilla sticks and freshly baked chocolate.

Emma savored the feeling of kinship she felt as she was hailed by kitchen servants performing their morning labors. It was foolish to be touched by something as mundane as having her name called out and being wished good morning, but the easy camaraderie affected her. Was the warm fullness centered in her chest similar to what a family member might experience?

Emma recalled her position. Despite Gideon's assurances, her presence here was temporary. Her true security lay in hoarding her income until she could invest in Jayne Stoneworthy's school or find another means to live independently. Until that goal was accomplished, she would forever be a transient participant in innumerable households. The only real sense of belonging she would ever know was unalterably linked to her ability to stand alone. If she was ever to have a secure place within society, she had to carve it for herself. In the end, she could depend only upon herself to accomplish this goal, for there was only herself to make her way in the world.

It was to her benefit to remember that, just as she now stood at the kitchen's perimeter of bustling servants, so did she live on the outer perimeter of this household—a passing member of a staff that would remain after she was gone. If anything, Gideon's actions in her bedchamber had made her situation more tenuous. Now that his passion had cooled, he probably regretted the momentary insanity they'd shared and regarded her as an unfit teacher for his niece. She wished she didn't agree with that assessment.

Mrs. Graves and Mrs. Foster stood huddled around the oak table.

"That's the most beautiful birthday cake I've ever seen. Those pink rosebuds look real enough to have been clipped from the garden."

Emma stepped forward and saw the cake under discussion. A cluster of plump pink roses cascaded across the ivory-colored frosting that covered the three-layer cake.

"You're right, Mrs. Foster." Emma resisted the temptation to stick her finger into the frosting bowl and help herself to the creamy mixture. "That's a magnificent cake. Whose birthday is it?"

The housekeeper sighed. "Mr. Broadbent's."

Mrs. Graves winked conspiratorially. "He doesn't know we've found out about it. He's running a dozen errands we've declared urgent."

"With him dashing about town," Mrs. Foster added, "we'll be able to finish our surprise without him finding out what we're up to."

Again Emma thought she detected a special warmth for the butler in Mrs. Foster's soft voice. The slender widow's bright blue eyes added a special charm to her somewhat ordinary features.

"Do you have candles to put on the cake?" Emma inquired.

"Unfortunately, no," Mrs. Foster replied. "And there was no way to ask Broadbent to purchase any. He'd have won-

dered why we needed such small ones. The man is much too
sharp to attempt to trick him.''

"That's true," Mrs. Graves agreed. "Not much gets past
him.''

"But the cake should have candles," Emma protested.

"And how are we going to buy them without the expense
being approved by our butler?" the cook demanded.

"We could spend our own money," Emma suggested.

"I'm certainly willing to contribute," Mrs. Foster said
quickly.

"As would most of the staff." Mrs. Graves finished frosting the cake with a flourish. "But there's still the matter of
those guards letting us out of the house. You know how they
are. Why, I reckon it would be easier to be pardoned from
prison than for one of us to take the carriage to town.''

Emma considered and discarded several solutions to their
dilemma. "Wexton's Mercantile is within walking distance.
If the guards were somehow distracted, I could slip out the
gate unnoticed.''

"Aye, the mercantile isn't that far," Mrs. Graves said reflectively. "You could be there and back in less than an
hour.''

"Oh, but when Broadbent finds out, he'll be greatly displeased," Mrs. Foster observed uneasily. "Mr. Cade informed us he expected the staff to follow Broadbent's instructions, and he specifically told us to get his personal
permission before leaving the premises.''

"What he don't know won't hurt him," the cook pointed
out pragmatically. "I agree with Miss Step. Our little party
tonight will be a lot more festive if we have candles for him
to blow out.''

From the housekeeper's uneasy expression, it was obvious
she was torn between obeying orders and doing something
special for him. "What kind of distraction were you thinking
of?''

Emma smiled. Fortunately, the widow Foster was more interested in doing something special for Broadbent than in ad-
hering to overly strict rules. As far as Emma was concerned,

the housekeeper's choice was the correct one. Just because a woman might be interested in a man, didn't mean she was obligated to comply with his every whim. In the long run, such servile behavior surely would prove damaging to his character. Over time, he would develop the mistaken notion that he needn't concern himself with the opinions of others. In short, he would become impossible.

Emma moved to the window above the sink and picked up a cloth. Rubbing industriously against the pane of glass, she cleared a circle. Covered from her throat to her feet in a flowing blue wool cape, Courtney danced on tiptoe as she tossed a red ball to Duncan. The dog leaped skyward and clamped his teeth around the reddish blur before it touched the back lawn. Amused guards stood in clusters, watching the animated play between the girl and the animal. Emma imagined she could hear the laughter that obviously bubbled from the girl's curved mouth.

"Our guards seem to have diverted themselves. With your help, I could be back from the mercantile before anyone discovers I've left."

Emma strolled to the table and picked up the bowl in which the frosting had been mixed. Scarcely aware of her actions, she employed the tip of her forefinger to maximum advantage and scooped up a generous glob of the creamy mixture. As she closed her lips around her finger, she surrendered the bowl to the housekeeper's outstretched hand. Mrs. Foster took a swipe of the rich frosting and passed the bowl to Mrs. Graves, who also took her turn scraping up a dab of the sugary concoction.

Again Emma reminded herself that she didn't have a permanent place among these women, but her heart wasn't in the self-admonition. What harm was there be in pretending she belonged among them? And that on Elijah's next birthday, and the ones to follow, she would be here for the celebrations?

Protect your heart.... The stern counsel came from a lifetime of small and large disappointments, yet she couldn't summon the determination to remain aloof from her fellow co-workers.

As the sweet taste of vanilla slid down her throat, she thought of Gideon. Her stomach clenched. She knew that, if he took her into his arms and kissed her again, she would be unable to deny either herself or him the sensual fulfillment of having him inside her.

Gideon dismounted Warrior. Nat Walker ambled toward him.

"So you finally decided to come home."

Gideon tipped back his hat and tried to ignore his aching butt muscles as he led his quarter horse to the stables. It had been a couple of years since he spent so much time in the saddle. "Everything quiet around here?"

"Naturally," Nat replied cockily. "With me overseeing things, nobody would dare cause trouble."

Despite his exhaustion, Gideon smiled. His eyes burned with sweat and too little sleep. He wanted a hot bath, one of Mrs. Graves's home-cooked feasts, a cheroot, a glass of brandy and a ten-hour stint in his bed.

Emma's face tried to gain a foothold in his thoughts, but in keeping with his vow to extinguish her from his mind, he ruthlessly shattered the beguiling image.

"Your easy days here are going to end for a couple of weeks. Hunter wants you back at the ranch."

Nat's features sobered. "More rustlers?"

"Not exactly," Gideon replied grimly. "Someone's taken up the sport of shooting the cattle in their tracks. They don't even make sure they're dead before riding off. Once they're convinced an animal is going to die, the bushwhackers are gone, leaving the cattle to suffer a slow, miserable death."

"Bastards."

"You got that right," Gideon said bitterly. "That they're willing to kill off the herd at no profit to themselves means someone's out to destroy Hunter and The Double H."

"You, Hunter and Burke have all been hit hard. Do you

think it's a coincidence the three of you happen to lead the Guardsmen?''

Gideon led Warrior into the barn. Substantially dimmed daylight sifted through the windows. The raw smell of freshly shoveled horse dung, loose hay and oiled harnesses and tack leather filled the air. Despite its pungent quality, Gideon preferred the earthy mixture of aromas to the stench of decaying fish he'd known working on the docks.

"It's hard not to notice we've been the targets of most of the trouble that's happened in the area. Things seem to be coming to a head, though." Gideon released Warrior's cinch and removed the saddle. "Last night we caught two men poking around Taggert's mine. At first they said they were looking for directions to another claim. After some hard questioning, one of them obliged us with details he left out of the first version of his story."

"What's his name?"

"Mitch Dundree." Gideon jerked off the saddle blanket and reached for a short-bristled brush. "You know him?"

"Name has a familiar ring." Nat rubbed his jaw. "I seem to remember Seth Bennett and someone named Dundree used to hit the saloons together."

"The same Bennett who worked for Hunter a year or so ago?"

The lines in Nat's sun-weathered face deepened. "Yeah, and I recall another hand who tagged along when they went town-prowling. Joe Randell."

The back of Gideon's neck tingled. "Joe still works for Hunter."

"He's never ridden on any Guardsmen business. Guess he hasn't earned the boss's trust."

"Considering how thing's are shaping up, I'd say Hunter's judgment is sound."

Nat's blue eyes narrowed. "Always did figure someone on the Double H had to be supplying information to the rustlers."

"Burke and Hunter need to know about this. Warrior's

beat.'' Gideon led the animal to a trough, carefully monitoring how much he drank. "I'll take the buckskin and—"

"Hell, Cade, you look as limp as a neck-wrung rooster."

"Thanks."

"It wasn't that many years ago you were a city dude trying to work your way up to tenderfoot."

"Only ten." Both Gideon and Burke had grown immune to the good-natured taunts from Westerners who, to hear them brag, had ridden before they learned to crawl. "But then, who's keeping track?"

"Don't be getting on your high horse. I still remember that first roundup you and Burke tagged along on. It's a miracle we're not still chasing those stampeding steers. Trust a city dude to yell to high heaven because his bathwater's a little nippy."

"I froze some damn important real estate in that river."

"So we all heard."

Gideon knew he'd never live down the fiasco of spooking a couple hundred head of cattle. "You and Jefferson Jones should spend more time together. You both share the same pitiful sense of humor."

"Ah, you know I'm kidding. You do okay for a stall-fed broomtail."

"Now that's something a man might like carved on his tombstone."

"When the time comes, I'll be sure to pass that on."

"You're all heart, Nat."

"Just to prove it, I'll drop by the bank and let Burke know about the connection between Dundree, Bennett and Randell. Then I'll ride out to The Double H and fill Hunter in on things."

"I can do it." Gideon's backside wasn't in the offer.

"Never doubted it, but I've got cabin fever, and a ride through town sounds mighty good."

"A ride through town that includes a bottle of that rotgut you call whiskey and a few minutes at Lusty LaSalle's—that's your standard cure for cabin fever, right?"

Nat stunned Gideon by flushing. "Naw, I don't mess around with that stuff anymore."

Gideon couldn't have been more shocked if the lanky cowboy announced he was sailing around the world. "Are you coming down with something?"

Nat scuffed the tip of his boot in the loose straw. "Maybe, but it ain't a physical ailment—exactly."

"Is this one of those times I'm supposed to follow the code of the West and mind my own business?"

The cowboy's features flushed redder. "I reckon you'll find out soon enough, so there's no point in hedging. That woman of yours is hell-bent on getting religion once a week, rain or shine. I don't recollect how it happened, but somehow I got dunked in the Setchee River by the preacher. Everyone said I was baptized—born again, they call it.

"So now I don't chew, spit, or scratch my privates when I got an itch, not in public, anyway. No more t'rantula juice or forn'cating for me, either. No sir, according to the preacher, it's the good book, good deeds and a good woman that keeps a man on the straight and narrow. I don't know how, but that woman of yours has poleaxed the bunch of us."

Even if this was just Nat's colorful way of speaking, one thing had to be made clear. "I don't have a woman. If you're referring to Miss Step, she's my niece's tutor, nothing else." It was a pleasure to make the correction and know he meant it. Miss Emma January Step had been relegated to her proper place, that of an unremarkable member of his staff. As he congratulated himself on his superior self-control, the last of Nat's words registered. "Are you saying some of the other men were dunked?"

"Baptized," he corrected glumly. "And it wasn't some, it was *all*. Every last one of us ended up in the Setchee."

Gideon tried to hide his smile. Instead of looking like someone heaven-bound, the cowboy's expression suggested he'd received his marching papers to a hotter, less exalted sphere. "When she discovers what's happened to her most loyal customers, LaSalle will probably declare a day of mourning."

"She's already done it. She hung black material over the door and at her winders, so did the 'Got Ya' and the 'Plucked Turkey.'"

"I'm sure you'll all be better off in the long run," Gideon said, wanting to offer hope to a man who'd clearly lost his moorings.

Nat pointed his raised forefinger at Gideon's chest. "You're laughing now, but I bet that changes right soon."

"I'm not laughing," he protested.

"Wait till that woman of yours works her female wiles on you."

"I told you she's not my woman." Gideon damned the sudden rise in temperature he experienced when he said the words *my woman.*

"Yeah, and skunk piss is for drinkin'." Still holding his stiffened finger like a loaded gun, Nat poked Gideon's shirt-front. "Don't let her get you in church, and you might escape the dunking. But there's no way you're going to escape that sweet-looking, sweet-talking, sweet-smelling female sashay-ing through your house all day long and sleeping in a nearby bed all night. No way a-tall. Before you know it, your spurs will be dragging across your tongue, and your hankerings will be harder than a horny toad's dried balls."

A barb of jealousy as sharp as the jagged wire strung across the Double H slashed Gideon. "Sounds as if you've been doing some looking and hankering of your own."

Wearing an amused grin, the cowboy shook his head. "Seems to me you're a mite more interested in that particular *employee* than the other folks you got working for you. To ease your mind, I don't poach another man's game. Besides, I've got my eye on a different filly. Too bad Lyman Thornton doesn't share my outlook."

Nat's joking barb grew jagged hooks. "What's Thornton got to do with Miss Step?"

"Since you've been gone, he's become a regular visitor. Dropping in for afternoon tea has become a habit."

Gideon forgot his aching muscles and his vow to brick Emma's image behind a carefully structured wall of indifference. Where had she gotten the misguided idea that she could entertain male admirers in his home? He'd hired her to tutor Courtney, not bat her eyelashes and swish her skirts for Thornton's benefit.

"Is he here now?"

"Naw, he usually honors us with his ugly puss around two o'clock."

"I'll take you up on your offer," Gideon said abruptly. "Let Burke and Hunter know how cozy Dundree, Bennett and Randell are. If Dundree's ready to exercise his jaw and tell us who's giving him orders, we might actually get back to living normal lives."

"Give me five minutes with him and I'll have him bellering like a bull calf in a briar patch."

"He'll have to be more articulate than that for the judge to hear his confession."

"As long as he has most of his teeth and a whole tongue, Judge Deeks will understand him clear enough."

"Save the questions for tonight, when Burke, Hunter and I show up. Between the four of us, we'll get to the bottom of things."

Nat headed toward his horse. "I could always sniff around and find out where Bennett and Randell are hanging their spurs."

Gideon turned to the house. "Don't attract any attention," he called over his shoulder. "We don't want to tip our hand."

"You can count on ol' Nat to handle things. I never let you down before, and I ain't fixing to now."

Gideon had ample confidence in Hunter's foreman. He didn't, however, have much confidence in his own ability to curb his irritation with Emma. He stalked to the front door and turned the knob. Nothing happened. It took a second to register that it was locked from the inside. Scowling, he grabbed the knocker and pounded loudly. His mood was such that he resented the ensuing wait. He didn't like admitting that, after his last ardent encounter with Emma, his brain had been so scrambled he forgot to take a key. Again.

Just as he was about to give up and head for the side entry, the door swung open.

"What in blazes took you so—" He broke off when he realized he was addressing his housekeeper instead of Broadbent. He quickly amended his greeting. "Good day, Mrs. Foster."

She executed a hasty curtsy. "Good day, sir."

"It appears we have you working double duty this afternoon."

She smiled nervously. He sighed. The last thing he wanted was to terrorize his reserved housekeeper. No, he planned on using his heavy guns on Emma, whom he anticipated terrorizing quite thoroughly.

"I don't mind, sir."

"I appreciate your attitude." Despite his beastly mood, he forced himself to smile. Looking alarmed, Mrs. Foster stepped back. Evidently, some of his displeasure leaked through his gritted teeth. "Where's Broadbent?"

"G-gone."

He frowned. "When do you expect him back?"

"I…um…I'm not sure."

"Did he tell you where he was going?"

She wiped her hands on her starched apron, then tucked them behind her back. "Which time?"

Gideon felt as if he'd stepped into the bizarre world Lewis Carroll wrote about more than a decade earlier, the one with the Cheshire cat. "How many times has Broadbent absented himself today?"

"Well, uh, there were those errands he had earlier."

"Am I to gather he finished them and returned?" Where was Emma? She who deserved the brunt of his foul mood, not poor Mrs. Foster.

"Uh, yes, he did come back."

There was a long moment of strained silence. Gideon swallowed an oath. What had happened to his normally competent housekeeper? Why was she acting as if she expected him to bite her?

"And?" he prompted, digging for more patience.

"And what?" she asked around an audible gulp.

Gideon struggled for patience. "And didn't he tell you where he was going and when he would return?"

"Well...I guess he did."

The last thing Gideon expected to feel upon returning home was the overwhelming urge to dismiss the benign Mrs. Foster.

"Madam, are you being deliberately obtuse?"

She licked her lips. "I suppose I am."

Her painfully honest response took him by surprise. "Why?"

"Be-because when I answer your question, I know you're going to be..." Her words trailed off.

Gideon realized his housekeeper was genuinely afraid, and assumed what he hoped was a tranquil expression. "What am I going to be?"

"Angry," she whispered. "Very angry."

"At you?"

She nodded jerkily. "And Mrs. Graves."

"What exactly have you and the cook been up to?" The edge of his impatience ebbed as he visualized the women sneaking into his library and helping themselves to his imported brandy.

"Well, we...uh...helped Miss Step slip away so she could walk to the mercantile."

The urge to smile died an immediate death. "You did *what?*"

Mrs. Foster promptly raised her apron and buried her face in it. "Oh, I know we shouldn't have, but it seemed like such a little thing. Then Broadbent came back and he...he *yelled* at us!"

What with the sobbing and the apron muffling the rush of words, it was difficult to decipher their meaning.

"Compose yourself, Mrs. Foster."

She raised her tear-stained face. "Broadbent called us stu-stu-stupid *females!*"

The overwrought woman looked as if she were about to give way to another bout of weeping. Unfortunately, he didn't have the time to see her through it. "When did Miss Step leave for the mercantile?"

The housekeeper sniffed. "It's been hours."

"How many?"

"Four."

"And you say she walked there?"

"Yes."

"Alone?"

"Y-yes."

"I left specific instructions that no one was to leave the residence without Broadbent's permission, did I not?"

She nodded miserably. "We were fixing a surprise for him, though, and if we told him about it, the surprise would be ruined."

Gideon closed his eyes. *Women.* Sometimes they acted so sensibly a man was lulled into believing they were capable of rational thought. "How long has Broadbent been gone?"

She hiccuped. "An hour."

"Did he take any of the men with him to help find Miss Step?"

Her trembling hands visited the apron's pockets. A crumpled handkerchief emerged. She blew vigorously. "He went by himself."

Which explained why Nat hadn't known about Emma's disappearance. "Mrs. Foster, I want you to listen very carefully."

She shoved the hankie back into her pocket. "All right."

"If Miss Step comes back before Broadbent or myself, she's to remain here. Under *no* circumstances is she to leave. Do you understand?"

"Y-yes."

"Good. See that *she* does, also. Inform Broadbent that I've taken four guards. We'll search the city on horseback. Courtney is to remain indoors for the rest of the day. Can I count on you to do as I've asked?"

"Yes, sir."

He looked at the woman's reddened eyes. There had been a time when he would have trusted her implicitly to follow his orders. He headed outside. There had been a time when his household and staff had performed with well-synchronized efficiency. *B.E.* was how he thought of it. Before Emma.

He strode through the kitchen. Duncan—who was supposed to remain outdoors—was gnawing contentedly on a tightly wound ball fashioned from red braiding.

"It's nice to know someone's happy," Gideon muttered.

The hound raised his head. Two streams of drool dripped from his jowls. *Don't take your bad mood out on me. I've had my share of hard luck, and you don't hear me complaining.* Duncan didn't express his canine philosophy aloud, but his unblinking eyes transmitted the message clearly enough.

"If you knew how stupid you looked with that pink bow on your head, you'd be howling your head off. These women have turned you into a lapdog. If you had any pride, you'd get away before they start dressing you in ruffles."

Duncan licked his chops and reclamped his jaws around the ball. Clearly, the animal was bored with the one-sided conversation.

"She's reduced me to talking to a no-account mutt."

Gideon stomped outside. The door slamming behind him didn't begin to release a portion of the anger that churned within him. When he got his hands on Emma January Step, he was going to exact his pound of flesh from her for putting him through this hell of uncertainty.

He was in the barn, wrapping his fingers around the pommel, when reality struck. Emma had escaped the brick wall of indifference behind which he had tried to imprison her. The hot blood pumping like newly released lava through his veins testified to that.

If he put his hands on her to throttle her, could he trust himself not to cave in like a badly dug mine shaft and finish what he'd started in her bedchamber?

Damn. Damn. Damn.

He finished saddling the buckskin and headed toward the

mercantile. Between now and when he laid eyes on Emma, he had a lot of mental bricks to reset in new mortar. Too bad he couldn't utilize some of the ones the workmen had left lying around. They had to be made of sturdier material than he'd been using.

Chapter Sixteen

Emma turned her face to the sun. It was a beautiful summer day. After being cooped up in what she'd come to view as Cade's Fortress, a wonderful sense of freedom lightened her step. The soles of her walking shoes clattered indecorously against the boardwalk. She was making the sound on purpose, letting the world know she'd escaped for a couple of hours of blissful independence. If she had had a drum, she would have banged it.

Her morning errand hadn't been accomplished as quickly as she anticipated. Maybe that was why she was in such good spirits. While at the mercantile, she'd run into Jayne Stoneworthy.

Jayne had been euphoric at the news that her uncle was mailing her a bank draft for a large sum of money. She'd only recently learned her parents had loaned him the funds years earlier. Now, when she desperately needed money, the incredible windfall was hers. The bank draft would make it possible to open her school more quickly than planned, and she would have enough capital to keep it running for almost two years *without* depending on a large number of students the minute her doors opened.

In the brief interim before the draft arrived, Emma had insisted on loaning her friend sufficient money to pay her creditors. They had celebrated Jayne's good fortune with a leisurely lunch in a hotel dining room. Emma had returned to Wexton's and bought the candles. She'd strolled the aisles of the mercantile until she found the perfect gift for Broadbent.

She smiled at the strange turn her day had taken. She'd begun the morning determined to hoard her savings, making no expenditures whatsoever, so she could have the financial security for which she longed. Scarcely half a day had passed, and those good intentions had flown out the window.

Being outside had probably addled her senses. But, after she talked to Jayne, a new spirit of optimism had soared within Emma. Things weren't all that bleak between herself and Gideon. She'd let their horrible parting make her forget the magical passion that had proceeded it. Even as her stomach quivered, she knew there had been more than just lust on Gideon's part. If he'd only been driven by physical urges, he wouldn't have denied himself the satisfaction of coupling with her.

He must care for her...just a little. She'd discounted the possibility of marriage between them. Frankly, she'd always doubted any man would want her for a wife. If her own parents hadn't loved her enough to keep her, it stood to reason there was something wrong with her. Whatever this inner blemish was, it rendered her unfit to be...loved.

Yet, in his own possessive way, Gideon *had* loved her. With his body. Her skin grew hot. He'd practically worshiped her. And when his solemn eyes glittered with dangerous intent as he pressed his mouth to that most intimate part of her, she'd surrendered more than her flesh. She'd surrendered her soul. And her heart.

How cowardly she'd lived her life. Until now, she'd taken only two significant risks. One had resulted in her becoming Gideon's employee. The other had landed Gideon Cade in her bed. Considering those earth-shattering outcomes, logic dictated that she hoard her victories and return to her conservative ways. Yet she'd done the opposite. Within the past hour, she'd loosened the purse strings of her nest egg to help Jayne and bought a gift for Elijah.

Her organized plans for the future no longer seemed unalterable. Confused by the unsettling currents that buffeted her, Emma felt as if she'd thrown her fate to the wind. The sun, the people strolling along the boardwalk and the passing carriages seemed to whisper that life itself was an unpredictable venture. Perhaps its most worthwhile rewards went to the brave. If that was so, it was past time to start taking risks—with life, with Gideon.

"Whoa!"

The whoop exploded like a gunshot from the street. Emma's heart clanged against her ribs. A flurry of movement erupted beside her. She spun around and raised the lumpy parcel she carried to her chest. A huge buckskin horse strained against tautly held reigns, rearing up on its hindquarters and pawing the air. Its back hooves dug sharply into the dirt road.

Emma stepped back, shielding her eyes against the bright sunlight that framed the unfolding drama. The rider, a dark, bearded blur, was covered in trail dust. With a smooth economy of motion, he quickly brought his high-spirited mount under control. Before she could offer a sigh of relief, the man charged straight at her.

For a panicked moment, she froze. Then her brain incited action. She jumped to the side. The animal's hooves thundered onto the boardwalk. The rider leaned toward her. Her scream was cut off in midcry. A powerful arm cinched her waist, jerking both her and her clutched parcel off the ground. After arcing upward for an airborne second, she found herself unceremoniously plunked sideways across her assailant's saddle.

Let me go! When she had sufficient breath, she intended to issue the command aloud.

"Hold still. You're going to end up in the dirt."

Emma struggled to free herself. It was broad daylight on a residential street. Surely someone would come to her rescue.

"Let me go!" At last she had enough air to demand her release.

The madman's grip tightened. She felt the air being squeezed from her and was forced to choose between fainting and holding still.

"Emma, you're making a spectacle of us. Sit sideways on my lap. There's enough room on the saddle for both of us."

Gideon Cade's harsh voice settled over her like a cloud of swarming wasps. Stunned by his near-violent assault, she tipped her face toward him. Her twisted bonnet allowed a glimpse of one glaring eyeball, a slice of his thinned lips and a small portion of his black, stubbled jaw. A chill pinched her heart. Fragmented though her view was, she could find nothing in Gideon's hard-edged face to remind her of the passionately tender man who'd bound her to him in the most primitive way imaginable.

"Gideon, what on earth has come over you?"

His broad hand shoved her head toward his chest. "I'm the one who'll be asking the questions, Miss Step."

With that snarly answer, he urged the horse forward. Emma's cheek was plastered against his hot, damp shirtfront. A strong blend of masculine scents swirled around her. His right arm was wrapped around her waist, and his right hand gripped the reins. His other leathered palm slid beneath her skirts and rested like a smoldering ember on the flimsy material that covered her thigh.

No one observing them from the street could see where the roaming hand had wandered, but she was fiercely conscious of its clandestine presence scant inches from... She trembled, especially in the moist place that had already experienced his scintillating trespass.

The sound of his heartbeat reverberated in her ear. Inexorably she relaxed against him. She had no idea what had transformed him into a raging dragon. Whatever had wakened the beast within Gideon Cade wasn't mere anger. With her bottom snugly fitted to his groin, she knew other powerful forces seethed within him.

Neither spoke as they rode the short distance home. Outside the gate, Gideon eased her from his lap. She felt his powerfully bunched shoulder against her back as his strong arm looped around her waist and lowered her to the ground. The soles of her shoes barely touched the dirt before he stood beside her.

"Are you ready to tell me what that was all about?"

"That's your trouble, Emma. You don't listen. I told you, I'm asking the questions."

"But—"

"Emma!" He snapped her name with the stinging impact of a curse. "Go to the library and wait for me."

"I refuse to obey the orders of a deranged man."

He stepped forward. She meant to hold her ground, but her lily-livered feet inched backward.

"If I'm deranged, you can take full credit for it." He ground the words out through lips that looked narrow and mean. "The next thing I want to see is your backside in motion as you march into the house."

Or else?

She eyed his slashed eyebrows, saw the muscle flexing along his implacable jawline and the restless sparks flashing in his fierce gaze. And even though she willed her tongue to speak up, it cowered behind trembling lips.

"No detours," he continued brusquely. "No stopping along the way and exchanging pleasantries with anyone you chance to meet."

He gripped her shoulders and turned her toward the house. "Practice being humble, Emma." The suggestion reached her ear on a hot whisper. "Have a hankie ready. Tears might soften me up."

He gave her a firm nudge.

She looked over her shoulder. "You don't scare me, Gideon Cade."

"Then you're not as bright as I thought."

Another nudge sent her walking. "I'll bring a hankie, all right," she muttered, loud enough for him to hear. "So I can lend it to you."

She didn't look to see if that last bit of bravado had an impact on his beastly temper. She had no idea what had set him off. One minute he was a fire-breathing lover with devilish hands that could induce an angel to abandon her wings. The next instant—or, in this case, several weeks later—he could turn so nasty, mulish and contrary as to tempt a saint to snatch up a plank of wood and whack it over his thick skull.

On the way to the library, she spied a half-dozen somber faces peeking through doorways and around corners. A few wore pasty smiles she supposed were meant to bolster her courage. They had exactly the opposite effect.

When she entered the study, its tomblike silence amplified her internal disquiet. Gideon's unexplained anger set a like tempest brewing within her. How dare he vent his fury—on a public street, and at home where her fellow servants could overhear his rantings! He *was* a lunatic.

Evidently, she wasn't to have long to stew over his impossible behavior. Scarcely had she accustomed herself to the quiet study before Gideon stalked into the chamber, carrying a chip the size of Gibraltar on his shoulder.

The last time he swept into a room with such force, it had been her bedchamber. This afternoon he didn't look remotely interested in a kiss, or anything else of a romantic nature.

Without speaking, he slammed the door behind him and glared at her from his imposing height. His large hands rested upon his lean hips. He put her in mind of a painting she'd once seen of a helmeted warlord with a castle to storm. Gideon's pummeled Western hat might not be made from metal, but his forbidding expression could easily have been cast from iron.

"I suppose the terms of your last will and testament apply only in the event of your death." It felt good to stand up to him, even though the wobbly squeak that laced her observation grated on her nerves.

"You thinking of sending me to my Maker, Emma?"

"In your present state, he wouldn't have you."

Gideon closed his eyes and drew a deep breath that expanded the black material of his shirt. A moment later, when his eyelids raised, it was obvious that he'd regained a measure of control. At least she wasn't staring into twin lava pools. Now it was merely a minor conflagration that blazed at her from his hostile gaze. He yanked his hat from his head and hurled it to a chair.

"What I had in mind," she explained, "was one of those legal documents I've heard about that would permit me to declare you a public menace and have you sent to a mental asylum. And perhaps, if the climate were mild enough, a moat with man-eating alligators could be provided."

"You don't have any idea how angry I am, do you?"

She rolled her eyes. "I'm not stupid."

"Glad to hear it."

Where his hat had protected his forehead, the trail dust ended in a straight line above his eyebrows, leaving a foolishly endearing strip of clean skin. She steeled herself against the absurd urge to press a warm, damp cloth to his face. The scoundrel didn't deserve a dollop of coddling.

"Just because you're upset about something doesn't give you the right to gallop down a street and terrorize an unsuspecting woman."

He arched an eyebrow. "You have a knack for understatement, Emma, but if you're feeling terrorized, we're on the right track."

She threw up her hands in frustration. "As long as you're speaking English, why not make sense?"

"You were present when I told the staff no one was to leave this house without notifying and securing permission from Broadbent."

"Is that what this is all about? You're up in arms because one of your employees had the temerity to disobey one of your niggling little orders? That some insignificant worm of a servant *dared* to defy the great and all-powerful Gideon Cade?" She began to pace. "I can't believe it! You almost ran me down and made mincemeat of me with that brute of a horse you were riding, hauling me onto the crazed beast's back. The scene you created was—"

"Emma."

Softly uttered, but delivered with awesome portent, her name stopped her in midtirade. Her mindless steps had placed a padded chair between them. She was grateful for its protection.

"Yes, Gideon?"

His left eye twitched. "If there's any ranting to be done, I'll do it."

"I don't care for your manner. You're entirely too overbearing and pugnacious."

"You'll have to excuse my lack of patience. I used the last of it dealing with Mrs. Foster. You'll have to make do with what's left."

For the first time, Emma looked beyond his belligerent mood and saw the new lines of fatigue that marked his face. His cheeks were more sharply carved than the last time she'd seen him. How long could he keep up the grueling pace he'd set for himself? To become upset over such a minor infraction showed he'd reached the end of his reserve. She knew how cranky she became when she missed even one night's rest.

In a gesture meant to pacify, she smiled. "We both seem remarkably adept at expressing our displeasure."

His features remained stubbornly set.

"Perhaps, we should take turns venting our anger," she ventured gently. How difficult could it be to cajole him from his foul mood? After all, her actions hadn't warranted this magnitude of censure.

"Don't even attempt to cajole me, Emma."

She took offense at being read as easily as a first-year primer.

"I wouldn't dream of it."

"We're not leaving this room until you understand when I issue an order I damn well expect to be obeyed."

"I knew *that* the moment I laid eyes on you," she assured him with forced cheerfulness. She was going to either humor him from his black temper or bash him over his head with a lamp. She'd leave the choice to him. "As I surmise it, the problem is that you issue too many commands. I suggest you employ a more selective approach. Naturally, you must take every precaution to protect Courtney. And I agree that it's a good idea to have members of your staff check with Broadbent before leaving the premises. A well-run house must be a house of order, after all."

Gideon couldn't believe it. Emma was *lecturing* him. That

she could dismiss her reckless behavior and attempt to instruct him on how to run his own home showed she needed to be taken in hand.

Two things kept him from attempting to shake some sense into her. The first was that she looked so damned cute standing in his library with her green bonnet askew and a smudge of dust on her cheek that he found it next to impossible to keep his train of thought.

The second restraint was the memory of what happened whenever physical contact occurred between them. He might not have spent his life in the West, but Gideon knew no man had been designed to sit in a saddle while battling a horse, a woman and an erection.

"I told you once I don't like being lectured," he reminded her, striving to keep his voice gruff. "I'm also not interested in hearing your views on the finer points of running my household. The only pertinent matter that needs clearing up is why you deliberately disobeyed me and left the premises unescorted."

"I had an errand."

He rubbed his palm over his eyes before speaking. "Now wouldn't be a good time to bait me, Emma."

"Today is Elijah's birthday," she explained, her tone unexpectedly conciliatory.

"Who the devil is Elijah?" Gideon demanded, remembering abruptly what Nat had said about Lyman Thornton hanging about. Just how many men did Emma have on the string?

Her eyebrows rose in surprise. "Broadbent, of course."

It had been so long since he heard his butler's name, Gideon had almost forgotten it. "Put me out of my misery and tell me how this is connected to you sneaking out of the house."

"Do you have a headache?"

"My head is fine, or it was until I ran into Mrs. Foster."

Emma's earlier vexation seemed to have mellowed. Damn, he wished he knew what had caused the change. The knowledge could come in handy when taming viragoes.

"You seem tired. Perhaps we should continue this discussion after you've had an opportunity to eat and rest."

So that was it. Emma's softened manner was based on pity. It didn't say much for his manhood, but he liked her softness any way he could get it. He experienced a reluctant kinship with Duncan. A woman's gentle handling made being domesticated almost appealing.

"We're not having a *discussion*. I'm giving you a dressing-down."

He tried to put some steam in the statement, but his unfortunate choice of words spoiled the effect.

Emma flushed. "I thought you'd already done that."

Evidently, she, too, was having difficulty expressing herself coherently. The pink blush tingeing her cheeks bloomed bright red.

"I mean," she continued, obviously disconcerted, "just now, not a few weeks ago when you…"

Her eyes silently begged for rescue. Who was going to rescue him?

"Let's get back to the subject at hand," he suggested. "What does Broadbent's birthday have to do with anything?"

"Everything," Emma replied, obviously as relieved as he was to drop the subject of what had transpired between them in her bedchamber. "Mrs. Graves baked a splendid cake. To make the occasion more festive, I suggested candles. Unfortunately, there were none available, so I offered to dash off to the mercantile."

"You didn't want to tell Broadbent about the candles because he would have found out about the cake?" Gideon hazarded.

Emma nodded. "So you see, I had no choice. It wouldn't have been much of a party without the candles. And as I'm here in your library safe and sound, I think it's best we forget the unfortunate incident."

"Do you?"

She set the bulky, string-tied paper bundle on his desk and stepped toward him. "You really look worn-out, Gideon. Perhaps you should have a nap before you eat."

Perhaps I should have you... "It's not going to be that easy."

"What isn't?"

"Getting off the hook." He closed the distance between them and, even as he damned himself for his stupidity, he took her small, competent hands into his. He remembered her woman's touch when she'd shyly wrapped her fingers around him. "As Courtney's potential guardian, you had no right to take the risk you did."

The reprimand was little more than a croak. Emma's face lifted. He told his body to behave itself.

"But, it really was a small thing, Gideon. No harm was done."

"*Great* harm was done," he corrected. "I want your promise you'll never disregard one of my orders again."

Despite his mental command, the blood in his veins rendezvoused at a predictable location.

She licked her lips. His skin tightened against his tensed muscles.

"I promise I'll never leave the house without informing Elijah," she amended quietly.

That wasn't good enough, was it? He'd brought her into the library to put the fear of Judgment Day into her, not let her off with some namby-pamby warning.

"You're not taking the threats against me seriously enough."

"On the contrary, I regard the threats against you and Courtney as extremely serious. But truly, Gideon, if you weren't so exhausted, you would realize no one is interested in me."

I'm interested.... "You're not a little girl to be spanked or sent to bed without any dinner for being rebellious, but it's obvious you don't understand the vicious nature of the animals we're up against."

He still held her hands gripped in his. Why couldn't he let them go?

"I understand you're carrying too many burdens for one man to bear. Would it hurt if you set them aside for a while?

Let me order a bath for you. While you're freshening up, I'll have Mrs. Graves prepare a tray. After that, you can get the sleep you've obviously denied yourself."

I'd rather peel that green-and-white striped dress off you and take you right here on the library floor. He had to do something, say something, to break the thickening spell of desire that was making a hash of his thoughts.

What had happened to that brick wall he'd spent the past three weeks working on?

"Is that the advice you give Lyman Thornton when he comes to visit? Do you offer to ease his burdens?"

Her hands struggled like captured birds to regain their freedom. He released them.

"I consider Lyman your acquaintance, not mine. I've only been cordial to him because I didn't see the benefit of adding another enemy to the long list you've managed to compile."

"You expect me to believe that cozying up to one of the richest men in Denver has been on my behalf?"

"For a reason I find incomprehensible to understand now, I was looking after your interests."

"By calling him by his first name?"

"Gideon, you're becoming overwrought. Perhaps you ought to sit down. I'll pour you a glass of sherry."

The tick he'd developed in his left eye returned. It infuriated him that the angrier he was, the more serene she seemed to become.

"I am not *overwrought*, and for your information, I *despise* sherry."

"Calm yourself," she said soothingly. She had the effrontery to take him by the arm and guide him to a chair. "The first night we met, I recall you required spirits to settle your nerves."

"Emma, you're not listening."

She headed off in the direction of his liquor cabinet. "Of course I am, Gideon."

"I will not have you shirking your duties as Courtney's tutor and entertaining male admirers in my house!"

She spun around and faced him. Finally, he'd gotten her attention.

"I would never shirk my duties where your niece is concerned."

"What do you call gallivanting all over town while you're supposed to be conducting her studies? What do you call serving private teas to that damned nuisance Thornton? A conscientious discharge of your responsibilities?"

Her face was pale. Tears misted her beautiful gray eyes. Too late, he remembered her lost family and the stock she put in being found worthy.

"I've spent hours pouring over Courtney's lesson plans. There's a stack of them on your desk to read, when you get around to it. Never for a moment have I forgotten she's the reason I'm here." Her words were choppy, on the verge of tearful.

"Emma—"

"I work very...hard..."

Her throat worked but she didn't continue. Instead, she fled the room and left him to his own miserable company.

He hadn't meant to make her cry. Yet he didn't go after her. The weeks they'd spent apart hadn't been long enough. They both were still raw from what had happened in her bedchamber. No matter how he tried, he couldn't regret that night.

He would give her a couple of hours to harden her heart against him. He'd use the time to shore up his own defenses.

Heaven help him, he didn't want her to succeed, not when he doubted his own resolve.

Heaven help them both.

Chapter Seventeen

Later that afternoon, Emma headed for the stairs. A quick glimpse into the mirror before she left her bedchamber had revealed red and swollen eyes that still burned from the useless tears she'd shed.

No one had disturbed her since she fled Gideon's wretched company several hours ago. She supposed Courtney and the servants were being considerate of her bruised feelings. Emma's isolation made her feel as if she were suffering from a communicable illness that others feared contracting. Her only illness, however, was a teary susceptibility to Gideon Cade's criticism. Once she cured herself of that she would be back to normal.

Emma entered the library and shut the door behind her. It would take only a moment to retrieve the parcel she'd left behind in her haste to escape Gideon. The aromatic scent of tobacco proved an unwelcome discovery. Emma scanned the chamber again, assuming Gideon must be present. She braced herself for a disdainful greeting.

"Miss Step!"

The startled yelp came from the direction of the east windows, one of which was raised. Obscured from immediate view, Courtney stood beside the pulled draperies. The green dress she wore blended in with the velvet folds. Guilty surprise flashed across her features. She held one of her uncle's cheroots. A lit one.

"Courtney, what—"

The library door opened. Emma's spirits plummeted. A perfectly horrible day was about to become even worse.

Garbed in a black suit, clean-shaven and looking as if he were ready to take on the world, Gideon Cade strode into his study.

"Emma. Good. You've decided to be sensible. We need to clear up this misunderstanding. First of all, please accept—"

Emma watched Gideon's razor-sharp gaze swing toward the windows, where some subtle gesture from his niece must have alerted him to her presence there.

He looked at the girl, then stared at the cheroot. "Courtney?"

Emma sat down. Instead of the chair's cross-stitched cushion, however, her bottom connected with an uncomfortable lump. The sound of crackling paper informed her that she'd sat on her forgotten parcel.

"Uh, Uncle Cade, I thought... That is, I..." Little puffs of smoke escaped the girl's parted lips and nostrils.

He inclined his head. "Yes?"

"Well, what I mean to say is—" A spasm of coughs interrupted her. "This isn't what it looks like."

"I'm relieved to hear that."

The girl rushed forward and placed the narrow cigar in the heavy crystal dish on her uncle's desk. She put her hands behind her back and smiled wanly.

The smile was not returned. "Go ahead, Courtney. I'm waiting for your explanation."

Emma's heart went out to her student. Answering to Gideon Cade was a bit like pleading one's case before an ill-natured dragon. No matter how one fared, one was bound to come away singed.

"I came into the library to fetch a book, and happened to see the cheroot you'd left unattended."

"Did you?"

Emma's gaze swung between the girl and the man.

"I remember thinking how…dangerous it was, so I decided to put it out. Before something caught fire."

"How did you plan to extinguish it?"

"Umm…the usual way."

"By smoking it?"

The girl flushed. "Well, I was a bit curious about what it would feel like to…uh…puff on it."

"And what did you discover?"

Courtney made a face. "It smells better than it tastes."

Gideon shifted his attention to Emma. The luxury of being an innocent spectator disappeared. "Am I to assume you saw nothing wrong with my niece's experiment, Miss Step?"

"But Uncle Gideon, Miss Step barely entered the library before you did," Courtney said, hastening to Emma's defense. "The minute you finish lecturing me upon the evils of smoking, she'll start one of her own."

"There's been enough lecturing today. I doubt, however, there's been sufficient time devoted to studying. I'm sure Miss Step has an assignment to occupy you for the next hour. Please attend to it."

The girl bowed her head. "Yes, sir."

When her student left the room, Emma intended to be right behind her. Rising quickly, she reached for the wrapped package that had cushioned her bottom for the past few minutes.

"Not so fast, Emma."

Drat, couldn't anything go as she planned? "Was there something further you wished to discuss with me?"

"I'm sorry I made you cry."

He would say something to threaten the protective layer she'd wrapped around her heart.

"You should be sorry." She would not give way to another bout of tears. "I take my teaching responsibilities very seriously."

"I know."

Emma brushed the back of her hand against her eyes. "I suppose you think I'm responsible for Courtney taking up smoking."

"No."

"Well, I'm not." To emphasize the point, she continued. "I'm not sure I approve of grown men indulging in pipes, cigars or cheroots."

"Emma…"

"The only reason she probably picked up the smelly old thing was because she was bored. You have no idea what it's like to be confined inside this house day after day."

"I suppose I don't."

"You're gallivanting about the area, dressed like a gunslinger, riding rude horses and having nasty editorials printed about you."

"I have been gone a lot."

"Making sure no one waylays your freight wagons or robs one of your rail cars. The gold has to get through, no matter what."

"I'm paid good money to make sure that happens."

"And in the meantime, Courtney is growing up in a household of servants and bodyguards."

"She has you."

"But I'm not family. You're her only living relative. She needs to know you, to feel as if she belongs to someone."

"Are we talking about my niece's feelings or yours?"

Emma felt the blood drain from her face. "I'm discussing Courtney's welfare, of course."

"Of course."

The gentleness of his reply grated. Nor did she take kindly to the knowing look in his eyes. Gideon had proved himself to be a brute where she was concerned. It was too late to mend his ways.

"So what are you going to do about it?" she demanded.

He stared at her coolly. "At present, nothing."

"You mean things are going to continue as they have been?"

"Not exactly."

Was she finally getting through to him? "What's going to change?"

"For one thing, I intend to hire more competent body-guards."

"Good grief, you'll have to hire a new cook to help Mrs. Graves feed them all."

"Not after I fire the ones I already have."

Emma gasped. "You can't do that."

"I assure you I can."

"You mean let go of Harv, Lefty, Rube—"

"You don't need to run through the list. I know their names."

"Even you couldn't be cruel enough to fire such loyal and hardworking men." And to think, moments before she'd attributed him with a smidgen of human compassion.

"If they can't perform the job I hired them to do, they're gone."

"Now you sound like Lyman Thornton."

Gideon's expression clouded. "Your not-so-secret admirer and I share no common traits."

"You're firing those men because of me, aren't you?"

"They failed—"

"Please don't. I couldn't bear to have that on my conscience."

"Emma, you don't even know them," he said, in clear exasperation.

"That's not true."

"Don't tell me—along with the Mad Hatter, you've been inviting them to your tea parties, too."

"Of course not. You know as well as I do they prefer coffee."

"Try whiskey."

"That was in the past."

"Oh, yeah, before they got religion."

"Don't you dare make fun of them. I've found that, despite their somewhat gruff exteriors, they're rather…sweet."

"Sweet?" Gideon repeated, his tone openly skeptical.

"Now that we've gotten to know each other, they've overcome their initial shyness."

"They've never been called shy before."

"I think they were at first, but all that's changed."

"Has it?"

Gideon's habit of asking terse questions had never been one of his more appealing traits, but Emma forged on anyway. "Lem showed Courtney and me the most amazing tricks with his lariat. Harv is going to teach us how to rope fence posts, though with that monstrous brick wall under construction, we'll have to hurry. Rube and Nat are going to talk to you about Courtney and me learning how to ride. And Eb's been telling the most exciting stories about cattle roundups."

If anything, Gideon's features became more hostile. "What kind of roundup stories has ol' Eb been sharing?"

"The usual kind, I'm sure."

"About greenhorns starting cattle stampedes?"

Despite Gideon's gloomy expression, Emma smiled. "There were a couple of those."

"Were names named?"

"Honestly, I think you're missing the point."

"No, you've missed the point, by turning a bunch of the meanest, toughest hombres this side of the Missouri into a hymn-singing choir of nursemaids. I'm surprised they don't have pink bows pinned to their hats."

She crossed her arms. "You simply can't fire them."

"Why not? You've ruined them for the work they were hired to do."

"I won't have it."

Gideon's gaze sharpened. "I beg your pardon."

"Oh, don't get that commanding-general-about-to-order-a-firing-squad look. I know I can't make you do the right thing."

"Then the matter is settled."

"But once you've had an opportunity to reflect upon the issue," she continued determinedly, "I know you'll make the correct decision."

"And according to you, that's retaining the services of a dozen inept gunmen?"

"You know they're not inept."

Gideon shoved a hand through his hair. "The only way those men will stay is if you agree to do exactly as I say."

Even though she knew he didn't mean anything of a personal nature, Emma's stomach flipped over. What would it feel like to have Gideon order her to kiss him...to take off her clothes...to open her body to him as she'd done the night of fantasy they shared?

"I promise to do exactly as you say," she breathed.

He nodded in satisfaction. "I'm going to hold you to that, Emma."

"All right." The tips of her breasts tingled. "I've been thinking..."

"I'm sure you have."

"About our men," she elaborated.

"*Our* men?"

She nodded. "They work very long hours—from sunup to sundown."

"That's the way it is."

"I've been wondering if they might be due for a raise in salary."

"Five minutes ago I planned on firing the lot. Now's not a good time to try and negotiate so much as a plug nickel for their sorry hides."

"But it's something you'll keep in mind? For the future?"

"You do every little thing you're supposed to, and I'll think about it."

She supposed that would have to do but she envied Gideon. How would it feel to be the absolute master of one's world?

He gestured to a chair. "Sit. We need to talk."

Still holding the package, she did as instructed.

"What the devil is in that thing?" he asked, taking the chair behind his desk. "And don't tell me just candles."

"I found the perfect birthday gift for Elijah at the mercantile."

"I've known the man for almost twenty years and would be hard-pressed to think of something to give him. What did you come up with?"

"A new robe," Emma said, unable to curb her excitement.

"The evening he was guarding your castle gate against my intrusion, he—"

"My *what?*"

"Oh, that was how I thought of your house that night, as an immense castle, with a ferocious gatekeeper guarding the entrance."

"Thunderation."

"Considering the circumstances, it wasn't such a far-fetched observation. I recalled how frayed his robe was and thought he would appreciate receiving a new one."

"I'm sure he will." Gideon was touched by the continual acts of thoughtfulness she performed for the benefit of others.

As if struck by a new concern, her smooth brow furrowed. "You don't think it's too personal, do you?"

"What if it is? Broadbent is bound to appreciate it."

"It's my first gift, you see."

"Your *first* gift?"

"That I've given to someone," she explained.

Gideon didn't like the way his throat tightened. "I see."

"I wouldn't want to make him feel uncomfortable."

"I guarantee he'll be delighted." After Gideon spoke with his butler, Broadbent would damn well dance a jig to show his gratitude.

"Mrs. Foster is giving him a comb, and Mrs. Graves some tobacco for his pipe." Emma paused for a moment, her gray eyes alight with a bit of magic that Gideon couldn't begin to decipher. "I think Elijah realizes she has feelings for him."

Gideon was dumbfounded. "Mrs. Graves has personal feelings for Broadbent?"

"Mrs. Foster," Emma corrected. "I think they may be close to an understanding."

"What kind of an understanding?" he asked warily.

"A marital one, of course."

Emma's misplaced romantic imaginings were an example of sentiment run amok. "Nonsense—Broadbent has been a dyed-in-the-wool bachelor since his wife's death, almost two decades ago."

"Well, I say there's something brewing between them."

Gideon tried to visualize his delicately refined housekeeper keeping company with his gruff, burly butler. The image wouldn't form. "She's too short for him." Emma's sudden frown reminded him that she tended to be sensitive about her own lack of height. "Not, of course, that there's anything wrong with being short."

"I wouldn't know," she said ingeniously.

"Broadbent isn't the only one smitten."

"Don't tell me," said Gideon dryly. "Mrs. Graves has palpitations when Hennesy brings the coach around."

"No, but Nat Walker gets a sparkle in his eyes whenever Miriam Goodwin crosses his path."

"Nat Walker and Miriam Goodwin?" He laughed outright. "I've seen both their places. There's no way those two will ever get together."

"We shall just have to wait and see which of us proves right."

"Ah, Emma." Gideon's thoughts returned to her earlier words. "You received presents at the orphanage, didn't you?"

"Presents?"

He pointed to the bundle on her lap. "Even orphans must receive wrapped surprises at Christmastime."

"Some institutions might do that."

"But not yours?" he guessed curtly.

She shook her head. "When I worked for Mrs. Kenswick, though, I saved enough funds to buy apples, sweet cakes and walnuts. When I arrived at the orphanage to deliver them, a churchwomen's group was there singing carols. They'd made a patchwork quilt for each child. Someone else had donated peppermint sticks. It was the most festive Christmas Eve I ever experienced at Heartshorn."

Gideon distrusted the gritty pressure building in his eyes. He damn well knew he wasn't on the verge of tears. Still, the foreign sensation made him uncomfortable.

Instead of softening up his men, Emma January Step would be better served to develop a tougher hide of her own. This wearing-her-heart-on-a-sleeve business had to stop.

He cleared his throat. "Emma, did you observe how well I handled the situation with Courtney when I caught her smoking?"

Emma regarded him quizzically. "I noticed you didn't yell."

"That's because I remained in control." He pushed back his chair and stood. "That's one of the major differences between men and women. Unless he's pushed to the very limits of his restraint, a man swears his allegiance to logic, not emotion."

"Really?"

He wasn't sure he trusted the subtle deepening in her gray eyes. "I admit we've had a rocky time of it. I also admit my self-mastery has failed more than once."

He shot her a penetrating glance to see if she was listening. From the pink gracing her cheeks, she was. "And I came close to losing my temper with you this afternoon."

"Close?"

He flushed. "All right, I went over the edge. I said some things that were uncalled-for. You're an excellent tutor. If anything, I would say you've pushed yourself too hard. You're not on trial here. You have nothing to prove.

"What I'm saying is that life is more agreeable when emotions are kept in check." In the face of her silence, he felt prodded to continue. "I would like to chart a new beginning based on mutual respect and restraint."

Gideon might believe that was possible, but Emma wasn't convinced. Any man who would sweep a resisting woman into his arms while on horseback didn't know the first thing about control. He seemed to expect a response. The sensible course was to agree with him. Yet the overwhelming urge grew within her to do or say something that would shatter his precious control into itty-bitty pieces.

She sighed with what she hoped was just the right amount of humility. "I would like my life to run more smoothly."

Gideon looked visibly relieved. For a moment, Emma had second thoughts about trying to provoke him. Despite the fact that he'd bathed, changed his clothes and shaved, the fatigue still showed in the fine lines at the corners of his eyes.

"Then we shall begin again."

She stood, her parcel clutched beneath one arm, and extended her hand. "Let's seal the agreement with a handshake."

He accepted the gesture. She made sure the pad of her thumb gently stroked his skin as she stared deeply into his eyes.

He cleared his throat and broke contact. She had no intention of letting him off so lightly. A dozen times her control had been superior to his. She wouldn't rest until he admitted as much.

"This must mean you've calmed down about Lyman Thornton's visits during your absence." She brought up the sore point with what she hoped was just the right amount of innocent cheerfulness.

"As I've left instructions he's no longer allowed on the premises, Thornton is a moot issue." Gideon rearranged several papers on his desk, then looked up. "Does that news distress you?"

"Hardly. I told you I only endured his company for your benefit."

"So you did. But didn't it make your heart go pitter-pat to think you were entertaining one of the 'noble' Guardsmen? I seem to recall you have a high opinion of them."

You're the one who makes my heart go pitter-pat. "I guess you talked to Broadbent."

"We had a brief discussion," Gideon confirmed. "He filled me in on what's been happening while I've been gone. There was no mention on his part of having developed an attachment to a member of my staff."

Gideon's smugness was becoming annoying. For his own good, he needed to be shown that he was an ordinary human being capable of losing his self-control.

Emma shifted restlessly. She was having a miserable time trying to get to sleep. No position she assumed granted her the least relief. Thoughts of Gideon's big, strong body kept invading her thoughts, if not her bed. Remembering his lecture, she wanted more than ever to shake his self-control.

It was so unfair that when her heart raced, the unfeeling lump within his chest beat with repressive steadiness. He was the one who'd forced himself into her serene world and torn it apart. Before he peeled her bedclothes from her and awakened a frantic need for fulfillment, sleeping alone hadn't been a chore. Now her insides and her outsides craved the things his mouth and hands could do. This time she wanted him inside her when her womb dissolved into a dozen shimmering waterfalls.

And she wanted his big naked body sprawled out on her sheets so that she could feel the rough texture of his skin beneath her fingertips. She wanted to taste him, to rub her naked flesh against his hairy body and lose herself in that pounding, cascading torrent of pure feeling.

She rolled onto her stomach. The sheet's friction did nothing to ease her emptiness. Nor was Duncan's sporadic barking conducive to falling asleep. Emma pushed aside the twisted blankets and got out of bed. She didn't bother turning up the lamp. Its banked light was sufficient to guide her to the terrace door. She stepped onto the balcony and called down to Duncan.

"Be quiet, you're going to wake up the whole house."

He raised his head and whined, then paced along the new brick fence.

"Come inside, Emma."

At the sound of Gideon's voice behind her, she whirled around. Her mouth was dry, but moist heat gathered elsewhere. "What do you want?"

Let it be me....

"A good night's rest," he answered, more shadow than form as he stood in her bedchamber. "There's a full moon tonight. Unless you want the men to have a clear view of you in your nightgown, you better come in."

Shivering, she did just that, closing the terrace door behind her. "I know you said Duncan needed to sleep outside, but he's making such a fuss no one's getting any rest."

"Bringing him in the house wouldn't make a difference."

"You're in my bedchamber," she pointed out on a breathless current of air, forgetting about the restless dog. "The last time you were here, you instructed me to shoot you if you returned."

"Fortunately, there isn't any need for bloodshed tonight. Unlike poor Duncan, I'm not governed solely by my instinctual need to rut."

Embarrassment flooded through her. She hadn't realized what the dog's problem was. Unlike Gideon, however, Emma was very much afraid she *could* be controlled by the instinctual need to mate.

"Uh, Gideon…"

"Yes?"

In her darkened chamber, she could barely make out where he stood. "I'm not sure that my terrace door latches properly. It's caused me some concern. Will you please check it?"

"Of course."

"I'll see to the lamp," she offered. She went to the nightstand and increased its brightness.

For the first time, she was able to clearly see Gideon. It was obvious he'd hastily thrown on a pair of britches and a white shirt. The upper garment hung loosely about his powerful shoulders, exposing his softly furred, muscular chest.

Remembering what Gideon had said about her nightgown becoming transparent if lit from behind, she continued to stand with the lamplight pooling around her. His dark gaze moved over her as thoroughly as his skilled hands had the last time he was in her room.

After apparently looking his fill, he shifted his attention to the door. He presented his broad back to her as he rattled the latch.

"There does seem to be something wrong."

"There does?" she asked in surprise, drawing closer.

"It wants to stick."

She stood behind him. Without quite knowing how it happened, she found herself leaning toward him. Her hands drifted beneath his loose shirt. She caressed the strongly defined muscles that played across his back. His skin was smooth and hot.

The rattling stopped.

She pressed her cheek against the material of his shirt and inhaled his clean, musky scent. Reaching around him, she let her fingertips stray to his waist. The only sound was that of their heavy breathing.

Spurred by a growing need that overwhelmed her, she pushed up his shirt and pressed a kiss to his back. A groan punctuated his labored breathing. He was so beautiful, so strong, so perfectly opposite from her, made to penetrate where she ached to receive, made to bring her body to trembling surrender.

She felt his rock-hard tension beneath her mouth and fingers. Some semblance of sanity got through to her that he was merely enduring her exploration. She didn't want it to be true. But she couldn't ignore his lack of participation. If he intended to, enough time had passed for him to reach for her. Hot shame coursed through her. This was the end, the absolute end between them. She could never face him again, not after this debacle.

Shocked by her wanton behavior, Emma unpeeled herself from him and tried to creep away. At the last moment his hand coiled around her wrist.

She stood with her head bowed, feeling his stare on her. She damned the lamp she'd turned up. The chamber's brightness made it impossible to hide.

"You should have shot me." The gritty words made no sense. He drew her palm to the front of his trousers. Heat pulsated against her. "This is going to be hard and quick. I'll make up for it next time."

The sound of ripping fabric bruised her ears. Stunned, she looked down at her own nakedness. His dark hands moved over her breasts. His head lowered, and his mouth closed around a nipple. She whimpered and writhed against him. His fingers sank into her buttocks. He clutched her closer. She couldn't stop moving against him.

"Oh, baby, you're already there, aren't you?"

"Please…"

With her legs wrapped around him, he backed her against the bedroom door. His tongue plunged into her mouth. "I could make this better.…"

"I can't…wait."

"It's too new for you to know how to control it."

Again she tucked her face into his shoulder. Her only relief came from rubbing against him.

"It's all right, honey. If you're there, take it. I'll hold you."

His guttural endearment sent her racing over a cliff. She twisted against him, shuddering. He swallowed up her surrender in hungry kisses that carried her to the distant shore of release.

She knew she'd found land when her weakened legs drifted to the floor. He caressed her lovingly, deeply, and she arched against him.

"Oh, Gideon, when you do that, I can't breathe, I can't think."

"You're so responsive, it makes my head swim."

"When we're alone in a room, I keep hoping you'll touch me."

"Honey, when you tell a man something like that, you can bet he's going to deliver."

Made self-conscious by the room's brightness, her nakedness and Gideon's intimate stroking, she tried to bury her face against his chest again.

"None of that."

"But it's embarrassing," she said on a quick inhalation of breath as he sent a new flurry of tremors ricocheting through her.

"It's beautiful. You're beautiful. I like the way your sweet, hot body goes crazy when I touch you."

"And your talk of control?"

"I am in control. You're the one who can't hold still."

She didn't like the sound of that, but there was no way to

clear her senses while he continued to work his delectable magic.

"We're going to finish this...um...the right way, aren't we?"

"The minute I get you in bed, the pants come off, and I come in."

"That's how I want it," she confessed, driven dizzy by his slow, steady assault.

"And that's exactly how you're going to get it. Tomorrow."

Her back arched. "What?"

"Ssh, now, honey." He eased her to the floor. "We've only got a couple of minutes before we're interrupted."

His mouth cherished her. Hot tears seeped past her clenched lashes. When freedom came, Gideon's palm covered her mouth. The salty taste of his callused flesh became part of the shattering experience.

The shudders were still coursing through her when a knock at the door sounded. "Miss Step...er...would Mr. Cade happen to be inside?"

"He damn well wishes he were," Gideon said, sotto voce.

He quickly uncurled to his feet and picked her up as easily as if she were a discarded pillow.

"I'll be right with you, Broadbent," he called out.

Emma found herself back in bed. Gideon took a long, leisurely and definitely proprietary look. "I want you ready by ten tomorrow morning. Wear the lavender gown I had made for you."

There was another discreet knock at the door. "I'm coming, Broadbent."

Emma propped herself up on an elbow. "I don't understand."

"Then I'll explain. You've just been utterly and irretrievably compromised."

Emma stared at him, dumbfounded. "I'm fairly certain I compromised you."

"So be it. You shall be the one to rectify it."

"Rectify it, how?"

"The usual way, with a preacher and church service."

"You're talking about marriage."

He bent over and kissed her hard. "You're an astut woman, Emma."

"But…" It was impossible to sort through her confuse thoughts. "You *hate* the idea of marriage."

He straightened. "The choice seems to have been taken from my hands."

Chapter Eighteen

The choice seems to have been taken from my hands.

The sting of Gideon's cynical parting remark haunted Emma the rest of the night and the following morning. She adjusted the cuffs on her fitted jacket as she strode to the schoolroom.

When she dressed this morning, she'd deliberately chosen one of her most conservative new outfits, a dark gold linen jacket and matching walking skirt. Its only ornament was the dark brown braiding about the skirt's and jacket's cuffs. The white blouse had a simple round collar.

Emma stepped into the classroom, feeling both professional and competent. Strange how clothes could affect a person's attitude. She consulted the watch pinned to her bodice. Two minutes past 9:00 a.m. She would have to remind Courtney about the importance of punctuality.

Struck by the house's silence, Emma sat behind her desk and awaited her tardy student. Usually, by this time, the maids were busily engaged performing their morning chores, and softly pitched conversations could be heard.

Hurried footsteps echoed in the hall. Emma prepared a calm smile for Courtney. Without slowing, however, the steps sped past the open door. Emma sighed and tapped her fingers on the desk. If she was occupied giving a lesson, it would be easier to forget about Gideon's cold-blooded proposal.

It hadn't been a proposal. But then, a man as dedicated to his cherished self-control as Gideon Cade was couldn't be expected to ask a woman to marry him. Oh, no, he was too adept at issuing ultimatums. Well, this was one time she wasn't going to jump because he said to. He was her employer. He couldn't order her to become his wife.

"Miss Step, what on earth are you doing in here?"

At Courtney's question, Emma started. Thank goodness, now she could focus on something besides her confused thoughts. "Good morning, I was beginning to think I was going to have to come and fetch you."

"Fetch me?" Gideon's niece repeated, clearly astonished. "Everyone is waiting for you downstairs."

Emma noticed her student wore a pastel blue organdy gown.

"Are you certain they're waiting for me?"

Courtney nodded enthusiastically. "Congratulations, Miss Step. I'm so happy you and Uncle Gideon are getting married. It's as if we're going to become a real family."

Emma couldn't bring herself to spoil the girl's happiness. Gideon was the one who'd gotten up her hopes. He could be the one to dash them.

"Is your uncle downstairs?"

"Oh, no, he's already left for the church."

"But he can't be gone!" Emma protested, alarmed that events were spinning out of control.

Courtney's young face became solemn. "You do love my uncle, don't you?"

Emma looked into her student's hopeful gaze and knew she was on thin ice. "I've grown very fond of him."

Fond of being held in his arms and having him breathe fire into me.

"Fond enough to marry him so we can be a family?"

There was that word again. *Family...* What she'd always yearned for but never possessed.

Emma swallowed. "Well..."

Courtney went to the large globe and turned it slowly. "Remember the day we talked about living in olden times? I said

I would have been a princess and a knight would have fought
in a joust to win my hand in marriage?"

"Yes."

"Well, I know that was make-believe. Things like that
don't happen nowadays." The girl sighed. "Maybe they
never did. But I've been thinking that maybe real life is better
than those old stories about chivalry and such things. I mean,
if a real man like my uncle and a real woman like yourself
fall in love and get married, then that's how families are
started. Babies get born. And there's uncles and aunts and
maybe even grandparents. Sometimes, anyway. And I
thought… Well, if you and Uncle Gideon had a baby, then I
would be an aunt or a cousin or something." Courtney looked
from the globe to Emma. "And we would all belong together.
For real."

Unshed tears blurred Emma's vision of the earnest girl. The
poignant memory stirred of how it had felt to be alone, but
to wish with every fiber of her young heart that she belonged
somewhere, to someone—that one day her mother or father
might appear at the orphanage and say, "There's been a terrible mistake. We want our little girl back. We need her."

Emma pushed back her chair and stood, holding open her
arms for Courtney. There was a slight hesitation, then a swirl
of organdy. Emma hugged the young woman as if she were
a small child. At first the unfamiliar embrace felt awkward,
then the self-consciousness eased. Emma patted her student's
back.

"It's all right to believe in happy endings."

Emma didn't know how long they stood before a cough
sounded at the doorway. She looked up and, through misty
eyes, saw a very dapperly attired Elijah Broadbent.

He cleared his throat. "Miss Cade, they are saving a place
for you in the carriage."

Courtney straightened and wiped her eyes. "I'll see you at
the church, Miss Step."

As the girl passed Elijah, he presented her with a crisp
white handkerchief. She took it, and several moments later
they heard her energetically use it.

Elijah's busy eyebrows knit as he studied Emma's dress with obvious misgivings. "You look more like a temperance woman on the picket line than a bride, Miss Step."

Emma flushed. "I don't believe I shall become a bride today."

She expected him to contradict her statement, but he didn't.

"So you're teaching Mr. Cade what it's like to eat humble pie in front of all Denver. The newspapers will chew him up for being left at the altar. He'll be a laughingstock from here to Chicago. You're going to show him which one of you is calling the shots now, Miss Step."

"I'm not doing this to embarrass him," she objected.

"I would say 'humiliate' is closer to the mark. The man won't be able to hold his head up without being laughed at everywhere he goes."

"You're deliberately overstating things to make me feel guilty."

"Why would I do that? We're good friends, you and I."

"You used to call me Emma!"

"Emma is a soft name, tender and sweet—if you get my drift. I've never known an Emma who would break a man's heart."

"He doesn't have a heart. He has a hard, sharp-edged stone that sits right in the middle of his chest."

"Aye, he's a hard man. Seems to me, though, he's brought a bit of nightly pleasure to one female in this household."

"Elijah!"

"He doesn't have a reputation for forcing himself on unwilling women, but I suppose no one really knows what goes on inside a bedchamber, except the man and woman involved."

Force? Emma squirmed. If there had been any force or coercion, it had come from her.

"Don't be thinking ill of me for talking straight to you, missy," he said doggedly. "Speaking of hearts, there's hard, and then there's *hard.* I can't imagine what it's going to do to the young woman who raced out of here when her dreams are crushed."

It's going to break her heart.

"And to think of how tough things have already been for her, losing her parents like she did, and—"

Emma couldn't bear to hear another word. "Elijah Broadbent, you are a shameless manipulator."

"Maybe so, but I've never broken a young girl's heart."

Emma didn't know which disturbed her more, the thought of a proud man like Gideon being made a laughingstock or poor Courtney having her hopes for a family destroyed.

"All right, I won't stand Gideon up at the altar."

"Well now, that's pleasing news."

"Don't start celebrating. I'll show up, but I'm not guaranteeing there's going to be a wedding."

"You're a feisty woman, Emma. That's the truth. But I got to tell you, my money is on Mr. Cade."

"Oh, stop grinning, you old fox. Before I leave this room, I want a promise from you."

He blinked owlishly. "What kind of promise?"

"I want you to apologize to Mrs. Foster for yelling at her yesterday. It wasn't her fault I went to the mercantile."

"Of course, I'll apologize to the good woman. Uh, by the way, thank you for the robe. It's a mighty fine garment."

Emma was astonished to see Elijah blush. "There's one more thing."

"What's that?"

"I want you to tell Mrs. Foster that you care for her every bit as much as she cares for you."

The butler turned redder. "You can't force a man to do something like that."

Emma raised her chin.

Elijah's expression became bleak. "When you poke your nose into a man's relations with females, you're tampering with fate."

"Your *word*, Elijah."

He heaved a mighty sigh. "You've got it, Emma."

Emma had no idea how the news had gotten out about the impromptu wedding ceremony Gideon had created out of thin air, but the church was packed.

The moment the organist caught sight of Emma and Elijah entering the church, the woman promptly pumped a fast-paced rendition of the ''Wedding March.'' Emma had planned to have a private word with Gideon. With a hundred pairs of eyes watching her walk down the church's center aisle, she was going to have to come up with a bolt of inspiration to end this farcical charade.

The organ's strains ended abruptly when Emma stood before Reverend Hobbly and Gideon. She glanced frantically around, seeking that flash of inspiration. One would think all kinds of divine currents wafted through a church. Surely a convenient miracle was just waiting for her to pluck it from the air. She needed to concentrate.

''Who gives this woman?''

''I do.''

A lump caught in Emma's throat when she realized Elijah was acting as her father.

''We are gathered here today to—''

''*Wait!*'' she yelped.

Sounding like the fluttering of a hundred birds' wings, whispers blew across the chapel. As if he were carved in stone and utterly immune to the muffled exchanges, Gideon's expression was one of polite interest.

''Did you have something to say before I begin, Miss Step?''

Where there had been a flurry of excited whispers before, now a grand silence descended.

Emma looked into Gideon's proud gaze.

''Uh, yes… That is, I do have something to say.''

''We're waiting.''

Emma closed her eyes. ''I think Denver is a very nice town.''

Evidently, despite the deathly-silent pool into which her statement fell, someone had trouble hearing it.

''Eh, what did she say?''

''*Denver is a very nice town!*''

''Addled, is she?'' asked the obviously hard-of-hearing

man, with more sympathy than Emma thought her ridiculous statement deserved.

The ceremony continued without further interruption. There was the preacher's booming recitation, Gideon's steady, firmly spoken responses, and her own faintly uttered replies.

Gideon's mouth, possessive and thorough, captured hers. There was a humming in her ears. The floor tilted. And she hung on for dear life.

Then organ music flooded around her. She and Gideon seemed to leave the church on a wave of good wishes and shouts of encouragement. The familiar faces of their body-guards appeared among the crowd. At some point, Gideon reached out and drew Courtney beside him and Emma.

The rest of the afternoon passed as a blur. Somehow, Mrs. Graves and the other kitchen servants managed to prepare and serve a grand buffet of varied dishes. Emma found herself introduced to two incredibly handsome and dynamic men— Burke Youngblood and Hunter Moran. Identified as Gideon's business associates, they seemed vaguely amused by the sud-denness of his marriage.

The crush of guests had scarcely begun to thin before Gid-eon took her arm and escorted her upstairs. Emma knew she was blushing, but couldn't help herself. Her new husband's less-than-subtle intention to get her alone in an upstairs bed-chamber did not go unnoticed among their remaining guests.

The fact that it was Gideon's bedchamber and not her own did little to soothe her sensibilities. He walked into the room ahead of her.

"Wait." She stood on the other side of the doorway.

He looked at her inquiringly. "Are you about to tell me you think Denver is a nice town?"

She flushed. Would she ever live down that foolery? "I'm waiting for you to carry me."

He stared at her intently. "I remember a time when you objected strenuously every time I did so."

"This is different."

"Is it?"

She tapped her foot. "I intend to begin as I mean to go. There's a threshold here. I'm waiting for you to carry me across it."

"Are you?"

"You know, you've an annoying habit of asking terse questions."

"Do I?"

"Thank you for proving my point. Now, are you ready to start acting like a husband?"

"You have no idea how ready." With that bold promise simmering in his gaze, he stalked toward her.

When he swept her into his arms, her stomach plunged giddily and her arms went around his neck.

He looked down at her. "Is this what you had in mind?"

His strength made her feel feminine and soft. "Oh, yes."

"Then I'm happy to oblige." He carried her easily across the symbolic patch of hardwood floor, then kicked the door shut behind him. "Any particular place you want me to set you down?"

"Here is fine," she said dreamily. He lowered her to her feet. Their gazes locked. She looked away first. "I guess we should go back downstairs."

"*What?*"

"We can't stay up here," she told him, embarrassed that he didn't understand how indelicate it was for them to be alone in his chamber.

He shrugged off his jacket, letting it fall where it landed. "Why the hell not?"

"Because it's the middle of the day, and we just got married."

"What am I missing?"

"Everyone will think we're…" Emma's words dwindled as she watched Gideon sit down. "Why are you removing your boots?"

He didn't look up. "I'm a civilized man."

"Ha! I'm certainly willing to debate that."

He peeled off his socks, then stood. His hands went immediately to his belt. "Have I mentioned that when you say, 'Ha!' it excites me."

That novel disclosure gave her pause. "What do you mean?"

Having unfastened his belt, he untucked his shirt and began to unbutton it. "I'm not sure. But when you say it, something vibrates inside me, and I have this overwhelming urge to get you naked."

It was hardly a romantic observation, but the thought of him wanting her as much as she wanted him satisfied something elementally female within her.

His shirt joined his jacket. Shirtless and barefoot, he projected a predatory aura of raw masculinity.

"Gideon, we really have to talk before things go any further."

He moved toward her, a mask of implacable resolve hardening his features. "Dearest Emma, I'm civilized enough to take off my boots before I make you my wife in every sense of the word. But there's no way I can hold things together long enough for us to have a chat."

His lean, tanned fingers slid beneath her jacket and moved down her shoulders, forcing the garment from her in a single motion. "I used up all the control I had the last two times we were together. There's nothing left."

With his hair-roughened chest scant inches from her nose, Emma sighed. "I suppose I should consider it a victory of sorts that you're admitting your precious control is hanging by a thread."

He unfastened her blouse's top pearl button. "Nothing's hanging by a thread. All I can think about is making you ready in the shortest time possible. We'll get to the niceties later."

In the blink of an eye, her blouse was gone. Because of the design of her front-lacing corset, the tops of her breasts were pushed up and exposed.

He seemed riveted by the sight. "Damn."

"It's very rude for you to look at me and swear. I can't

help the way I'm built. Besides, you never complained before.''

He ran the callused pad of a fingertip between the cleft separating her breasts. ''How is it you have no idea how remarkably beautiful you are?''

''There's no reason to say I'm something I'm not because you want me.''

He pressed a moist kiss on each white mound before raising his head. His glittering gaze took her breath away. ''You'll get the words later. All I've got to give you now is me.''

His mouth came down on hers with a hot, wet urgency that pushed speech beyond the realm of possibility. The only sounds were those of clothing being swept away, ragged gasps, and deep, bone-melting groans. Somehow they were both naked in his huge bed. His hands seemed to be everywhere. She tried to keep up with him, to touch him as freely and intimately as he stroked her. She failed. There was a power and urgency to him that overwhelmed her.

He took possession of her body; there was no other way to describe it. Whatever had built within her before and been released was nothing compared to the writhing tumult gathering within her now. Gideon's single-minded assault awakened a pulsating river of sensation that swept over her sensitized nerve endings with the wild fury of a breaking storm.

His lips moved across her breasts and hips. When he positioned her for a fiercely intimate lover's kiss, she cried out. He was indescribably gentle, and she was caught more deeply in the raging current. The first shimmering tremors of an upward crest spiraled through her.

Gideon must have sensed she was on the brink. He rose above. His magnificent, naked body glistened with perspiration. His face was harshly sculpted—strange and familiar, beautiful and dangerous. He eased her thighs farther apart. She saw the full length of him. A shiver of fear cooled some of her ardor. Even though he probed delicately, she tensed, bracing herself for the pain that logic dictated must accompany his penetration.

As if sensing her apprehension, he paused above her,

poised for his ultimate possession. The bunched muscles of his powerful upper arms and shoulders testified to the toll his restraint took upon him.

"Don't tense up, honey. You're ready for me. I can feel it."

He looked fierce, almost warriorlike, but he spoke tenderly.

She reached up and ran her fingertips across his shoulders. He closed his eyes and groaned, sinking deeper inside. Then he withdrew with agonizing slowness, only to repeat the movement. Each time he advanced, he claimed new territory. Each time he retreated, he left her panting for his return.

"Can you... Can you..."

"Can I what?" he growled.

"Can you kiss me while you...do it."

"Anything to oblige a lady..."

His mouth slanted against hers. The kiss slammed into her, hitting her hard enough to take her breath away. His tongue stroked her, penetrating, retreating. She bucked against him. Gideon's finesseful loveplay disintegrated. He groaned again. One strong hand clamped the back of her head, the other her hip.

As he claimed her in the ultimate act of possession, she knew it was *he* who was possessed. His powerful body lost itself to a surging cadence of primal need that raked him with its savage claws. Even so, after the first moment of pain, he didn't hurt her. Despite the frenzied desire that tore at him, he must have maintained an awareness of her vulnerability. Then there was no thought at all, not of him, not of herself. There was only the glorious, golden descent into a warm sea of sparkling froth.

He shuddered into her, his shout one of exultant satisfaction.

Emma drifted from the sweeping peak of fulfillment, feeling as if she were cocooned in a blissful bubble. This dragon-lover of hers mated well.

"That was a long time coming." His gritty voice popped the lazy bubble. He eased himself onto his side and stared at her with such satisfaction that she couldn't help smiling.

Surely no conquering warrior or dragon beast had ever looked so pleased with himself.

"Not so very long." She rolled to her side. Several dull aches made their presence known. "You've known me for less than three months."

"Considering I wanted you the first time I laid eyes on you, it's been a long wait."

She curled against him, secretly pleased that he made no move to cover himself. It wasn't every day she chanced to gaze upon her very own dragon-lover. There was much for her curious gaze to feast upon. "You were perfectly awful to me the first time we met."

"That didn't keep me from wanting to know what you tasted like."

Emma blushed. "I should think that question has been answered."

He chuckled. With her cheek resting against his chest, the sound reverberated in her ear. "Who would have guessed I would be brought down by such a prickly little thing?"

"I'm not sure I like being called prickly. And really, Gideon, surely by now you realize I'm not little."

He leaned forward and kissed the tip of each breast. His gesture so enchanted her, she nuzzled his chest. "You're just right."

His words brought tears to her eyes. How long had she wished someone would say that? But in her dreams, it was always her parents who delivered the magic utterance.

She cleared her throat. It wouldn't be wise to get sentimental. Gideon probably wasn't talking about such esoteric things as her heart and soul. No doubt he was referring to how compatible they were physically. It still astonished her that she had been able to accommodate him. Pushy man that he was, he'd probably made the extra room for himself.

They needed to talk, Emma thought drowsily. She would rest her eyes for a few minutes and see what her new husband had to say for himself about their rushed marriage and what the future held. Her eyelids drifted shut.

"Thank you, Emma."

"You don't have to thank me, Gideon," she breathed sleepily, stifling a yawn. "I'm sure I enjoyed it as much as you did."

"I'm thanking you for showing up at the church, honey, even if you didn't wear the lavender gown."

"I wasn't going to," she admitted, enjoying the boneless languor that had settled in her limbs.

"I would have come after you, but I appreciate you making things easier."

Easier... Yes, that was how life would be, now that she had her very own personal fire-breathing dragon.

Chapter Nineteen

Beneath Lyman Thornton's dress shirt, perspiration dampened his armpits. The sensation was both novel and uncomfortable. Lately, however, a subtle tension accompanied these meetings between him and his associates.

"I still say if Gideon Cade were dead, we could move in and take over his operation." Lyman knew it was a sign of weakness to repeat himself in order to make a point, yet he was unable to stop himself.

Winslow Dilicar, owner of Denver's largest newspaper, leaned forward in his leather chair. "I admit there was a time when eliminating Cade held great appeal. I've used the force of my newspaper empire to discredit him with the public by accusing him of leading the Vigilantes. A few years ago, we could have helped ourselves to his freighting empire, but that time has passed."

Frank Sutton nodded. Always pragmatic, the cattle baron could be counted upon to cut his losses and follow the most practical course of action. "I don't like the idea of losing out on that sweet deal any more than you do, Thornton, but like Dilicar says, it's time to move on. We've got a shot at taking over Hunter Moran's cattle operation. I say we take it."

Lyman jumped to his feet and began to pace. "I can't believe you want to walk away from a fortune in gold. Gideon

Cade is just one man. With our connections, and the men we've got working for us, we can finish him off."

"I'm afraid I must correct you, Thornton. It appears Cade has his associates, just as we have ours. It's obvious he and Moran have formed some kind of partnership. Burke Youngblood also seems to have forged an alliance with them. We tried to break Cade and failed. I'm not saying we will give up. We can come at him from a different angle, by going through Moran or Youngblood first."

Lyman shook his head. "I tell you he's never been more vulnerable than he is now. You must have heard he got married this morning." It was hard to choke out the loathsome announcement. "His mind isn't on business. He's as easy a target as he's ever going to be."

"You got a personal grudge against him that's eating your craw?" Sutton demanded.

The rancher's unpolished manner repelled Lyman. "We're equal partners, Frank. I don't answer to you."

"Quite so." Dilicar got to his feet. "Perhaps we've been hasty in writing off Cade. I tell you what, why don't you put together a plan, and we'll see what we can do?"

"I'll do that."

"Fine, fine." Dilicar kept his hand on Lyman's back and escorted him to his office door. "Well, you'd best get busy with those plans."

When the door closed on Thornton, Frank Sutton was frowning at his cigar. "I thought we'd decided to lay low with Cade."

"So we did." The businessman crossed the chamber and pushed open another door that hadn't been fully closed. "Come in, Wallis."

Sutton stiffened. "No one's supposed to know about our meetings."

"Relax, Frank. This is Grant Wallis. He's worked for me before."

Sutton considered the nondescript man. He was of average height, with medium brown hair and a slight build. There was

nothing remarkable about him, until one noticed his cold, col-
orless eyes. "So what's the deal?"

"I'm sure I'm not alone when I say that Thornton's attitude
of late has become...unreliable."

Frank puffed on his cigar. "From the time he botched killing Cade and ended up murdering his brother and wife,
Thornton's been a weak link. And that business with the
stage—there was no call to kill the passengers."

"I spoke personally with one of the men involved in that
fiasco. He told me Thornton was looking for excitement and
participated in the robbery."

"The fool!"

Dilicar nodded. "It was his call that the passengers were
killed. Naturally, the man who shared this story is no longer
alive. I admit Thornton was an asset in the past, but as with
the Vigilantes, I think his usefulness is at an end. I hate dis-
banding the Vigilantes. Creating them to kill off the outlaw
rabble and keep our own men in line made life easier for us.
Hanging renegade cattle rustlers without interference from the
law has worked well for you, Frank, but we have to move
with the times, and times are changing. Wallis here is an
expert at tying up loose ends. I think it's time we consolidate
our partnership, don't you?"

Frank liked things simple. "I'm right pleased to meet you,
Wallis."

After a drink to seal the bargain, Frank picked up his Stetson and left Dilicar to his schemes. When the rancher stepped
into the street, he nodded at one of the many men he paid to
watch his back. Trust and Frank Sutton weren't even passing
acquaintances.

Leaving his sleeping bride alone in bed to respond to
Broadbent's discreet summons wasn't Gideon's first choice
as to how to occupy his wedding day. Still, he assumed his
butler wouldn't have disturbed him unless something serious
had come up. Gideon searched the room for his discarded
clothes and dressed. As he closed the bedchamber door softly
behind him, he promised himself that one way or another he

was going to get his life under control. Making love to Emma was at the head of his list of daily miracles.

Thirty minutes had passed since Broadbent's knock on the bedchamber door before Gideon stepped into the library, he was greeted by the sight of his restrained housekeeper locked in a very *unrestrained* embrace with his butler.

Gideon would have closed the door and left them to their privacy, but Mrs. Foster, sensing the intrusion, opened her eyes, saw him standing in the doorway and shrieked.

Broadbent released her immediately and spun around, thrusting her behind him in a naturally protective gesture. "Sir!"

Somehow, this is Emma's fault, Gideon thought, as he confronted his red-faced butler. *My household used to run as smoothly as a well-oiled clock. Now, around every corner I find unchecked chaos.* For the life of him, Gideon couldn't understand his cheerfulness in the face of the unpredictable future looming before him.

"Well, Broadbent, what have you to say for yourself?" Actually, it wasn't that unpleasant an experience to catch his usually unflappable butler off balance. The episode put Gideon in mind of the first time he'd encountered Emma. She and that hellhound of hers had certainly taken some of the starch from Broadbent's collar.

"I...ahem..."

"I was dusting!" Mrs. Foster announced with sudden inspiration, shaking her feather duster to prove the point.

"If you've finished with my butler, I would like a private word with him."

The pink-cheeked housekeeper looked years younger as she hurried from the room. For that matter, so did Broadbent.

"I assume your intentions are honorable."

Broadbent's jowls quivered with offended dignity. "I am not a callow youth to be grilled."

"Save your intimidating tactics for the staff. Mrs. Foster is a genteel lady. I won't have her sensibilities trifled with."

"You've never concerned yourself with such matters in the past."

"I'm a married man now. I have higher standards."

Broadbent looked pointedly at the clock on the mantel. "What an amazing transformation, considering you've only been wed a few hours."

"Nevertheless, I expect you to tread lightly with Mrs. Foster's heart. Emma thinks the woman has tender feelings for you. Marry her, and there's bound to be a raise in it for you."

"My own feelings are such that a bribe will *not* be necessary."

"It's the damnedest thing, isn't it, Broadbent."

One bushy brow inched upward. "What, sir?"

"That two crusty old bachelors like us should find ourselves with two lively females ensconced in our lives."

Broadbent straightened and adjusted his coat. Only the slight twitching of his lips revealed his amusement. "Speak for yourself, sir. I have always considered myself a *robust* specimen."

His butler's turn of phrase reminded Gideon that his bride was waiting for him in bed. "As soon as you tell me why you knocked on my door, you can get back to wooing Mrs. Foster."

The older man withdrew a folded note from inside his jacket. "It's from Youngblood."

Gideon quickly scanned the message's contents. At first Burke's bold scrawl was merely a series of words:

Have the men who killed Jonathan and
Cynthia at Taggert's mine.

Until it lifted, Gideon didn't realize he'd been gripped by shock. The stunned moment of lost time passed. His heart started beating again. The air returned to his lungs. It was over. His search had finally ended. Justice would be served.

"You also received a telegraph wire from Philadelphia," Broadbent said. "It was delivered a few minutes ago."

Gideon had trouble focusing on anything other than Burke's message. "What?"

The butler picked up a sheet of paper with a series of neatly printed block letters. "This was delivered before you came downstairs."

Anything other than the monumental news he'd just received was bound to be anticlimactic. Still, Gideon reached for the paper. That his hand shook didn't surprise him.

To: Mr. Gideon Cade, Denver, Colorado

In response to your request for information regarding the parents of Emma January Step delivered to the Burnby Heartshorn Foundling Home on date specified. Be advised both parents deceased. Further details to follow by U.S. Post. Both sets of grandparents and large number of surviving family members living in New York City, unaware of Miss Step's existence.

Detective Russell Hendrix

"Is something amiss, sir?"

Gideon looked up. "It appears my wife isn't as alone in the world as she's believed."

"In-laws, sir?"

"A large number of them, according to the detective I engaged to try and unravel my wife's unorthodox beginnings." He folded the sheet of paper and slid it into his shirt pocket. "I'm not going to share this revelation with her, however, until I've had these people investigated. There's no need for her to know if she comes from a line of derelicts."

"I'm not certain she would view things in quite that light."

"As her husband, I have the responsibility to protect her from anything or anyone who might cause her distress."

"I understand, sir."

"Gideon?"

At the sound of his name, his head snapped up. Deliciously disheveled and looking thoroughly loved, his bride stood at the library doorway. A shaft of uneasiness struck him at the thought she might have overhead the conversation she'd interrupted.

"Yes, darling?"

She blushed prettily. Even though conflicting emotions surged inside him, he couldn't help smiling. Her incredible brown hair had been brushed back, but errant tendrils had their way, curling around her flushed face. Her lips were swollen, her eyes shiny. The collar of the white blouse she'd put back on was uneven, as were the buttons. Her jacket and skirt showed the wrinkled evidence of their cavalier treatment. All in all, he'd never seen her look more fetching.

Even as he admired his bride, the sweeping battle of his clashing feelings tore at him. His head pounded with the exultant expectation of confronting and killing his brother's murderers. Emma wasn't alone in the world. Other people had the claim of blood relationship with his wife. His heart pounded only with the need to protect her and keep her safe. And his body... His body wanted to possess her again.

"I woke up and missed you," she said, with an endearing sweetness that affected the way he breathed.

Broadbent coughed. Emma's blush became scarlet.

"Oh, I thought you were alone."

Obviously seeking to spare Emma further embarrassment, Broadbent excused himself.

"We're alone now," Gideon said softly.

He experienced the urge to take her into his arms and prove she was really his. Even as he told himself that such urges were indicative of hotheaded youth, not the reasoned response of a mature adult, he moved toward her.

"I missed you," she repeated, artlessly. Gideon wanted to perform some heroic act to dazzle her into loving him.

"It's only been a few minutes." There was no reason for her to know that his mind had become a morass of sentiment. If he pretended to be logical, his thoughts might actually behave that way again.

She entered his embrace as naturally as if she'd being doing so for a lifetime. His arms closed around her. He liked the way she leaned into him and rested her cheek against his chest.

"Why did you leave?"

"Broadbent had something important he needed to discuss with me."

Instead of the telegram, Gideon felt as if he'd poked a red-hot branding iron into his pocket. The scorching heat should have burned Emma's cheek. Nevertheless, he had no intention of sharing her family history with her until he knew it would bring happiness.

"I heard the knock on our bedchamber door," she said, slipping her hands inside his jacket and looping her arms around his waist, "but I was so sleepy I couldn't move."

Again, her honesty affected him more powerfully than any of the practiced flirting to which he'd been subjected in the past. "Believe me, I didn't want to leave our bed, either."

"What are your plans now?"

Her dulcet purr was provocative enough to summon a dead man from the grave. The thought's black irony seeped into his consciousness. He was about to make the opposite come true. He was going to send three men to their graves. To lay claim to such a brutal goal while holding his sweet Emma seemed blasphemous. Gently, he extricated himself.

"I hope I never have to turn down such a charming invitation again, honey. But something's come up that I have to take care of."

I can't be late for my appointment as executioner.

Again, to harbor such a black thought while in Emma's presence seemed to violate a natural law of existence.

Emma sensed Gideon's distraction. Whatever his mind was on, it certainly wasn't her. She told herself it was foolish to feel hurt that her new husband of less than four hours would rather concentrate on business than on her. Her feelings were tender enough from their recent lovemaking, however, to need reassurance. Had she pleased him?

And then there was the need to understand why he had insisted she marry him. Was it simple lust? Their marriage bed had proved beyond any doubt that Gideon Cade was a passionate man to whom the physical act of coupling brought intense pleasure. But a man of his wealth and position didn't have to marry to acquire such pleasure.

"Would I sound too much like a wife if I asked when you thought you would be finished with your business?"

Strong emotion flashed in his gaze. Mystified by its intensity, she wondered what competed for his attention on his wedding day.

"I hope to be home by nightfall."

"I'll have Mrs. Graves set aside a plate for you."

Emma was at a loss to explain the cold formality that had invaded their conversation. Being newly married and having no personal experience with intimate discussions, she had no idea how to ease the awkwardness that had sprung up between them.

"I will try to...hurry things," he said.

Without warning, one of the library panes shattered into shards of flying glass fragments. Gideon leaped toward her, pulling her into his arms and drawing her down to the floor.

"Are you all right?"

His hoarse demand hurt her eardrum. "I'm fine."

He leaned on an elbow and surveyed the room. Amid a pool of broken glass lay a red brick.

He released his hold. "Stay here."

Apparently unconcerned about his own safety, he rose lithely to his feet and approached the window. The sound of a woman's hysterical screaming and Duncan's frenzied barking poured through the jagged opening.

"Let me go! He has no right to live, no right to sit in judgment of others! He killed my Harry!!"

Broken sobs followed. Duncan's spate of wild barking ceased. Goose bumps scraped Emma's skin. It was impossible to hear such heartrending suffering without having a sympathetic reaction. The poor soul was lost in a world of terrible grief. Despite Gideon's order, Emma got to her feet. This grieving woman posed no threat to either herself or Gideon.

"What's going on, Rube?" Gideon called through the window.

"This here lady said she had a delivery for the kitchen, but when she got to the side of the house she started acting crazy.

She began yelling and grabbed one of those loose bricks and threw it through the window.''

"Bring her inside.''

By the time Emma got to the shattered window, there was nothing to see. Gideon turned around. "I suppose I'm going to have to resign myself that you refuse to obey orders.''

"The worst possible fate for a man like you would be to have a wife who mindlessly obeyed your every command.''

"Remind me to have you explain that later.''

The sound of boots thundering down the hall and a woman's weeping turned their attention to the doorway. Rube and Eb entered, each holding one arm of a middle-aged woman dressed in dirt-stained calico. Her brown hair hung in limp clumps around her lined face. It was hard to tell if the men were supporting or restraining her.

"Please come in,'' Gideon said, speaking directly to the woman. His voice was calm, his manner controlled.

Her lost gaze focused on him. Rage and hatred replaced the emptiness. "You're him, aren't you? You're the one leading those murdering vigilantes.''

Gideon drew closer. "I'm *not* a Vigilante. As far as I'm concerned, they're as despicable as the criminals they claim to hunt down.''

"You killed my husband, the father of my children!'' She lunged toward him, almost breaking free of the strong men who held her. Clearly, Gideon's denial had no impact.

"The newspapers say you are. They wouldn't lie. You had no call to hang Harry! He weren't no rustler!''

Gideon motioned to his men. "Don't hurt her.''

The implacable lines of her husband's expression tore at Emma. She knew him well enough to know he would never be a part of such a craven group as the Vigilantes. It astonished her that she could have ever doubted him. The papers were wrong. Gideon was incapable of savage vengeance. To be falsely accused by this distraught woman of killing her husband and the father of her children must cause Gideon great pain.

"I know what's been printed about me. All I have is my

word that I'm not associated with the Vigilantes. That won't bring your husband back.''

The woman strained against the hands that gripped her arms. Anger-driven fire flashed briefly in her gaze before giving way to a terrifying blankness. She sagged suddenly, catching her captors off guard. It took the full strength of both men to help her to a chair.

"You're right. Nothing will bring Harry back. He's gone. Gone…''

Emma went to her and put her arm around her shoulders. "I'm so sorry.''

"What's to become of us without Harry?''

The plea sounded as if it came from a little girl. Emma wished it was possible to offer an answer that would make the pain and the fear go away. Life had taught her, though, that no simple answers existed. A person simply kept going. That small act of endurance brought one to the next day. That was how life was lived. One day at a time, with the hope no person would be asked to endure more than he could bear.

"I'm so sorry,'' Emma said again. "I can only imagine your pain. I want you to know my husband is telling the truth. He isn't a Vigilante.'' Emma looked up and found herself imprisoned by Gideon's penetrating stare. "I could never love a murderer,'' she said softly. "My husband is no murderer.''

She'd never told a man she loved him. With a start, she realized she'd never said those words to another human being. Just as she was unprepared for the exquisite rush of warmth she experienced, she was unprepared for the tortured look that twisted her husband's bleak expression.

Chapter Twenty

Two hours later, Emma watched a workman set a replacement pane of glass in its new slot. Touched by the cooling afternoon breeze, she shivered. Dark storm clouds gathered overhead, offering a portent of the first rain they'd had since the night Gideon had climbed to her terrace. Courtney had gone inside moments before. Duncan snoozed nearby.

Emma gathered her shawl close to her. The woman who'd entered their lives so dramatically had identified herself as Mary Speyer. It was difficult to tell if she still believed Gideon was responsible for her husband's death. The emotionally exhausted woman was asleep in a guest room. Mrs. Foster watched over her.

Emma wished there had been an opportunity for her and Gideon to talk before he left. Driven by a restlessness she didn't understand, she'd slipped outside for fresh air. She'd told Gideon she loved him, which was a bit like peeling off the protective covering of her skin. A person shouldn't be expected to make such a declaration without getting something in return—like an admission from her husband that he loved her, too.

Of course, she knew better than to expect that. Still, he could have taken her into his arms and said something kindly.

She would have settled for "I think we shall get along well together."

A drop of rain struck Emma's cheek. Absently she brushed away the moisture. Realistically, she probably *wouldn't* have settled for such a tepid response. "I've decided life would have been boring without you, Emma. I'm ready for some excitement."

Better, but hardly adequate.

"Without you, my life has no meaning. I love you with every fiber of my being."

Definitely what every new bride deserved to hear from her groom. Until she reminded him, he hadn't even thought to carry her over the threshold. That could mean one of two things. Either he hadn't considered her worth the effort, or the only thing on his mind had been making love to her. For his sake, it had better be the latter.

Gideon stood outside Taggert's cabin. Four years of his life was about to come full circle.

"You okay, Cade?" Jefferson asked.

"Fine. You're sure they're the ones?"

He needed confirmation before he exacted revenge.

"When they found out Dundree had already told us they were in on it, they confessed real quick. Seems like they didn't want to end up with vigilante justice. Considering the alternative, being turned over to the authorities is sounding mighty good to them."

What the cowboy didn't say was the men wouldn't have been so forthcoming with their confession if they knew their fate rested in the hands of the brother of the man they'd cut down.

Gideon opened the door and stepped inside. It took a moment for his eyes to adjust to the lack of direct sunlight. He didn't know what he'd expected to feel when he saw Jonathan and Cynthia's killers. What he found was three sullen men who'd been bound hand and foot. They sat on the rough-planked floor, with their backs against a log wall.

There was nothing extraordinary about them. The three could have been any ill-kept drifters passing through Denver.

What had he expected—the crazed look of evil incarnate? He shook his head. He'd been around long enough to learn that most of what passed for evil couldn't be separated from what passed as good.

He waited for a surge of righteous rage to overtake him, waited for the kind of blood lust that had crowded his mind and heart in the weeks, months and years since he buried his brother. He needed the white-hot sizzle of rage to settle in his gut. He could see himself jerking each man to his shackled feet, could feel his fist pounding into them again and again.

As he stood there, waiting for the incendiary flash of raw hatred to loosen his pent-up fury, he heard a quietly spoken but clearly audible voice.

I could never love a murderer...

He looked around the crude cabin for Emma, since it was her voice he'd heard. The guards and the bound men stared at him. Sweat beaded his face. He knew he was the only one who'd heard the softly spoken utterance.

He closed his eyes and willed himself to act—or at least to say something—but a strange paralysis invaded his limbs. An almost desperate inner awareness told him that if he failed to take his vengeance now, he never would.

The self-defeating temptation rose in him to lay down his terrible burden, to forget the crime he'd pledged himself to avenge and choose instead Emma's healing love. His warring feelings pulled him toward radically opposite destinies.

"Cade, you okay?"

It was the second time he'd been asked that in as many minutes. With a surge of ferocious will, Gideon leaned forward and yanked one of the men toward him. Unprepared for the assault, the man faltered on his bound feet.

"So, you like shooting, do you?"

The question was torn from the darkest, most savage part of him. He'd set himself on a path from which he would not be deflected—even if it meant losing what he'd so briefly had. Emma's heart.

* * *

"Mrs. Cade?"

It took a moment for Emma to realize that the gaunt and grizzled stranger was speaking to her.

She'd been about to return to the warmth of the house through the kitchen. Perhaps sharing cinnamon rolls and hot cocoa with Courtney would, at least temporarily, divert her from the uncertainty plaguing her impetuous marriage to Gideon.

"Yes, I'm Mrs. Cade."

He glanced around the yard, then leaned close. "You gotta come quick."

A numbing sense of foreboding fell upon her. "Why? What's wrong?"

"Mr. Cade's been shot. Bad. He's asking for you."

The earth stopped. She couldn't think, dared not feel. Instinctively she moved toward the gate. Her legs lost their strength. It didn't matter. Had the stranger not assisted her, she would have crawled. When she was helped into a coach, dimly registered was its black outline and costly maroon interior. Her world shrank to the time it would take to reach Gideon.

He couldn't die. That was unthinkable. Her throat sealed shut. Clammy sweat chilled her skin. The coach's lurching movement aided in maintaining her sanity. At the brisk rate the horses were being pushed, it wouldn't be long until she was with Gideon.

All at once, her mind was alive with questions. "What happened?"

The man glanced at her before his gaze slid away. "I told you, he got shot."

That the bearer of this ominous news couldn't meet her stare added to her alarm. "I don't know your name. Who are you?"

He tugged at his battered hat with scarred fingers. "Jonah."

"Jonah, is there a doctor with him?" Surely, if there had been time to get her, they'd summoned a physician.

He regarded her from sunken eyes, then blinked. "I 'spect by now they got one."

"Do you know where he was struck?" Not his heart or his head, she prayed. Let it be an arm or a leg. Let him live. She'd take him alive any way she could have him, and she would bully him into feeling the same way.

"I think it was his chest," Jonah said noncommittally.

Dear Lord... She sank back against the bouncing seat and silently pleaded for Gideon's life to be spared. Since time had lost all meaning, she had no idea how long it was before she began to bargain and promise everything she could think of to preserve her husband.

Gradually, the distance they'd covered crept into Emma's fear-tossed thoughts. She brushed away the tears. "Jonah, how much farther is it? It seems as if we've been traveling for hours."

"That's because you got yourself a shock. We ain't gone far."

She looked out the window. Wild terrain swept past them. Her companion must be used to covering great stretches of territory. Despair gripped her. "We're going to be too late."

"Maybe," Jonah said practically. "Won't know till we get there."

Too late... Emma didn't want to give up hope. To give that up was to give up on life. But an undeniable truth uncoiled within her. Fate had never overly concerned itself with her welfare. Why should it start now? Maybe she was supposed to be unhappy. Maybe that was the natural order of things. By falling in love with Gideon, even if he didn't love her, she must have skirted too close to happiness. Perhaps there was a law, written on some forgotten stone tablet in some barren wasteland, stating that Emma January Step was meant to live her life alone.

She realized she was feeling sorry for herself and said a hasty prayer of apology. She had so much to be thankful for.

There were the new friends she'd made working in Gideon's household, the growing affection between her and Courtney, and... What would any of it matter without Gideon?

Emma closed her eyes. The coach had slowed for its ascent up the steep mountain path. In the distance she thought she heard a dog's bark. She prayed again.

"Whoa! Whoa!"

Just when she'd begun to despair of them ever reaching their destination, the coach finally came to a halt.

"We're here, Mrs. Cade," Jonah said.

She saw the uneasy look in his eyes. Did he think Gideon was already dead? *Don't let it be true.... Don't let it be true....* She mentally repeated the litany over and over.

Jonah opened the door. Emma touched his checked sleeve. "No matter what happens, I want to thank you for bringing me."

His wide eyelids lowered, then raised. "Ma'am, it's a rough, cruel world out here. Sometimes a man has to do things to stay alive that he sure wishes he didn't have to." His prominent Adam's apple worked spasmodically. "Good luck to ya."

Other than to note that she was entering a spacious log cabin, Emma paid scant heed to her surroundings. Once she was inside, her gaze swept the large room, searching for her husband, who'd been too badly hurt to bring to town. There was no sight of him. A keening sense of hopelessness welled within her. If she didn't see him soon, she thought she might die.

The cabin door slammed shut, and she spun around.

Lyman Thornton stood before her. "Emma, it's so good to see you. I apologize for our lodgings." A sweep of his arm encompassed the room and its furnishings. "I assure you this is a temporary resting place."

Gideon knew something was wrong the moment he dismounted Warrior and led him to the back gate. The house was ablaze with lights, and the men he'd hired to guard the place watched from their vantage points with rifles raised.

Feeling as raw and battered as if he'd kept an appointment with Satan in hell, Gideon was met by Nat before he'd taken two steps.

"They got Emma."

The bottom fell out of Gideon's world. He placed a hand on Warrior's saddle for support. "What happened?"

Stupid question. It didn't matter what had happened. It only mattered that they get her back.

"Whoever it was struck from the east entrance."

"What about the guards?" *Forgive me, God, I don't care about them.*

"Lefty and Eb. They were knocked unconscious."

Emma would care. She'd adopted them. If they were killed, she would grieve terribly. He couldn't bear the thought of his tenderhearted bride grieving.

Gideon rubbed a hand over his eyes. "When was she taken?"

"Several hours ago."

The night sky had dried since the recent rain. Gideon forced his mind to work. His wife might possess a tender heart, but she also was blessed with a streak of bravery. She deserved a husband of comparable grit. He swore by all that was holy that she would have him.

"Have you alerted Burke and Hunter?"

"They know. Except for the guards watching over Courtney, every man we've got is searching for her." In a gesture Gideon recognized as unnatural for the wrangler, Nat reached out and touched his shoulder. "We'll find her."

Gideon's hands clenched. "You got that right."

"Come now, you didn't eat anything last night." Lyman smiled as genially as if he were her host for an afternoon tea. "Try some of Roscoe's eggs. The man works magic on a cookstove."

Emma shook her head. The smell of the eggs made her stomach roil. "I'm not hungry."

Lyman sighed. "My dear, I realize you've experienced a bit of upheaval, but a mature person adapts to life's unexpected changes."

The strangeness of Thornton's attitude continued to disorient Emma. He seemed to believe there was nothing extraordinary about kidnapping her and holding her against her will. No amount of argument last night had convinced him to let her go. She'd wondered briefly if he was touched by madness.

In the wee hours of the morning, as she lay stiffly upon a bed in the other room, she'd reached her chilling conclusion. He was as sane as she was. He'd simply laid out a scheme of how he thought things should be, and his monumental conceit prevented him from accepting the fact that he couldn't impose his will upon others.

At least Gideon hadn't been shot. That horrible lie had been concocted to get her to go with Jonah. Emma knew it was foolish to be disappointed by the man's perfidy. Jonah was a stranger to her and had probably led a life of criminal behavior. Still, she'd trusted him.

"I still don't understand why you've kidnapped me." She picked up the fork and prodded the eggs. "Do you expect Gideon to pay ransom to get me back?"

"Oh, I'm sure he would pay a fortune to retrieve you, but that's not why I've claimed you." He pulled up a chair and sat across the table from her. "You must realize from my number of visits that I'm hopelessly smitten, Emma."

Bile rose to the back of her throat. "I thought everyone in Denver had heard that Gideon and I are married. I love him."

Thornton nodded reflectively and rubbed his jaw. "I'm sure you think you do, but he's clearly railroaded you into becoming his wife. Some men are impossibly arrogant and always expect to have their way. Over time, though, I'm confident your feelings will transfer to me." He smiled. "Until that happens, we'll be isolated from the company of others."

That he could calmly speak such insanity shook her to the

core. "Lyman, surely you realize you can't make someone fall in love with you, nor can you kidnap someone." She gestured with both hands for emphasis. "It's against the law!"

"Stop saying kidnapped," he snapped, clearly losing his patience. "You will cease all nagging and whining." He pushed back his chair and stood. "As for the law, it's for ordinary people, not me. Life's triumphs go to men who boldly take what they want. I wanted Loutitia's academy gone and a new hotel built on that site so I made it happen."

Emma looked at him in horrified astonishment. "You burned down the school?"

"Naturally I had someone else do it." His tone continued to be conversational. He evidenced no remorse for the heinous act. "Loutitia and her stupid academy were a waste of valuable real estate. Since I kept her financial records, it was easy to make her believe she was on the verge of bankruptcy."

"But why burn it down? People could have been killed!"

"The old building had to come down. The insurance that covered its loss provided me with a handsome bonus. As for possible deaths…" He shrugged. "The man who set the blaze was a professional. He assured me everyone would have sufficient time to get out alive." Thornton's features suddenly became grave. "I must admit during the few minutes I thought you'd perished in the flames, I was extremely displeased with his performance. I'd decided that, if you had been killed, he would suffer the same fate."

Stunned by Thornton's confession, she could think of nothing to say at first, then, "I can't believe you're truly a Guardsman."

He threw back his head and laughed. "Of course I'm not one of those moronic crusaders. I was simply fishing for information that afternoon we took tea together. I've suspected for sometime that your former husband, however, is involved with them."

"He's not my former husband!"

"Calm yourself," Thornton ordered, his earlier geniality

fading. "Gideon Cade is a dead man. Any part he's played in your life is over. I've been forced to kill in the past, and there's little doubt I will be obliged to do so in the future. My earlier attempts on your late husband failed, but my next one won't."

Emma's mind reeled. "Are you saying that you played a role in his brother's murder?"

"An unfortunate accident," Thornton admitted with all the regret of a a a man apologizing for a sneeze. "I had no hard feelings toward Jonathan or his charming wife. Mistakes do happen."

Sickened by Thornton's horrible revelations, Emma sat speechless before him. It had become inescapably obvious that he lacked all true human emotion. There was no guilt to be found in him, nor any compassion. She had the chilling sensation she was speaking directly to Satan himself.

The cabin's front door swung open. The thought flashed that Gideon had come for her. Hope surged, then died when a stranger stepped into the room.

Lyman grabbed the rifle propped next to the table. "Who the devil let you in here? This is private property."

"It's good to see you're on guard, Thornton. Dilicar sent me out to lend you some assistance."

"I don't need any help," Thornton said suspiciously. "Everything here is under control."

Not closing the door behind him, the cold-eyed stranger stepped farther into the room. "This Cade's woman?"

"I don't know who the hell you think you are, but—"

The man extended his hand. "The name's Wallis. Dilicar brought me in to make sure Cade doesn't escape the net we've set for him."

"*I* set the damned net. Dilicar was willing to let Cade live."

"Now that you've got his woman, I'd say that changes things." Wallis inched farther into the cabin. Without apparently realizing he was doing so, Lyman retreated, yielding space. "You send him word yet on where to find her?"

"Not that it's any of your business, but that's the last thing I'd do."

Wallis walked boldly to the stove where a pot of coffee sat simmering. He withdrew it from the warming burner and poured himself a cup. "Why bait the hook if you aren't going to use it?"

"She's not bait. I don't need to draw Gideon to this cabin. With her missing, he's going to be taking all kinds of risks trying to find her. The last thing he'll be doing is watching his back."

Taking a cue from Wallis, Emma began to move slowly toward the open doorway. Lyman's attention was focused so fully on the stranger who'd invaded his territory that he seemed unaware of her movement. She wondered if Lyman realized how their visitor had pushed back his suit coat and how accessible he'd made his pistol.

The bitter taste of fear settled in her throat. She'd never felt death's presence before, but this mountain cabin was thick with lethal menace. She was only a few feet from the doorway.

"Emma, your eggs are getting cold," Lyman informed her gently. "It will hurt Roscoe's feelings if they go wasted."

Frustration tore at her. Then, to her absolute astonishment, Duncan bounded through the doorway into the cabin.

"Who let that mutt in here?" Lyman asked in disgust. He crossed the room and took Emma's arm. "Sit down and—"

He never got the rest of his command out. Duncan's low growl was his only warning as he leaped toward the man who'd unwisely gripped her arm. Lyman brought the butt of the rifle down with sickening impact against the dog's skull. With a cutoff yelp, Duncan dropped to the floor.

Emma jerked free and threw herself over the dog's still body. "You monster!"

A gun blast exploded in the cabin. Emma's ears rang with the reverberating thunder. Lyman Thornton's bloody body collapsed beside her. In dazed shock, she looked toward Wallis.

"I'm sorry you had to see that, but I had no choice. Thornton needed to be brought down."

Emma swallowed. She didn't believe this cold-eyed stranger had come to rescue her. Unlike Jonah, whom she knew to be a villain and still had difficulty disliking, the man who towered above her invoked no particle of human trust. The eerie sensation crawled across her flesh, testifying that she was looking into death's pitiless gaze.

"And I apologize for what I must do next. Please understand, I use violence only as a last resort." He raised his revolver. "I promise to make this quick. Believe me, you won't feel a thing."

Emma stroked Duncan's warm fur and closed her eyes. *Goodbye, Gideon...*

Two gunshots rang out. She cringed, waiting for a burst of pain...

"*Emma!*"

Gideon's raw shout was more welcome than a heavenly choir. Like an apparition from a nightmare, he staggered into the room. Blood covered his left arm. She rose unsteadily and reached for him.

No! This can't be real. You can't have arrived to save my life, only to lose yours....

His strong right arm clamped around her. "Dammit, woman, the next time I tell you to stay put, you better do it."

Hot tears spilled from her eyes. "Oh, Gideon, how can you jest at a time like this?"

The big, stupid man. Didn't he know he was about to die?

His rough laughter embraced her. "You're alive, darling, and I've got you. What better time to celebrate?"

"But you've been shot." *And you're going to die!* She didn't voice that thought. Better to let his last few moments be unfettered by despondency. "There's a bed, you need to—"

"There'll be time enough for that when we get home, honey."

Hope stirred. "Do you think you'll be able to make it home?"

He brought his mouth down on hers for a possessive kiss. "You can bet on it. You're not letting the sight of a little blood make you fainthearted, are you? Hell, I've nicked myself shaving and suffered more damage."

She stared into his eyes. They glowed, but not with delirium. Gideon was going to live. She kissed him back.

"Everything all right in here?"

The sound of Nat Walker's voice brought Emma back to her surroundings. The image of Thornton savagely striking Duncan cut through her thoughts. She began to struggle to get free from Gideon.

"Whoa, where are you going?"

"Oh, Gideon, Lyman killed Duncan." She looked down at the floor, to the dog's still form. "He was so brave." She knelt down, brushing away the new tears. "He came to my defense as if he'd been trained to do just that."

Gideon lowered himself to one knee and ran a palm across the dog's fur.

Emma looked up. His complexion was chalky, his features grim.

"Honey, he was a fierce little warrior on your behalf. Remember that."

Gideon swayed. Nat was there to help settle him on the floor.

"Now don't you go and panic on me, Mrs. Cade. Your husband's too big and ornery to let a measly little bullet in his arm take him down. He's just feeling faint from all the blood he's lost."

"Let's take him home, Nat."

"Ma'am, I would say that's just the place for him."

"I didn't faint," came Gideon's low-voiced denial.

Walker helped him to his feet. Emma gathered Duncan into her arms. It might be the last thing she was able to do for the noble hound, but she would see he had a magnificent burial.

A faint whine reached her. She lowered her head. A wet

tongue weakly scraped her cheek. More tears, a lifetime of tears, broke free.

"Oh, Duncan…"

As she walked to the black coach that had brought her to the cabin, Emma was astonished to see Jonah standing sheepishly to the side of it.

He raised a bony hand to forestall anything she might say. "I'm right sorry for what I did. After I left you, I got to feeling so low, I couldn't take it. For the first time since I was a boy, my conscience got to pestering me something fierce. I can't explain it, but I had to tell your husband what I'd done and where you were."

Emma didn't know what to say.

Gideon's voice emerged from inside the coach. "I can explain it. You can't kidnap or terrorize an angel without paying a severe penalty."

"What's the penalty?" Jonah asked nervously.

"The angel insists you accompany her to paradise, isn't that right, darling?"

Nat's big hands gently reached for Duncan. He laid the wounded dog on the floor and then helped Emma inside the carriage.

"Anywhere you are is paradise." She settled herself beside him. "Lean on me."

Gideon's strong arm came around her. "There's something else a man needs to know when dealing with angels."

"What's that?"

"He can't fall in love with one and keep his black heart intact."

She picked up Duncan and placed him in her lap. "You're not making any sense."

"Of course I am. For the past four years I've lived and breathed for one thing. Justice."

"Against the men who killed Jonathan and Cynthia?"

"That's right. And I wanted to exact it myself."

Emma went still. "Like a vigilante?"

"Exactly. But then I got tangled up with a little sprite—"

"I'm not little," she corrected, lest he think he could get away with such slanderous statements.

"A luscious angel," he amended obligingly. "I learned a heart cankered with hatred can't love. And I had to love you, Emma. There wasn't any choice at all."

"Oh, Gideon, I've ached to hear you say that." What need had she for pride at this point?

"And I've ached to be able to say it. Hell, if I weren't hurting so bad, I would shout it. I love you, Emma January Step Cade. And I thank God you fought your way past my gatekeeper and stormed my castle. Just as I thank God for the sweetest justice any man ever received this side of heaven."

Epilogue

Christmas Eve, Philadelphia

Six-year-old Georgiana Daniels clutched the Christmas stocking filled with nuts and candies to her small chest. "Tell me again, Miss Smith. Where am I going?"

The woman smiled at the dreamy-voiced child. Too much excitement in one day for one so young, the teacher thought. Yet who could blame the girl for being exhilarated by the wondrous changes ahead of her?

"You've been adopted, Georgiana. A man and a woman in a place called Denver are going to be your new mama and papa. You're going to have a big sister and live in a fine house."

Clara Smith had worked for three years at the Burnby Heartshorn Foundling Home. The changes made in the past few months, since the institution had been bought by a wealthy Western financier, were almost magical in nature. Where there had been scarcity and harshness before, abundance and generosity reigned. She thought she could work here for the rest of her life and be happy. In the past month alone, three adoptions had taken place.

"What's my mama's name again?" The child snuggled sleepily into the new sheets and blankets that adorned the soft new mattress of her new bed. Everything about Heartshorn was becoming new.

"Emmaline." The woman eased the stocking from the child's embrace and left the room.

"Are you awake, Georgiana?"

Georgiana rolled to her side. Despite the darkness, she squinted toward the bed next to hers. "I'm still awake, Rebecca."

"I'm sure gonna miss you when you're gone."

The four-year-old's voice trembled. Georgiana pulled back her blankets. "Come and get in bed with me."

The girl launched herself beside Georgiana beneath the covers. As she cuddled the trembling child next to her, Georgiana struggled to speak. "Maybe I shouldn't go, Becca. We've been friends forever. Who's going to take care of you when I'm gone?"

"You gotta go. There's a mama and a daddy waiting for you. It wouldn't be right to disappoint them."

Tears came to Georgiana's eyes. She loved Becca with all her heart. Georgiana hugged the girl to her. "I'll only go because once I'm there, I know I can talk them into adopting you, too."

"Oh, Georgiana, do you really think you can?"

The six-year-old tried to blink back her tears. "It's only fair that, if they keep me, they take you, too."

Becca relaxed against her. "Then we would be together forever."

"Cross my heart and hope to die," Georgiana whispered.

Christmas Eve, Denver

"I'm so excited, I can't stand it."

Gideon watched his wife run a silver brush through her thick brown hair. Love unfurled in his chest. He didn't know if he would ever get used to the powerful feelings Emma stirred within him. He moved toward the dressing table. "That's just what every husband likes to hear when he enters his bedchamber."

Emma's soft laughter erupted. "You do excite me, darling But I'm not talking about your magnificent body or the fac I'm privileged to lay in the arms of a noble Guardsman eac night."

"I don't know how noble I am." He set the small package he carried on a nearby table and stepped behind her, placing his hands on her shoulders. The sheer fabric of her nightgowr outlined her gently ripening figure. He'd never seen her sc radiant. He leaned forward and cupped the small fullness tha cocooned their growing baby.

"You are the most beautiful woman on this earth."

Again her soft laughter spilled over him. "I gave up months ago trying to convince you I'm as ordinary as oatmea for breakfast."

"Hush, I won't have that kind of blasphemy spoken in this house. Angels deserve higher praise."

"Are we back to that again?"

"Always." He rubbed his jaw against the silken crown of her hair. "I brought you a present."

She laid aside the brush and rested her head against him. "You don't have to keep buying me gifts."

"It's Christmas Eve."

"With you, every day's Christmas Eve."

She sighed as if struggling for patience, but he saw the flash of enthusiasm in her gray eyes. He handed her the gaily wrapped package and watched her reflection as she tore off the pink bow and pushed aside the colorful paper. He briefly tracked the bow's descent. It landed next to the bottle of French perfume he'd given her last week. The bow seemed symbolic, a token of his surrender to the tenderness his wife loosed within him.

When she saw what he'd given her, amusement and tenderness filled her gaze. "Gideon, I fear you're becoming absentminded." She held up the intricately carved silver hand mirror. "This is the seventh mirror you've given me in as many months."

"And I'm going to keep giving them to until the evidence is too plainly revealed for you to deny. You are beautiful."

She turned toward him. He stepped back and drew her into his arms. "Hmm…" Her fingers played across his chest. His groin tightened. "Am I also tall? I've always wanted to be, you know."

He kissed her smooth forehead. "The vastness of your height takes my breath away, honey."

Her giggle made him want to strip away their clothing and have her crying out his name. He swallowed. Now that she'd begun to show, he wasn't so sure of himself with her.

The maneuverings of her fingers unbuttoned his shirt. He closed his eyes and wondered how he'd gotten himself into this mess. When he married her, he'd thought his days of abstinence had ended. Unfortunately, with her pregnancy, he was no longer sure that was the case.

"What I'm excited about is Nat and Miriam agreeing to bring our precious adopted Georgiana back with them on the train when they return from their honeymoon."

"I can't believe those two got married. Thanks for not saying I told you so."

"I wouldn't dream of it. Won't Georgiana be surprised when she learns she's going to have a little baby brother or sister?"

"Oh, yeah, that will be a big surprise," he said weakly, wondering how long he could feel Emma's fingertips caressing his chest without going mad.

She rubbed her pinkened lips against one of his nipples and then blew softly. His hands became fists. He figured he could take a lot of her loving before he started blubbering for mercy.

"I wish Dr. Hadly had given me permission to travel there."

"Pregnant women don't belong on trains," Gideon told her. He wondered if he could trust himself enough to fondle her breasts. They were tender now, he reminded himself. He needed to be especially gentle. He wished he'd asked Hadly how long a man could consort with his pregnant wife, but that seemed something a husband should already know.

"Is something wrong?"

He looked down. A frown gathered between Emma's delicate eyebrows. "Wrong?"

"You're not being very cooperative. I'm not going to have to seduce you again, am I?"

Her teasing in the bedroom never failed to arouse him. How was it that such a prim and proper woman could give herself so freely? She was still shy about some things, but when he got her hot and bothered, she held nothing back. He saw the pink outline of her nipples through her nightgown and swallowed.

If he couldn't have this discussion with the doctor, he would have it with Emma. "Honey, I'm so ready for you, I hurt. But what with the baby coming, we're probably going to have to start…uh…being careful."

"It's a little late for that," she pointed out saucily.

"Yeah, well, I wouldn't want to hurt…anything."

"The only way you could hurt me would be to let me go on aching without you inside me."

He looked into her suddenly wise woman's eyes. "You're sure?"

"Very." Her hand moved to the front of his trousers. She touched him with provocative boldness.

"I love you, Emma."

The tears in her eyes threatened to unman him. "Oh, Gideon, how did I ever live before I met you?"

Humbled, he brushed away her tears. "That's the question I ask myself every morning I wake up beside you."

"You even gave me back my family," she said thickly.

"It was my pleasure, darling. My pleasure."

How do I tell you what you've done for me? Emma took her husband's hand and led him to their bed. "I received a letter today from my mother's parents. They're planning on being here for the birth."

"I got a wire that your father's folks are making the same plans."

"What do you think will happen when they meet after all these years?"

"They'll be feeling a lot of different things—sorrow that they withheld permission for your mother and father to marry, grief that their son and daughter died so tragically of influenza, and regret that their granddaughter grew up in an orphanage, far away from the love and material wealth they would have provided, had they known of your existence. I think happiness will win out. They're going to be reunited with their granddaughter, and there will be a new baby for them to get to know."

"And Courtney and little Georgiana will be a part of it all."

"We'll make sure of it, darling," Gideon promised, knowing that having Georgiana in their home would heal much of Emma's childhood pain, just as loving and nurturing their own baby would.

He picked up his wife and carried her to their bed. "When I met you, I thought you were aptly named."

"What do you mean?"

"Miss Step," he murmured, laying her down and stretching out beside her. "I recognized your potential of being the biggest misstep I'd ever taken."

She touched his cheek. "And was I?"

"Darling, you're the rightest thing that ever happened to me."

He lowered his head and gave himself up to the joy of loving Emma.

* * * * *

Author's Note

Cade's Justice is set in Denver, Colorado, in a magical time period accessible to authors of fiction. My next two books will also take place in Denver during this period. Burke Youngblood and Hunter Moran are the heros. As with all my stories, I blend elements of reality and creativity to build a "let's pretend" world of romance and adventure where my heros and heroines resist falling in love all the way to paradise. "The Guardsmen" of Denver are purely fictional creations. Sigh...

Harlequin® Historical

Coming in December
from Harlequin Historical

A Warrior's Bride

Award-winning author Margaret Moore
creates another exciting story
set in medieval times!

A WARRIOR'S BRIDE (ISBN 28995-2)
available wherever Harlequin Historicals are sold.

WELCOME TO *Love Inspired* ™

A brand-new series of contemporary inspirational love stories.

Join men and women as they learn valuable lessons about facing the challenges of today's world and about life, love and faith.

Look for:

Christmas Rose
by Lacey Springer

A Matter of Trust
by Cheryl Wolverton

The Wedding Quilt
by Lenora Worth

Available in retail outlets
in November 1997.

LIFT YOUR SPIRITS AND GLADDEN YOUR HEART with *Love Inspired* ™!

Steeple
Hill™

LI1297

Coming in August 1997!

THE BETTY NEELS
RUBY COLLECTION

August 1997—Stars Through the Mist
September 1997—The Doubtful Marriage
October 1997—The End of the Rainbow
November 1997—Three for a Wedding
December 1997—Roses for Christmas
January 1998—The Hasty Marriage

COLLECTOR'S EDITION

This August start assembling the
Betty Neels Ruby Collection. Six of the
most requested and best-loved titles have
been especially chosen for this collection.
From August 1997 until January 1998,
one title per month will be available to avid
fans. Spot the collection by the lush ruby red
cover with the gold Collector's Edition banner
and your favorite author's name—Betty Neels!

Available in August at your favorite retail outlet.

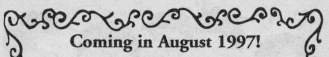

HARLEQUIN®

Look us up on-line at: http://www.romance.net   BNRUBY

Ring in the New Year with

New Year's Resolution:

FAMILY

This heartwarming collection of three contemporary stories rings in the New Year with babies, families and the best of holiday romance.

Add a dash of romance to your holiday celebrations with this exciting new collection, featuring bestselling authors **Barbara Bretton, Anne McAllister** and **Leandra Logan.**

Available in December, wherever Harlequin books are sold.

HARLEQUIN®

KEY TO MY HEART

Unlock the secrets of romance just in time for the most romantic day of the year—Valentine's Day!

Key to My Heart
features three of your favorite authors,

Kasey Michaels,
Rebecca York
and Muriel Jensen,

to bring you wonderful tales of romance and Valentine's Day dreams come true.

As an added bonus you can receive Harlequin's special Valentine's Day necklace. FREE with the purchase of every *Key to My Heart* collection.

Available in January,
wherever Harlequin books are sold.

DELTA JUSTICE

A family dynasty of law and order is shattered by a mysterious crime of passion.

Don't miss the next exciting book
as the Delacroix family mystery unfolds in:

Every Kid Needs a Hero
by Candace Schuler

Widower Matt Taggart had a couple of kids to raise and not a lot of time for headstrong, jet-set women like Jax Delacroix.

Jacqueline Delacroix had succeeded beautifully doing a man's job in a man's world. But back home she was running into the same old Southern family expectations. This time, though, they were coming from little Amy Taggart...and her irresistible dad.

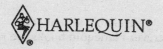

HARLEQUIN®

HARLEQUIN WOMEN KNOW ROMANCE WHEN THEY SEE IT.

And they'll see it on **ROMANCE CLASSICS**, the new 24-hour TV channel devoted to romantic movies and original programs like the special **Romantically Speaking—Harlequin™ Goes Prime Time.**

Romantically Speaking—Harlequin™ Goes Prime Time introduces you to many of your favorite romance authors in a program developed exclusively for Harlequin® readers.

Watch for **Romantically Speaking—Harlequin™ Goes Prime Time** beginning in the summer of 1997.

If you're not receiving ROMANCE CLASSICS, call your local cable operator or satellite provider and ask for it today!

Escape to the network of your dreams.

See Ingrid Bergman and Gregory Peck in *Spellbound* on Romance Classics.

ROMANCE CLASSICS

Born in the USA

Every month there's another title from one
of your favorite authors!

October 1997
Romeo in the Rain by Kasey Michaels
When Courtney Blackmun's daughter brought home Mr. Tall,
Dark and Handsome, Courtney wanted to send the young
matchmaker to her room! Of course, that meant the single
New Jersey mom would be left alone with the irresistibly
attractive Adam Richardson....

November 1997
Intrusive Man by Lass Small
Indiana's Hannah Calhoun had enough on her hands taking
care of her young son, and the last thing she needed was a
man complicating things—especially Max Simmons, the
gorgeous cop who had eased himself right into her little boy's
heart...and was making his way into hers.

December 1997
Crazy Like a Fox by Anne Stuart
Moving in with her deceased husband's—*eccentric*—family
in Louisiana meant a whole new life for Margaret Jaffrey and
her nine-year-old daughter. But the beautiful young widow
soon finds herself seduced by the slower pace and the much-
too-attractive cousin-in-law, Peter Andrew Jaffrey....

**BORN IN THE USA: Love, marriage—
and the pursuit of family!**

Available at your favorite retail outlet!

HARLEQUIN®   Silhouette®